MW00782609

Rewriting the Rules

NICOLE CRYSTAL

Rewriting the Rules

NICOLE CRYSTAL

Copyright © 2024 by Nicole Crystal

Library of Congress Cataloging-in-Publication Data

Names: Crystal, Nicole, author.
Title: Rewriting the Rules
Description: First Edition
ISBN: 979-8-9902866-3-4 (trade paperback) |
ISBN: 979-8-9902866-4-1 (trade hardback) |
ISBN: 979-8-9902866-6-5 (Special Edition, paperback)
ISBN: 979-8-9902866-5-8 (ebook)

This is a work of fiction. Names, characters, places and incidents either are the product of the author's imagination or are used fictitiously, and any resemblance to actual persons, living or dead, business establishments, events or locales is entirely coincidental.

For those who refuse to believe in love.
Enjoy.

1

Arden ♥

Now, December 13th

I stab listlessly at the salad I forced myself to grab, my stomach twisting with anxiety. I'm barely holding back panicked sobs, gruesome images flashing relentlessly—the first responder's somber tone telling me the devastating news, blood-smeared accident photos making bile rise in my throat, my vibrant little sister broken and unmoving when I first saw her in that hospital bed. A twenty-car pileup on the highway…where *I* should have been driving, not her.

I wrap both arms around my heaving ribs, trying desperately to gulp enough air and clamp down the hysterical screams clawing up my raw throat. Even the thought of choking down a single bite makes waves of nausea roll dangerously.

Cora's stable now. She's upstairs sleeping, I tell myself again. *The doctors think she'll fully recover in time.* A broken wrist, some cuts and bruises. She's one of the lucky ones, based on the cries I've heard echoing from the hallway all evening.

But none of it steadies the panic attack building as I sit here alone. Everything feels seconds from unraveling completely. I'm barely holding together, attempting to stop imagining all the tragic what-ifs that can still go wrong, trying to stop feeling so responsible for her pain.

The day was a mess, starting with breakfast, when I was reminded about my forced fate—moving to Florida after graduation to join our parents at their new condo. Last Christmas, the part of me who wanted to find a middle ground agreed. But with the final semester starting in a few weeks, I'm not as convinced. Was that what propelled me to shut down? To bring up the leadership final I needed to finish, with the hope Cora would volunteer to drive them to the airport instead of me? It worked. And now I'm here, wishing I'd never opened my stupid mouth. I should be up there in that hospital bed, not Cora.

I scan the cafeteria desperately, seeking any diversion from reliving today's trauma for the thousandth time. But my frantic gaze freezes on an achingly familiar face, sending an icy spear of betrayal through my already ravaged heart.

Because, sitting a mere six feet away, looking unfairly handsome as always, is none other than Mark Bell. The man who pushed me away without explanation and pretended I didn't exist for an entire year afterward.

That cocky playboy is the last person I want to see right now.

Bitterness churns as I recall our night together last December. I guess I should be careful asking for *any* distraction.

As I debate slipping away unnoticed, Mark shifts in his seat, eyes blowing wide as they catch mine. Alarm flashes across his stupidly perfect features.

Shit.

Not the place he expected to see me, obviously.

Panicked, I drop my gaze to the table, throat tightening. Maybe Mark doesn't even remember me. We were together all of five hours, and they clearly meant nothing to him. He'll just keep ignoring me, right?

Wrong.

I brace myself as his shoes appear next to me on the carpeted cafeteria floor, and I notice his large knuckles grip my table.

Thank you, universe! I can totally handle an awful trip down memory lane on top of everything else going wrong today. No problem.

"Arden Cooper?" Mark's gentle rumble hits like a body blow. *Put on your perfect veneer, girl. Don't let him see you vulnerable.* But it's no use. When I glance up, seeing the concern swimming in the chocolate depths of Mark's eyes, I can't prevent the tears that spring forth against my will. As much as I wish his genuine empathy didn't effortlessly shatter me, one comforting look has me breaking into the pieces I've barely held together all day.

"Arden, hey. What's going on? Are you okay?" His normal charismatic tone is replaced by something gentler, almost sweet. And I hate that I secretly want to wrap myself in it.

At Mark's gentle question, the last threads of my composure loosen completely.

"My sister...she was in a car crash earlier," I gasp between sobs.

Mark murmurs my name, tentatively reaching for my trembling hand. I cling desperately as the dam inside me crumbles. He was the solid comfort I unloaded my secrets and dreams to on a whim one night last year. And however foolish, his compassion reaches me like a lifeline amidst the trauma threatening to drown me.

I'm shaking as I describe the morning, the waiting room, seeing Cora so helpless. Mark's hand tightens on mine as I weep brokenly over how close I came to losing my baby sister. Her car was pinned between three others. The pictures of the mangled steel flashing on the news testify to what could have happened.

As if sensing my spiral towards hysterics, Mark opens both arms questioningly. Without thinking, I fall into his solid chest, clinging desperately to this near stranger's comfort because I have no one else. Our parents are stuck in Florida until tomorrow.

Eventually, my ragged sobs quiet to hitched breaths. Mark's hand rubs gentle circles on my back, murmuring comfort. I vaguely process coffee cups being dropped at our table, appreciative when Mark passes one to me without a word.

I cradle the warmth with clammy hands, exhaustion hitting fully as the adrenaline drops. Sipping the bold liquid, I feel marginally more human facing Mark's compassionate stare. Am I breaking down in front of him *again*?

"Sorry. I'm not usually so dramatic," I mumble embarrassingly.

"You don't seem like the dramatic type, Arden," Mark insists lightly. "So, please don't apologize. You've been through a lot today. No one can hold up forever alone." His dark eyes radiate only kindness—no judgment or alternative agenda. "I'm happy to sit here and talk—or stay quiet—as long as you need."

My natural instinct is to raise the guard I've prudently crafted for men like Mark Bell, to spit back some comment about how he couldn't make time for me before, and to flee before revealing any more vulnerabilities. But the quiet care in Mark's expression stops me. Instead, I slowly unburden what's been swirling inside my mind. The guilt consuming me because Cora took my place driving our parents to the airport. My worry over the surgery she'll now have tomorrow. The challenging morning after we said goodbye to our childhood home in the suburbs, and my parents left for their new place in Florida.

By the time I finish, the weight on my chest feels slightly lighter, like voicing my fears out loud released some of whatever power they had. Mark listens intently, interjecting only thoughtful questions, holding more emotional intelligence than I knew he had.

Actually, that's a lie.

He's proven he could listen, that he's more than just a pretty face.

I mean, isn't this how it happened last year at the party? He approached me, flirted, and then showed genuine concern. And like a girl who thought she'd found a diamond in the rough, I let him see the real me. Heck, Mark was the one who gave me the confidence to finally tell my parents I didn't want to go to law school. In one night, he'd infiltrated parts of my heart I didn't even know existed.

Then he vanished. He shattered those newly found pieces before they even had a chance to take root.

I take a long drink of coffee, desperate to shift the dynamic from trauma and tears. "What about you, Mark? Living it up post-graduation?"

A cloud passes over his expression before he shrugs. "Oh, you know...same old. Work, parties, bar, keeping the rotation moving."

His generic playboy answer seems trained, unwilling to let go of his guise and show the additional layers I know exist. I don't know what compelled me to offer my troubles to him freely, but I wish he felt comfortable doing the same.

I tentatively reach for his hand, struck by how natural the contact already feels despite our rocky history. "Mark, why are *you* at the hospital tonight?" I probe gently.

Pain flickers briefly in Mark's eyes. "My roommate was in an accident earlier, too," he admits softly. "Car caught fire. He barely got out in time." His haunted gaze shifts toward two men clutching coffee cups nearby. "Those two...they're his brothers."

Guilt spears through me. Here I spilled my pain selfishly, while he comforted me, despite his friend's crisis.

As I open my mouth to apologize again, Mark twists his fingers into mine, squeezing gently.

"Hey, you're fine. I'm glad to be here for you, Arden."

Did he just read my mind?

I stare, almost dumbfounded, as his dark eyes turn tender.

"After everything, it's the least I can do." He chews on his lip, dropping his gaze. "I, uh...maybe I could get your number? In case you ever wanted to talk more or..."

My number?

Heat rushes to my cheeks as vivid memories from our night together flood back unbidden: Lying tangled in his sheets, the warmth of his skin against mine, his husky voice as he tossed me his phone to enter my number, the searing press of his lips...

Don't go there, Arden!

I hastily shut down the treacherous thoughts before wishful thinking trumps logic.

Definitely time to rebuild those walls.

"It's probably still in there. Unless you deleted it," I answer with forced casualness.

"Yeah..." Mark glances up, rubbing his neck.

Is he thinking about that moment, too? The electric anticipation between us when I typed in my number? The unspoken promise of something more?

I hesitate, the crestfallen look on his face tugging at my heart despite my better judgment.

Softening slightly, I offer a tentative olive branch. "But really...thanks for coming over. I guess I didn't realize how much I needed that hug."

A hug. The words feel foreign on my tongue, too intimate, too revealing.

But Mark's genuine smile in response warms me in a way I'm not ready to acknowledge. "Then I'll give you a call. We could grab coffee sometime. Or, uh, if you ever wanted to give those pants back..."

My gaze drops to the flannel pajama pants I have on—his pants. The soft fabric suddenly feels like a brand against my skin.

Damn it.

"Maybe if you'd called last year, you could've gotten them back sooner," I deflect, my voice tight as I grapple for composure, reminding myself *why* I still had them. Mark ignored me as if his life depended on it.

Forcing a polite smile, I back away. "Anyway, I should head back upstairs. Take care of yourself, Mark."

As I turn to leave, Mark's hand gently catches my wrist. "Arden, wait." His eyes search mine, a flicker of regret passing over his face. "I know I messed up last year. But seeing you here, now...I don't want to make the same mistake twice."

I hesitate, my heart yearning to believe him despite the armor I've put back up. "I...I need to focus on Cora right now, Mark. But maybe, when things settle down, we could..." I trail off, unsure of what I'm even suggesting.

Mark nods, understanding. "I'll be here whenever you're ready." He releases my wrist, but the warmth of his touch lingers as I walk away, leaving a bittersweet ache of what could have been settling in my chest.

2

Mark 🌑

One Year Prior, December 9th

The icy glare from the woman dressed as Black Widow flashes a clear warning—she's noticed my shameless flirting. Not that it took much effort on my part. Captivating female attention is a reflex sharpened from years of watching my parents' endless infidelities. One I exert without intention now.

Still, Little Miss Widow Maker over there scrutinizing me is...intriguing. Everything about her screams buttoned up, from her self-assured posture to her sexy, yet conservative, costume. She's not my usual ditzy, easy conquest. Something about the defiance sparkling in her eyes ignites my curiosity, drawing me to her.

I murmur a vague excuse about needing a drink to the sophomore girl draped over me. Detaching my forearm from her grip, I cross the room and casually brace myself against the wall next to the woman in black.

I flash my most charming smile, keeping my tone low. "There must be something wrong with my eyes, because I can't take them off you."

After a humorless laugh, she gives an exasperated sigh. "Because every girl dreams of cheesy pickup lines," she mutters dryly, dark, coffee eyes ticking up to mine. "Is it really that easy?"

"I got your attention with it, didn't I?" I counter, letting my gaze travel slowly down and back up every curve of her body. "Can I at least get a name for the lady monopolizing my thoughts tonight?"

Something flashes in her eyes—Satisfaction? Amusement?—before they narrow with a resigned huff. "Arden. I'm Arden Cooper."

"Arden," I repeat, savoring how her name rolls off my tongue like a forbidden treat. I offer my hand, letting my fingertips graze hers a moment longer than strictly necessary. "First time here? Think I'd remember a sexy, bubbly bombshell like you."

She rolls her eyes so hard I'm afraid they might get stuck in the back of her head. Taking a sip of her drink, she fights to keep a straight face, but the delicate pink blooming on her cheeks gives her away. She's digging this banter.

"Not my usual scene. But when I heard there was a Christmas costume party, I couldn't say no," she deadpans, lifting her cup in a mock salute.

"Glad you like it. It was my suggestion. Thought it might...inspire some creativity." I flash her my patented panty-melting grin, relishing the flicker of appreciation in her eyes before she blinks it away. "I'm Mark, by the way. But you probably already knew that."

She lets out a throaty laugh that hits me straight to the core. "Oh, I know who you are."

My reputation precedes me, as usual. But I'm not letting this sassy goddess off that easy. "And what exactly have you heard about me...Widow Maker?" I lean in, close enough to catch the faint scent of her perfume, an irresistible mix of vanilla and sin.

Arden arches a perfectly sculpted brow, her lips curving into a smirk. "Oh, I've heard plenty, Pirate Playboy. Enough to know that, if you're hoping to plunder some booty tonight, you'd be better off setting your sights on easier targets. Like that fairy princess over there, who's been undressing you with her eyes all evening. I'm sure she'd be more than happy to walk your plank."

I clutch my chest in mock offense, but I can't deny the sting of her rejection. This girl is proving to be a tougher nut to crack than I anticipated. "Ouch! Ye wound me, lass. And here I thought we were having a moment."

"A moment?" She scoffs, but there's a glimmer of amusement in her eyes. "Please. I'm just enjoying the free entertainment. Watching you work the room, laying on the charm thicker than your guyliner...it's quite the spectacle." Her gaze rakes over me appreciatively, lingering just long enough to set my blood on fire. "Though I must admit, it looks rather exhausting, putting on that performance all night long."

A surprised laugh bursts from my chest. This cheeky little minx, calling me out on my bullshit while eye-fucking me like I'm the last piece of candy in the dish? Oh, it is *on.*

"Aye, 'tis a heavy burden, being this devilishly charming." I grin, letting my accent slip into a playful pirate brogue. "But fear not, me saucy—"

"Okay, that's enough of that," she cuts me off with a snort, but I catch the way her cheeks flush ever so slightly. "Don't you have some poor, unsuspecting damsel to go deflower?"

"Nah." I wave a hand dismissively. "I'd much rather continue this delightful chat with you. In fact, I can't think of anything better."

Arden bites back a smirk, her eyes glinting with a challenge. "You're incorrigible."

"And you're loving it," I shoot back, letting my gaze burn into hers. "What do you say we continue this conversation somewhere a bit more...intimate?"

Arden holds my stare before flashing a coy smile and leaning close enough that her breath feathers my ear. "In your dreams, Pirate Playboy."

She starts to pull away, but before she can make her grand exit, a drunken party-goer stumbles into her, sloshing their drink all over Arden's sexy black costume. She gasps, jumping back as the sticky liquid seeps into the fabric.

"Oh my god, I'm so sorry!" the drunk girl slurs, swaying on her feet. "I didn't see you there!"

Arden grits her teeth, clearly trying to maintain her composure. "It's fine," she says tightly, but I can see the frustration building.

Sensing an opportunity, I grab a few napkins from a nearby table. "Here, let me help you with that," I offer, dabbing at the damp spots on her costume.

She swats my hand away, her cheeks flushing an adorable shade of pink. "I've got it, thanks," she mutters, but I can see how her hands tremble slightly as she blots at the stain.

"C'mon, let's get you cleaned up," I insist, placing a gentle hand on the small of her back. "My room's just upstairs, private bathroom and all. I can even rustle up some dry clothes for you."

Arden's eyes narrow, flashing both suspicion and intrigue. "Oh really? I'm supposed to believe you're just some Good Samaritan?"

I shrug. "Can't a guy be chivalrous without ulterior motives?"

She snorts, rolling her eyes. "In my experience? Rarely."

"Well, allow me to change your mind." I flash her my most winning smile. "No funny business. Just trying to help that damsel in distress you mentioned."

Arden raises an eyebrow, a reluctant smile tugging at her lips. "I can handle myself just fine."

"Oh, I don't doubt that for a second," I chuckle. "Just come with me."

She hesitates for a moment, then sighs dramatically. "Fine. Lead the way, Pirate Playboy. But I'm warning you, any funny business and you'll regret it."

As we weave through the crowded room, a thrill of excitement hits at the thought of getting her alone in my room. Sure, I promised to behave, but a little harmless flirting never hurt anyone, right?

Once we reach my room, Arden beelines for the bathroom, shutting the door firmly in my face.

I smirk, shaking my head. Should've expected that.

After a few minutes, I knock gently. "Coast clear in there? I come bearing gifts." I crack the door, waving a pair of flannel pants and an oversized tee. "Thought you might want something comfier than that damp costume."

Arden eyes the clothes suspiciously. "Let me guess, your 'favorite' pajama pants?"

I grin, caught. "What can I say? I'm a sucker for the classics."

She rolls her eyes but snatches the clothes anyway. "Don't get any ideas about how to get these back."

"Wouldn't dream of it." Though my thoughts are already well underway.

I retreat to the bed, surprised by the nerves twisting in my stomach. Since when do I care about impressing a girl beyond getting her into bed? But there's something about Arden that makes me want to be...better, somehow. To be someone she might actually like.

Arden emerges a few minutes later, swimming in my clothes. The oversized shirt hangs loosely off one shoulder, and the pants are rolled up adorably at her ankles. Her dark hair tumbles around her face in messy waves, making her look less like a seductive temptress and more like a soft, rumpled dream I never want to wake up from.

Damn, I want her to like me...Actually like me.

I clear my throat, trying to keep my voice steady despite the way my heart's racing. "You know, as tragic as it is about your costume, I gotta say, this look? It works for you." I gesture vaguely at her outfit, my casual tone belying the heat I feel creeping up my neck. "You could pull off the casual girlfriend costume if anyone asks."

Casual girlfriend? WTF, Mark?

Arden snorts, tugging at the oversized shirt. "More like 'Just Rolled Out of Your Bed.'"

I can't help the grin that spreads across my face. "Is that an offer? Because I'm more than happy to help make that look more authentic."

A pillow flies at my head, which I catch with a laugh. Arden's trying to look stern, but I can see the smile she's fighting. "Keep dreaming, Romeo."

"Oh, trust me, I will," I wink, patting the space next to me on the bed. "But in the meantime, how about we make those dreams a reality? We could throw on a movie, wait out the chaos downstairs. Unless you're eager to show off those stylish new pants to the masses?"

Arden hesitates, and I can practically see the gears turning in her head. She's tempted, I know it.

"Wow, first your room, now your bed? Your game is strong tonight, Pirate Playboy. Do you ever quit?"

I hold up my hands in mock surrender. "Hey, I'm just being a good host. Two friends, hanging out, watching a movie." I pause, then add with a smirk, "Unless, of course, you ask nicely."

Arden raises an eyebrow skeptically. "Friends, huh? Is that what we're calling this now?"

I lean in, voice low and teasing. "Well, that depends. What would you like us to be, Arden?"

Arden's eyes widen slightly at my question, a flush creeping up her neck. She recovers quickly, though, crossing her arms with a challenging smirk. "I didn't come tonight for titles, just entertainment."

"Fair enough," I lean back, reaching for the remote. "Prepare to be entertained, then? I promise I'll keep my hands to myself...mostly."

Arden hesitates for a moment longer, then sighs dramatically. "Alright, Romeo. But I'm choosing the movie."

"Wouldn't have it any other way, Juliet," I grin, tossing her the remote.

My heart does a little flip as Arden settles onto the bed next to me, close enough that I can feel the warmth radiating off her skin.

As she settles onto the bed next to me, close enough that I can feel the heat radiating off her body, I struggle to keep my cool. She flips through the options, eventually settling on a horror flick.

"Horror? Didn't peg you for a scary movie fan," I tease, nudging her shoulder.

She shrugs, a mischievous glint in her eye. "What can I say? Your theme inspired me."

As the movie starts, I can't help but steal glances at her. Something about the way she looks in my clothes, all sweet and messy and adorably grumpy, makes my chest feel strangely tight.

I shake my head, trying to clear the unfamiliar sensation. *Focus, Mark.* You've got a girl in your bed. This is no time to be catching feelings.

But as Arden nestles closer, her head resting on my shoulder, I'm hit with a realization that knocks the wind out of me: I don't want this night to end. And that terrifies me more than any horror movie ever could.

3

Arden ♥

Now, February 22ⁿᵈ

I stifle an eye roll as Craig shrugs off yet another invitation to dance. What possessed me to drag this pragmatic stick-in-the-mud here on my birthday night? Surely, I'm not still clinging to childish dreams that he might suddenly let loose on the dance floor with me.

I glance at my phone, thinking about all the other items on my color-coded planner I could be working on right now—thesis papers, job applications, dreaming of a future after graduation, anything but staring aimlessly.

At least the band is as incredible as promised. But noticing the happy couples twirling nearby, I wonder if my perfect partner exists—an effortless blend of daring and intellect to match my speed.

Steady Craig is great on paper. He's the reliable scholar my high-achiever parents would applaud. The voice of reason, uncorrupted by adventure, spontaneity, or a desire strong enough to pull me onto the dance floor on my special night. And glimpsing his pained expression now, he clearly finds my choice of birthday activities torturous.

I guess it's good that this casual fling with Craig was never meant to be serious. In less than three months I'll be heading to Florida. This interim thing between us was only supposed to be light fun, something to occupy our nights and spark intelligent conversation. But now that we're here, I'm stuck watching this lukewarm companionship go down in flames on my favorite night of the year.

Since when did my list of attributes for dates start to consist of passion and impulsiveness?

Oh, right. That Christmas party two Decembers ago.

Before then, I was content with predictable. Somehow, in one night, Mark Bell sparked needs I didn't know I had. He made me feel alive. At first, anyway.

So why am I still thinking of him?

Because he was different when you saw him at the hospital, a small voice cries.

Ugh. Maybe I should have responded to Mark's texts when he asked to meet up last month. I mean, he did keep his word this time.

Craig shifts, blessedly interrupting my wayward spiral towards could-have-been. Before overthinking, I offer to grab drinks. Because, honestly, I need a minute away to properly analyze why the hell my thoughts all end with that infamous playboy again.

Just enjoy the night, Arden. Have fun solo if you need to. You've never needed anyone else before.

I straighten my silk and sequined dress, floating toward carefree laughter and hypnotic chords. But before I make it too far, strong hands grasp my hips and pull me back against a firm chest.

Seriously? Can't a girl dance alone these days?

My breath catches as I'm swiftly spun around.

No.

Three inches from my wide-eyed stare is the ever-infuriating, ridiculously handsome man of my nightmares and fantasies. Mark smirks, arms flexing beneath his painted-on, designer button-up, revealing those too-tempting muscles.

Damn, I forgot what he looked like dressed up. So much for getting over those dreams. Or the hurt of his disappearing act after our night together last year.

"I must be in a museum because you, babe, are a work of art," he tosses out casually.

I scoff, crossing my arms despite my heart pounding dangerously in my chest. "Babe? Wow, Mark. It's nice to know you haven't lost touch with the ladies. Come to see if I need rescuing tonight? Or just stringing me along again?"

Hurt flashes briefly before he fixes a charmed grin. "Actually, I wanted to ask about your sister. How's she doing?"

I blink, shocked by the sincerity in his voice. "She's...she's doing better. She recently finished rehab and went back to campus for the semester. I'm going to visit her in a few weeks."

"Good. I'm happy to hear that." His dark eyes sweep down my body shamelessly. "Now that you can't use her as an excuse, maybe you can tell me why a certain firecracker keeps ignoring all my texts?"

Me? Ha.

"I'm surprised you didn't move to the next on the list," I respond dryly, glancing down at his forearms jutting off my hips like branches leading to the forbidden fruit. *Has he gotten sexier? Is that even possible?*

I reach for my usual composure, not wanting Mark to see how much his attention can ruffle every one of my feathers. "But as much as I'm enjoying this reunion, I should probably get drinks and head back to my date."

"Right. Your date." Mark glances over his shoulder at the table where Craig ignorantly stares at his phone. "The guy who sent *you* to get drinks? Come on. Even I'm better than that."

I bark out a surprised laugh. *So he did notice me.* "You? Better? Oh, *babe*, you couldn't handle me."

His grin only widens. "Damn, I miss that sassy tongue."

I retreat a clumsy step and his smile falters, something more genuine replacing it. "Don't go. Can we talk for a minute?"

I lift my chin, reaching for confidence I don't feel. "Talk? Last time we talked, it didn't exactly end well."

Images of our night together, followed by months of his silence, flash through my mind. They're a stark contrast to the steadying presence that held me together at the hospital weeks ago.

Mark leans closer, his breath fanning my ear. "But everything before that was pretty spectacular, and you know it."

Same cocky playboy, I remind myself. But he's not wrong…

Mark anchors his hand on my lower back, reading my traitorous thoughts, and guides us toward a quieter corner of the bar. "C'mon. I won't keep you from that boring date of yours too long."

I stare up at his sparkling brown hues, my heart skipping at the mischievous glint in his eye. "Exactly how long have you been watching me, Mark?"

Mark huffs a nervous laugh, his gaze slowly trailing my body in a way that makes my skin tingle. "Didn't miss you when you walked in, if that's what you're asking."

I hum, synapses firing rapidly at the thought of this god-like man noticing me as we continue weaving through the crowd. I'm hyper-aware of every touch, of the way his body brushes against mine with every step. It's intoxicating and terrifying all at once, a reminder that our chemistry needs no refreshers.

Mark halts us near a shadowy booth, spinning to face me with uncharacteristic vulnerability. "Look, Arden, I know I'm probably the last person you want to see right now, but I couldn't let another moment pass without saying this." He takes a deep breath, his fingers tentatively intertwining with mine. "I'm sorry. For everything. The way I treated you that night, the radio silence afterward. I was an ass, and you deserved better."

I arch an eyebrow, fighting the urge to melt at his touch. "Wow, an apology from Mark Bell? Did I miss the news about Hell freezing over? Or did you just run out of willing women to charm?"

He winces, a rueful smile playing on his lips. "Yeah, I had that coming. Probably deserve worse, if we're being honest."

I study him, searching for any hint of insincerity, but find only genuine regret in his eyes. It's disarming, and I find it hard to resist the whisper to surrender to this confusing man.

"Your support at the hospital meant a lot," I admit softly, my gaze dropping to our joined hands. "I should've responded to your texts, but...I couldn't risk being just another notch on your bedpost."

Mark's thumb traces gentle circles on the back of my hand. "You could never be 'just' anything, Arden. You're...different."

I can't help but laugh. "Different, huh? Is that your new pickup line?"

"Hey, I'm trying here," he chuckles, but there's a nervousness to it I've never heard before. "What do you say we start over? Maybe with you actually answering my texts this time?"

I bite my lip, torn between self-preservation and the allure of second chances. "You really have impeccable timing, you know that? Showing up on my birthday of all nights. At least the band's made it tolerable."

Mark's eyes widen comically. "Wait, it's your birthday? And you're spending it with Mr. Personality back there instead of me? That's it, we're having a do-over. Right now."

I roll my eyes, but can't suppress my smile. "You're impossible."

"Part of my charm," he grins, tugging me gently towards the bar. "Come on, birthday girl. Let me buy you a drink. As friends," he adds, seeing my hesitation.

"Friends," I echo, ignoring the little thrill that runs through me at his touch. "Just friends, Romeo. Don't get any ideas."

He leans in close, his breath hot against my ear. "Too late, Juliet. I'm full of ideas when it comes to you."

As he pulls back, his eyes dancing with something dark and more intense, my skin prickles with awareness.

Before I can gather my wits, Mark turns to the bartender, his charisma on full display. "Two shots of your finest tequila, please. It's the birthday girl's special day."

I sputter, caught off guard by his bold announcement. "Mark! You can't just..."

"What?" he shrugs, handing me the shot with a wink. "Can't make this night special? Relax, Bubbles."

I raise an eyebrow, fighting back a smile. "Bubbles?"

"For that bubbly personality of yours, I enjoy so much," Mark says, clinking his glass to mine. "Happy birthday! Cheers to new friends and new nicknames."

"Cheers to twenty-three, Trouble," I respond, raising my shot.

"Trouble?" Mark echoes, his eyes sparkling with amusement. "I like it. Suits me, don't you think?"

"Definitely," I agree, knocking back my shot and relishing the burn of the tequila as it slides down my throat. "You've been nothing but trouble since the day we met."

Mark's fingers trail down my arm, leaving a path of heat in their wake. "Ah, but you love it. Admit it, Arden. Life's more fun with a little trouble in it."

My response sticks in my throat as a busty blonde slithers up, interrupting us with possessive familiarity.

"Here you are! I've been looking all over for you," she coos, red nails digging greedily into his arm.

My smile falters, my stomach twisting with the all-too-familiar sting of betrayal.

"Gwen…hey," Mark says tentatively, eyes barely leaving mine.

I flash back instantly to that first bewildering interaction at his frat party, where initial sparks between Mark and me died abruptly with the arrival of a clingy redhead at his bedroom door. His hasty dismissal of me, how he'd so quickly turned his attention to someone else, hits me in a sickening wave of memories.

How could I be so naïve?

I force myself to meet the blonde woman's dismissive stare with as much dignity as possible. Because, clearly, Mark hasn't lost his charming touch with *all* women.

"Anyway, I should get back…" My tone, thankfully, emerges nonchalant as I gesture vaguely toward my table. I take a step backward, refusing eye contact with either of them.

"Arden, wait!" Mark reaches for my wrist, dislodging his pouting date's hand. "It's your birthday, please just—"

I wave him off, humiliation and anger roiling dangerously inside. "It's okay, Mark. We really do have terrible timing," I bite out, not waiting for him to respond.

As I walk away, head held high, I second-guess myself. Am I overreacting? Did Mark stop me only to apologize? He never said he wanted anything more.

Still, the sight of that blonde draped all over him, the casual indifference with which he'd greeted her…it was all too familiar, too painful to ignore.

Back at the table, and out of Mark's sight, I barely resist the childish urge to stomp my feet.

Craig glances up from his phone, furrowing his brows at my huffy expression and empty hands. "Everything alright, Dee? You seem a bit flustered."

I exhale, forcing breezy detachment. "Oh, just ran into an old…friend."

Craig's eyebrows raise slightly. "Friend? I don't think I've seen you this worked up over a friend before."

I'm about to respond when Mark materializes at our table, running a hand through his hair in a way that's frustratingly attractive.

"Arden," he says, his voice low and urgent. "I screwed up. I should've told you I was here with someone. But it doesn't change anything I said earlier. And yeah, we have terrible fucking timing."

Craig's eyebrows shoot up, his gaze ping-ponging between us. "Um, what's going on?"

I sigh, gesturing between them. "Craig, this is Mark, the friend I ran into. Mark, meet Craig. My date."

Mark barely acknowledges Craig, his eyes locked on mine. "Arden, please. Don't shut me out again."

I laugh, the sound brittle and sharp. "That's rich coming from you, Mark. Shouldn't you be off charming Miss America over there?"

Craig clears his throat, clearly uncomfortable. "Arden? Is everything okay?"

Before I can answer, Mark jumps in, his tone oddly formal. "Look, I came over to invite you both to join us up front. It's Arden's birthday, and my roommate's band is playing. Thought she might want to meet them."

His hand finds my shoulder, his touch almost pleading. "Come on, Arden. Let me make it up to you. Don't let me ruin your night."

Craig glances at me, a hint of concern in his eyes. "What do you want to do, Dee? It's your birthday celebration."

My celebration? Twenty minutes ago, I couldn't pry him from this booth. Introduce another guy vying for my attention, and suddenly, he's happy to join.

I bite my lip, torn between lingering hurt and the magnetic pull I still feel towards Mark despite it all. Finally, I nod. "Alright, fine. But only because I want to meet the band."

Mark flashes an irresistible dimpled grin, but it fades quickly when Craig shockingly hops up and grabs my hand.

As we follow Mark towards the VIP section, Craig squeezes my hand. "Just say the word if you want to leave."

I'm sure that's exactly what he wants me to do. Leave.

I offer a grateful smile. "Let's just enjoy the night, yeah? Who knows, maybe we'll even get you crowd surfing."

Craig chuckles, shaking his head. "I think I'll leave the wild antics to you. I'm more of a cheer-from-the-sidelines kind of guy."

At least he's self-aware. Not like Mr. Arrogance ahead of us.

As we enter the VIP section, I risk a glance at Mark, only to find his gaze fixed on me, intense and full of unspoken meaning. And, yeah, there's no question which man could make me lose all inhibitions on the dance floor tonight.

I quickly glance away, refusing to let myself get pulled back in by his charm.

But as he introduces us around, his hand ghosting over my lower back, I feel that same spark ignite between us.

This night is far from over. And with Mark Bell around, anything could happen.

And damn it, if that isn't as thrilling as it is terrifying.

.

4

Mark

Now, February 22nd

She's the one fucking girl I turned down. The only girl I've had in my bed, completely ready and willing, that I walked away from. The one that's haunted my dreams ever since, a constant reminder of what could have been, what I was too scared to reach for.

It took me months to even look at another woman after meeting her, months of drowning myself in working out, studying, and booze. Anything that would erase the memory of her skin against mine, her laughter in my ear, or the way she made me feel like, for once in my life, I wanted more than sex.

Because, fuck, if I wasn't seeing rings, wedding bells, and white picket fences when I kissed her. So I ran. I pushed her away like she wasn't the best thing I'd ever had in my bed.

Then, when I was finally back to my usual self, my armor firmly in place, she showed up again, bawling into my shirt, confiding in me, making me want to comfort instead of charm. She had me thinking I should be someone who stays beyond the hookup, someone who selflessly cares for a woman instead of seeking the next fleeting high.

Is that why I'm desperate for her attention tonight? Finally ready to explore this? Because seeing her here, in the flesh, close enough to touch, to taste...it's like a fucking revelation. I want it all. I want her.

The biting comeback perched on my tongue melts away as Arden's eyes roll skyward dramatically, her full lips thinning in that signature sass that already drives me crazy. My pulse kicks into overdrive, imagining far more enjoyable reasons I could provoke those reactions—maybe tracing that tempting mouth with my fingers and tongue until she's breathing my name in a heated mantra.

But I gave up that opportunity. Now I'll have to earn it back.

When she stopped responding to my texts two months ago, I convinced myself she was gone for good, that I'd fucked up beyond repair. But somehow, I'm being gifted another chance. And with one glimpse of her in the bar light's glow, I'm ready to send every other woman packing without a backward glance.

I hide a smirk, a twisted sense of satisfaction curling in my gut as I watch Captain Generica struggle to hold her interest. Judging by his floundering attempts at conversation, he's out of his depth. The realization that she's as unimpressed with him as she is with my text game probably shouldn't fill me with such possessive pride. But sue me, it does

Now I just need to figure out how to keep those soulful brown eyes on me...and how to lose Gwen before she ruins everything with her clingy bullshit.

Why'd I choose tonight to finally ask someone out? *Our fucking terrible timing, that's why.*

As we enter the VIP area, I guide Arden with a light touch to her lower back, trying not to grin like an idiot when I feel her slight shiver. I lean in close, introducing her to the band's friends, my voice low and intimate.

When Jake's ballad starts playing, I see my chance. "Hey," I murmur, offering my hand. "Dance with me?"

Arden's eyes widen, caught off guard. She glances around, biting her lip and driving me crazy. "I...I don't think that's a good idea, Mark."

The rejection hits harder than I expected. Usually, I can charm my way into or out of anything, but Arden? She sees right through me. And damn it if that doesn't make me want her even more.

Baby steps, I remind myself. *Rome wasn't built in a day, and Arden Cooper's trust won't be won back in a night.*

I nod, forcing a smile. "No worries. Maybe later?"

I wave over a waitress, hyperaware of Arden settling in next to me, her thigh brushing mine. Just as I'm about to order, a honeyed laugh cuts through the air like nails on a chalkboard.

Gwen.

Before I can react, she's in my lap, arms around my neck like a python. "Marky!" she coos, loud enough for the whole VIP section to hear.

I wince, trying to maneuver out of her grasp without causing a scene. Arden probably assumes this clinging act is more than what it looks like, that I'm some taken man. I scramble to explain, to find the words to tell her that Gwen means nothing to me.

But before I can speak, Gwen catches Arden's attention, tapping her on the shoulder. giggles, cutting me off with a pout. "This one likes to play hard to get. I've been trying to pin him down for months."

Hard to get? More like I had to get over seeing Arden...again.

Gwen punctuates this little act by fingering my collar inappropriately. "Come on, babe. Let's dance!"

"I'm not really in the mood," I bite out, barely containing a smile as Arden's head whips in my direction.

As Gwen pouts, I drain my beer, wishing I could drown myself in the amber liquid and forget this whole fucking mess. Maybe I should've just asked Arden to ditch this place with me earlier. Then again, knowing her, she probably would've told me to go to hell.

Make her comfortable. Make her like you.

I spot Jake's girlfriend, Tessa, nearby and seize the opportunity for a distraction. "Hey, Tessa! Come meet my friends." I gesture to Arden and her date, whose name completely escapes me. *Shit.*

"Arden," I manage, then falter. "And, uh..."

"Craig," Arden supplies, her tone clipped. "My date."

I wince internally. *Nice one, Bell.* "Right, Craig. Sorry, man."

Trying to salvage the situation, I quickly add, "Tessa here is Jake's girlfriend. You know, the lead singer of All Rhoades?"

Tessa, bless her, jumps in with a warm smile. "It's great to meet you both!"

I watch Arden carefully, hoping for a reaction. Her eyes light up as she glances between Tessa and the stage, and I feel a surge of relief.

"Wait, you're dating the singer?" Arden asks, genuine interest coloring her voice. "That's so cool. They're absolutely killing it up there."

Tessa beams, clearly pleased by Arden's enthusiasm. "Aren't they? I'm so glad you're enjoying the show. You should tell them yourself—they'll be down after this song."

I lean back in my seat, watching the exchange unfold with relief and admiration. Leave it to Arden to find common ground and forge a connection with a total stranger.

Gwen's nails dig into my shoulder, demanding attention, but I barely notice. I'm too caught up in Arden's laugh, the way her eyes crinkle at the corners when she smiles. And right now, she has me wanting things I've never craved before.

The moment the band steps off the stage, Tessa is on her feet, waving them over with an excited grin. "Guys, come meet Arden and Craig! Arden's a big fan."

Jake leads the way, his eyes lighting up as he spots me. "Mark! I wasn't expecting to see you here tonight, man. I thought you had other plans." His gaze darts to Gwen and then Arden, a silent question in his raised brow: *How did you manage to get Arden here, and why is Gwen still around?*

Most people assume the women rotating through my life are nameless, interchangeable. But Jake knows specifically about Arden. He knows about our exchange in the hospital and my pursuit afterward in an attempt to make up for behaving like such as asshole last year. And he knows she's played me the previous two months the same way I play everyone else…by ghosting them.

I shrug, aiming for nonchalance. "Plans change. You know how it is."

Jake chuckles, shaking his head as he greets Arden and Craig. "Nice to meet you both. Though I think I've heard of you before, Arden."

Thanks, Jake. Like I need any more reasons to crawl beneath this table tonight.

My face goes crimson as I catch Arden's smirk, but she plays it off, offering her hand like the comment never happened. "Likewise. Seriously, you guys were incredible up there. I can't believe it took me this long to see you play."

As Jake, his two brothers Owen and Thomas, the drummer Chris, and Arden fall into easy conversation about the band's music and influences, I can't help but watch Craig hover at her side, his hand resting possessively on her thigh.

I need to get control of myself. Arden's not mine, no matter how badly I might want her to be. I made that clear a year and a half ago when I told her to leave.

The reminder makes me sick to my stomach, and for a moment, I'm tempted to run far away from this complicated tangle of emotions. But that's what I did before. And as much as I tried, I couldn't forget her. There's no hiding from whatever this connection is, especially now that I've tasted it again. Or really want to taste it again…

Perhaps sensing my tension, Gwen drapes herself over me again. "Babe, I'm bored," she whines, her voice hitting my last nerve. "Let's get out of here, go somewhere more...private."

I'm about to tell her to find some other poor sap to latch onto when I catch Arden watching us from the corner of my eye, her expression unreadable.

Fuck. This is not how I wanted this night to go.

Extricating myself from Gwen's octopus-like grip, I lean forward, determined to salvage what's left of this train wreck of an evening. "So, Craig, what do you do? How'd you and Arden meet?"

It's a desperate attempt to shift the focus and show Arden that I'm interested in her life. That I'm not just some dick only out for one thing.

Craig blinks, looking startled to be addressed directly. "Oh, uh, I'm a senior. Pre-med," he says, puffing up his chest a bit. "Arden and I met through a mutual friend. We've been seeing each other for a few weeks now."

There's a note of pride in his voice, a subtle marking of territory that has me working my jaw unconsciously. But I force myself to nod, to smile like it doesn't fucking kill me to imagine him with his hands on Arden, his lips on her skin.

"Pre-med, huh? That's impressive, man. I barely survived Biology 101."

Arden snorts softly beside me, and I glance over to find her watching me with a wry smile.

"If I remember, didn't you get a degree in exercise science? I think you might've passed biology," she comments, her eyes sparkling with humor. "Or did you charm the TA into giving you extra credit to pass?"

Damn, her memory is fantastic. But I'm just as guilty of clinging to every word we exchanged that fateful night. The way she confided in me about her internal struggle regarding law school, the desperation in her voice as she yearned to be seen as more than the sum of others' expectations—those raw, vulnerable moments are seared into my mind, unforgettable and profound.

"Guess my secret got out, then," I joke, grateful for her lifeline. "Though I earned every one of those pity points."

Arden laughs, the sound warming me from the inside out, and I can't help but grin back at her, feeling lighter than I have all night.

But the moment is short-lived, broken by Craig pointedly clearing his throat. "Well, as fun as this has been, I think it's about time we called it a night, don't you, Dee? Early lab tomorrow and all."

Did I get under his skin?

"No, stay," Owen, Jake's oldest brother, chimes in, his eyes glinting with mischief. "A little birdie mentioned it's your birthday, Arden. We can't let you leave without a proper celebration."

"Yeah," Jake agrees, a smug grin spreading. "And I'm dying to hear more about how you and Mark met. It's not every day he brings *friends* around."

I kick his leg under the table, shooting him a warning glare as I lift my beer glass in a hasty toast. "How about we save that story for another day? Just focus on Arden tonight. Besides, don't you guys need to get back on stage?"

Owen checks his watch and nods, but the knowing look he shares with Jake tells me this conversation is far from over.

"Oh, I want to hear," Gwen purrs. "Sounds juicy."

I gently pry her hand away, my jaw clenching with barely concealed irritation. *If only she knew how quickly I'd abandon this entire bar if Arden asked.*

I shrug, keeping my tone casual. "We just met at a party, that's all."

Gwen's eyes narrow, clearly seeing through my flimsy explanation. But before she can voice her displeasure, I catch a conspiratorial gleam in Jake's eye as he leans toward the mic, a wicked grin spreading across his face.

"Hey, Sadie's!" he calls out, his voice booming over the crowd. "Before we get back to the music, I wanted to give a special shout-out to the birthday girl in the house tonight." He points toward Arden, his grin widening. "Where's the lovely Arden Cooper?"

As the spotlight swings her way, her eyes widen in surprise. Then the band launches into a lively rendition of 50 Cent's "In Da Club," and the entire bar erupts in a chorus of laughter and cheers.

Swept up in the moment, our entire section surges toward the dance floor. As I move to follow, I notice a glaring absence: Arden's date, Craig, lingering by the table, a scowl etched on his face. A surge of petty satisfaction courses through me at the sight. *Looks like Mr. Pre-Med isn't much for birthday serenades,* I muse.

Then Arden steals my attention. Her body moves effortlessly, swaying to the beat. And when her eyes find mine across the crowded dance floor, time seems to stand still. She arches a brow, a silent dare, a challenge to see who will break the connection first.

As if I could. As if I'd ever want to.

I'm helpless, my eyes glued to her with an almost physical magnetic pull. A wicked grin plays on her lips as she catches me staring, and I feel my body react, a searing heat coursing through my veins, igniting every nerve ending.

Fuck, I want her. Want her with a desperation that borders on madness.

Gwen's hand clasps mine, trying to tug me in the opposite direction, but I pull away, my eyes never leaving Arden. Gwen can't compete with the glittering dark eyes of the firecracker rocking the dance floor.

"Mark!" Gwen hisses, her voice sharp with anger. "If you walk away, you can kiss this ass goodbye."

Her words fade into nothing as I push through the crowd, drawn to Arden like a moth to a flame.

And when she throws me a daring smirk over her shoulder, her hips swaying in a way that steals my breath? I know I'm a goner.

To hell with the consequences. To hell with anything that tries to keep me from her.

As if he can read my thoughts, Jake chooses now to switch songs, the opening notes of Usher's "You Got It Bad" pulsing through the speakers. I catch his knowing grin from the stage and flip him off subtly, even as I send up a silent thank you.

Because the song has Arden spinning into my arms, her body pressing deliciously against mine, her fingers trailing sparks down my chest. And when she laughs breathlessly, her eyes telling me she knows exactly what the lyrics mean, I'm lost.

I've got it bad, alright. So fucking bad it hurts.

But with her here, smiling up at me like I'm the only man in the world? The ache in my chest feels less like pain and more like promise.

My hands find her hips, pulling her closer until there's no space left between us. The heat of her body seeps into mine, intoxicating and overwhelming in the best possible way. We move together like we were made for this, like our bodies were designed to fit perfectly against each other.

Arden's fingers slide up my chest, curling around the back of my neck. I lean down, my forehead resting against hers, our breath mingling in the scant space between our lips.

"Arden, do you have any idea what you do to me?" I murmur, my voice low and rough with want.

Her eyes flutter closed briefly, her tongue darting out to wet her lips. "I might have an inkling," she breathes, her hips pressing harder against mine.

Fuck, I can't think straight when she's this close. Her body, her scent, the way she feels pressed up against me—it's all driving me insane. To hell with holding back.

I dip my head, my lips brushing against hers in the barest whisper of a kiss. And for one perfect, heart-stopping moment, I swear she leans into me, a soft sigh escaping her mouth.

But then she's pulling back, her hands sliding down to my chest, gently but firmly putting space between us. I blink, dazed and confused by the sudden loss of her warmth.

"Mark..." Her voice is soft, tinged with regret. "We can't. Just friends, remember?"

Just friends. The harsh reminder of the line I'm desperately trying not to cross.

I catch the glimmer in her eye, the teasing curl of her lips. She's not rejecting me, not really. She's reminding me that this, whatever it is between us, must be taken slowly. That trust needs to be earned, not rushed.

So I take a deep breath, letting it out in a rueful chuckle. "Friends. Right. I can do that."

Arden's smile widens, her eyes sparkling with something that looks dangerously like affection. "Good. Because I like having you as my new friend, Trouble."

I grin, my heart so full it feels like it might burst. "I like being your friend, too, Bubbles. More than you know."

As the song fades out, as the spell of the moment slowly dissipates, I realize the truth in those words. Being Arden's friend, someone she trusts and confides in, might just mean everything to me.

But as she steps out of my arms with a coy smile, a thought whispers through my mind, fierce and unshakable in its certainty: Arden Cooper, you might not be mine yet. But someday? Someday, you will be. Even if you don't know it yet.

5

Arden ♥

Now, March 2nd

My phone chimes just as I'm walking out of my final class for the day. I glance at the screen, thoughts already swirling with anticipation. I bite my lip, mentally preparing myself for whatever witty comment Mark just sent, now that we're on daily texting terms.

It's been a week since our almost-kiss at the bar, and I can't seem to shake the memory of his lips hovering just inches from mine, the heat of his breath mingling with mine. I'd be lying if I said I hadn't replayed that moment a thousand times, wondering what would have happened if I'd closed the distance and surrendered to whatever pull consumes us.

But I didn't. And now, here I am, trying to navigate the murky waters of friendship with a man who sends flirty texts that toe the line of "platonic."

I should end whatever this is and protect my heart from the inevitable fallout. But every time I resolve to cut ties, Mark finds a way to draw me back in with a well-timed joke or a sweet comment that has my heart swooning. And for some unknown reason, I want more. More of his teasing banter, more of his undivided attention, more of the way he makes me feel like I'm the most important person in his life.

Case in point: the current message on my phone screen.

Mark: *Hey Bubbles, got a craving for pasta and hate eating alone. Wanna grab dinner?*

Is Mark...asking me out? Just the two of us?

A thrill of excitement hits. But just as quickly, doubt creeps in, reminding me why getting involved with Mark Bell is a recipe for heartbreak. He's a player, a serial charmer who's left a trail of broken hearts in his wake. Not to mention, I've already been burned by him once.

Do I really want to risk getting caught up in his games again?

But even as I try to talk myself out of it, I can't deny the part of me that's desperate to see where this could go—the part that's been dreaming of his touch, his kiss, since we first met.

Taking a deep breath, I type out a response before I lose my nerve.

Me: *What happened to Gwen? Or the other countless groupies that follow you around?*
Mark: *Just you.*

Two simple words, but they're enough to send my heart soaring and my doubts retreating to the back of my mind.

Maybe it's foolish. Maybe I'm setting myself up for another fall. But right now, all I can think about is the promise of an evening spent in Mark's company, lost in the depths of his dark eyes and the warmth of his smile.

I grin, my fingers flying over the keyboard as I shoot back a playful response.

Me: *Wow! You really know how to sweep a girl off her feet when asking her out. No cheesy pick-up line this time?*

Mark: *So confident it's a date? Thought this was just friendly.*
   Francesca's at 8. See you there.
Me: *So assured I'll show?*
Mark: *You can't resist me.*

Heat floods as temptation wars with common sense. Because his response is 100 percent accurate, and as much as I can tell myself it's just an innocent dinner, I know it's a carefully laid seduction trap. If I go, I'll need to armor up against those dark, devilish eyes that cause my reservations to crumble so quickly. I may have thrown caution to the wind last year, believing he'd want something more than an empty hookup, but now...now I know better.

Or do I?

Me: *Guess we'll find out in a few hours.*
Mark: *I'll have the drinks waiting.* 🥂
Me: *Such a FRIENDLY thing to do.*
Mark: *Oh, I'll be on my best friendly behavior.* 😏 *See you soon.*

I slide my phone back into my pocket, trying to convince myself this is just a casual dinner between acquaintances, not some candlelit romance. But the grin spreading across my face as I think about having dinner solo with Mark on our not-a-date is a dead giveaway. Who am I kidding? Agreeing to a round two with Chicago's heartbreaker-in-chief is probably the definition of insanity.

With a sigh, I rush home, determined to find the perfect outfit that says, "I don't care what Mark thinks," while simultaneously making me look irresistible. After an hour of wardrobe changes and self-pep talks, I finally settle on a v-neck, long-sleeve dress that hugs my curves, paired with cute flannel leggings and sultry knee-high boots. The mirror reflects a woman who looks damn good—dressy enough for a date, casual enough for a friendly dinner.

As I approach the restaurant, the tantalizing aroma of garlic and herbs fills the air, making my stomach grumble in anticipation. I take a deep breath, smoothing my clammy palms down my jacket. It's just dinner with an incredibly gorgeous man who can make me weak in the knees with a single glance—no big deal, right?

But as the hostess leads me through the restaurant, the soft glow of candlelight dancing across the tables shatters my illusion of casualness. *Candles, really?* This isn't just a casual meet-up. This is a full-blown, hearts-in-eyes, rom-com-worthy date.

And then I see him.

Mark rises from our table, his smile capable of melting glaciers. The low lighting accentuates his chiseled features and the mischievous glint in his eyes.

With gentle movements that contrast the intensity in his gaze, Mark helps me out of my coat. The hostess takes it away, but I barely notice, to caught up in the depths of his dark eyes, acutely aware that I'm in big, capital "T" Trouble. The kind of trouble that comes with a soundtrack of sappy love songs and a montage of longing glances across crowded rooms.

"You showed," Mark teases, his dimples flaring with a playful grin. "I was starting to worry you might actually stand me up."

I raise an eyebrow, trying to ignore the way my pulse races at his proximity. "And miss out on the chance to witness the legendary Mark Bell charm in action? Never."

He chuckles, pulling out my chair. As I sit, he leans in close, his breath tickling my ear. "You look beautiful tonight, Arden."

Heat rushes to my cheeks, and I suddenly find the nonexistent wrinkles on my dress absolutely fascinating. When I finally gather the courage to meet his amused stare, I volley back daringly, "I'm impressed, Mark. I didn't think you'd bring your *friends* to such a swanky place."

"What can I say?" He grins, taking a sip of his whiskey. "I wanted to make tonight special. And a place this nice deserves pleasant company for once."

His fingers trail shivery sparks down my wrist, making me bite my lip to stifle a gasp. I quickly grab my menu, using it as a shield. *Yep, that's the look that drives me crazy.*

"Well, I hope I meet your elevated standards," I manage, peeking over the top of the menu. "You've certainly exceeded mine so far, minus the cheesy lines you probably used to sweet-talk the hostess."

"Cheesy lines? Me?" He drops his voice to a tempting whisper. "Tonight, my charm is only for you."

Damn him. If he keeps this up, I'm in serious danger of melting into a puddle right here at the table.

Our playful banter flows effortlessly as we navigate the menu, Mark's quick wit and charming comebacks leaving me grinning from ear to ear. When the waiter arrives, Mark's confident demeanor sets the tone for a pleasant exchange. He asks for the waiter's opinion on the best wine pairings, valuing their expertise and creating a warm, inclusive atmosphere. I can't help but admire the way he puts everyone at ease, his natural charisma shining through in every interaction.

Mark leans in as we wait for our entrées, his gaze intense and focused solely on me. "So, tell me, how are the plans for law school coming along?" When I nearly choke on my wine, he adds quickly, "That was the plan, right? Law school after graduation?"

He remembers that? I take a sip of water, composing myself. "Oh, yeah. It was. But not anymore. I actually...changed direction."

Mark's eyes sharpen with curiosity. "Really? What's the new plan, then?"

Just as I open my mouth to respond, our food arrives, the tantalizing aroma of the dishes momentarily distracting us from the conversation. Mark thanks the waiter, his attention quickly returning to me, eager to hear about my new path.

"I changed my focus to consulting, actually," I admit. "One of my professor's early careers had a dramatic impact. After graduation in May, I'm heading to my parents' place in St. Pete and found an amazing company in Tampa. My final interview is in a few weeks."

It sounds crazy, admitting out loud that I'm chasing dreams instead of following the safe, well-trodden path to success.

"I've been researching the company for months, trying to learn everything I can about their business model and recent projects. I even contacted a few alums who work there to get their insights. I want to be as prepared as possible for this interview."

Mark's eyes widen, and for a moment, I brace myself for the same skeptical response I've gotten from everyone else. But then he lets out a low whistle. "Wow, Arden. That's some serious dedication. No wonder you're crushing it in your classes and landing dream job interviews."

I shrug, the pride evident in my smile. "I've always been a bit of an overachiever. When I set my mind to something, I give it my all and don't accept failure."

Wow, did I just say all that out loud? I swirl my pasta, needing to shift the topic before Mark thinks I'm too intense like everyone else.

"What about you? Still breaking hearts and taking names now that you've finished school?"

Mark shakes his head, a rueful smile playing on his lips. "Nah, I hung up the jersey. Both on the field and off."

I raise an eyebrow. "Oh, really? And who are you now, Mark? Aside from the kind of guy who takes women to fancy restaurants to impress them instead of their fraternity bedroom."

"That room seemed to please you just fine, if I remember correctly," Mark responds, grinning. "But in all seriousness, I took a job as an athletic trainer last summer. Recently, I started partnering with some of the pro sports teams around town, assessing injuries and designing rehab programs."

"Wow, Mark. That's actually...remarkable."

He shrugs, but I catch the glimmer of pride in his eyes. "Figured if I can't be out there on the field myself anymore, I might as well help other athletes stay in top form."

I tilt my head, curiosity piqued. "No more baseball? What happened?"

A shadow crosses his face, and for a moment, I think he might brush off the question. But then he sighs, his gaze turning distant.

"Shoulder injury last spring. I probably could've pushed through it, but..." He pauses, jaw clenching. "Truth is, I was looking for an out. Baseball was my dad's dream, not mine. He was always pushing me to be the best and go pro. Never mind what I wanted."

My heart clenches at the pain in his voice. I reach out, covering his hand with mine. "I'm sorry, Mark. That must have been tough."

He stares at our joined hands for a long moment before meeting my gaze. "It was. But it also made me realize something. I spent so long chasing his approval, trying to be the man he wanted me to be. I lost myself in the process."

I nod, thinking of my own situation. "It's like being trapped in someone else's story, isn't it? Always trying to live up to their expectations?"

Mark's thumb traces circles on my hand, his eyes distant. "Exactly. I'm done being a character in someone else's plot. It's time I write my own story."

"Well, this new chapter suits you," I say softly, a smile tugging at my lips. "Don't get me wrong, the cocky athlete routine had its charm, but this caring, supportive side? It's... intriguing."

Mark's eyebrow quirks, a playful glint in his eye. "Careful, Bubbles. Keep talking like that, and I might start thinking you're angling for a job as my personal therapist."

I laugh, the tension easing. "And what would that entail, exactly? Weekly sessions of stroking your ego?"

His knee bumps mine under the table. "So many directions to take that," he teases, quickly adding, "But I'd rather hear more about you."

Mark listens as I tell him about my decision to leave the law school track and about Cora's recovery. It's nice, having this kind of conversation, feeling like I can say whatever comes to mind without fear of judgment. And glancing up at his attentive stare, something shifts, an entirely new kind of heat blazing between us.

But then reality crashes back in, and I pull away, mentally scolding myself. What am I doing? I can't get swept up with Mark Bell. We're oil and vinegar.

"Sorry," I mutter, "I didn't mean to dump all that on you."

Mark leans forward, his eyes searching mine. "Arden, you can always be yourself with me. The real you. Baggage and all."

His sincerity catches me off guard, and I feel my carefully constructed walls start to crumble. *How does he know just what to say to disarm me completely?* "I'm enjoying getting to know you too," I admit. "More than I expected."

Mark's smile is radiant. "Well, then, let's keep surprising each other."

"Yeah," I breathe, lost in the warmth of his gaze. "I guess we will."

As we walk out into the cool night air, Mark's hand brushes against mine. His eyes are full of unspoken promises, and I find myself wanting to take that leap. To believe that maybe, just maybe, we could be something more than a fling.

"So," Mark says, his voice low and teasing, "whatever happened to Mr. Tall, Dark, and Boring from the bar?"

I let out a shaky laugh, both relieved and disappointed by the change in subject. "Craig? Yeah, that fizzled out before I even made it home that night."

Mark's grin widens. "Can't say I'm disappointed to hear that."

"What about you?" I counter. "Did you and Gwen kiss and make up after her little tantrum?"

Mark pauses, his eyes flickering to my lips before meeting my gaze with an intensity that makes my breath catch. "Nah, wasn't worth it. Not when I've got my sights set on someone far more intriguing."

I try to ignore the flutter in my stomach. "Oh? And here I thought I was special."

"Trust me, Bubbles, you're in a league of your own," Mark says, his smile softening. "In fact, I was thinking...the guys and I do movie nights on Tuesdays. Horror flicks, ironically. And since you like them so much, I thought that maybe I, uh, could get a do-over from last time?"

I smirk despite myself. "Horror movies? In March?"

He shrugs, a hint of vulnerability in his eyes. "It was kind of our thing growing up."

His too? I try to ignore the tightening in my chest at this new piece of information.

"Think you could keep your hands to yourself this time? I seem to recall some rather 'friendly' cuddling last year."

Mark holds up a hand. "Hey, in my defense, you were the one who jumped into my arms at the first sign of danger."

I scoff, trying to ignore the heat rushing to my cheeks at the memory of being curled up in his arms, wearing his clothes. "Please, you were just using it as an excuse to cop a feel."

Mark grins, leaning in conspiratorially. "Well, it did have that added benefit. But if you're worried about my wandering hands this time, you could always bring a chaperone."

I laugh, shoving him playfully. "What, like a stern nun with a ruler? I think I can handle you on my own, thanks."

"Ooh, kinky," Mark teases, eyes twinkling. "I like where your mind's at, Bubbles."

"Down, boy," I retort, rolling my eyes even as I fight a smile. "I swear, you're like a dog with a bone."

"Woof," he deadpans, before his expression turns sincere. "But really, Arden, I promise to be on my best behavior. Scout's honor." He holds up three fingers solemnly.

"You? A Boy Scout? Now that I'd pay to see."

"I'm full of surprises," he winks. "Stick around, and you might uncover a few more."

I try to keep my tone casual, despite the warmth spreading through my chest. "I'll think about it. But this better not be some elaborate ploy to get me alone in your room again."

Mark catches my hand in his, his thumb stroking over my knuckles in a way that makes my skin tingle. "You're not a game, Arden. You never were. But if you need me to promise, I will."

The earnestness in his eyes catches me off guard, and for a moment, we just stand there, hands entwined.

Finally, Mark steps back, smiling ruefully. "Come on, let me walk you home. It's late, and I'd feel better knowing you got back safely."

I roll my eyes, but can't help feeling touched by his concern. "I can take care of myself, you know."

"Oh, I'm well aware," he grins. "But humor me, just this once?"

Something in his tone makes me soften. "Fine, but don't make a habit of it. I don't need a personal bodyguard."

As we start walking, Mark bumps my shoulder playfully. "Shame. I was rather looking forward to seeing you in that Black Widow costume again."

I elbow him gently, failing to suppress my smile. "Keep it PG, hotshot. We're in public."

He laughs, the sound rich and warm in the cool night air. We continue in comfortable silence, our arms brushing occasionally as we navigate the quiet streets. Too soon, we arrive at my building, and I feel a pang of disappointment at the thought of saying goodbye.

"Well, this is me," I say unnecessarily, fiddling with my keys to prolong the moment.

Mark nods, his gaze drifting over my face like he's trying to memorize every detail. "Thanks for giving me another chance and meeting up so last minute. I had a really great time tonight."

I swallow around the sudden lump in my throat, my heart feeling too big for my chest. "I did, too, Mark."

He smiles, reaching out to tuck a stray curl behind my ear. The gesture is tender and intimate, and I find myself leaning into his touch without thought.

"See you soon," he murmurs, his fingers lingering on my cheek. With a final, gentle caress, Mark steps back, shoving his hands back in his pockets. "Sweet dreams, Arden Cooper."

And then he's turning away, disappearing into the shadows of the night. I stand there, watching him go, my heart racing and my skin tingling from his touch.

Somewhere between the drinks and getting here, the careful dance of flirtation and restraint we abided by all night, I realized the truth I've been trying so hard to deny.

I'm falling, hard and fast, and completely against my better judgment. And the scariest part?

I'm not sure I want to stop.

6

Mark ⚾

Now, March 13th

Jake smirks, drizzling butter over the freshly popped popcorn. "So, think your new *friend* will grace us with her presence tonight, or is she back to giving you the cold shoulder after your totally platonic, not-at-all-romantic, birthday dinner?"

"She didn't know it was my birthday, so keep your trap shut. And, yeah, she'll be here." I chug my beer to disguise the nerves creeping as the minutes inch closer to her arrival.

Why am I acting like this is the first time I've invited a girl over?

"Damn, dude, I've never seen you so worked up. Better alert the media their most eligible bachelor is finally hooked on a woman," Jake teases, munching popcorn with a knowing grin.

"Please, we're just friends. Remember?" I retort, tossing kernels at Jake's too-smug face. "And don't think I've forgotten about your little stunt with that Usher song last month. You're lucky no one else picked up on your less-than-subtle matchmaking attempt."

"Oh, come on! It was perfect," Jake protests, his laughter trailing me into the kitchen. "I'm just glad Owen didn't murder me afterward."

Right then, Owen bustles in, arms loaded with beer and snow dusting his hat. "Whoa, it's getting nasty out there!" He pauses, taking in my death glare aimed at Jake. "Uh-oh. Is Jake teasing you about your lady troubles again?"

"I do not have lady troubles," I grind out, snatching a beer from Owen's stash with enough force to send the bottles clinking together.

"Sure, keep telling yourself that, Loverboy!" Jake hollers, dropping the popcorn bowls onto the table in front of the couches.

I clench my jaw, his words hitting a little too close to home. Because denying my growing feelings for Arden has become a full-time job lately. And with the impending visit to my parents' next weekend, I need all the self-delusion I can muster.

Pasting on a carefree grin, I stroll back into the living room. "Aww, Jay, no need to be jealous. I've got plenty of love to go around."

Jake snorts, tossing a throw pillow at me. "Please, Hotcakes, you couldn't handle all this."

"Oh, I don't know," a familiar voice chimes in, causing us both to turn. "I think Mark might surprise you. He's got hidden depths."

Oh, shit.

Arden stands in the doorway, snowflakes melting in her hair, a mischievous glint in her eye. She steps inside, closing the door behind her. "Though you guys might want to consider locking up. You never know what kind of trouble might wander in off the streets."

I feel a grin spreading across my face. "Trouble, huh? And here I thought we were inviting in a little slice of heaven."

Jake rolls his eyes dramatically. "And there he goes, laying it on thick. You want some cheese with that wine, Mark?"

Arden laughs, shrugging off her coat. "Don't mind him, Jake. I find his cheesiness oddly endearing. Like a puppy trying to impress its owner."

"Hey!" I protest, but I can't keep the smile off my face as I grab her jacket. "I'll have you know, I'm more of a wolf than a puppy."

"Sure you are, Hotcakes," Arden winks. "Though I don't brave snowstorms for just any canine."

Tessa appears in the hallway, taking in the scene with amusement. "Did I miss something?"

Jake, ever helpful, pipes up. "Oh, you know, just Mark professing his undying love for me. Again."

I flip him off good-naturedly. "You're just mad you're losing your cuddle buddy." Turning to Arden, I soften. "What can I get you to drink?"

"Beer's fine," she says, following me to the kitchen.

As I grab a few bottles, Arden leans in close, her breath tickling my ear. "I like this host-with-the-most vibe you've got going on."

I suppress a shiver, forcing my voice to stay steady. "Careful what you wish for. I might just make a habit of it."

Her answering grin is wicked, and it takes every ounce of self-control not to pull her in for a kiss right then and there.

As we settle onto the loveseat, Jake queues up the movie and flips off the lights, plunging us into intimate darkness. I can't help but feel like everything's falling into place. And if the way Arden's thigh presses against mine is any indication, this night might just be the start of something amazing.

Friends, Mark. Just friends.

Clearing my throat, I try to sound casual. "So, how was the visit with your sister last weekend? Any wild freshman parties?"

Arden's eyes sparkle in the flickering light of the TV. "Wouldn't you like to know?"

My jaw clenches involuntarily. *Is that jealousy, Mark?* "Bet you had your share of nineteen-year-old college guys targeting you all night."

She chuckles, squeezing just above my knee. "Funny, wasn't I *your* target once upon a time?"

Jake and Owen's snickers don't even phase me as the memory of that night hits me like a freight train. Arden, sprawled across my sheets, her lips swollen from my kisses, my name falling from her mouth like a prayer.

Fuck, I was an idiot to let her go. Worse, actually. I told her to go.

But I can't admit that now, so I let my arm drape across her shoulders as I press my mouth to her ear, whispering for her alone. "Trust me, Arden, you're way more than a target."

Jake, ever the mood-killer, chimes in with a smirk. "So, Arden, Mark said you liked horror movies. Any specific reason? Besides the obvious appeal of cuddling up to Mark during jump scares."

Arden rolls her eyes, smiling. "Ha ha, very funny. If you must know, it was my freshman roommate. We were both homesick, and cheesy thrillers became our go-to comfort movies. I guess it just stuck with me."

My jaw drops, and I stare at her in disbelief. "Wait, seriously? Horror movies are your comfort films?"

She shrugs, a shy smile playing on her lips. "I know, it's weird. But there's something about the predictable scares that's... soothing, I guess?"

I shake my head, a grin spreading across my face. "Arden Cooper, you are full of surprises."

Jake clears his throat pointedly. "Well, well. Looks like you two have more in common than just unresolved sexual tension."

I shoot him a warning look, but Arden just laughs, her cheeks pink. "Alright, enough chatter. Let's start this movie before I come to my senses and bail."

As the movie kicks off, Arden snuggles closer, resting her head on my shoulder. The scent of her shampoo fills my senses, a tantalizing blend of vanilla and something uniquely her. I have to physically restrain myself from burying my face in her hair and inhaling deeply.

The eerie music surges on-screen, and Arden's hand finds mine, her fingers intertwining with my own. I give her hand a gentle squeeze, relishing the way her palm fits perfectly against mine. The warmth spreading through my chest has nothing to do with the horror on screen and everything to do with the woman beside me. And for the second time, I find myself hoping this night never ends.

It's a sweet torture, having her so close but not being able to touch her the way I desperately want to. By the time the credits roll, I'm wound tighter than a spring, every nerve ending in my body attuned to the woman beside me.

How did I ever turn her down? What the fuck was I thinking?

Her. I was thinking about her.

Jake flips the lights on, stretching with a yawn. "Nice pick, guys, but I think it's bedtime for me and Tes."

Arden smooths her rumpled hair, her shy smile flashing. "Yeah. I should probably get going, too. Thank you all for letting me crash. This was fun."

"Come back anytime," I blurt on instinct.

Arden peers up, surprise flashing, no doubt from my overly eager offer.

"Guys, it's getting bad outside," Owen comments, garnering our stares. Behind him, thick snow falls, illuminated by the city lights outside the window.

I glance at Arden, unease piercing me as I imagine her heading home.

Owen checks his phone, his brow furrowing. "Looks like we've got about five inches of snow already, and it's coming down fast." He glances at Jake and me, a pleading look in his eyes. "Mind if I crash on your couch tonight? I don't think heading up north's a good idea."

"Mi casa es su casa, buddy," I reply, but my attention is solely on Arden. "There's no way you're going home in this, Bubbles."

"So much for that promise, huh?" Arden raises an eyebrow, a defiant gleam in her eye. "But, seriously, I'm not that far."

Before I can argue, Jake, Owen, and even Tessa chime in, their voices overlapping in a discord of poorly veiled eagerness.

"You can totally stay here, Arden! The couch is super comfy."

"I'll make Jake sleep on the couch. You can stay in the room with me."

"Yeah, or you could bunk with me. I promise I don't snore...much."

I shoot them a quick glare, my jaw clenching. "Seriously?"

Turning to her, I soften my tone, reaching for her hand. "If you're uncomfortable staying here, let me drive you home. I want to make sure you get there in one piece."

Arden hesitates, her teeth biting her lower lip in that maddeningly adorable way. "I don't know, Mark. I don't want to be any trouble..."

"Nonsense," I assure her, gently squeezing her hand. "I'm just looking out for my girl—uh, I mean, my friend."

Smooth, Bell. Real smooth.

But Arden just smiles, a pretty blush staining her cheeks. "Okay, if you're sure. We should probably go, then, before the roads get any worse."

Grabbing my keys, I guide her to my car, the possessive caveman in me, preening at the thought of ensuring her safety myself.

Even though she's less than five miles away, the drive to her apartment is a white-knuckled affair—my sports car fishtails on the icy streets. I keep our speed slow, my heart in my throat every time we hit a patch of black ice.

When we finally slide into her parking lot, I'm half-tempted to throw Arden over my shoulder and carry her to her door.

Because that wouldn't be overkill at all.

"Well, that was... exciting," Arden says, her voice shaky but amused.

I laugh, the tension easing. "Just adding to the night's thrills."

As we make our way to her building, the snow falling heavier now, Arden turns to me with an unreadable expression. "Mark, I...I don't think you should drive back in this. It's too dangerous out there."

My heart races at the implication. "Are you...inviting me to stay?"

She bites her lip, a blush creeping up her cheeks. "I just...after Cora's accident, I couldn't live with myself if something happened to you. Plus, my roommate's out for the night, so..."

"Arden," I say softly, "are you sure?"

She nods. "Just behave yourself," she says, starting up the stairs. "Besides, I have some pajama pants you can wear."

Oh, if only she knew how impossible behaving myself will be.

As we enter her apartment, the air between us feels charged, like the calm before a storm. Arden busies herself in the kitchen, her movements slightly jerky.

"Drink?" she asks, her voice a touch too high. "I've got wine, beer, water..."

"Whatever you're having is fine," I reply, leaning against the counter and trying to appear more calm than I feel.

Arden uncorks a bottle of wine, her hands trembling slightly as she pours, and I wonder if she's as affected by this situation as I am.

"So," I say, accepting the glass she offers, "this is quite the turn of events, huh?"

Arden laughs, the sound a bit strained. "Yeah, who would've thought? Mark Bell, spending the night at my place. Platonically."

I raise an eyebrow. "Platonically? Is that a challenge?"

She rolls her eyes, but I catch the hint of a smile. "Don't get any ideas. I'm just being a good Samaritan."

As we settle on the couch, wine in hand, I can feel the tension slowly ebbing. This is Arden, after all. The woman who can match me quip for quip, who sees through my bullshit.

"Arden," I say softly, "talk to me. What's going on in that beautiful head of yours?"

She's quiet for a moment, her fingers tracing the rim of her wine glass. When she looks up, her eyes are filled with a vulnerability that takes my breath away.

"This is dangerous, isn't it?" she whispers, her thumb grazing my lower lip in a feather-light touch.

I swallow hard, understanding exactly what she means. "Arden, last year, I…" I can't finish the admission, so I subtly shift direction. "What would you have said if I'd asked you to stay that night?"

Arden's fingers knit through mine. "You didn't cross lines without permission, if that's what you're asking. I knew what I was signing up for. But I'll admit I don't often fall victim to empty hookups."

Because she thinks that's all it would've been.

I smooth her knuckles, gut twisting with shame. Should I tell her the truth? That it was never just a hookup for me? That the thought of waking up next to her, of having something real and meaningful, scared the ever-living shit out of me?

"I don't do the girlfriend thing. Never have," I confess, daring to meet her eyes.

Arden nods, disappointment flickering briefly.

I let out a painful sigh, deciding I need to be honest. "Remember how I mentioned my parents at dinner? There's more to that story." I pause, gathering my thoughts. "They were high school sweethearts. Got pregnant with me at seventeen. My mom...she resented my dad for 'trapping' her, as she put it."

Arden squeezes my hand encouragingly as the words pour forth in a torrent after being dammed up for years. "As I grew up, I watched their love turn bitter. My mom wanted to find out what she missed out on until it turned into a don't ask, don't tell policy. Any affection they once had soured into passive-aggressive jabs and behind-closed-doors fights. They stayed together 'for the kid,' but..." I trail off, shaking my head.

"Mark," Arden says softly, her hand cupping my cheek. "I'm so sorry you had to experience that."

I lean into her touch, drawing strength from her warmth. "It messed me up, you know? Made me hesitant to form any real connections outside of baseball and the Rhoades. I swore I'd never chain myself to someone only to wake up one day full of regret and resentment."

"But you're not your parents, Mark," Arden says, her thumb brushing my cheekbone. "You get to choose what kind of relationship you want."

I rub her hand, anxiety spiking. Because the way my pulse races holding her, the way I crave shielding her from all hurt...it feels terrifyingly close to a four-letter word I promised I'd never say. A word that only brings pain and disappointment.

I meet her gaze, vulnerability raw in my voice. "Do I? Because every time I start to feel something real, I panic. I push people away. Like I did with you that night."

Understanding dawns in Arden's eyes. "Is that why you asked me to leave?"

I nod, shame hitting violently. "You terrify me, Arden."

She raises an eyebrow, a hint of amusement in her eyes. "I terrify you? That's the best pick-up line you've used yet."

I chuckle nervously, trying to lighten the mood. "Well, you know, your wit is pretty formidable. A guy's gotta protect his ego."

Arden rolls her eyes, but there's a softness in her expression. "Right, because the great Mark Bell is so easily intimidated."

"Hey, I'm more sensitive than I look," I protest weakly.

She studies me for a moment, her gaze thoughtful. "So, what now? Are you going to push me away again?"

I swallow hard, the question hitting closer to home than I'd like to admit. Because doesn't it all end up in heartbreak anyway? "I don't know," I answer honestly. "I'm not great at this whole...vulnerability thing."

Arden nods, understanding in her eyes. "Neither am I, if we're being honest. It's easier to keep people at arm's length, isn't it?"

"Yeah," I agree softly. There's a moment of silence, heavy with unspoken emotions. Then, curiosity gets the better of me. "Have you? Been in love? Let someone get that close?"

She's quiet for a moment, a wistful expression on her face. "I thought so, once. But now...I'm not so sure. I always imagined true love would be all-consuming, you know? The kind of passion that defies logic and reason."

Does she feel it too? This pull between us that challenges everything I've ever thought?

I'm about to ask more when she adds, almost as an afterthought, "It doesn't really matter now, anyway. I'm leaving for Florida in two months. It's not like I'm looking for anything serious."

Right. How'd I forget that? Her interview for the company in Tampa.

"Two months, huh?" I counter, trying to keep my tone light despite the sudden heaviness in my chest. "That's plenty of time for me to charm you into staying."

Arden rolls her eyes, but I catch the hint of a smile. "Please. Your charm has an expiration date, remember? How long did you say your longest relationship lasted?"

I chuckle, tucking a strand of hair behind her ear. "Touché. I am a master at avoiding complications." For a brief moment, I let myself get lost in her stare, imagining a future where this could be normal—holding her every night, waking up to her smile. It's terrifying and exhilarating all at once. Even if I know it's only a dream.

"But maybe I'm due for a change?" I add softly, the words slipping out against my better judgment.

Arden raises an eyebrow. "Oh? And what brought on this sudden desire for personal growth?"

I meet her gaze, allowing another moment of sincerity to slip through. "Let's just say I've got some pretty compelling reasons to consider it."

Arden looks away, a faint blush coloring her cheeks. "It's late," she murmurs. "And as therapeutic as this has been, we should probably get some sleep."

She stands, and I follow, hyperaware of her every movement as we make our way to her bedroom. At the threshold, I pause, memories of our last encounter flooding back.

I can't let that happen again.

"Arden," I start, my voice low. "I just want to be clear...I'm not expecting anything. We can just sleep."

She turns, surprise flickering in her eyes before a smile tugs at her lips. "Of course, this is platonic after all. Though I should ask, who are you? Because you're definitely the Mark Bell I met last year."

I laugh, the tension easing slightly. "Just trying to win some challenge this stunning brunette tossed out."

She presses a folded pair of familiar pajama pants into my hands, smirking. "Here. Try not to seduce me in your sleep, okay?"

"No promises," I wink, accepting the pants.

When the door clicks shut behind her, I slide on the forgotten pants, my body buzzing with anticipation. A few minutes later, Arden emerges in a soft cotton pajama set that shouldn't look as sexy as it does. I have to physically restrain myself from reaching for her.

This night is going to be the sweetest kind of torture.

As Arden flips off the lights, I ease beneath the covers, holding them up invitingly. I exhale as Arden slides into the sheets, settling beside me. Staring at her silhouette with only the dim light of the window creates an aura of intimacy I should've better prepared myself for.

"This okay?" I ask, my voice rougher than I intended.

Arden nods, shifting slightly. "Yeah, it's fine. Although you could've made it easier on me and kept your shirt on."

I can't help but grin. "Just evening the playing field, Bubbles."

Her fingers trace a path down my chest, and I have to stifle a groan. "You call this even?"

I catch her hand, bringing it to my lips for a quick kiss. "Careful. You're playing with fire."

She laughs softly, nestling closer. "Goodnight, Mark."

As Arden's breathing evens out, I find myself staring at the ceiling, my mind racing. I'm supposed to be guarding my heart, but with Arden in my arms, it feels like a losing battle.

I'm in trouble, I realize. Deep, inescapable trouble. Because despite my best efforts, I'm falling for Arden Cooper. And I have no idea what to do about it.

7

Arden ♥

Now, March 14th

A husky voice caresses my ear. "Rise and shine, Bubbles."

My sleep-fogged brain clings to the fading strands of an incredibly vivid dream starring a certain magnetic charmer. As awareness creeps in, hints of manliness tease my nostrils.

I blink awake slowly, my heart stumbling over itself. *This isn't a dream.* Mark's here. In my bed.

Mark's hand still grips my waist with immense heat, reminding me that last night wasn't imagined either. I peer up to find him watching me, his dark eyes soft with unconcealed tenderness that repeatedly steals my breath.

"There you are." His hand slides up my back, trailing warmth in its wake. "How did you sleep?"

I grapple for normal brain function. Snippets of last night's sleepy confessions replay on a loop like exquisite torture. How we somehow made it through without ripping each other's clothes off still boggles my mind.

I clear my sandpaper throat. "Honestly? Great."

Mark chuckles, sending vibrations into parts of my body that still believe I'm in my not-PG dream. "Me too, surprisingly." At my coy silence, his grin widens. "Feel free to invite me over for sleepovers anytime. Platonic or otherwise."

Before I freshman-with-first-crush splutter in response, Mark presses a fleeting kiss to my forehead and starts to roll off the bed. *Someone's in a ridiculously good mood.* My fingertips drift up, skin tingling where his lips touched as I push through the sleepy haze.

"I should've told you last night, but I have a client appointment this morning. I didn't want to slip out without saying anything," he says casually, his muscular chest way too close to me.

"Yeah, of course," I mumble, reality slowly making it way into my brain.

It's Wednesday.

Reluctantly extracting myself from the warm cocoon of blankets, I freeze, my eyes widening at the sight before me. Mark, in all his shirtless glory, is lazily stretching, his flannel pants—my flannel pants—riding low on his hips.

Sweet baby Jesus, is this real life?

I avert my gaze before I spontaneously combust, stretching myself. *Two can play this game.* "So, what's the verdict on the great snowpocalypse outside?"

Mark's eyes dart to my midsection as my shirt rides up, his cheeks flushing adorably before he quickly looks away. "Oh, uh, heard the plows going by earlier. Probably fine by now."

He busies himself with gathering his clothes, his neck turning an impressive shade of red. I smirk, unable to resist teasing him a little.

"Feeling a bit flustered this morning?"

Mark's head snaps up, his eyes narrowing playfully. "Flustered? Me? Never. I'm the epitome of cool, Bubbles."

I can't help but laugh, heading towards the kitchen. "Right, and I'm the Queen of England. Coffee before you brave the arctic wasteland out there?"

He follows, leaning against the counter with that infuriatingly charming grin. "Well, if Her Majesty insists, who am I to refuse?"

As I start the coffee maker, I toss over my shoulder, "Don't let me keep you from your adoring fans. I'm sure they're lost without you."

Mark folds the borrowed pajama pants with exaggerated care. "Trust me, the Rookie I'm training is anything but an adoring fan. And I definitely considered playing hooky. More than once."

I slide a steaming mug towards him, my heart doing a little flip as his fingers brush mine.

He takes a sip, his eyes closing in bliss. "Mmm, this is amazing. You're a coffee goddess, Arden Cooper."

I shrug, fighting a smile. "Just another one of my many talents."

There's a comfortable silence as we sip our coffee. Something's shifted between us, a new understanding that I'm not quite ready to examine too closely.

Mark breaks the quiet, his voice softer than usual. "You know, I could get used to this. The banter, the coffee...it's nice."

Can he read my mind?

I nudge his shoulder, ignoring the warmth blooming in my chest. "Careful there, Hotcakes. Your ego might not fit through the door if I keep this up."

Mark feigns offense. "My ego is perfectly sized, thank you very much."

"Sure it is," I tease, taking a sip of my coffee.

The silence lingers, and I find myself lost in a daydream where Tuesdays could be movie nights together, and this could be our every Wednesday. The thought doesn't scare me nearly as much as it when I left for Mark's apartment last night.

"So, when's the next movie night?" I ask, stepping closer to where my color-coded calendar hangs on the wall. "Are they every Tuesday?"

Mark follows my gaze, his eyes landing on the circled date. "Usually. But I won't be there next week. I'm in Arizona for spring training." He taps the square marked "final interview" next Thursday. "But that's your big day, right? The Tampa gig?"

I blink, surprised he remembered. "Yeah, it is. Good memory."

His smile is soft, almost tender. "Well, you know, it seemed important to you."

Warmth blooms in my chest, but it's quickly overshadowed by a sinking realization. "Wait, did you say you'll be gone next week?"

Mark clears his throat, his hand rubbing the back of his neck. "Uh, yeah...heading out Friday for about a week. Baseball season's about to start. My schedule's crazy...pretty much through October."

Disappointment settles unfamiliarly. *Since when do emotions dictate your reactions, Arden?* I paste on a breezy façade, determined to maintain my composure. "Well, bring me back a cactus souvenir. You know, for when I nail this interview." I poke his arm playfully, ignoring the sudden urge to drag him back to my bedroom and keep him here.

Get a grip, Arden. It's a week. I've gone months without seeing this man, and now I'm acting like I can't handle a minute without him. Besides, we didn't actually say this was anything more than friendship. It's not like anything serious happened between us, even if a larger part of me than I'm willing to admit wishes it would have.

Mark's eyes crinkle at the corners, that signature charm on full display. "How about we celebrate your job offer when I get back? I'm booked Friday and Saturday, but Sunday's wide open."

"You sound so confident we'll be celebrating," I reply softly.

"Because they'd be stupid not to hire you. You're brilliant." He taps my nose, taking a step back.

"I should probably head out," he says, slipping on his shoes. "Thanks for letting me stay over. Last night was...well, it meant a lot to me."

The sincerity in his voice catches me off guard. "Yeah, it was...nice," I manage, cursing my inability to form coherent thoughts.

Mark's fingers graze my cheek as he tucks a strand of hair behind my ear. "Think about next Sunday, okay?" His thumb trails along my jawline, his eyes intense. "And crush that interview."

I laugh, still amused by his good mood. "When did you turn into Mr. Supportive?"

His eyes sparkle good-naturedly, making my insides flip in response. "Apparently, I wake up disgustingly upbeat next to you."

"Well, try not to forget it when you're hanging out with all Arizona groupies. I still expect my daily dose of inappropriate texts," I tease, ignoring the twinge of something that feels dangerously like jealousy.

Mark's grin turns wicked as he tugs me closer, his broad chest pressing against mine. "Trust me, Bubbles, you're not easy to forget."

He tucks more flyaway strands behind my ear, his gaze searching mine. Then, his thumb traces my lower lip, and I can't help but lean into his touch. My eyes flutter closed, and I find myself hoping, praying that he'll close the distance between us.

The tension builds, electric and all-consuming. I part my lips, ready to throw caution to the wind...

And then a loud, insistent knocking shatters the spell. We jump apart, startled by my neighbor's booming voice as he hollers about a misdelivered package.

Mark laughs ruefully, the sound easing the tightness in my chest. "Terrible fucking timing, huh?"

He shakes his head, squeezing my hand one last time before letting go. "Good luck with the interview prep, Bubbles. Can't wait to hear how it goes."

I nod, speechless, as I watch Mark walk away, already missing his presence.

What is happening to me?

Closing the door softly, I lean against it, my legs suddenly weak. Mark's scent still lingers, wrapping around me like a bittersweet embrace.

In a daze, I make my way to the bedroom, collapsing onto the rumpled sheets that still hold the imprint of our bodies. Staring up at the ceiling, I try to make sense of the whirlwind of emotions swirling inside me.

Last night, we crossed a line. We went from casual acquaintances to...what? Friends? Lovers? Something in between?

I squeeze my eyes shut, remembering the way Mark held me, the raw vulnerability in his voice as he shared his deepest fears and insecurities, and the way his touch set my skin on fire, making me crave things I'd never dared to want before.

But in the harsh light of day, reality comes crashing back in. I'm leaving for Florida, chasing the career I've finally dared to dream about. And Mark...Mark doesn't do relationships. He said so himself.

So why can't I shake this feeling that we're meant to be something more?

I press my palms against my eyes, trying to stem the tide of unwanted emotions. I'm not the girl who gets swept up in romantic fantasies. I have to focus on my goals and my carefully constructed plans.

But even as I try to convince myself, a small, traitorous part of me whispers that maybe the life I've dreamed about isn't the only thing I want.

Now, the only question that remains is what I'm going to do about it.

8

Mark

Now, March 23rd

I take another swig of the beer in my hand, staring at the glowing device lit up with messages about tomorrow's party and suggestions of "meeting up."

I scroll past one from a girl I vaguely remember from last semester, offering to "make my wildest dreams come true." I snort. Unless she's got a time machine that'll take me back to my pre-Arden era, I doubt she's got the skills.

"You good, man? Or still dazed from all that Arizona heat?" Jake's assessing stare bores into mine knowingly until I paste on a strained grin.

"Peachy. Thanks for asking. Just trying to figure out how I'm going to survive this baseball kick-off party without my trusty wingmen now that you guys are too cool for school." I down the remnants of my beer, eyeing them suspiciously as their halfhearted excuses fill the air.

"I mean, seriously though, I show up for dinner to celebrate Thomas's summer internship... and now you're all too mature for campus ragers?" I bite out a sarcastic laugh. "Guess this washed-up has-been will relive former glory days solo."

I stare at the empty bottle in my hand, mentally prepping for the impending doom that awaits me at my parent's house.

Why did I think staying there was a good idea again? I glance at the empty beer bottles on the table. *Oh, right. I was trying to be responsible—silly me.*

"Alright, boys, I'm heading out. Please tell your parents thanks for inviting me. It was nice to see them again, even if their offspring are a bunch of party poopers."

"You know you can stay here," Owen adds casually, nodding toward the basement couch I spent one too many adolescent nights on.

I exhale gruffly, raking both hands through my hair. "I promised I'd make an appearance since I'm in town." I keep my tone purposefully light despite the apprehension coiling tighter. "If I bail, I'll never hear the end of it."

After goodbyes, I shuffle reluctantly toward my childhood home next door, each step heavier than the last. Glancing up at the dark windows from the driveway, I wonder if the universe has taken pity on me and I'll be able to crash in peace tonight.

Slightly tipsy and already feeling like Sunday is too far away, an idea pops into my head. I pull up my favorite text thread. Arden's. If I'm gonna be forced back into college party land tomorrow, why not invite along the one bright spot guaranteed to improve the experience? Or at least provide a do-over from my dumbass move last year. There's no harm in that, right?

Me: *Any chance you're free tomorrow night?* 😬

I hit send before I overthink the impulse invite. I've never *invited* a girl to a party before, but the thought of having her pressed against me all night sounds infinitely more enjoyable than dealing with drunk twenty-year-olds vying for a piece. Especially when memories of Arden sleeping in my arms has my mind derailing, thinking of tantalizing ideas to persuade my favorite firecracker with another sleepover.

My phone chimes, and I glance down eagerly as warmth floods for reasons I still don't completely understand.

> Arden: *Sry, game night planned with some friends. Desperate to see me?*
> Me: *Just in need of another therapy session.*
> Arden: *I should start charging. Feeling taken advantage of.*
> Me: *We should talk about a payment plan then. Could put you on retainer.*
> Arden: *Interesting… Might need to chat that one live.*
> Me: *Sunday over breakfast?*
> Arden: *I'll order hotcakes.*

Anticipation still flutters as I step across the threshold into my parents' place. But any hopes of a drama-free night turn to ash as laughter—my mother's, but not my father's—filters down the dim corridor.

I halt abruptly, bile scorching my throat as the intimate scene registers. Some over-muscled twenty-something is wrapped around my scantily clad mother. At my explosive entrance, they spring apart, the broad-shouldered figure chilling my blood to ice.

Because I know that strong jaw and cocky grin.

"Bryce, what the actual fuck?" I bite out without thinking. Disgust curdles my stomach, seeing one of my high school teammates shamelessly groping my smirking mother.

At their fumbled excuses, resentment spurs a caustic retort as I head further away from their make-out session. "Guess I shouldn't be shocked by anything these days. You always were desperate for ass."

"Mark, stop!" my mother commands, standing up. "I didn't realize you'd be back so early. I wouldn't have…" She trails off, but her words lie.

I'd bet this was purposeful. To remind me that I have no true friends besides the family next door.

"Yeah, well, here I am," I rasp tightly. "Since you're clearly busy, I'll just head to bed."

I start to turn on my heel, but she pulls me back. "No, stay. I'll grab drinks. Tell me about things. Did dinner go all right?" She makes for the kitchen, calling back over her shoulder. "Oh, and I mentioned to Lanie you were in town. She wanted to drop by and say hi. Said she misses you."

Lanie...my high school casual-sex-only friend. As if I needed this night to get worse.

"Lovely," I mutter, scrubbing my neck roughly as I try not to vomit the dinner I just choked down.

Bryce clears his throat, mumbling something about being desperate for pieces of ass. *Fucker.*

I reluctantly accept the offered beer, taking a long swig, wishing it was something stronger. Like bleach. Anything to erase the memory of Bryce's hands on my mother's—never mind.

Refocusing on my mother's smirk, I return to her comment. "I wish you hadn't told Lanie, Mom. I'm tired and not up for company."

She stifles an amused laugh. "Please. Since when don't you have time for female admirers?" Her sharp gaze turns calculating. "Unless a new girl is occupying that fleeting attention span of yours...?"

I grit my teeth, not ready to admit I have a secret crush. She'd probably twist it into something ugly. So, instead, I glance down the hallway, shifting topics. "Dad around tonight?"

My mother's lips thin subtly. "He sends his regards but had obligations tonight." She smooths her dress needlessly. "But he did want you to call, Marky. He's proud of your new big-shot career mending million-dollar athletes."

Despite lingering anger, warmth hits me at my father's rare pride. Then again, that's why I threw myself into baseball so much in the first place. The need to feel good enough after feeling like such a mistake all my life. The reason for their misery.

Bryce pipes up. "So, uh, yeah, hear you're like some huge athletic trainer now? Working with pro teams and everything?"

I take another drink. It's not exactly how I planned to catch up with a former friend, but it could be worse. At least my mother is acting civil since he's here. "Yeah, first full season. I just got back from spring training last night."

"That's awesome, man!" Bryce grins, taking a swig from his bottle. "Living the dream, getting to hang with major league stars, huh?"

"After the glitz wears off, it's mostly just long hours and cranky athletes," I admit, chuckling despite the scenario.

Before Bryce replies, the doorbell chimes ominously. I shoot my mom a long glare, reading her innocent shoulder shrug.

"Did you seriously just tell her I was here?" I grit out tightly.

But her poorly veiled scheming is soon confirmed as Lanie steps inside. I squeeze my eyes shut, bracing myself.

"Wow, it feels like old times," Lanie comments, spotting both me and Bryce.

"Guess so," I add dryly.

Lanie laughs airily, greeting me with a hug, her nails brushing my elbow flirtatiously. "What's it been, Mark? Six months since I've seen you?"

"Sounds right." My tone is clipped as I scratch my neck awkwardly, desperate for an escape. "Well...it's great to see you both, but if you don't mind, it's been a long week. I hope you all enjoy catching up."

I leave them all puzzled by my abrupt departure as I head into my former childhood room. But before I even fall onto the mattress, I hear footsteps inching closer.

Lanie raps her knuckles softly. "Hey, mind if I come in?"

No rest for the weary. Then again, my mother's comment wasn't wrong. It's not like me to avoid a sure thing.

I swallow a groan, reluctantly twisting the handle. "Hey...sorry, just tired. What's up?"

Lanie sidles past me into the room, shutting the door gently behind her as warning bells blare in my mind. "I just miss you, Marky. Your mom tells me you're quite the globetrotter these days."

I sigh, leaning against the wall, trying to maintain a casual demeanor despite the growing unease in my gut. "Didn't realize you and my mother had become such good friends. You know what she does to me."

She trails one nail up my arm, eyeing me through lowered lashes. "I know...she just comes into the office sometimes. She's been keeping me updated on my favorite shortstop." Her other hand reaches to trace my stubbled jaw daringly. "It would be nice to see you around here more often again."

I shift subtly away from her caress, pulse elevating, though not from anticipation. The familiar flirtation that once thrilled me now feels strangely hollow compared to Arden's last week.

"Yeah, the job's pretty demanding. I'm not around much these days..." I trail off, scrambling for a way to let Lanie down easily without hurting her feelings or revealing too much about my changing heart.

At Lanie's pout, I soften my tone, old habits compelling me to be gentle with her emotions despite my lack of interest. "But it's good seeing familiar faces when I'm in town. We had some fun back then, didn't we?"

Lanie hums, pressing closer eagerly at my diplomacy. "Lots of fun." Her suggestive tone hints at recreating previous escapades, her hand drifting lower.

Panic rises in my throat. I'm leading her on. *I suck at this...Saying no.*

As Lanie's fingers graze my waistband, I grasp her wrist gently but firmly, stopping her in her tracks. "Lanie, wait."

She looks up at me, confusion and hurt flickering in her eyes. I take a deep breath, wondering if I can get away with a sudden case of food poisoning. Or spontaneously join the priesthood—anything to escape this awkward trip down memory lane. But I decide on the truth, choosing my words carefully.

"I'm sorry if I gave you the wrong impression, but...things are different now." I hold her gaze, trying to convey my sincerity. "I'm not the same guy I was back then."

Then, as in six months ago. Our last hook-up.

Lanie's brow furrows, her voice small. "Different, how?"

I exhale slowly, running a hand through my hair. "It's just...I can't do this."

How did I *ever* do this?

"Seriously?" she chokes out. When I remain silent, her eyes widen. "Oh my... There's someone else, isn't there?"

I nod slowly. "I think so."

Because, yeah, if Arden wants something more, I'm all in.

Lanie takes a shaky breath, a sad smile on her lips. "Well, she must be quite something if she has you turning down sex for once."

"Guess I'm starting to realize I might've had it wrong all along," I murmur, more to myself than to her.

Lanie hums, chewing on her lip. "I'm just disappointed it wasn't me."

Fuck. Is that what she wanted all this time? Have others?

When I remain silent, unable to form a response, Lanie huffs and walks away. The sound of the front door closing echoes through the house, leaving me alone with my thoughts.

I slump against the wall, guilt washing over me. I've been inconsiderate, even if what Lanie and I had wasn't love. But beneath the remorse, there's a glimmer of something else—a quiet certainty that I'm finally on the right path.

Almost unconsciously, I find myself reaching for my phone. Jake answers on the second ring, the background noise fading as he steps away from his brothers.

"Mark, you just left. What's up?"

I let out a hollow laugh. "Yeah, about that...Got a minute?"

As I recount the events since leaving—the awkward encounter with my mother and Lanie's unexpected revelation—Jake listens patiently. When I finish, there's a moment of silence before he speaks.

"Sounds like you've had quite the last thirty minutes," he says, a hint of amusement in his voice. "But let me get this straight—you turned down a sure thing because of Arden?"

I run a hand through my hair, frustration seeping into my voice. "I know, I know. I sound completely whipped by a girl I kissed over a year ago. What if I'm just caught up in the chase? What if we hook up and all those feelings just...poof, disappear?"

Jake chuckles. "Maybe...or maybe you've stumbled onto something legit. I mean, you're admitting to catching feelings. I feel like I don't even know you anymore."

His words hit home, and I feel a mix of fear and excitement bubbling up inside me. There's nothing I want more than the intoxicating high of Arden's unexpected presence in my life... even if it means risking a hardcore faceplant, no matter where it leads.

"So you think it's worth taking a shot?"

"How many times do I have to tell you yes for you to finally believe me?" Jake says, his tone growing serious. "I've never seen you like this. I mean, I literally told you a year ago to act on this and your sorry ass waited until I was laid up in a hospital."

I let out a heavy sigh, pinching the bridge of my nose. "Since when did you become the fucking love guru, anyway?"

Jake laughs. "Hey, someone's gotta knock some sense into that thick skull of yours. Now, quit your moping and get your ass back over here. We'll strategize your next move to charm the pants off that girl...but first, we're gonna need more beer."

9

Arden ♥

Fifteen Months Ago, December 9th

As the movie credits roll, I stretch lazily, suddenly aware of how close Mark and I have gotten throughout the film. Our shoulders are pressed together, our legs tangled under the blanket he draped over us halfway through. It's cozy and intimate in a way I hadn't expected when I first agreed to stay.

Still, this isn't me. I don't go to parties like this, let alone end up in the bedrooms of guys like Mark Bell. I've spent years creating my perfect college persona, the one who attracts the pre-med or pre-law type. Men who think like me. Ones who spark intelligent conversation, not sidelong glances and cheesy pick-up lines.

Then again, these last two hours tell me Mark may not be who I initially assumed.

"So," Mark says, his voice low and warm in the dim light. "Too scared to leave?"

I turn to face him, our noses almost brushing with the movement. "Sorry to disappoint Pirate Playboy, but I've seen that one before. Not afraid to walk back to my place, if that's what you're asking."

Something flickers in Mark's gaze, a hint of vulnerability that catches me off guard. But before I can dwell on it, he's grinning at me, his eyes twinkling with mischief. "Fine, but you're not leaving just yet."

"Oh, really?" I tease. "Why's that?"

Mark trails his fingers down my side temptingly. "Because I'm not done getting to know you."

I bite my lip, trying to ignore the butterflies in my stomach at his words. *God, sexuality is a powerful thing.* I reframe my thoughts. I can handle this. I can be in the room I promised myself I wouldn't end up in, tangled up with the man I've heard stories about since I was a freshman.

"What else do you want to know?"

His gaze falls to my lips, his own curving into a suggestive smirk. But then, as if catching himself, he shakes his head, his expression softening. "For starters, why don't you tell me how a girl like you ended up here tonight? Or were you just curious about the rave reviews?"

I let out a startled laugh. "Unfortunately, I didn't get the 'rave reviews.'" *However, no one mentioned being disappointed.* "A friend from class convinced me. Said friend started making out with some blonde and left me to fend for myself. Then you showed up, trying to wow me with your cheesy pick-up lines."

"Yet you're in my bed," he answers plainly, his stare not wavering.

Seeking a distraction, my gaze catches on the lone picture frame nearby—three grinning boys with a younger, carefree Mark at the center, likely brothers or childhood best friends. It makes me wonder how much more there is to this man I quickly judged earlier tonight.

Mark's hand finds mine, stealing back my attention. "Why'd you really show-up here? Call it a hunch, but I don't see you as the type to be convinced to do anything you don't really *want* to do."

"Accurate assessment most days," I say quietly, glancing at our entwined fingers. *Damn him for seeing through me so easily.* And the way he's looking at me, all soft and genuine? Maybe that's why I feel propelled toward honesty.

"My life's kind of a mess lately," I admit. "I guess I was looking for a distraction, something different than what I'm used to."

"Distraction?" he asks. I look up, noticing something tender in his expression. "Care to share what has that pretty mind so burdened?"

I take a deep breath, steeling myself for the confession weighing on my heart. What I haven't shared with anyone. "It's just...I grew up believing my future was already laid out. Graduate, attend law school, and become some hotshot attorney like my parents. But lately...I don't know. It doesn't feel like what I want, like I've just been going along with it to get their approval. Now, they want me to do some summer program at their firm. I had the interview yesterday, and it was so...empty."

I place my head in my palm, suddenly embarrassed to have said all that out loud. He probably thinks I'm crazy for not taking the sure thing. "I'm not sure why I just shared all that."

"You're fine, Arden," Mark says empathetically, stroking my knuckles soothingly. "But that's a big realization. Have you talked to your parents about it?"

I half-laugh, half-cringe. "Ha. They've invested so much in this future they've envisioned. I can't disappoint them now. They'd probably disown me."

Mark shifts closer, arm wrapping around my shoulder. "Hey, if you're feisty enough to put arrogant athletes in their place, I'm pretty sure you can handle anything. No offense to your parents, but I meant what I said earlier. Doubt you'd follow someone else's dreams willingly."

Heat wraps around me with the look Mark's giving me, like I'm truly being seen for the first time. "What makes you so sure you know me at all, Pirate Playboy?"

He huffs, tilting my chin up toward his. "I may not understand you yet, Arden Cooper, but I can understand parental pressures."

"Oh, really?" I volley playfully to disguise my sudden desire to taste his delicious-looking lips. "Somehow, I pictured star athletes coasting easily through childhood glory."

Mark's mouth twists wryly, pulling back slightly. "Please. Maybe in certain areas. But my parents consider my baseball scholarships wasted if I don't go pro. No room for simply enjoying the game on my terms."

My palm covers his, newly intrigued by the man underneath the casual veneer he wears. "Hmm…thought you were just some sports major. Didn't realize you dabbled in armchair psychology, too."

"Exercise science, actually," he corrects, lips quirking.

Medical? Not what I expected.

Interest sparks as I trace his knuckles. "Brains and brawn? Impressive."

"How do you think I got the most intriguing girl at the party into my room?" Mark retorts, dramatically flexing.

I laugh, tossing a pillow toward his still-flexed bicep. "Please, I didn't come up here just to inflate your ego."

Mark catches it swiftly, eyes dancing. "Yet here you are. On my bed. Telling me how much you need a distraction." His nose skims my throat, eliciting a sharp inhale. "I think you're secretly craving me."

My composure splinters dangerously, whispers urging me to give in—to be his, if only for tonight.

"Maybe I'm waiting to see if actions back up all those shameless boasts," I respond playfully, grabbing the pillow again and smacking it across his too-smug face.

Howling, Mark topples sideways onto the mattress. "Oh, it's on now, Widow Maker."

Next thing I know, he's kneeling above me, pillow raised dramatically as I shriek. Laughter echoes amidst our breathless battle as more pillows are found and tossed between us.

Finally, I pin Mark, pulse racing, straddled on top of his distracting thighs.

The heated stalemate steals the air and reason, leaving only the burning awareness of his palms on my hips and the dark promise flashing in his smile.

What'd I start?

"Give up?" I rasp thickly.

His grin grows sinful. "I never surrender, babe." In one swift move, Mark flips me beneath him, his muscular weight lusciously trapping me now instead. He hovers over me, both our chests heaving as electricity charges intimately between us.

I tilt my chin defiantly, rallying sassy bravado to mask my thudding pulse. "Guess your famous endurance is more hype than substance after all," I tease, trailing a deliberate fingertip down his throat.

Mark's eyebrows shoot up in surprise. "Awakening my competitive side, Arden?" His eyes flash daringly before he bends closer, breath fanning my flushed cheek. "I've got all night. My stamina isn't the issue."

I lower my voice, batting my lashes playfully. "Promises, promises...but something tells me you're all talk."

Mark's grin goes wicked as his mouth hangs above mine daringly. "Want to bet on how long it'll take before you're sighing my name?"

I swallow hard, fighting to maintain my composure. "Probably less time than it'll take for you to toss me aside."

A flicker of something—hurt? surprise?—crosses Mark's face. Before I can dwell on it, he reaches for his phone, holding it out to me with an expectant look.

"What's this?" I ask, eyeing the device suspiciously.

A slow, devastating smile spreads across Mark's face. "Your chance to prove me wrong. Put your number in. I want to see you again."

My heart races as I take the phone, fingers trembling slightly as I type in my information. Mark tosses it aside carelessly, his attention laser-focused on me once more. *Is this really happening?*

"Better?" he asks, his voice husky.

I lift my chin, meeting his eyes. "It's a start."

The playful banter fades, replaced by a crackling tension that makes the air feel electric. Mark's gaze drops to my lips, and I find myself unconsciously leaning closer. Slowly, almost reverently, he brings a hand up to cup my cheek, his thumb brushing over my bottom lip.

I shiver at the contact, unprepared for the magnetic pull I feel towards him. It's like we're two opposing forces, destined to collide.

"Arden," Mark murmurs, his voice low and rough with desire. His eyes search mine, a mix of want and vulnerability in their depths. "Tell me to stop, and I will."

Stop? The thought seems absurd. It's like he's ignited some craving in me that I never knew existed, and I've never wanted anything more. I lean into his touch, my own hand coming up to tangle in his hair.

"Don't stop," I whisper, tugging him closer, needing to feel his lips on mine.

Mark's eyes darken, a predatory gleam overtaking them. And then his mouth is on mine, hot and demanding. I moan into the kiss, arching as he fully lowers himself to me. Mark growls, our bodies becoming a tangle of limbs as we fight for control. I nip at his bottom lip, relishing the way he groans into my mouth.

And, wow, the effect I have on him, the way he seems to come undone at my touch as much as I do his.

Mark's hand slips beneath my shirt, his calloused fingers leaving trails of fire on my skin. I'm lost in a haze of sensation, drowning in the taste and feel of him. I've never let myself surrender so completely to desire, never allowed myself to be consumed by passion. But with Mark, I want to let go, to give in to the hunger burning between us.

"Where have you been all my life, Arden Cooper?" Mark rasps, his teeth and tongue trailing down my throat.

Where have I been?

I gasp as he tugs me upward, dragging my shirt over my head and pressing kisses lower still. I've never enjoyed being so ravished by a man, so appreciated in the most unadulterated way. It's intoxicating, addictive, the way he's solely focused on me.

His damp lips trace the edge of my bra, and he groans in pleasure. *He's enjoying this, enjoying me.* The knowledge makes me feel powerful and desired in a way I never have before.

I yank at the fabric of his costume, desperate to feel his skin against me. When it pulls free, Mark simply tosses it aside carelessly.

And then we're pressed together, chest to chest, skin to skin.

I roll us over, straddling his hips as I take control once more. I like the way his eyes widen in surprise, the way his hands flex on my thighs. I rock against him, reveling in the friction, in the way his breath hitches and his fingers dig into my flesh.

"Arden," he groans, his head falling back against the pillow. "Damn, baby."

I lean down, my hair falling in a curtain around us as I brush my lips over his jaw, his cheek, the corner of his mouth. "I'm just getting started, Pirate Playboy."

And I intend to make this a night neither of us will ever forget.

As his lips find mine again, an incessant knock echoes into the room.

Mark jerks back as if burned, his eyes wide and panicked. "Fuck," he mutters, running a hand through his disheveled hair.

I blink down at him, my mind hazy with desire and confusion. "What's wrong?"

"Mark? You in there?" a male voice bellows, followed by another knock. "Chelsie's been looking all over for you."

I shift as Mark scrambles off the bed and grabs a shirt off the dresser. The frantic energy rolling off him is a stark contrast to the passionate, confident man of just moments ago.

"Mark?" I try again, reaching for him. "What's going on? Who's Chelsie?"

He flinches away from my touch, and the rejection stings like a slap. "She's no one," he says, his voice strained. "It's just… Fuck. I'm sorry, Arden, but I can't do this. You should go."

"Go?" I echo, disbelief and hurt warring in my chest. "But I thought… I mean, we were just…"

A feminine voice joins the one outside, high-pitched and whiny. "Mark, baby, come on. I've been looking all over for you! I thought we were something special."

Mark closes his eyes briefly, looking pained. "Please, Arden. Just go. This…this was a mistake."

Mistake? He's damn right it was a mistake. One I'll never make again.

I'm just another conquest, another girl to be used and discarded when something better comes along.

God, I've been stupid.

"Wow," I say, my voice trembling with a dangerous cocktail of anger and humiliation. "And here I thought you'd kick me out *after* you fully had your way with me."

"Arden, that's not…" Mark starts, but I'm already off the bed, snatching the shirt from the floor and pulling it on with jerky movements.

"No, I get it," I say, my tone brittle and sharp. "You're done with me. Message received, loud and clear."

I grab my bag and head for the door, my heart shattering with every step. I pause with my hand on the knob, looking back at him one last time. "You know, I really thought you felt something when you kissed me. But I guess that was part of the act, too, huh?"

I don't wait for his response, yanking the door open and pushing past the surprised faces on the other side. I hurry down the stairs, my vision blurry with tears I refuse to let fall. I won't give him the satisfaction of seeing how much he's hurt me.

Outside, the cool night air does little to soothe the ache in my chest. I wrap my arms around myself, feeling exposed and vulnerable in a way I never have before. I let myself believe that Mark and I had a genuine connection, that he saw me as more than just another notch on his bedpost. But in the end, I was just a fool, another girl coerced by his charm and good looks.

As I make my way back to my dorm, I vow never to let myself be taken in like that again. I'll guard my heart more carefully, build up walls to protect myself from players like Mark Bell. And if I ever see him again, I'll make damn sure he knows just how little he means to me, even if it's a lie.

Because the truth is, walking away from him tonight feels like leaving a piece of myself behind. And I hate him for making me feel this way, for giving me a glimpse of something beautiful and then snatching it away.

But what hurts the most is the sinking certainty that, come tomorrow, he'll have forgotten all about me, just like every other girl he's had.

And that's a pain I'll carry with me for a long time.

10

Arden ♥

Now, March 24th

"Earth to Arden..."

Mandy's singsong voice snaps me from my current daydream. "Yeah?"

"Girl, what's up? You seem distracted," she says casually.

That's for sure.

I paste on a smile, clearing the cards off the coffee table, not ready to admit Mark's text from yesterday has been on my mind our entire game night.

"Just thinking about graduation," I mumble, attempting to perk back up. Because, really, graduation's part of what's on my mind. I'm moving to Florida in less than six weeks. I shouldn't get involved with anyone now. And there's no way Mark Bell meant something long-term by his "retainer" comment. That's just wishful thinking.

Josh, one of our mutual friends and my former pre-law frienemy, glances up, catching my brooding eyes with a hesitant smile. "I got roped into checking out some campus party tonight if you're not ready to turn in," he offers lightly. "Happy to split a ride. It could help clear your head before diving back into dense textbooks tomorrow."

Go to a party with *Josh*?

I mean, sure, we used to be close back when I was still on the lawyer track. But we haven't hung out much since I abandoned that career path and all the extracurriculars that went with it. I bite my lip anxiously, glancing warily at my roommate, Mandy, for support. She holds her hands up in defeat. "I think we're in for the night," she says casually, patting the thigh of her girlfriend, Zuri. Her hopeful eyes look at me encouragingly. "But Arden, you should go with Josh. Have fun for a bit. We'll clean up here."

My logical brain conjures all the pros and cons. On the one hand, it'd be nice to get away from my racing thoughts and act like a typical senior for once, but on the other, I know there's only one person who'd capture my attention tonight. And Josh isn't him.

I huff a breath, grappling for brightness I don't quite feel as I give in. "Well, I guess one drink couldn't hurt." Ignoring my unimpulsive nature, I let Josh tug me to my feet. Mandy's answering cheers do little to reassure my decision.

Just have fun for once, Arden. Stop over-analyzing everything.

Grabbing an Uber, I attempt casual small talk with Josh. "So, how are you and Rachel? Figuring out post-graduate plans?"

Josh turns, jaw dropping slightly. "Oh, you didn't know? We, uh, broke up just after the holiday. She's heading west for law school, and I'm going south to Miami. Figured it was best."

I flush, internally cursing Mandy for not telling me ahead of time. "Josh, I'm so sorry. If I'd have known. I'd never—"

"No, it's cool," he insists, cutting me off. He slides closer to me in the back seat unexpectedly. "Arden, I should admit, the reason Mandy invited me tonight was because I told her I kinda…well, I've had a thing for you for a while, and I didn't want to leave without telling you."

Oh. I stare, caught completely off guard. I think back to last year, the late nights spent poring over case studies and quizzing each other on legal jargon. There were moments when I thought he might have been interested in more than just friendship—a lingering glance, a brush of his hand against mine but I always chalked it up to sleep deprivation and stress. Besides, he'd been dating Rachel since sophomore year.

"I just thought you were out of my league before," Josh continues earnestly. "Too intimidating, I guess. But now that we're not competing for the same internships and clerkships, I thought maybe…" He trails off, looking at me with a hopeful expression.

I swallow hard, forcing a smile. Josh is a great guy—intelligent, driven, and undeniably handsome. In another life, I might have been thrilled to hear him confess his feelings. But now, with a particular athletic trainer consuming my dreams, it rings hollow.

"I'm flattered, Josh. But there's only a few weeks of classes left," I deflect.

"Maybe we can just spend some time together? See what happens?" he asks hopefully. "Mandy mentioned you were going to Florida, too."

My fists clench involuntarily in my lap, and I feel trapped by his unexpected romantic attention. *Why did I think this was a good idea?* I should've just stayed home, continuing my daydream about breakfast tomorrow.

"Josh, I don't…" My thoughts trail off as I recognize the house we pull up to.

This has to be a mistake.

But as Josh exits the car, offering me his hand, I realize this is where he intended to go. I let him pull me from the car, my jaw dropping as I take in the scene. In front of me, touting cheerful spring blooms, is the brownstone representing one of my biggest "what-if" regrets. The night Mark Bell somehow saw straight through my icy armor and made me feel dangerously cared for…at least for all of five hours.

"This is where the party is?" I ask, my tone coming out more clipped than intended.

Josh glances between the house and me. "Yeah. Is there a problem?"

I bite my lip harshly, willing composure. Surely, being here is just a coincidence.

Or not. I think back to Mark's text yesterday. *Why did he ask if I was busy?*

I blurt out words without thinking. "What's the party for?"

"Kick-off to baseball or something, my freshman year roommate—"

Shit.

I don't hear the rest of what he says as I practically run toward the house. Weaving through the sea of partiers, I scour the rooms until I finally spot the face etched permanently behind my eyelids.

Mark leans casually against a wall sporting fitted designer attire, his roguish laugh drifting above the loud music as some smiling brunette leans closer.

Jealousy and disappointment coil in my stomach. Of course Mark's here trolling for new conquests—that's who he is. Why did I think he'd change after our unintentional sleepover last week?

Memories of our night together flood my mind unbidden—the tender way he held me, the vulnerability in his eyes as he shared his fears, the electric spark of his touch against my skin.

Standing there, frozen in disbelief, my mind spins like a hamster on a wheel. *I thought Mark and I had something special, a connection that went beyond his usual playboy antics.* But seeing him here, in the very place where we first met, flirting with someone else... it's like a cosmic joke at my expense. *Is he still the same man who left me high and dry?*

My gut tells me to make a run for it before he spots me, to save myself from the inevitable rollercoaster of falling for a man who's as commitment-phobic as a claustrophobic in an elevator. But then I think about his message again.

Did he want me to come *with* him? *Here?*

Before I can figure out my next move, Mark notices me, his heavy stare dragging up my frame disbelievingly. In the space of a heartbeat, longing, fury, and regret all battle fiercely in the eyes glued only to mine now.

It did mean something.

Just as I'm about to step forward, a hand presses against my back.

Josh leans in close, his voice laced with concern. "Arden, you okay? You ran off like you saw a ghost."

I'm about to respond when Mark materializes in front of us, his signature smirk firmly in place. He gives Josh a once-over before his gaze trails deliberately down my body, setting my skin on fire. "Are you tired yet? Because you've been running through my mind all day."

I bite back a smile at his shameless pickup line. "Is that so? And here I thought you'd be too busy with your fan club to think of me."

"Then let me make it clear, Bubbles." Mark reaches out, running a finger down my bare shoulder, leaving a trail of goosebumps in its wake. "Grab a drink with me?"

Beside me, Josh clears his throat pointedly, his brow furrowed in confusion. "Uh, sorry to interrupt whatever this is, but Arden, you can't seriously be buying into this guy's act. You have to know his reputation."

I feel a flare of irritation at Josh's condescending tone. I flashback to our joint classes, the way he always assumed he knew better than me, even when I was right.

I step closer to Mark, my arm brushing against his. "I appreciate your concern, Josh, but I can handle myself. Mark and I are...friends."

Josh scoffs, his gaze hardening as he looks at Mark. "Right. Friends. Just be careful, Arden. Guys like him, they're only after one thing."

Mark bristles at the insinuation, but before he can say anything, I loop my arm around Mark's. "Thanks for the advice, Josh. But I think I'll roll the dice on this one. Now, if you'll excuse us, I believe Mark owes me a drink."

Mark grins, spinning us around and tossing a parting shot over his shoulder to a gobsmacked Josh, "Don't worry, I promise to have her home by curfew."

As Mark's hand finds the small of my back, heat sizzles through my body like bacon on a griddle. But instead of leading us toward the kitchen, he steers me into a dim side room, pressing me against the wall.

"Did you end game night early just to come find me? Or did I interrupt a date?" he rasps.

I tilt my head, meeting his smoldering gaze with a coy smile. "Maybe I was worried about you. You know, since you needed that therapy session. And now that we're in person, we can chat that retainer."

Mark licks his lips and my eyes inadvertently track the movement. "Happy to pay however you see fit."

I bite my lip, heat pooling low in my belly at his suggestive tone. "I'm sure we can come to some sort of arrangement."

Mark's eyes darken, his forehead dropping to mine. "You have no idea what you do to me, do you? I haven't been able to think straight since leaving you. Waking up with you in my arms, feeling your soft skin against mine...it's been torture not being able to touch you the way I want to."

His confession steals the breath from my lungs, my heart hammering against my ribs. *We're really doing this, admitting what we actually feel.*

"Mark..." His name escapes my lips, a breathless plea, a question and an answer all in one.

"Tell me you feel it, too, Arden. This thing between us. Tell me it's not just in my head."

His eyes search mine, seeking validation, needing proof that I'm just as lost as he is.

I swallow hard, my fingers curling into the fabric of his shirt. "It's not just you."

"Thank God." A low growl rumbles in his chest, his hand sliding up to cup my jaw.

He inches closer as every nerve ending in my body screams for him to close the distance, to finally give in to the desire that's been building between us for weeks.

But just as we're about to surrender, the door crashes open, shattering the moment like a sledgehammer to glass.

Mark jumps back, his body still shielding mine, a protective stance that speaks volumes as we turn to face the intruder. It's one of his former roommates—the one who interrupted us last year, standing outside Mark's bedroom door.

Damn, the irony.

The former roommate takes in our compromising position, eyes widening. "Shit, sorry, didn't mean to interrupt," he stammers, a knowing smirk spreading across his face.

I feel my cheeks flush with embarrassment, but Mark just sighs, running a hand through his hair in frustration.

"Jesus, Trevor, your timing..."

"The poker game's about to start," Trevor replies casually as people filter into the room.

"Shit. Now?" Mark sighs, his disappointment evident as he turns to me, an apology written on his face. "I'm so sorry. I completely forgot about the game. Kind of a season tradition."

I wave off his concern, trying to ignore the way my body is still buzzing with unresolved tension. "It's fine. I'm the one who randomly showed up."

He looks torn, his gaze darting between me and the growing crowd in the room. "I can bail, you know. Say the word, and I'll tell them to deal me out."

The offer is tempting, but I know this night means a lot. And if I'm being honest, the idea of watching Mark in his element, all cocky swagger and devastating charm, is more than a little appealing.

"And miss the chance to see you in action? Not a chance, hotshot." I grin, running a finger down his chest teasingly. "Besides, I'm curious to see if your poker face is as good as your pickup lines."

Mark's eyes flash with heat, his hand capturing mine and bringing it to his lips. "Oh, trust me, Bubbles. When it comes to you, all bets are off."

Behind us, Trevor clears his throat pointedly. "Yo, Bell, you playing or what? Bringing your new girl? Need to know how many seats I'm dealing for."

Mark's gaze circles my face before reluctantly turning toward Trevor, pasting on a strained smile for his audience. "Deal us both in."

He turns back to me, his expression softening as he brushes a thumb across my lower lip. "I'm not ready to part with you yet. Though, I should warn you. It's strip poker."

I attempt to disguise my shock as a cough, not fooling Mark, as a wicked grin spreads across his face. "Change your mind and want to leave?"

I force calmness. I can do this. Live a little. After all, I wanted spontaneity, right?

"Nope. In fact, why don't we make it more interesting?"

Mark raises an eyebrow, intrigued. "What did you have in mind?"

I lean closer, pressing my lips to his ear. "What do you want?"

Mark chuckles, his fingers skimming below the hem of my skirt. "If I win, I get to do what I should've done more than a year ago. Take you home and worship every inch of your gorgeous body until you're screaming my name."

I have to bite back a moan, my thighs clenching at the mental image he's painted. Determined not to let him have the upper hand, I slide my hand up his chest, toying with the buttons of his shirt.

"And if I win, you have to take me on an actual date. Friday night," I murmur.

"With pleasure, babe." His hand finds the small of my back, leading me toward the crowded table. "Hell, if I win, we can go on a date, too."

My stomach somersaults at realizing this isn't just some one-time thing. He wants more, too.

Somehow, I manage to maintain composure as I sit, meeting his molten stare. "Sure you want to cross this line? There's no going back."

"Positive, Arden," he confirms, voice rich with promise. His hand finds my thigh beneath the table. "We can talk about that retainer over breakfast tomorrow."

A part of me knows that this is a dangerous game, that the stakes are higher than just a few articles of clothing. I'm risking my heart, my carefully laid plans, and everything I've worked so hard for.

But another part of me, who comes alive under Mark's touch and thrills at his bold challenges, is ready to throw caution to the wind and see where this wild ride takes us.

So bring it on.

Win or lose, tonight is going to change everything.

11

Mark

Now, March 24ᵗʰ

My leg bounces impatiently under the table, attention torn violently between the alluring woman at my side and the crinkled cards I've hardly glanced at. My restraint hangs by a thread, mentally unprepared to see her tonight.

I'd planned for breakfast tomorrow, being able to casually admit that I wanted more than friendship and that I'd be willing to take things slow. But now? Having her in my element as she eyes me like a damn snack, all I can think about is splaying her across this table and running my hands possessively down every inch of her skin in sinful worship until she begs for more.

Fuck…it's been way too long.

The laughter at the table pulls me from my sultry fantasies as a man across from us reluctantly peels off his shirt. I need to get my shit together, keep some composure, or I'll wreck this before it even begins.

Arden's wandering nails drag fire up my inner thigh, causing more restraint to crumble as she offers a coy smile. So much for slow…because one truth became clear tonight: I'm all in on this feisty woman.

As more rounds get played, I stretch subtly just to watch Arden's gaze track the strip of exposed skin above my waistband.

I can't resist leaning closer, teeth nipping at her ear. "Already wanting me shirtless, beautiful?"

I trail my fingers down her leg, reaching her bare skin. As I do, she crosses her legs, trapping my hand firmly between the skin I'm aching to see bare and flushed.

"No shirt means I'm one step closer to winning," she teases, heated gaze turning to meet mine.

When the next round of poorly dealt cards claims me as an unfortunate victim, I peel off my shirt, relishing when her teeth snag her lower lip and her dark eyes glimpse the newly exposed skin of my torso shamelessly.

As attention moves to another player shedding clothing, Arden presses her hand to my abdomen, slowly teasing lower. "Still confident, hotshot?"

I rein in a feral groan, nearly coming undone by her lethal tempting.

And when Arden loses, my breath catches as her blouse hits the floor, her tempting curves barely caged by a black lace tank top. Appreciative murmurs register faintly, but my attention is solely captivated by this striking goddess taunting me.

"Still think you'll win?" I challenge, letting my knuckles graze north below her skirt.

Her sharp inhale rewards my boldness, even as she maintains modest composure for onlookers.

"Please. Get those dreamy eyes ready to give the crowd a show." Arden fakes an exaggerated yawn, trailing nails down my bare back in explicit promise. "I'm just getting started stringing you along."

I nearly choke. And just when I'm ready to toss all pretense and kiss that smug grin off her face, audience be damned, Arden's friend Josh materializes across the table.

Who the fuck is this guy and why was she here with him?

"Getting quite intense in here, huh?" Josh remarks, openly leering at Arden.

Arden glances up at him with a forced smile, her hand pressing on my thigh as if sensing my rising irritation.

Josh's smirk cuts through as another player tosses off clothing. "Lucky break for you ladies tonight, hmm? The local heartthrob here seems eager to give us all a show."

His deliberate jab elicits muffled laughter and envious looks my way. I grit my teeth, heat creeping up my neck as anger and humiliation wage war inside me. I've spent years cultivating my reputation as a smooth-talking player, needing women to expect the inevitable. I'd be gone by morning. But having it thrown in my face like this, in front of Arden...it feels cheap.

I glance at Arden, trying to gauge her reaction, but her expression is unreadable, her gaze fixed on the cards in her hand.

Sensing blood in the water, Josh presses on ruthlessly. "Tell me, Mark, how many ladies have you sweet-talked this smoothly before? You've got to be racking up impressive numbers by now. I mean, come on, how many women here have been charmed by this man?"

The derisive chuckles, waving hands, and shouted agreements around the room all feel like punches to the gut.

I scrub both hands roughly over my face, shame and outrage burning hot under my skin. I want to defend myself, to tell Josh he doesn't know a damn thing about me or what I feel for Arden. But the words stick in my throat, choked by the painful knowledge that he's not entirely wrong.

I brace myself for more callous potshots, for Josh to lay bare all my past indiscretions and warn Arden away. And the part of my brain that knows she's too good for me whispers maybe she'd be better off if he did.

Arden's steady voice cuts through the tension before I can sink deeper into self-loathing. "Real nice ambush, Josh," she remarks coolly. "Jealous that I'm sitting here with him instead of you?"

Josh flushes, his smug grin faltering as the table's attention shifts. I bite back a smirk, my chest swelling with a mix of gratitude and awe at Arden's fierce loyalty.

She leans closer, her dark eyes meeting mine. "I think we're done here. Take me home."

Then she's standing, holding out her hand in invitation. Without hesitating, I thread my fingers into hers with a rush of possessive satisfaction.

Let anyone else think what they want about my reputation. This woman's opinion is all that matters.

I grab our discarded shirts and let her lead me out without a backward glance, already thinking about the reckless games she and I can play behind closed doors.

Arden shivers as the cool spring air hits us outside. Without thinking, I drape both shirts over her, smiling at the appreciation flickering in her expression.

Maybe I can be the gentleman she deserves.

"Thanks," she murmurs, pulling my collared shirt around her middle.

As I request a ride, I catch her glance down at the too-big shirt, shaking her head with a rueful smile.

"What? You should be used to wearing my clothes by now." I tease, reading her mind.

She smirks, a playful twinkle shining in her eyes. "It's you I'm not sure I'll ever get used to."

"No?"

Arden steps closer, her hand cupping my cheek. "Josh was out of line, you know. What he said about you...it wasn't fair."

I lean into her gentle touch, my chest tightening. "He wasn't entirely wrong, though."

Her brows furrow. "Don't let him get into your head."

"No, I—" I exhale, needing to get this out. "I know I have a reputation. I've done things I'm not proud of, hurt people without meaning to. And I don't know if I can ever be the guy who deserves someone like you, even if it's just for a few weeks."

Shame hits, and I look away, saved by the approaching car. We climb in, and Arden slides close, tilting my face toward her.

"Hey," she says softly, her thumb brushing my skin. "I'm not perfect either, you know."

I scoff, a wry smile tugging at my lips. "Really? Your perfectionism is too hard to handle? However will I cope?"

She rolls her eyes, grinning. "Funny. But seriously, sometimes I can be caught up in my own goals that I forget to actually live. To appreciate what's right in front of me." She chews on her lip momentarily, eyes softening. "Look, I'm just trying to say that we all have a past. But the guy I'm with right now? He's different from the one I met last year. And I kind of like him."

She likes me. Past and all.

I close my eyes for a minute, finding the right words. "I don't know if I can be more than *that* guy, Arden."

"You already are," she whispers, her forehead pressing against mine. "If you weren't, there's no way you would've survived a night in my bed without kissing me."

I laugh softly, meeting her gaze. "I just don't want to hurt you."

"I know," she whispers, her nose nudging mine. "But I'm a big girl. Let me decide what I can handle."

I tighten my arm around her, pulling her closer. "Arden, I—"

The driver pulls up to my apartment, cutting off my confession. I help her out, and we pause just outside the entrance, the air between us crackling with possibility, the thought from the car already forgotten.

Because here we are. Just the two of us. Alone.

I reach for her face, my hands embarrassingly unsteady. Her skin is warm, soft, and I swear I can feel her pulse quickening under my touch. I lean in, trying to play it cool despite the nerves threatening to overtake me.

"Listen, we don't have to do anything. I can call you another ride if—"

Her fingers trace my jaw, effectively shutting me up as they ghost over my lips. "I'm sure, Mark. I'm staying."

Holy shit.

I take a deep breath, letting her answer sink in. *She wants this. Me.*

I move closer, giving her time to back out if she wants. Our lips are so close I can feel the warmth of her breath, the anticipation becoming a physical ache.

Then Arden lets out this soft little sigh that absolutely wrecks me, and our mouths collide.

It's like someone lit a fuse. One second we're barely touching, and the next, we're all hands and mouths and desperation. I pour everything I've been holding back since seeing her again into the kiss. I can't stop, can't get enough of her. Still, I need her closer, need more of her.

When we finally come up for air, we're both panting. Arden's lips are swollen, her eyes a little dazed, and it takes every ounce of my self-control not to dive back in for another taste.

"Wow," she breathes, a small smile playing at the corners of her mouth.

I grin back, feeling like I might actually burst. "Yeah. Wow."

Arden glances away briefly, nose crinkling adorably. "So, are we gonna stay outside or…"

I search her face, suddenly nervous again. "If you come up…I mean, are you sure about this?"

She arches an eyebrow, her smile turning playful. "After that kiss? You really think I'm going anywhere?"

And just like that, my last shred of hesitation evaporates. I grab her hand, fumbling with my keys as we practically race to my apartment. We stumble through the door, laughing and kissing, hands roaming as we shed layers of clothing.

As I taste her again, sweeter than I ever allowed myself to imagine, I silently thank whatever cosmic force brought Arden back into my life. Because this? This is too good ever to deny again.

Whatever consequences tomorrow brings, whatever fall-out comes down the road, I don't care. Tonight, I'm hers.

12

Arden ♥

Now, March 25th

Mark's urgent kiss steals my breath before the door clicks shut, igniting a fire within me that's been smoldering since our first encounter. As he lifts me effortlessly, I wrap my legs around his waist, losing myself in the delicious friction of our bodies pressed together.

When we finally surface for air, I'm dizzy and needing more. Mark cradles me against his broad chest, his fingers tracing the curve of my cheek with a tenderness that makes my throat tighten.

"God, Arden," he murmurs roughly. "You taste even better than I remember."

I can't help but smile, pressing a soft kiss to his lips. "Funny, I was just thinking the same thing about you."

But even as I melt into his embrace, doubts creep in, whispering that I'm not ready for this. That falling for a man with a playboy past is a surefire recipe for heartbreak, no matter how much I try to convince myself otherwise. My career should be my priority, not chasing a fairy tale ending with a guy who's probably broken more hearts than I can count.

But how can something that feels this right be wrong?

As if sensing my hesitation, Mark pauses, his eyes searching mine. "Hey, we can take this as slow as you want. I'm good just kissing you all night."

Does he really mean that? That beneath all that cocky bravado beats the heart of a true gentleman?

I trace his jawline, affection flooding as he leans into my touch. "It's not that I don't want this. Believe me, I do. I just...I think maybe we should ease into things. Savor it."

Mark's eyes, dark with passion, lock onto mine. His voice is husky, barely controlled. "Whatever you want, Arden. Just tell me."

The raw need in his tone sends shivers down my spine. I struggle to form coherent thoughts as his lips ghost along my neck. "Base by base?" I manage to whisper.

A low growl rumbles in his chest. "A baseball metaphor for foreplay? And I thought I couldn't want you more."

Leave it to this man to use sexual banter to ease the building tension.

I laugh breathlessly, my hands fisting in his shirt. "Shut up and kiss me again, Hotcakes."

He obliges, capturing my lips and leaving me dizzy with want. When we finally break apart, gasping for air, an idea strikes me.

"Shower," I blurt out, my inhibitions lowered by desire.

Mark pulls back slightly, his eyebrows raised in surprise. "Shower?"

I shrug, trying to appear nonchalant despite the heat rising in my cheeks. "Well, we both kind of smell like a frat party right now. And...it might help us cool off. Or not."

His eyes darken impossibly further, his hands tightening on my hips. "You sure about this, Arden? That's pushing a few bases at once."

The fact that he's checking in, making sure I'm comfortable, only intensifies my want for him. "I'm sure. We don't have to head for home. Just...see where it leads?"

A slow, wicked grin spreads across Mark's face. "Lead the way, Bubbles. I'm all yours."

He follows me down the hall, but as we close ourselves in the steamy room, I realize how naïve I am to the desire pooling inside. When Mark fully sheds his remaining clothes, I poorly stifle a gasp as his boxers come off, seeing him fully bare for the first time.

He grins as I avert my eyes like some inexperienced teenager, attempting to ignore the evidence of his desire now on bold display.

"I can just stand and watch if you'd rather. If this is too much." His tone is sincere despite how his gaze lingers appreciatively on my body.

You asked for this, Arden.

Before overthinking, I unclasp my bra and shimmy out of my underwear, kicking both out of the way. "Nope. I'm good."

Mark inhales sharply at my impromptu striptease, his stunned attention glued below my neck.

I tip his jaw up pointedly, patting his cheek twice. "Eyes are up here, slugger."

"Sorry, babe. It's just…" He blinks, fighting an obvious desire to lower his gaze as his hands run up and down my bare hips. "My imagination didn't do you justice."

I laugh at his open admission, reaching for flirty to mask the growing anxiety of being fully exposed. "Hmm, you've thought about me naked?"

"More times than I should admit."

His arm snakes around my middle, pulling me closer as his mouth finds mine unhurriedly. He draws me into the warm spray with him, his strong hands traversing my body, not to claim but to appreciate.

I want him, want whatever this is becoming, with a desperation I've never known.

I watch water droplets trace Mark's impressive body as he shifts, his erection pressing against my thigh.

"Mark…"

The cool tile at my back contrasts deliciously with the heat of his body pressing against mine, and I arch into him, craving more.

"Next base, okay?" he asks softly, trailing kisses down my jaw. His fingers glide down my body, brushing my thighs until they open to him.

He pauses, frantic brown eyes meeting mine as he waits for my answer. I bite my lip, nodding, the tension between my legs now a physical ache.

Mark gentles his mouth above mine as his fingers crawl like a burning fire up and down my skin, scorching wherever they touch until they reach their destination.

"I can't tell you how long I've wanted to do this," he breathes, the tips of his fingers just barely brushing against my sensitive center. "How many nights I've laid awake thinking about what it'd feel like to touch you."

Then they plunge deep within me, seeking and finding the need radiating there.

I gasp at the sensation, gripping Mark to keep upright. He dips his head to mine, his other hand caressing my breasts. He teases each nipple before lowering his mouth to capture each one tenderly.

"Tell me this isn't a fucking dream," he whispers, gaze locking with mine as fiery desire glimmers in his depths.

"Oh, you're dreaming, alright," I rasp. *And damn if I'm not dreaming, too, fantasizing about more nights like tonight already.*

Then he moves lower still. His fingers tease inside me as his lips press below my belly button. "Too fast? Or can I taste you, too?"

I moan, fisting my hands into his hair to steady myself as his tongue hits the inside of my thigh, a sinful promise of what's to come.

"Tell me this is okay, babe…need to hear you say it."

"Yes! Please, Mark," I cry out madly.

His amused laughter rumbles against my flushed skin. "Are you begging for me already, Bubbles?"

"Oh, stop gloating," I pant between breaths.

Mark peeks up at me through lowered lashes, a mischievous grin playing on his lips as he gently lifts my leg over his shoulder. "Not gloating. Just enjoying."

And judging by the look in his eyes, I'm about to be enjoying it, too.

Damn, I'm in trouble. The kind of trouble that has me reaching for anything to hold on to, prepared for the fall I'm about to take.

He leans in, his tongue darting out to taste me, and I nearly jump out of my skin. Yeah, this man knows exactly what he's doing. He circles my throbbing clit with his tongue, teasing and tantalizing, turning me into a writhing, whimpering mess. I'm pretty sure the neighbors can hear me, but at this point, I couldn't care less.

The room starts to spin around me as his tongue works its magic, pushing me closer and closer to the brink of ecstasy. The sound of the water cascading down our bodies mingles with my gasps and moans, creating a steamy soundtrack that would make me blush if it didn't feel so damn amazing.

"Mark," I pant, my fingers tangling in his hair. "Please… I need…" I can't even form a coherent sentence, my brain short-circuiting from the overload of pleasure.

He slips another finger inside me, moving in a relentless rhythm that has my vision blurring. His tongue continues its assault on all my most sensitive spots, and I'm pretty sure I'm going to combust. *Death by orgasm. What a way to go.*

I'm teetering on the edge, my body wound tighter than a coiled spring, when he does something absolutely wicked with his tongue, and I shatter.

"Mark!" His name spills from my lips like a prayer as I'm tossed over the edge, pleasure crashing over me in blinding waves.

Mark slows, adding gentle pressure until my body turns to jelly in his arms. With a final kiss to my inner thigh, he stands, holding me against him as I try to remember how to function like a normal human being. His hands brush softly against my skin, soothing any remaining tension like a magic elixir.

He tilts my chin up, his eyes meeting mine, and I swear I could drown in those pools of molten desire. "I've got you," he whispers, his voice rough with emotion. "I've got you, Arden."

"What about you?" I ask in a raspy voice, my throat raw from all the moaning and screaming. *Real sexy, Arden.*

He stifles a laugh against my cheek, his breath tickling my skin. "Babe, you could simply touch me right now, and I'd probably finish."

A sinful grin spreads across my face as my hand finds him again, stroking his rock-hard length. He exhales with a desperate need, his hips bucking into my touch.

"Is that a challenge?" I ask, rubbing his shaft along the wetness still seeping out of me.

"Arden, baby..." he gasps, rising to his tiptoes, his eyes rolling back in his head. "You don't have to..."

But I don't stop, my hand moving faster, building up a steady rhythm. He whispers my name, consuming my mouth with his, his kisses desperate and needy. He mutters urgent pleas, begging for release, until finally, he stiffens, a string of worship spilling from his lips as he comes undone from my touch.

Mark stills, emotions too powerful for words glinting darkly in his searching eyes. He smooths back my wet hair, his touch infinitely gentle, as if I'm something rare and precious.

"You're beautiful, Arden Cooper. Absolutely perfect." The tender reverence steals my breath as he places a soft kiss on the corner of my mouth, tugging me beneath the spray of the water.

He reaches for the shampoo, meticulously working a creamy lather through my hair. I practically purr under the sensual care, my eyes drifting shut in bliss. *Who knew washing hair could be so erotic?* Concerns for what happens now slowly seep away, replaced by a bone-deep contentment and a growing certainty that this moment is one of a growing list with Mark Bell that I'll compare any other man to for the rest of my life.

Mark bundles me in a plush towel, eyes dazed. "Still up for that sleepover? It can be just cuddling," he chances lightly, pressing a quick kiss to my cheek.

"Cuddling?" I murmur, pressing a hand to his bare chest, "If you keep spoiling me like this, I might never leave."

"Is that a promise or a threat?" he responds, chuckling.

I loop my arms around his neck, not able to stop smiling. "Both."

But our moment is cut short by a sharp tap on the bathroom door.

"Mark, you in there?" bellows a voice I vaguely recognize as Jake's.

We freeze, eyes widening comically.

"Go figure, interrupted by another knock on the door," I whisper with a soft laugh.

"Not this time," Mark promises before calling over his shoulder, "Go away, Jake. I'm busy."

"Dude, seriously?" Jake's anger seeps through the door. "We spent all night talking about how much you want Arden, and then you bring another girl back here the next night? Not cool, man."

I raise an eyebrow at Mark as color creeps up his neck. But he isn't mad. More like amused. He holds up a finger, mouthing "one sec" before cracking the door open, careful to keep me hidden from view.

"Jake, listen—"

"No, *you* listen," Jake interjects, his voice rising. "I thought you were finally ready to stop playing games and go after what you really want. But if you're gonna fall back into your old habits, I'm done giving advice."

I clamp a hand over my mouth, shoulders shaking with silent laughter as Mark tosses me a wink.

"Jake, I believe you remember Arden?" Mark says, pulling me back into his arms.

Jake's mouth drops, eyes darting between my towel-clad form and Mark's smug grin. "Oh, shit. Uh, my bad, you two."

"No worries, Jake," I say sweetly, leaning forward to pat his arm. "It's nice to know Mark has such a caring and supportive roommate."

Mark snorts, wrapping me tighter against his chest. "All right, that's enough bonding for one night. If you don't mind, Jake, Arden and I have a sleepover to get back to."

Jake holds up his hands, backing away with a knowing smirk. "Say no more. Just keep the noise down, yeah? Some of us had to work and want to get some sleep."

"No guarantees," Mark calls after him, kicking the door shut and pressing his lips to mine.

I laugh against his mouth, my heart soaring with giddy happiness. "You're terrible, you know that?"

"Yup," he agrees, grinning down at me. "But don't pretend that you didn't totally enjoy that."

"Hmm, knowing you're completely smitten over me?" I tease.

"Something like that." He grins, taking my hand and leading me down the hall to his bedroom.

I take in the details of the room as we step inside. It's neater than expected, with a few trophies shelved on the wall. The bed is unmade, dark blue sheets rumpled invitingly. I spot a different photo on the nightstand and move closer. It's not the younger Mark from last year, but one of him in his graduation gown with Jake and two older adults.

"Is this your family, with Jake?" I ask, picking up the photo.

Mark comes up behind me, his chin resting on my shoulder as he looks at the picture. "Jake's parents, actually. Ruth and John. They're probably closer to me than my own."

I lean back into him, struck by the wistful note in his voice. There's so much I still don't know about this man, so many layers to uncover. The thought is both thrilling and daunting.

"Let's get some sleep," he offers lightly.

As we curl beneath the sheets, Mark's fingers trace gentle patterns on my skin, lulling me into peaceful drowsiness.

"Any regrets?" he murmurs into my hair.

"Why? Looking to step up to the plate again? I'm not sure I can handle another round of your...batting practice."

He chuckles, the sound rumbling through his chest. "Just checking on you, babe. Making sure I didn't break you beyond repair."

I glance up, frowning playfully. "Cocky, much?"

Mark flashes his charming smile. "With the way you reacted? Definitely."

"Yeah, well, don't let it go to your head. I'm not stroking your ego any more than I already have," I respond, rolling my eyes indulgently.

Mark's grin turns wicked. "Oh, you can stroke anything of mine anytime you want."

I groan, burying my face in his neck. "You're impossible."

He laughs, his arms tightening around me. "Don't pretend like you don't love it."

I peek up at him, my heart skipping a beat.

Mark's expression turns tender as he realizes what he said. He runs a finger down my cheek with gentle reverence. "Hey, we can figure everything out as we go, okay?"

I whisper, "Okay," even as my mind starts analyzing the situation, weighing the pros and cons like a complex equation.

Pros: Incredible chemistry, a deep connection, and the excitement of exploring a new chapter together.

Cons: The uncertainty of our future, with my impending move and Mark's packed schedule. And, of course, Mark's notorious commitment issues.

Does this all equate to heartbreak in the end?

Sensing my overactive brain, Mark tilts my chin toward his. "Let's talk tomorrow. Just enjoy the night for now?"

I nod, forcing a smile and settling back against Mark's chest.

Tomorrow, I silently vow, *I'll put some rules in place. No falling in love, no talking about forever, and just living in the moment, enjoying what we have while it lasts.*

I won't let myself get swept away by fairy tale dreams. I'll enjoy the ride, but I won't forget that all rides eventually come to an end. And when this one does, I'll be ready. I'll have my rules, my armor, to keep my heart safe from the impact.

But for now, for tonight, I'll allow myself to bask in the warmth of Mark's embrace, to imagine, just for a fleeting moment, that this could be something real, something lasting.

A girl can dream, right? Even if she knows she'll have to wake up eventually...

13

Mark 🏐

Now, March 25th

I blink against the brightness, my eyes adjusting to the sight of Arden on the pillow beside me. Her dark hair is splayed out in a messy halo, and I can't resist brushing a stray lock from her cheek, marveling at the softness of her skin.

If I thought I was giddy waking up to her last week, I don't even know how to describe what I'm feeling right now. Like waking up in heaven? Or maybe I'm still dreaming?

Arden stirs as I trace my fingers down her arm, her eyelids fluttering open to reveal those striking coffee-colored eyes that steal the air from my lungs. As she stretches, her limbs brush against mine beneath the covers.

"Morning, beautiful," I rasp, my voice still rough with sleep. "Please tell me having you here isn't just my wildest fantasy."

Arden's laughter rings out, bright and clear as a bell, her wandering hands tracing sparks down my bare chest. "Two sleepovers, and I'm already starring in your fantasies? You really can't get enough of me, huh?"

I tug her closer, my laugh rumbling against her temple. "I thought I admitted that last night." I nip her skin playfully to avoid letting my tone reveal too much.

Her fingers glide further down my torso, pausing as they brush over my stretched boxers. She hums, flashing a coy smile.

I lazily trace the hem of her shirt, flirting dangerously with the upper thighs that brushed mine all night. "What can I say? I'm waking up next to you in my t-shirt."

Her sharp inhale burns hotter as I picture the curves hidden below the cotton barrier between us. It's too easy to imagine trailing kisses down to where the fabric ends…knowing what it tastes like. But I'd only push more of the boundaries we haven't fully outlined.

So, instead of capturing her mouth the way I want to, I run my thumb along it. "Still good for breakfast?"

It's not typically my style. But everything with Arden is different. Better somehow.

Arden strokes my stubbled jaw. "Sleepover plus breakfast afterward? Maybe we are still dreaming."

I tap her nose playfully before rolling out of bed. "There's a nice café across the street." I pull on discarded jeans, beaming at the vision of her lying in my bed. "Unless you'd rather eat in? I'm happy to cook up something here, too."

Arden looks up slyly as she pulls herself out of the bed. "Suppose going out saves your kitchen some hazard damage."

"Trying to say I can't cook?" I tease, laughing brightly.

"Can you?"

I watch as she pulls on her skirt from last night, then twists my t-shirt into a knot, letting it hang loose.

"Breakfast out it is. But fair warning—" I smooth both palms down her sides suggestively. "—if you keep looking unfairly sexy wearing my clothes, there's no guarantee we'll make it to the café."

I relish her pleased flush before forcing distance between us. "Let me grab a shirt so public indecency laws stay intact," I add, tossing a playful wink over my shoulder before rummaging through my dresser.

But when I turn to face Arden again, my grin falters. She's worrying her lip, a pensive expression replacing her earlier humor. The shirt dangles, forgotten from my fingers as I search her features, trying to decipher the sudden shift in her mood.

"Everything okay?" I ask gently, taking a step closer.

Arden crosses the room in a few swift strides, words seeming to catch in her throat before she blinks them away. "Just hungry," she announces, tugging me insistently toward the door before I press further.

But whatever I just saw looked a lot like hesitation, or worse...regret.

As we settle into the booth, I find myself tracing patterns on Arden's wrist, a nervous habit I didn't even know I had. The silence stretches between us, comfortable yet charged with unspoken questions.

Finally, I take a deep breath. "So, I've got to ask... What made you change your mind about me? After those months of radio silence, why'd you agree to dinner?"

Arden's eyes meet mine, a hint of a smile playing at her lips. "Honestly? I wanted to see if that guy I met at the hospital was the real deal." She pauses, taking a sip of coffee. "That, and... well, let's just say our little encounter at the bar was a pretty potent reminder of our chemistry."

I lean in, my heart doing a weird flip-flop thing I'm not used to. "Arden, I'm flying blind here. I've never... I mean, waking up and still wanting to be around someone? That's new territory for me." I run a hand through my hair, feeling uncharacteristically vulnerable. "But this thing between us? I can't ignore it. I don't want to."

Arden's hand finds mine, her touch gentle. "God, Mark. How do you do that? Say exactly the right thing at exactly the right moment?" But there's a flicker of something in her eyes–regret? Fear?–that makes my stomach clench.

She bites her lip, and I brace myself for what's coming. "It's just...I'm leaving after graduation. I need you to understand that."

As she starts explaining her dreams, her five-year plan to open her own consulting firm, I feel a mix of pride and disappointment swirling in my chest. This is the Arden I've been getting to know–passionate, driven, determined to forge her own path.

It hits me then: she's breaking free from the life others planned for her, just like I did with baseball. How can I even think about asking her to reconsider?

I push down the selfish part of me that wants to beg her to stay, focusing instead on the fire in her eyes as she talks about her future.

"Speaking of your grand plans," I say, aiming for a lighter tone, "how'd that interview go on Thursday? You left me hanging. I thought we had a deal about updates."

She exhales, fidgeting with her coffee cup. "It went...really good, actually. I should hear something this week."

I lean closer, unable to keep the pride from my voice. "They'd be idiots not to snatch you up, you know that, right?"

Arden blushes, ducking her head. "Thanks, it's just..."

I tilt her chin up, meeting her eyes with a grin. "What? You're realizing you can't bear to leave all this behind?" I gesture to myself dramatically.

She rolls her eyes, but I catch the hint of a smile. "Something like that. I just...I'm enjoying getting to know you, spending time together."

And damn if my heart doesn't do a backflip at her words.

I get it now, why people write songs about this stuff, why a part of me still wants to run for the hills. This woman could absolutely wreck me.

But I tried running once, and look where that got me. I'm in too deep now.

I tuck a strand of hair behind her ear, my voice softer than I intended. "Okay, then. Let's see where this goes. Make some unforgettable memories before you leave."

She tilts her head, a playful glint in her eye. "Are you suggesting a spring fling, Mark?"

"You could never be a fling, Arden Cooper." I kiss her nose to take away from the truth of my confession.

She leans back, her gaze searching mine before resolve flashes. "Okay, Romeo. But if we're doing this, we should set some ground rules. Try to avoid getting hurt."

"What kind of ground rules?"

And why does the thought of me hurting her again make me want to beg for forgiveness already?

Nervousness flickers briefly in Arden's brown hues, and I bite my tongue.

"We have six weeks until I leave. How about we keep it simple? No promises of forever or expectations. No declarations of love. No asking me to stay. We make memories, like you said."

I let her rules sink in.

No forever. Easy. I don't want something long-term.

No expectations. I don't have any, so okay.

No falling in love. I'm not sure I know what love is, so maybe that's manageable, avoidable. I hope.

No asking her to stay. She's leaving after graduation. Why does that already make my chest ache? Does that mean rule number one won't be as easy as I think?

You're getting ahead of yourself. You're assuming she sticks around and doesn't dump your sorry ass before the six weeks are up.

I force my usual confident charm, accepting her terms. "So, no tiny Bell-Coopers in our imminent plans, then? I think we're on the same page."

"Tiny Bell-Coopers?" Arden shakes her head in amusement before resting it on my shoulder. "But we can add that to the list if you think it's necessary."

"I mean, six weeks is basically forever, so you never know."

Her laughter rumbles against my shoulder. "Talk of kids aside, something tells me the time won't be nearly long enough."

I press my lips to her temple, breathing in the smell of her hair. The scent immediately takes me back to the shower last night, off massaging her scalp after... *Yeah, I might need more than six weeks, too.*

I swallow the thought down, tilting her chin toward mine. "Well, in that case, I better step up my game. Can't have you getting bored of me."

Her nose crinkles adorably. "Bored? You're like a walking, talking entertainment center."

I raise an eyebrow, a grin tugging at my lips. "Is that so? Well, you ain't seen nothing yet, baby. I've got moves that'll keep you on your toes."

Arden snorts, her laughter filling the cafe. "Moves, huh?"

As our conversation shifts to light and playful topics, like me showing off my famous running man dance to the entire restaurant, I wonder what the hell I've gotten myself into. Because there's not a thing I won't do to make this girl smile.

Six weeks. I've got six weeks to show Arden how unforgettable I can be. Six weeks to make memories that will last a lifetime.

So, game on. That's a challenge I'm determined to win.

I drift back to my apartment, still floating from the unbelievable day with Arden, no matter how terrifying.

As I barge inside, Jake glances up from a textbook and immediately breaks into laughter. "I'm guessing that goofy-ass grin means your night went well?"

I toss a pillow at his head even as heat creeps up my neck. "Get your mind out of the gutter. We just talked…" At Jake's deeply skeptical look, I amend, "…Okay, and maybe some other stuff."

"Because I didn't hear half of it," he mutters, rolling his eyes dramatically.

I sink onto the couch opposite him, sighing pleasantly. "I didn't know when you'd be home."

"And that would have changed something?" Jake shuts the book, laughing as I stare blankly. "Exactly what I thought. Now, maybe you can fill me in on how all that happened? Or should I make assumptions after our conversation Friday night?"

I rake both hands roughly through my hair, grappling with how to summarize the emotionally packed hours with Arden. "She, uh, actually showed up at that party. The baseball kick-off."

"Arden? Was back at your old house?" At my fervent nod, his eyes narrow thoughtfully. "So, did you ditch all your former teammates and disappear upstairs again with the spicy lawyer right away or…?"

"God, am I that predictable?" I scrub my jaw, returning a playful smile. "But strip poker, actually."

"Your skills, man," Jake says breathlessly, practically rolling with laughter. "Although I have to admit, I doubted miracles existed for romantic disasters like you."

I huff a tired laugh. "Thanks for the vote of confidence, jerk." Softening my tone, I meet Jake's gaze. "But in all seriousness, I did tell her the truth…that I wanted to make something work, at least until she graduates."

Jake whistles lowly. "Look at you committing to someone!" His expression turns serious as he studies me. "I know it's scary as hell, and you don't think stuff like this lasts, just don't hold back, okay? She seems to like you. The actual you."

I shake my head, trying to lighten the sudden knot in my throat. "Being all wise on me again, Jay?"

He shrugs, a cocky smirk on his face. "What can I say? I've got hidden depths, too. Maybe I'll write a song about it."

I laugh, shoving him playfully. "Stick to your own stories. Like the mystery girl who saved you in that car accident last December."

Jake stiffens, turning serious. "Hey, I told you that in confidence. I don't need Tessa getting upset about a girl my concussed brain might've imagined. I didn't even get her name."

The tension eases as we change topics to Jake's love life rather than mine—still, his words from earlier echo in my mind long after our conversation. *Don't hold back. She likes the actual you.*

And just like Jake's imaginary angel from the accident, part of me still can't believe this is real. That a girl like Arden— intelligent, funny, gorgeous, and way out of my league—would give a guy like me a chance. And I'll be damned if I'm going to screw it up.

Even if it means letting her go eventually.

14

Arden ♥

Now, March 27th

My gaze stays glued to the clock as the professor's droning voice turns to irritating white noise. I've barely heard a word all hour, my scattered thoughts replaying the call I received before class combined with the anticipation of seeing Mark for the first time since waking up blissfully tangled in his arms two days ago.

But even our flirty texts and the promise of his lips on mine can't undo the growing unease in my stomach, knowing this—whatever we're calling it—has an expiration date etched in stone.

The job offer I've been dreaming about since my parents' ultimatum is only a reminder. I should be elated, over the moon. I got both: Appeasing my parents and the consulting gig I spent a year and a half researching and fantasizing about. All my post-graduate goals are falling into place, the validation of how hard I've worked to get out of the shadow of my parent's reputation and expectations.

And it wasn't easy. It came with compromise.

When I finally gathered enough courage to tell my parents last winter that I wanted something different from their carefully crafted vision of my future as a high-powered attorney, they panicked.

Their response? A thinly veiled attempt to regain control: move home for six months post-graduation or face the daunting prospect of repaying my entire college tuition.

I can almost hear their voices now, a mixture of disappointment and determination. "You're not thinking clearly," they said, as if my desire for a different path was a temporary lapse in judgment. Their strategy was clear—wear me down with constant pressure, disapproving glances, and not-so-subtle hints about reconsidering law school. And when that failed? Well, the threat of crippling debt is a powerful motivator.

So, I agreed. I threw myself into finding the perfect consulting job near St. Petersburg, a step towards independence while still appeasing their wishes.

And until a few weeks ago, I never looked back or questioned it.

Now, with movie night looming, and the growing desire to see the man I'm falling so quickly for, I'm wondering how easy it will be to say goodbye. Am I racing headlong into heartbreak?

The practical side of me knows that going all gaga over Mark like some swooning teenager isn't part of my carefully constructed plan. Sexy smiles and irresistible charm were never factored into the equation.

Maybe I should ghost tonight. Blame midterms or a nonexistent study group. Slowly start extracting myself before either of our feelings wanders into dangerous territory.

Then again, that's why I set rules. *No expectations. No falling in love.* Besides, Mark's not the type to beg some girl to stay. He made that clear. Two days after I get my diploma, he'll probably have already moved on to the next wide-eyed girl throwing herself at him. And I'd be wise to remember that.

This is just for fun, I remind myself as the class is finally dismissed. But even as I repeat the phrase, I know I'm kidding myself. I'm already hooked on his brand of trouble. Despite how much I've tried to protect myself, Mark makes me feel seen and appreciated in a way I've never known with anyone else—not even my parents. And I'm helpless to resist, powerless to do anything except head straight into the flames, reasonable excused be damned.

Reaching the apartment, muffled sounds of guitars drift into the hallway. Taking a deep breath, I rap my knuckles against the wood. Ready or not, here I come.

The music stops abruptly, followed by hushed voices before the door swings open, revealing a surprised Jake.

"Arden! Didn't expect you so soon," he says, glancing at his phone.

I check my watch, wincing when I realize I'm over an hour early. *So much for not looking desperate.* "Sorry, I wrapped up with class and didn't pay attention to the time. I can come back later if—"

Jake chuckles, waving me in. "Nah, don't worry about it. Come on in. Mark should be back soon anyway."

As I step inside, Jake calls out to the living room, "Hey guys, look who's here!"

Owen's on a chair, guitar still on his lap and Tessa's sprawled on the couch with an open physics textbook.

Tessa's face lights up when she spots me. "Oh, thank God. Please distract me from all this musical creativity" she groans, gesturing dramatically to Owen.

I laugh, settling into an armchair. "And you couldn't have picked a better subject than physics to help?"

We fall into an easy conversation about classes and summer plans. Tessa animatedly describes her upcoming internship in New York, while Jake mentions Thomas's similar gig in Boston. It's nice, familiar. Like I've known them for years instead of weeks.

We're mid-laughter when the front door bangs open. We all turn as Mark freezes in the doorway, his shirt clinging to him with sweat, eyes widening as they land on me.

"You're...not supposed to be here yet," he says, a mix of surprise and something else in his voice.

I manage a flippant shrug. "Yeah, I, uh, finished class early. Thought I'd head straight over."

It's not entirely a lie.

And judging by the heated gaze sweeping over me, I don't think he minds.

A slow smile spreads across Mark's face as he tilts his head toward the hallway. "Well, I need to grab a quick shower, but...want to catch up for a sec first?"

Shower? The thought already has me floating closer.

Pause, Arden. Cram down this crazy desire before your heart goes supernova.

But logic doesn't stand a chance against Mark's focus behind closed doors.

The moment Mark's bedroom's privacy blankets us, his hands tangle into my hair, his lips claiming mine. I melt against him, wondering how I could've even considered canceling.

He breaks the kiss, trailing his lips greedily down my neck. "I've been craving your taste for days, baby."

I laugh softly, my fingers tracing patterns on his damp shirt. "It's been two days."

"Way too fucking long," he rasps, mouthing roaming lower.

Lustful desires cloud my brain until I catch his grad photo and snap back to reality. Graduation. Career. Moving. Saying goodbye. I stiffen, blinking the rest of the room back into focus.

"Mark, wait."

He freezes, his eyes snapping back to mine with an intensity that steals my breath.

I run my hands down his arms, buying time as I gather my courage. "I, uh...I got the job in Tampa."

Mark blinks, a whirlwind of emotions flashing across his face. "Arden, that's..." His voice cracks, and he clears his throat. "Of course they hired you. You're freaking amazing." He searches my face, his brow furrowing. "Why don't you seem excited? It's what you wanted, right?"

I force a smile, hoping it doesn't look as shaky as it feels. "No, I am excited. It's just...it makes everything feel real, you know? Like, this is actually happening."

The weight of it all settles on my shoulders—the accomplishment, the freedom, and the bittersweet realization that it's another step away from...whatever this is with Mark.

Mark nods slowly, his trademark grin slipping into place like armor. "Well, sounds like we've got something to celebrate, then. Our Friday night date is still on, right?

Our date. He still wants to keep his promise from the poker game? He still wants to continue this.

Maybe I can get lost in the hopeless fantasy a little longer, too.

"I'd like that," I murmur, unable to resist glancing at his lips. "Now, where were we before I rudely interrupted with my life-changing news?"

Relief flashes in Mark's eyes as his hands find my hips, walking me backward toward his perfectly made bed. "Well, I was about to get in the shower," he says, his voice low and teasing. "Unless…"

I laugh, swatting at his chest. "Go get cleaned up. Then we can do the whole 'how was your day, dear?' routine like normal people."

Mark's eyebrows shoot up in mock surprise. "Normal? Us? I'd rather have you tell me all about your day *in* the shower. You know you want to."

Heat flares into my cheeks as images of his naked body flash in my mind. I tamp down the sudden pool of want forming, knowing a repeat of Saturday night will only speed up our not-so-slow pace.

Instead, I laugh in amusement. "And risk another lecture from Jake? How about a raincheck when there isn't a room full of people behind your thin bathroom wall?"

He shrugs, kissing me briefly before stripping off his damp t-shirt. "So, you don't like an audience. Good to know." He doesn't wait for me to respond as he saunters toward the bathroom, muscles shifting enticingly with his cocky grin. "But if you change your mind, you know where to find me."

I clamp my hands together, afraid they'll reach for newly bared skin against my better judgment. Because, right now, Mark looks every inch like the unfairly sexy athlete who waltzes into random parties, capturing any woman's attention he wants.

Get ahold of yourself, Arden. Act like you're not already head over heels.

As the water turns on across the hall, I run a quick hand through my kiss-blown hair. Then, with a long exhale, I paste on a breezy smile and head back into the living room, trying to act like I wasn't just hard-core making out when I face everyone again.

But judging by the knowing grins I'm greeted by, I failed.

Still, I manage to hold it together with some semblance of coherent conversation. At least until Mark enters the living room minutes later, water droplets trailing temptingly down his neck and disappearing beneath his stretched shirt.

Stop acting like you've never seen a sexy man before! Or this sexy man who had your legs over…*nope. Not going there.*

I snap my jaw shut, feeling a fiery blush creep up my neck.

Mark towels off his hair, a sinful grin spreading at my obvious thoughts.

"See something interesting, Bubbles?"

I force nonchalance despite my flaming cheeks. "What, no! Just, uh, chatting about summer plans with Tessa and Jake." I wave vaguely towards the couple sitting on the couch.

Mark prowls closer, bracing his arms on either side of my chair, caging me in. "Uh-huh," he starts, voice dropping to a whisper against my ear. "Don't pretend like you weren't picturing me all wet and naked."

And wow, do I wish I was impulsive because, right now, my only thought is dragging him back to the bathroom and testing the acoustics more thoroughly.

The sound of the doorbell interrupts my crumbling restraint. *Thank God.*

Jake coughs into this fist. "Foods here, guys."

Mark smirks, pulling back to grab my hand. But his hot look promises more dangerous games await during the movie. "Saved by the dinner bell, Bubbles."

We fill our plates, settle onto the couch, and casually talk with the others. But each touch from him ignites hidden tension still simmering in my blood.

When Mark discretely trails his pinky up my thigh, I shoot him a warning glare.

He chuckles, shifting closer. "Is Friday really the soonest I can have you to myself again?"

He wants to see me sooner?

I swallow a bite of pizza, grasping for a distraction as arousal and uncertainty swirl. "Aren't you on the road this week? And I leave this weekend for that family cruise I mentioned. So, yeah, just Friday."

Disappointment flickers in Mark's expression before he flashes a suggestive smile. "You're sure I can't convince you to stay tonight? My flight doesn't take off until nine tomorrow."

I shoot him a look that says, "nice try," but his hand finds my knee, his touch electric even through my jeans.

"Fine," he murmurs, leaning close. "Guess I'll just have to make the most of our movie time."

"Careful. Admitting you want me around is a slippery slope towards forever." I wink, reaching for playful instead of overanalyzing.

Mark barks a surprised laugh. "What can I say? I'm a glutton for punishment. Your particular brand of chaos is growing on me." His voice softens. "I'll miss you while I'm gone, you know."

His admission catches me off guard, and I struggle to maintain my cool facade. "Well then, Friday should be quite the homecoming, huh?"

"Oh, you can count on it," Mark grins, his lips tantalizingly close to mine.

A pointed cough nearby reminds us we're not alone. *So much for not wanting an audience.* We jump apart, trying (and failing) to look innocent as we pretend to focus on the movie. But in the darkness, the air between us feels charged, alive with possibility as a realization hits. This isn't just some physical attraction sparked by flirty banter that can be severed at a moment's notice like I've tried to convince myself.

We were right. There's no going back.

When I shiver, Mark reaches for a blanket, wrapping it around us both. But the gleam in his eye tells me he has more than just my warmth in mind. His fingertips find the nape of my neck, sending sparks down my body that have nothing to do with the temperature.

As the movie progresses, his touches grow bolder. His hand on my thigh feels like a brand, even through my jeans. Then, after returning from a drink refill, I find myself tucked against his sturdy chest, the steady thrum of his heartbeat echoing in my ears. Mark's arm snakes around my waist, his fingers toying with the hem of my shirt, sneaking beneath to caress the bare skin of my hip. His teeth graze the shell of my ear, his breath hot and tempting, sending a shiver of desire down my spine.

This is a game.

I twist in his embrace, my lips hovering over the rapid pulse in his neck. "What are we, sixteen?" I tease, my nails raking down his chest, feeling the muscles tense beneath my touch.

Mark's sharp inhale fills the space between us, his grip on my hip tightening reflexively. Our eyes meet, the flickering light of the TV dancing in his darkened gaze. The pretense of watching the movie disappears, replaced by a silent challenge, a dare to see who will surrender first to the mounting tension.

"Keep testing me," Mark warns in a low rumble, "and I'll carry you to my room right now, audience be damned."

Emboldened by his words, I let my hand drift lower, my nails biting into the firm muscle of his thigh. "Thought we were taking this slow," I whisper, my lips brushing the stubble along his jaw. But even as I say the words, I press closer, the heat of his body igniting a reckless hunger within me.

Mark's breath shakes, his fingers digging into my hip. "Last warning, Arden." His eyes blaze with molten intensity, the promise of pleasure and surrender burning in their depths.

The rational part of my mind urges me to retreat, to salvage some semblance of control. Still, the ache building between my thighs drowns out all reason.

"But we'll miss the ending," I pretend pout, my tone dripping with false innocence as I rest my palm high on his thigh, my pinky finger grazing the inseam of his jeans.

A strangled groan escapes Mark's lips, his hand clamping down on mine as the credits begin to roll. The sound of conversation filters through the haze of desire, but Mark's still focused solely on me.

"You might have won this round," he concedes, his lips brushing the sensitive spot behind my ear, "but come Friday, I'm going to make you beg for mercy."

The dark promise in his words sends a thrill of anticipation through my veins, the ache of desire pulsing in time with my racing heart.

As others say their goodbyes, Mark and I remain knotted together on the couch, our bodies humming with unresolved tension.

Finally, after what feels like hours, Mark clears his throat. "I guess it's getting late, huh?" His murmured question hints that this pause is anything but casual. "You could still stay...if you've changed your mind."

It would be easy to say yes, to let him pull me to his bedroom and see what comes next. But I shouldn't. Not if there's any hope of slowing this fast and furious entanglement down. Friday, when I know I'll have a week away to recover, sounds like the better option.

"I should go," I whisper, my fingers lingering on his jaw. "But Friday..."

"Friday," he echoes, his expression full of promise.

He walks me to the door, our hands clasped tightly, neither wanting to let go. On the threshold, he pulls me in for a long goodbye kiss, his lips demanding and tender all at once. It takes every ounce of my willpower to pull away, my breath coming in shallow gasps.

"Goodnight, Mark," I whisper, my forehead resting against his.

"Sweet dreams, Arden," he replies, his thumb brushing my swollen lips.

Street lamps cast a soft glow on the sidewalk as I head home, but they've got nothing on the warmth spreading through my chest. Mark's stolen glances and lingering touches replay in my mind like a highlight reel of our budding romance.

Even though my practical side urges caution, my heart echoes louder, urging me to take a leap of faith. If these stolen moments with Mark are all we have, then I refuse to look back with regret.

Come Friday, I won't hold back. No more playing it safe. If our time is limited, I want every second etched into my memory, a reminder that taking risks is sometimes worth the potential for heartbreak.

15

Mark

Now, March 30ᵗʰ

I lean casually against the brick exterior, arms crossed, fixing my most charming grin. "So, I'm curious if you'd be willing to hit up a party at Trevor's before we head back. I might've promised I'd make a brief appearance."

Arden's grin hints at intrigued curiosity, even as she arches a coy brow. "Leave a nice dinner and head to some house party? Here, I thought you were only interested in luring me back to your bed."

I nuzzle closer until my nose skims her throat. "Oh, trust me, that temptation's still front of mind after your teasing Tuesday night, but I have issues with breaking promises. Stems from always being let down by my parents. Besides, I thought you might enjoy seeing me in my natural habitat first."

She laughs even as a shiver hits at my appreciative exploration. "Hmm, it sounds counterproductive to have me watch all your groupies fawning for your attention. But good to know you're trustworthy with your promises."

My teeth graze unfairly sensitive skin below her ear, enjoying how she leans into the touch. "Do I detect a hint of jealousy?"

Arden scoffs, her nails biting deliciously down my forearm. "That'd require me believing your inflated ego belongs to me in the first place."

I chuckle low in my throat, nudging insistently closer. "Maybe not officially. But something tells me your claws would come out if another trespassed on your territory."

"Probably not as sharply as yours would," she responds smugly before tilting my jaw toward hers.

"You know me too well already." I steal another greedy kiss and press my forehead to hers. "So what do you say?"

She sighs indulgently, brushing her thumb over my cheek. "We both know I'm helpless at denying you anything when you get that endearing look."

Her blunt admission hits me squarely in the chest.

"That so?"

"Um, hmm." She taps a spot next to my lips. "Think it's this dimple that gets me."

Chest bursting, I guide her mouth back to mine, speaking between kisses. "Just a quick appearance, then desperately needed one-on-one time. Promise."

She smiles against my mouth before stepping back and offering me her hand. "Since I know you don't make them foolishly…"

I entwine our fingers, unable to wipe the grin off my face as we amble into the night. The promise of Arden's attention at my side already has my exhilaration pumping, but as we near Trevor's place, an uneasy knot forms in my stomach.

Memories of those wild, carefree college parties bubble up, and I can feel the restless energy creeping back in. Glancing at the way Arden's scanning the room—and me—I wonder if she senses the same thing. If she's regretting agreeing to this.

Sliding my palm supportively around her waist, I dip close to her ear. "Just say the word, and I'll sweep you out of here faster than Cinderella at midnight."

In true Arden fashion, she flashes a self-assured smirk. "Still not that damsel in distress you're seeking, babe."

Babe?

With a wink, Arden spins away, hips swaying enticingly as she wanders deeper into the chaos solo. I can only stare, stunned, before Trevor blocks my view, waving drinks sloshing a vibrant red.

"Damn! That same chick leaving you slack-jawed, dude?" His suggestive look follows Arden's path across the room.

I take a swig from the cup, reeling in my instinctive reaction to bare teeth. "Careful, man. She'll stomp your ass with one of those heels."

Trevor chuckles, the insult not even piercing his arrogance as he responds, "Never thought I'd see Mark Bell on a leash for more than one night. She must be really good in the sack, huh?"

As his lewd remark fills the air, a sinking feeling settles in my stomach. I swallow another gulp of the bitter liquid. Is this what I used to sound like? Objectifying women without a second thought? The idea of karma has the liquor souring in my throat.

"Real gentleman don't kiss and tell, Trev." I tap him on the shoulder, downing the rest of the drink and stepping toward Arden. "Thanks for the invite tonight, but if you don't mind, I've got a girl to catch."

Pride and unease mix into a dangerous cocktail as Arden engages with the other partygoers, her natural charisma drawing them in. When one guy in particular sidles up a little too close for my liking, I start to make my way over, fully prepared to stake my claim. Then I pause, remembering how Arden called me out just before we got here.

Arden's a big girl. She can handle herself. Hell, she handled me with ease. And sure enough, after a brief exchange, she politely excuses herself, shooting me a subtle wink as she rejoins my side.

"Disappointed? You totally looked ready to play knight in shining armor," she murmurs, her fingers trailing teasingly down my shoulder.

I wrap my arms around her, pinning her close. "Guess I'm just not used to sharing you."

Arden laughs, the sound easing the last bit of tension. "Well, you better get used to it. I have no intention of playing trophy girlfriend."

Did she say girlfriend?

Realizing her mistake, her grin turns sheepish. "But I'll admit, I'm impressed with your maturity."

"And we're just gonna bypass that other comment?" I tease, nuzzling into her hair.

She slips her fingers into my waistband. "No idea what you're talking about."

I shake my head, not hiding my smile. "If that's how you want to play, what do you say we find somewhere I can show you all this growth and maturity I'm learning? Maybe somewhere more…private?"

Her answering grin is pure sin. "Thought you'd never ask."

Finally out of the house and alone, I pin Arden against the brick alley wall, hands roaming feverishly over the curves I've desperately wanted for days.

She briefly indulges my hungry exploration before gently maneuvering us down the shadowed street, smiling coyly. "Someone's excited."

I growl impatiently, nipping at her collarbone in retaliation. "Gotta make up for the next nine days you'll be gone. I can't have your thoughts wandering when some sun-kissed cabin boy smiles your way."

Laughing under her breath, Arden twines our fingers, increasing our pace. "It goes both ways, Hotcakes. Don't think I haven't noticed all those college girls eyeing your gym selfies on social media daily." She angles a heated look in my direction. "Although I won't deny that I'm enjoying your undivided attention tonight."

"You haven't seen the full extent of my attention yet." I increase my stride, towing a giggling Arden recklessly down the streets until my apartment door appears up ahead.

I tighten my grip as we reach the lobby, keeping Arden tucked close.

"Last chance if you want to tell me no. Because if you come upstairs with me, there's no guarantee I'll hold back tonight." I smooth her wind-tossed curls, thumb tracing her delicate jaw until she nuzzles instinctively into my palm.

Arden's eyes squeeze shut, and she huffs a helpless laugh. "God, Mark, it's insane how easily you unravel me." She shakes her head, her fingers subtly pulling mine toward the stairs. "Let's go."

I don't move, searching her coy smile. "Truly sure? No takebacks once I get you alone upstairs." My teasing tone barely masks the anticipation surging inside me.

Arden steps closer, walking tempting fingers up my torso, igniting trails of hungry sparks. "What if I confess taking you to bed sounds like the perfect way to end this strange but somehow amazing night?"

A ragged sound escapes at her sultry admission. "Well, in that case, Bubbles, I'm all yours for the taking."

She giggles as my lips meet hers briefly before I sweep her swiftly upstairs.

We stumble into my bedroom, our laughter fading as the door clicks shut behind us. The air shifts, now thick with anticipation, the charge between us sparking like a live wire as I back Arden toward the bed.

"Eager much?" Arden teases as my mouth descends on hers hungrily.

"Did you expect otherwise? You've got me wrapped around your finger," I confess, my hands skimming up her sides, feeling the heat of her skin through the fabric of her shirt. "And here I thought I was the one with all the game."

Arden quirks an eyebrow, her fingers toying with my belt buckle. "Oh, you've got game alright. Maybe you've just underestimated mine."

As my jeans release, dropping to the floor, I capture her wrists, pinning them above her head as I lower her to the mattress. "Careful there, champ. All these sports metaphors are making it harder to practice patience."

She huffs out a laugh, arching beneath me as her hips roll against mine in a deliberate tease. "Then don't," she taunts, her lips curving into a wicked smile.

Challenge accepted.

I crush my mouth to hers in a bruising kiss, all tongue and teeth and desperate hunger. She meets me with the same intensity, her fingers tangling in my hair, tugging me closer. I grind against her, the friction delicious and maddening all at once.

"Damn, Arden," I pant, tearing my lips from hers to blaze a trail of open-mouthed kisses down her throat. "I've never needed anyone the way I need you."

Her breathless laugh dies as my hands roam up her thighs, inching closer.

I rear back, my eyes raking over her with blatant appreciation. Her dress has ridden up revealing the lace underwear below, her chest is heaving with the tantalizing swell of her breasts. Her lips are kiss-swollen, cheeks flushed, and her eyes glitter with desire.

She's a fucking vision, and she's all mine.

"Yours for the taking," she mutters, her voice a mix of sass and genuine desire that's so uniquely Arden.

"Oh, I'll take you all right," I promise darkly. "I'll take you so hard and so deep, you'll be ruined for anyone else."

She grins, her tongue darting out to wet her lips. "You sure you can live up to that hype, Mr. Big Shot?"

I flash her a cocky grin. "Baby, I am the hype. And I'm going to blow your pretty little mind."

With that, I set to work removing her dress, my hands roaming greedily over every inch of newly exposed skin. She's perfection, all soft curves and supple flesh, and I want to touch and taste every single inch.

Arden's breath hitches as my fingers graze the lace of her panties. "Mark, please..."

I grin wickedly, hooking my fingers in the delicate fabric and dragging it down her legs. "Please what, baby? Tell me what you need."

Arden smirks, pushing against my chest and rolling us until she's straddling me.

Oh, fuck.

She trails her plump lips down my torso like they're fire.

"Since you were so kind to me last week," she whispers, her breath fanning lower and lower and lower.

Oh, fuck. Oh, fuck. Oh, fuck.

Arden grips the hem of my boxers, pushing them down.

"Babe, you don't have to," I rasp weakly.

With a glance up, she smiles and then takes me into her mouth, claiming complete control.

And damn, I love her in control.

When I can't take another minute without combusting, I grab her wrist and toss her softly to the mattress. "I appreciate it, but not how this is ending tonight."

She sighs as my cock presses against her teasingly. *Calm down, Mark. Don't shoot your load yet.*

"I want to feel you, to be inside you," I breathe heavily, pressing kisses down her jaw. "Tell me it's okay, Arden. Tell me you want me deep inside you."

I shift, the feel of her wet pussy nearly causing me to do something reckless like thrust into her bare, but somehow I refrain.

Her hands smooth over my shoulders, her nails biting into my skin. "Ruin me for anyone else, Mark."

Well, fuck. If that isn't a green light, I don't know what is.

I claim her mouth again, hot and filthy, as I reach into my dresser drawer and slide on a condom.

When it's on, and I'm positioned, the tip of my cock brushing her welcoming heat, I pause, drinking in the sight of her. "Christ, Arden. You're fucking perfect, you know that?"

She reaches for me, her palms sliding up my arms in a silent plea. "Then make me yours."

I grip her hips, a low groan rumbling in my chest as I cover her body with mine. "You're mine, Arden," I rasp as the tip of my cock presses against her slick heat. "All mine."

With a feral growl, I push forward into her molten heat. The sensation is damn near overwhelming, stealing the breath from my lungs. She's so tight, so wet, so goddamn perfect, it's taking every ounce of my willpower not to lose it right then and there.

And as I try to hold back, I know she's ruined me too. For anyone else, for anything less. Because this is more than just sex—it's a deep, soul-searing connection that has me questioning how I ever thought I could be satisfied with anything less.

And God help me, but I never want it to end.

I want to savor every moment, every gasp and moan and shudder of pleasure. So, I slow my pace, ignoring Arden's whimper of protest.

"Patience, baby," I murmur, biting at her earlobe. "I'm going to take my time with you. Make you feel so good you forget your own name."

She shivers beneath me, her eyes fluttering shut as I start to move again, my thrusts deeper, harder. I angle my hips, searching for that spot inside her that I know will make her see stars.

"Mark!" she cries out, her back arching off the bed as I find it. "Right there, don't stop!"

I growl, the sound primal and possessive. "Wouldn't dream of it, sweetheart."

I drive into her relentlessly, my hand slipping between our bodies to circle her clit. She's close. I can feel it in the way she tightens around me, her breath coming in short, sharp gasps.

"Give it to me, Arden. Let me hear you, baby."

She tightens around me, nails digging into my skin as her eyes roll back.

"Louder," I plea.

And then it's like a damn breaks. She's begging, cursing, yelling my name. Her prim and sophisticated words giving way to raw filth before her teeth sink into my skin and her body pulses beneath mine.

It's all the permission I need to give in and lose myself in her. My body trembles as I put everything I have into frenzied plunges. With each whimper of reached desire, she takes my breath away until I finally let go, let the thought of this…of being inside her, of her bare chest bouncing below me, of her smooth skin, of the juices flowing from her, consume me.

I collapse next to Arden as she curls into my chest, her body still trembling. I wrap my arms around her, holding her close as our racing hearts gradually slow to a steady, synchronized rhythm.

In the soft glow of the bedside lamp, I study her face, committing every detail to memory. The way her lashes flutter against her flushed cheeks, the gentle curve of her kiss-swollen lips, the stray curl that clings to her damp forehead, the way she leans into my touch, even in her sated exhaustion.

"Wow, babe. That was…just…yeah," I mumble absently, not able to put words together.

Arden hums contentedly, nuzzling deeper into my embrace. "I could get used to this."

I grin, tightening my arms around her. "Good, because we're just getting started, beautiful. Hope you're ready for round two...and three...and four..."

She laughs, the sound vibrating against my chest. "That needy?"

I roll us over so I'm hovering above her. "For you, definitely." I dip my head, nipping at the sensitive skin of her neck. "I've got big plans to leave you deliriously satisfied before your trip tomorrow."

Arden giggles, her fingers threading through my hair. "Give me at least five minutes to catch my breath."

"Fine, but not a second more. It's been way the hell too long."

She furrows her brows curiously. "Too long? What? Like a week or something?"

"C'mon, babe. I know I'm new to this, but give me a little credit," I request. "It's been almost six months."

Her mouth opens, and I nudge it closed.

"Noooo," she drawls, shaking her head in disbelief. "No way."

I tug at a rogue curl. "Fine, don't believe me, but I told you from day one, you have no idea what you do to me, Arden."

She stares at me for a long minute before her fingers run temptingly up my back, twisting into my hair. "On second thought, I think I'm ready for round two."

I chuckle, already trailing heated kisses down her neck. "That's what I like to hear."

As I lose myself in the soft warmth of her skin, the playfulness between us shifts, becoming something deeper, more intense. Because as much as I want to keep things light and flirty, to pretend that I'll be okay walking away from this, I know I won't. This is different. Arden is different.

She's the one I want to wake up to. To share everything with. To hold onto, even if it's scary as hell.

It hits me as she sighs beneath my touch—I'm in way too deep to back out now.

So I don't fight it. I dive in, getting lost in her skin, her taste, the sounds she makes. I push away thoughts of goodbyes and ticking clocks.

Right now, it's just us and this insane connection. And damn, it's worth everything.

16

Arden ♥

Now, April 6th

The cruise ship's lavish dining hall, with its crystal chandeliers and uniformed servers, should be a haven of tranquility. Instead, it's become a battleground for my future decisions. Having an adult drink with my parents sounded like a great idea…time to actually get them one-on-one and try, once more, to make them understand. But now, sitting across from their disapproving stares as they discuss my life choices for the umpteenth time, I wonder if I made a mistake.

"Arden, we simply want what's best for you," my father insists, the wrinkles on his forehead deepening with every word. His voice is a mixture of frustration and concern, and I know without even looking that he hasn't been listening to me at all. "A law degree is a solid foundation for any career."

Best for me or best for the image you have of who I should be? I bite my tongue, fighting the urge to lash out. This argument is nothing new, and no matter how passionately I try to explain my reasons, they refuse to hear me. They've had this vision of my future mapped out since I was a child, attending future career days at their firm. I wish I knew why it bothered them so much. Why they can't accept what I want?

"I already accepted the consulting position," I counter, the rebellion simmering in my chest threatening to boil over. "This isn't up for discussion again."

My mother's lips purse into a thin line, the pearls around her neck nearly choking with disapproval. "You're being shortsighted, darling. But if you truly refuse to go to law school, don't expect financial support from us. Start with whatever this entry-level job is, and hang around until they place you into some random city instead of the partner track at a location of your choosing."

Location of my choosing. That comment hits differently than it did at Christmastime. Chicago sounds perfect now. And what if this consulting firm places me somewhere else? Somewhere farther? Who will be there for Cora if I'm not around?

Still, I can't let "what ifs" stop me from pursuing what I want. I knew the consequences when I made my decision last year. I'll spend the summer in Florida with my parents and Cora. I'll finish the rotational program, and Cora will be back at school by the time I'm placed.

I take a breath, refusing to let them see me waiver. "The consulting route is my choice. I told you I'd stay six months, and I will." My voice is steady, even as my heart pounds a frantic rhythm against my ribs. "Now, if you'll excuse me, I think I'm going to head back to the pool and enjoy this final day at sea."

I finish my drink, not glancing back until I step onto the deck, letting the hot sunshine reach me like another world.

Keeping my head high, I walk to where I left Cora earlier, spotting her perched on the pool's edge. She's laughing, chatting it up with some bronzed spring breaker. And for as difficult as it is to see her as the nineteen-year-old she is, I smile, knowing this all could've looked very different had her recovery this past winter not gone as smoothly.

I slip onto the lounge chair and grab my book, attempting (and failing) to get further than a few words before my mind wanders off. Between spending too much time discussing my future and the man in Chicago still monopolizing my thoughts, this trip has been anything but refreshing. At least it's been a good chance to reconnect with my sister, not having seen her since my weekend visit to her university in early March.

"Hey, are you even reading that?" Cora's teasing voice pulls me out of my trance as I glance up wistfully. Seeing the answer written on my face, she rolls her eyes. "Mom and Dad back at it today?"

I agree hesitantly. "Among other things, yeah." I gaze at the boy she was chatting with, eager to change the topic. "What about you? You looked pretty intimate with Blondie over there."

Protectiveness kicks up as Cora's expression brightens. She glances shyly over her shoulder before responding. "Oh, yeah. Derek. He seems…nice."

When I fold my arms in silent assessment, she rushes to add, "Seriously? He's harmless, Dee. Besides, you don't have to watch out for me anymore."

Dee. The name she's called me since she learned how to speak. It only adds to the pang in my chest. Because she's right, she's an adult now. And despite my best efforts to stay in touch, she's been on her own this last year at school without me.

"Just be careful, Coco, okay?" I purposely throw in her childhood nickname, hoping she understands. She's always going to be my baby sister. The one I've looked out for my entire life.

Cora nods before offering a cheery smile and returning to Blondie's shameless flirting. A flicker of unease hits me as Beach Boy moves closer to my giggling sister. She looks so young, so innocent. And with our parents so focused on their own lives, it's always fallen on me to keep her safe, to be the one she can count on. Can I really leave her behind to chase my own dreams?

With a jagged inhale, I force my eyes back to the book in my hand.

I shouldn't be so quick to judge. I've lost my heart to the king of shameless flirting.

My phone buzzes with a new text. Speak of the devil...

The flutter in my chest gives away just how caught up I already am.

Mark: *Missing you* 😊

I smile at Mark's sweet message. But even as I type out a playful response, a small voice whispers that the distance between us is more than just physical. With every day that passes, every reminder of my responsibilities to my family, I feel like I'm being pulled further and further away from a life that could be, no matter how far-fetched.

Me: *Enjoying the views without you* 📸

I attach a photo of me peering over my sunglasses, unable to resist teasing him.

Mark: *You're cruel...* 🦉 *Send more?*

Laughter escapes, imagining the adorable pout he's probably wearing.

Me: *Shouldn't you be working instead of sexting, hotcakes?*
Mark: *Can't help it when I'm fantasizing about you in a bikini all day...*

My cheeks flush crimson, imagining the images in his mind. I decide to shift topics before I lose all composure.

Me: *How's the trip going? You'll be back for Easter still?*
Mark: *Lonely in this hotel room without you. Be home late
    Saturday. You?*
Me: *Same. Cora's staying over for Easter brunch on Sunday.
    Want to join?* 🍷 😋
Mark: *Tempting... Rather have you all to myself, though* 😏
Me: *Mandy will be gone. Cora's leaving early afternoon. Could
    make it worth your while if you come over...*
Mark: *Convinced. I'll be there with champagne ready* 🥂 *See you
    Sunday, sexy.*

I grin at the phone, butterflies taking flight, imagining our reunion. Two more days.

"Hey, Dee!" Cora's voice pulls me from the flirtatious texting. "You mind if I bail tonight? I think I'm gonna meet Derek at that party."

Again, maternal instincts flare. Playing Mom to Cora never felt like a game. It was more like a necessity, given our parents were at the height of their careers when she was born and weren't around much.

I set the phone down and turn to Cora, curious when she started making solo plans with virtual strangers. Probably when she hit puberty and I left for college.

"Party?" I repeat, suddenly seeing the adult sitting next to me. "They can get pretty wild, but if that's what you want to do, I can't stop you."

She stares at me, head tilting. "Why don't you come, too? I mean, doesn't dancing sound like more fun than a night of whale watching? Maybe it'll get your mind off what's his name…Mr. Hotty McHot Pants?"

I know she adds the last part to get under my skin.

"Oh, stop. Don't make me regret telling you about Mark."

Cora pretends to zip her mouth closed before coaxing gently, "So that's a yes, then?"

"Fine," I answer. As Cora's face lights up with gratitude, I add, "Only because someone's gotta keep an eye on you."

She rolls her eyes exaggeratedly as she returns to pool boy Derek. But even as she leaves, I'm smiling. I can juggle the heat of desire and the chill of concern. I always have. But right now, amidst the laughter of fellow vacationers and the scent of sunscreen and chlorine, I realize that, no matter where life takes me, this—the fierce love for my sister—is something better than any temporary man can provide.

Moonlight glints off the churning waves as Cora and I cross the festive deck toward the thumping bass. I smooth the slinky material of my dress, forcing down irrational concern as we enter.

The club is a sensory overload–pulsing lights, throbbing music, and the mingled scents of perfume and alcohol. I weave through the crowd, keeping an eye on Cora as she makes her way to the VIP area.

"Cora, slow down!" I call out, but my voice is lost in the din.

She glances back, flashing me an excited grin as we reach the stairs. The VIP balcony is slightly less chaotic, but the air is thick with cigarette smoke and spilled drinks.

"You made it!" a voice booms, and I turn to see Derek, the blonde guy from earlier, pushing through the throng of people to reach us. He throws an arm around Cora, and I feel a twinge of unease.

"Derek, this is my sister, Arden," Cora says, her eyes darting between us. "Arden, Derek and his friends."

I nod, offering a polite smile as Derek introduces us to a group of guys who all seem to blend together. Their gazes linger a bit too long for comfort, but I brush it off.

"Can I get you a drink?" one of them offers.

"I'm good, thanks," I reply, my tone firm but not unfriendly.

I scan the area, noting the various stages of inebriation around us. Cora seems to be having a good time, laughing at something Derek's saying. It's nice to see her relaxed, but I can't shake my protective instincts.

When Derek's hand slides lower on Cora's waist, I notice her smile falter slightly. It's subtle, but it's enough to set off alarm bells.

I make my way over, keeping my voice casual. "Hey, Cora, mind if I borrow you for a sec? Girl talk."

She looks up, surprise flickering across her face. "Um, sure. Everything okay?"

"All good," I assure her, flashing a smile at Derek. "Just need my sister for a minute."

He shrugs, stepping back. "No problem. Don't keep her too long, though."

As we move to a quieter spot, I lean in close to Cora. "You good? That guy seems a bit... handsy."

Cora rolls her eyes, but I catch a hint of uncertainty. "It's fine, Arden. I'm not a kid anymore, I can handle myself."

"I know you can," I say softly. "But if you need an out, just say the word. We can bail anytime. I just...I worry about you."

Her expression softens, and she reaches out to squeeze my hand. "I know you do, and I love you for it. But you have to trust me to make my own choices, okay? Even if they're not always the ones you would make. Now, try to have some fun."

As if the universe knew what I needed, my phone buzzes and Mark's goofy contact photo flashes on my screen.

Cora just smiles. "Talk to McHotty Pants. Stop worrying about me."

I laugh, as she shoves me away playfully.

"Fine. I'm going. Find me if you need anything."

Seeking solitude on the open-air deck, I swipe open the Facetime chat. Mark's warm gaze immediately fills the screen, his eyes sweeping over me appreciatively.

"Well, don't you look sexy," Mark's voice purrs through the phone. "All dressed up without me? That's just cruel, babe."

I smile, taking in his post-workout look. "Maybe I wanted to give you something to think about while you're in...where are you again? Pittsburgh?"

Mark's eyes flash playfully. "Careful, Bubbles. Two can play at that game." Without warning, he sets the phone down and tugs off his shirt, giving me a tantalizing view.

I roll my eyes, fighting to temper the sparks he ignites so easily. "Please. As if you don't have admirers in every city."

"Trust me," he shakes his head, his voice dropping low, "the only woman on my mind is you. This week's been torture."

"Yeah?" I bite my lip, warmth spreading through me at his words. "I might've missed you a little too."

We fall into easy banter, catching up on our nights apart. It's surprising how quickly I've gotten used to these calls, how much I look forward to them. Even with miles between us, Mark's attention makes me feel...seen.

Our conversation flows naturally until something catches my eye over Mark's shoulder. A group of guys are leading a clearly intoxicated girl out of the club. My stomach drops as I recognize the chestnut hair.

Cora.

"Mark, I gotta go," I blurt out, ending the call without waiting for a response.

Dread spikes through me as I take in Cora's state. She's swaying dangerously, leaning heavily on Derek, whose grip on her waist seems more possessive than supportive.

I'm moving before I even realize it, all thoughts of Mark and our conversation pushed aside by the urgent need to protect my sister.

"Get your hands off her!"

Derek glances at me lazily. "Chill out, we're just having some fun..." He makes no move to release Cora, her glazed eyes struggling to focus.

"Doesn't look like fun to me," I bite out.

Derek's friends shuffle their feet, clearly wanting no part of this. Still, he argues petulantly until fury overrides my attempts at diplomacy. I shove him back, extricating Cora from his loosened grip.

She collapses against me, her apologies muffled by sobs. My heart constricts, a mix of relief and guilt washing over me. I stroke her hair, whispering soothing words as we stumble away.

As the angry shouts fade behind us, I hold Cora tighter, silently vowing to protect her from the darkness that nearly swallowed her tonight. A shudder runs through me as I consider how differently this could have ended. If I hadn't been here, if I'd been drinking too...

The weight of responsibility settles heavily on my shoulders. I've always been the big sister, the protector, but tonight hammers home just how crucial that role is. It's not just about being there for the good times or offering advice on boys and classes. It's about being a lifeline when the world turns dangerous and confusing.

My phone buzzes insistently, and I know it's Mark. For a moment, I'm torn between the desire to hear his voice and the need to focus entirely on Cora. But that hesitation, that split second of divided loyalty, makes my decision clear.

No matter how strong my feelings for Mark, no matter how tempting the idea of a summer romance, Cora has to come first. She's not just my sister; she's my responsibility. And I can't abandon that, not even for the promise of love.

As I guide Cora down the stairs, I finally answer the call, wedging the phone between my ear and shoulder.

"Arden?! What the hell happened?" Mark's concerned voice cuts over the background noise.

"Cora. But I need you to trust me. We're heading back to the cabin," I rush out, pausing as she stumbles slightly.

Mark curses vehemently. "Is she okay? Did that punk try something? Just tell me where to find the bastard, I swear…"

Despite everything, his ferocious protectiveness makes me smile. "She'll be alright. Nothing that rest and water won't fix." *I'm hoping, anyway.*

Mark makes a dissenting noise but doesn't argue further. "Call me when you get her settled. I need to know you're both safe."

Warmth touches my strained smile. "I will. And Mark…thank you."

After getting Cora to drink some water and maneuvering her into bed, I step onto the balcony, not surprised that Mark picks up immediately.

"Everything okay now?" he rushes to ask.

I sigh, leaning against the railing and staring at the moonlit waves, the weight of my thoughts and fears resurfacing. "She's asleep. I think she'll be fine. But if I hadn't been there…"

"Don't go down that road," Mark urges gently. "You were there, and you protected her. That's what matters."

I nod, even though he can't see me. "I know. But it got me thinking. About Cora, and my family, and…and us."

There's a brief pause, and I can almost hear the gears turning in Mark's head. "What about us?"

I take a deep breath, trying to find the right words. "I just…I don't know how to balance my family's needs with what I want for myself."

"Arden," Mark says softly, his voice warm and reassuring. "I heard your requests loud and clear when we started this. I'd never ask you to choose between me and Cora."

Of course he's being understanding and patient and perfect.

I close my eyes, feeling a bittersweet tug in my chest. As comforting as his words are, they also serve as a reminder of the inevitable end to whatever this has become. The rules *I* put in place. And damn it if I'm not blurring them all. Because, yeah, I've fallen so deep for this man, I'm drowning.

I glance at Cora sleeping peacefully on the bed, wondering if Mark deserves someone better, someone who can promise more—longer—be less tethered to people who need her elsewhere or a dream she's chasing.

"Still there, beautiful?" Mark asks, pulling me from my spiraling thoughts.

"Yeah. Sorry. Just looking at Cora," I deflect, not ready to admit all the fears and doubts plaguing me. "But, really, thank you. For understanding. For being you."

For caring for me despite the walls I've put up.

"Anytime, babe. That's what I'm here for."

And, wow, do I wish I could do the same for him. To help him in some way so this wasn't all for nothing, to prove that I care about him, even if we can't have forever. At least not right now.

Because staring at Cora, I know I have to let him go—for his sake as much as my own.

17

Mark

Fifteen Months Ago, January 10th

I spot her across the crowded gym, barely catching the bar in my hands as my breath snags. Arden Cooper. She's staring down at the phone in her hands, headphones on, as she steps onto the treadmill. I watch her from my seated position in front of the mirror as memories of our heated interaction last month crash over me relentlessly.

I scrub a rough palm over my face, grappling to get control.

Did I really think I'd never see her again? That I could pretend she didn't exist?

And how'd I go so long before without ever noticing her?

She glances up, eyes facing the mirror. For a minute, I don't think she sees me, but as her shoulders recoil and her gaze drops, I know she does.

I slink along the wall, ducking behind a walled-off pull-up bar. Cowardly, I know. But facing her confident stare after the way I retreated from intimacy that night might finally shatter me. What could I even say after kicking her out?

Sorry, I panicked because you made me feel too much?

I hoist myself up, peering over the barrier I put between us. I can't tear my eyes away as Arden starts a steady jog. Watching the grace of her stride, I ache to run my hands over those slender curves again, to charm her sass until her eyes stare at me with only want. I squeeze my eyes shut, muscles shaking as I finally release my grip on the bar.

It's better that she believes I used her than to share these unwelcome feelings I can't escape. Safer if she hates me enough to ensure we both stay far away.

As I slump into the locker room, Jake corners me.

"Hiding from someone?" he teases, his sharp gaze sizing me up instantly. "What happened? Find out you accidentally slept with one of your new professors?"

I attempt to smooth my expression into casual indifference, spinning the lock in my fingers absently. "Don't know what you mean."

"Uh-huh. So this hide-and-seek game is part of your new workout routine?" Jake volleys back dryly. When I pointedly don't respond, he adds more gently, "C'mon, man, clearly something's eating at you."

I throw up my hands, the words pouring out in a rush. "Fine! There was... I met this girl at the Christmas party last month. I cut things off before anything happened, and now I can't stop thinking about her. She's here, and I'm fucking hiding to avoid talking to her. Pathetic, right?"

Jake makes a thoughtful sound, biting back a grin at my dramatic response. "I mean...hiding is a bit extreme. Never known you to be one who can't charm your way out of a situation."

At my answering scowl, Jake snorts. "Oh, these are actual feelings? My bad." He crosses his arms, leaning against the row of lockers. "Seriously? What's the real story? Why'd you cut things off?"

I recount the night I met her, our charged chemistry, admitting how I panicked after kissing her. Jake listens thoughtfully, finally speaking after we brave the winter chill, venturing back to his dorm room.

"So let me get this straight," Jake says, leaning back against his desk. "You met a girl you had a crazy connection with, had her practically naked in your bed, then you kicked her out?"

I wince at the blunt recap but nod reluctantly.

Jake lets out a low whistle. "Damn, man. That's cold, even for you."

"I know, I know," I groan, scrubbing a hand over my face. "I just... I freaked out, okay? It was too intense, too real. I didn't know how to handle it."

Jake's expression softens with understanding. "But now you can't stop thinking about her?"

I let out a bitter laugh. "Understatement of the century. bro. It's like she's under my skin, and I can't shake her."

"Sounds serious," Jake chuckles, dodging the pillow I throw at him. "Maybe the universe is trying to tell you something."

I snort, rolling my eyes. "Yeah, right. What's next, you gonna start reading tarot cards?"

"Hey, stranger things have happened," Jake shrugs, unfazed by my sarcasm. "Look at me and Tessa. Sometimes, you just gotta take a leap of faith."

"Says the guy who's so whipped he probably irons Tessa's shoelaces," I tease, trying to deflect.

Jake grins, puffing out his chest. "And proud of it, my friend. Love makes you do crazy things...like hiding out in a gym to avoid a girl."

"Whoa, whoa, who said anything about love?" I say, holding up my hands. "I barely know this girl. We didn't even hook up. Just made out."

Jake shakes his head, and I hate how well he can read me. "Keep telling yourself that, buddy. But I've known you since we were practically in diapers, and I've never seen you this worked up over a girl before."

I sigh, running a hand through my hair. "I don't know, man. I'm just...not built for the whole relationship thing, you know? I like my life the way it is."

"Sure," Jake nods, his tone skeptical. "That's why we're having this conversation, right?"

I shoot him a glare, but there's no heat behind it. "I hate it when you're right."

Jake laughs, clapping me on the shoulder. "Get used to it, brother. Now, are you gonna man up and talk to her, or do I need to be on my deathbed first?"

"Low blow, dude," I chuckle, shaking my head. But as I glance out the window, I can't help but wonder where Arden is, what she's doing. Maybe Jake's right. Maybe there's more to this than I'm ready to admit.

For now, though, I'll stick to the shadows. It's safer there. Even if a part of me whispers that I'm making the biggest mistake of my life.

18

Mark

Now, April 8th

I shuffle through the empty hallway impatiently, my pulse spiking just knowing I'm about to see Arden. No wonder she confused me so damn much last year...a week apart, and suddenly it's like I can't breathe without her.

Thank God for work and my three-day trip to Pittsburgh, or I might've been tempted to rent a boat and seek her out, if only to get a temporary fix.

I rake both hands roughly through my hair, trying to get a grip on these unfamiliar thoughts. Somehow, the time away only increased whatever magnetic stronghold Arden has over me. And it's fucking scary as hell.

Searching for composure, I knock on the door, delicious scents already wafting into the hallway. When an unfamiliar brunette appears in the doorway, I pause awkwardly until I remember Arden's sister stayed over.

"You must be Cora!" I hold out the bouquet I impulsively bought on the way over. "I've heard so much about you."

Her eyes widen in surprise as she grabs the stems. "You're Mark?" Her words are more of a question than a statement, and I'm not sure whether to be concerned or amused.

"In the flesh. Hopefully I meet expectations?"

"Oh, Cora, stop gawking. Let him inside," Arden calls teasingly from somewhere out of view.

Cora steps back, offering an inviting smile.

Entering the apartment, I catch a domesticated version of the ever-intimidating Arden Cooper. Even with oven mitts on, she's a force to be reckoned with. Enough so that all my sanity goes out the window as I stride toward her, wrapping my arms around her. Arden gasps softly at the force but melts against my chest, her vanilla scent drug-like in its aura. Setting down the bottle of champagne still in my hand, I claim her smiling lips fiercely, unable to withstand another second without her taste on my tongue again.

"I missed you too," she whispers, absently running her hands over her shirt when I finally loosen my grip. Her eyes dart to the person standing behind me and reality sets back in.

"Do you two need the room? I can go," Cora teases lightly, gaze circling the two of us.

Hell of a first impression, Mark. Way to go.

I flush, adding a few inches of space between me and Arden. "Sorry about that…uh, Happy Easter?"

Arden laughs, her face still pink from my over-the-top welcome-home kiss. "Mark, I believe you met my sister, Cora. Cora, Mark."

"Guess I see why my sister's been gushing about you, Hotty McHot Pants," she responds, tossing a playful wink.

"Huh?"

What did she call me?

"Come on. Let's eat while it's warm," Arden interrupts, mouthing something to her sister I can't see, then glances at me with a shake of her head as she brings the final egg dish to the table. I chuckle to myself, needing to ask about the story later.

"Food smells amazing!" I comment appreciatively when Arden sits down beside us.

And fuck, if the smile she offers doesn't have images of last week's sleepover flashing dangerously.

I pour glasses of champagne, attempting to make casual small talk to keep my wandering thoughts more PG in her sister's presence. "So, ladies, tell me about the trip."

They grin, both diving in to explain the different islands they visited as we start passing around food. They share a few stories of beaches and sights as we enjoy the quiche. Laughter flows freely as these two play off each other's sentences. It's strangely endearing watching how they admire one another rather than the loathing my family tends to hold for each other.

As brunch wraps up, a comfortable silence settles over the table. Arden glances my way, a playful glint in her eyes. "So, Mark, are you still thinking about heading to your family's Easter dinner tonight?"

I groan, leaning back in my chair dramatically. "Ugh, don't remind me. My parents decided to join the Rhoades' dinner last minute. And let's just say, it's not exactly a happy reunion when Bells are together."

Cora snorts, popping a blueberry into her mouth. "What, no heartwarming moments of family bonding over the ham?"

"More like passive-aggressive jabs over the honey glaze," I quip, earning a laugh from Cora. But Arden's sympathetic gaze has me wanting to open up more. "Mom can be...a lot. She has this way of making everything feel like a competition, and I'm always the one losing."

Arden reaches over, squeezing my hand. "I'm sorry I brought it up."

I shake my head, pausing as Cora's eyes light up across from us.

"Ooh, I know! Arden should go with you! She's, like, the queen of handling difficult people. Remember when you made our Aunt Karen cry at Thanksgiving, Dee?"

Arden? Meet my family? Why does that idea excite me?

Arden rolls her eyes, but I can see the corners of her mouth twitching. "Okay, first of all, I didn't make her cry. She just got a little...overwhelmed by my logical arguments."

I raise an eyebrow, intrigued. "Cora makes a good point. I'd pay to watch your sharp wit match my mother's blows." I meet Arden's surprised look, hesitantly hopeful. "What do you say, Arden? It'd be a shame to go without my therapist."

She taps her chin like she's considering it. "Spend my evening watching you squirm while I verbally eviscerate your mother? Tempting..."

"I'll make it worthwhile," I promise, waggling my eyebrows suggestively.

"Oh, stop," Arden scolds without any real threat, throwing her napkin at me. "But I guess I could tag along...if only to help with all that self-growth you touted last week."

Last week...at the party. Before...

I grin, not able to stop the flood of images at the mention of that night. "Have I mentioned lately how amazing you are?"

She smirks, tossing her hair over her shoulder. "Not lately, but I have been out of the country..."

Did she follow my line of thinking?

Cora looks between us, shaking her head in amusement. "You two are disgustingly cute, you know that?"

Arden and I exchange a glance, both fighting back smiles. "Yeah, we know," I say, leaning over to kiss Arden's cheek.

Arden laces her fingers through mine supportively. And I'm struck by certainty that this remarkable woman will stand steadfastly at my side, formidable as ever, regardless of whatever chaos awaits us tonight.

♥ ⚾ ♥ ⚾ ♥

I glance over at Arden in the passenger seat, giving her hand a gentle squeeze. "Thank you again for coming with. I'm sure this wasn't how you expected to spend your Easter."

Arden smiles softly, her thumb tracing circles over my wrist. "You know, I never told you this, but you were the one who gave me the courage to finally tell my parents I didn't want to go to law school last year."

I blink, surprised. "Me? How?"

She chuckles, shaking her head. "That night at the party, when we talked...you listened. Really listened. And you told me that I should follow my own dreams, not someone else's. It stuck with me."

I'm floored. The idea that I had such an impact on her life...it's humbling. Then again, this fierce woman never needed *me* to convince her anything.

"Arden…"

"Maybe this is my chance to return the favor," she says lightly, but I can hear the sincerity in her voice.

Chest tightening with emotion, I bring her hand to my lips, pressing a kiss to her knuckles. It's not enough to express what I'm feeling, but it's all I can manage right now.

After a moment, Arden clears her throat, her tone turning playful. "You know, maybe we should plan a signal or something? For when we need the other to intervene?"

I chuckle, glancing side-long briefly. "A signal, huh? How about I just start making out with you until it gets too awkward and they throw us out?"

"As tempting as that sounds," Arden says, swatting my arm, "I don't think Mrs. Rhoades would appreciate the dramatic exit."

Her nails trace delicate patterns down my arm as she sobers. "But really, Mark, thank you for trusting me enough to invite me into your world. I'm enjoying seeing these new sides of you."

The sincerity in her voice hits me hard. I wish I wasn't driving so I could look her in the eye as I respond. "I should be thanking you for seeing something here worth fighting for. For making me believe I deserve more than the toxicity I've been used to." I take an uneven breath. "Somehow, all of this feels easier with you by my side."

"Almost like together, we're unbreakable," she offers softly, and I can hear the weight of unspoken truths in her words.

I nod, gently tracing the delicate bones of her hand with my thumb. "Something like that."

As we pull up to the Rhoades' house, I feel my stomach twist with apprehension. Arden must sense my tension because she gives my hand a reassuring squeeze.

"We've got this, Mark," she says firmly. "I'm right here with you. And we can leave whenever you need to, okay? No pressure to stay if it gets to be too much."

I take a deep breath, fighting the urge to turn the car around. "No, we're here. Let's get this over with."

As Mrs. Rhoades ushers us inside with hugs and hellos, I guide Arden through the swirl of family members and into the kitchen. I grab us both a drink, wishing it was something stronger.

Arden leans in close, her voice low. "Remember, I've got your back. Just say the word, and I'll create a diversion. I've got a mean fainting spell in my repertoire."

I laugh, the tension in my shoulders easing slightly, but it all comes rushing back when I hear my mother's artificially sweet voice.

"Well, look who decided to grace us with his presence!" Her gaze sweeps over me before landing on Arden, her sharp smile faltering for a moment as she notices our joined hands. "And you've brought a guest!"

I squeeze Arden's hand, drawing strength from her presence. "Mom, this is Arden."

My mother's smile is all teeth as she pulls Arden in for a hug. "How lovely to meet you, dear." She turns back to me, her eyes glinting. "Marky, how on earth did you convince such a charming young lady to accompany you?"

I feel my jaw clench, but before I can respond, Arden's voice cuts in, smooth as silk.

"Oh, Mrs. Bell, I'm the lucky one here," she says, her hand resting on my chest. I glance down at her, surprised. "I mean, an intelligent, ambitious man who wants me to meet his family? I hit the jackpot." She turns to my mother, her smile genuine. "You must be so proud."

I stare speechless—game recognizing perfect game—as Arden stretches onto her toes to brush a soft kiss over my jaw.

This woman exceeds all my expectations. *Daily.*

"Please, call me Diane," my mother says, her eyes narrowing slightly. "Though I hope you know what you're getting into, dear. Mark's always been a bit...unpredictable."

I feel a hot surge of anger, but Arden beats me to the punch.

"Oh, I'm well aware," she says, leaning into me. "We met at a party, after all. But beneath that charming exterior? I found a kind, compassionate, driven man." She looks up at me, her eyes sparkling. "He's a catch in all the best ways."

My mother's gaze darts between us, clearly thrown by Arden's glowing praise and easy affection directed my way. For a moment, I think she might lash out, but instead, she gives a tight smile.

"Well, you've found quite the champion in this one, Marky. I hope she knows what she's signing up for." With that, Mom turns on her heel and stalks away.

My mother's gaze darts between us, clearly thrown off balance. Finally, she manages a tight smile. "Well, you've certainly found quite the champion, Marky. I hope she knows what she's in for." With that, she turns and walks away.

I turn to Arden, my heart swelling with gratitude. "Arden, I... That was... Thank you."

She grins, her eyes twinkling with mischief. "What? I only spoke the truth. Though I may have left out the part about your terrible dance moves and cheesy pickup lines."

I can't help but laugh, pulling her close. "You didn't seem to mind my dance moves that night at the bar."

"Probably because of the shots you kept offering," she teases, but her expression softens. "You okay?"

I nod, surprising myself with how true it is. "Yeah, I am." I brush a fleeting kiss to her temple, because this might be the first time someone's voiced appreciation for me beyond what my body is capable of. The first time someone told me I'm *worth* more.

Arden's smile is soft and warm. "Good. Because I want some juicy stories from the Rhoades' on you as a troubled teen."

I groan as she tugs me toward Owen, Jake, and Thomas. But embarrassing stories aside, I can't help but marvel at this incredible woman. And I'm helpless to fall deeper under her spell.

As the party winds down, I catch Arden's eye and give her a mischievous grin. "Hey, wanna see where the legend of Mark Bell began?"

She raises an eyebrow, a smirk playing on her lips. "Do I need a hazmat suit for this?"

I laugh, taking her hand and leading her out into the spring air. We walk next door, and I can feel her curiosity growing.

"Welcome to Casa de Bell," I announce, pushing open the front door with a flourish.

As we step inside, memories hit like a tidal wave—good and bad—as she walks inside. I remember the pride in my father's voice when I got into college on a full baseball scholarship, the fights my parents had in this room as I lay upstairs overhearing them, and the sound of the door being shut and opened with the constant rotation of mystery hookups.

I watch Arden take it all in, her eyes wide with interest.

"So this is where the magic happened, huh?" she teases, but there's a softness in her voice that tells me she understands the significance of this moment.

"Magic, mayhem, the occasional emotional breakdown," I shrug, aiming for nonchalance. "You know, the usual."

We make our way upstairs to my old room, and I feel a little exposed. It's one thing to show her the polished version of myself, but this? This is raw, unfiltered Mark Bell.

"You know, your dad's not too bad," Arden says softly, cautiously eyeing a wall of photos.

I think back to the few words he said during dinner: asking about my job, seeking projections on the baseball season, and not making a big deal about Arden being there with me.

"Not when he's around," I reply tentatively.

She hums, pausing at the only picture frame displayed prominently—me with the Rhoades from middle school.

"I remember this from your room at the frat house," she says softly.

I'm surprised she noticed, let alone remembered. "Yeah, must've brought it back here when I moved in with Jake."

She nods, her fingers tracing the outline of an old baseball trophy. "Most of my childhood stuff got tossed when my parents moved to Florida," she admits, a forced lightness in her tone. "Guess you'll never see all my cool adolescent keepsakes."

"I can only imagine what that room would've been like for the straight-laced Arden Cooper," I tease, pulling her back to my chest and wrapping my arms around her. "Gray walls? Debate trophies? Boyband posters with hearts drawn in Sharpie?"

She huffs a laugh. "Predictable, huh?" She elbows me gently. "Although you forgot the secret stash of teen romance novels."

"No way. Good-girl Arden reading trashy love stories? I don't believe it!" I gasp dramatically.

Laughing, she swats me away. "Oh, stop! Not like you didn't have questionable swimsuit model cutouts plastered on your wall." Arden spins around, lifting a coy eyebrow. "In fact, I'd be willing to bet there are dirty magazines in here somewhere. Closet, maybe?"

Before I can reply, she disentangles from my arms and moves toward the closet. I make a theatrical lunge to block her access as we dissolve into playful laughter, struggling for dominance.

I pin her to the ground, breathless, as she grins up at me. "I prefer my centerfolds live and in person now anyway," I quip.

Our laughter fades to a charged silence as we hold each other's stare, hip to hip, on my childhood bedroom floor. A sense of déjà vu washes over me, and memories of our first magnetic encounter flood vividly.

What if I'd never asked her to leave that night?

What if I'd chased after her months ago instead of giving in to fear?

If I'd had the courage that Jake tried instilling in me...

Now, having her here, in this room, I'm struck by how right it feels. Like she belongs here, in this part of my life I've kept hidden for so long.

My palms frame her face, grappling to voice the permanent mark this woman's left behind my barricades. But the promise I made her rings in my head... *Don't ask her to stay, don't fall in love, don't talk about the future.*

"Thank you," I offer softly, emotion cracking my voice. "For being here. For…seeing me."

Arden's fingers twist gently into my hair. "Thank you for letting me in."

I dip my head to hers, my mouth meeting hers tenderly. And in her arms, I let my kiss explain all the words I shouldn't say aloud.

Stay with me, Arden.

I'm in love with you.

19

Arden ♥

Now, April 18th

I stare blankly across Mark's dark room, thoughts racing despite how tired I am.

I should've known I wouldn't be able to sleep tonight after the day I had. Between the video call finalizing my start date at the consulting firm and my mother emailing me details about the move home in less than four weeks, chaos is circling in my brain. The carefully outlined calendar of the month's to-do's feel overwhelming as the blind certainties I used to cling to waiver nightly since Mark Bell shook up my world.

I think about my carefully constructed five-year plan and the picture I painted for myself. And it's all still what I want. It's just not the *only* thing I want anymore.

Huffing impatiently, I shift onto my side, facing a sleeping Mark, and indulge in the dangerous what-if daydream swirling relentlessly. What if, instead of separate paths post-graduation, we chase this connection? Would it last? Am I utterly hopeless thinking Mark would actually want a long-term girlfriend? And long-distance…forget it. This man craves intimacy like it's oxygen. There's no way texts and phone calls could suffice.

Laying my head on Mark's shoulder, I attempt to reframe my wandering thoughts and simply be present these final weeks. It's easier to do when Mark's warm exhales tease my collarbone, sending all logic out the window. But left in its place is the sudden fear that no one else can shelter me as completely as when Mark's arms surround me.

Mark stirs beneath me, pressing his lips to my forehead almost unconsciously as he murmurs, "Can't sleep?"

I nuzzle his neck again, tamping down panicked confessions threatening to spill free. "Just...overthinking everything as always."

Mark makes a sleepy sound of dissent, a calloused hand sliding temptingly lower now. "Mmm...you think too much, babe. How about I help distract that big brain a bit?"

Everything in me wants to melt into the welcoming oblivion those skillful hands promise. But unwillingly, visions creep in of how this could look weeks from now, someone else lying in this bed.

Mark's lips find the unfairly sensitive nerves below my ear, and the unpleasant images give way to the fiery yearning burning inside me. Because no logic or self-protection stands a chance against the drug of Mark Bell's devotion behind closed doors.

In the darkness, I cling tighter to the radiating heat no one else can rival, pushing away the tiny voice whispering that this intoxicating chemistry is love. We made rules for a reason, didn't we?

Mark's thumb traces my lower lip, his other hand sliding along my thigh. "Tell me what I can do to help you relax, baby."

I almost laugh. What can he do? Love me? Beg me to stay? More requests I can't actually voice. Because, deep down, I know I'd never forgive myself for giving up my goals on something that's not guaranteed.

We've been together a few weeks, not the years I've spent achieving straight A's. Not even the length of time I spent researching the firm I'm going to work for.

When I meet Mark's gaze, the intensity I find there makes my breath catch. It's not just desire—it's something deeper, something that scares and thrills me in equal measure.

He feels it, too.

Slowly, reverently, I trail my fingers over his face, mapping the planes and angles I adore—the stubble along his jaw, the arch of his brow, the fullness of his lips.

Mark's eyes flutter shut, a shaky exhale escaping him. When he opens them again, they're bright with understanding. "I know, Arden. It's not enough time. But don't pull away yet, okay?"

He gets me. Sees me. Knows me.

How is that possible?

"Just kiss me." There's a desperation in his voice that makes my chest ache, making me want to soothe his doubts more than my own.

I shift, lowering myself on top of him. Even in the dim light, I can see his silhouetted smile. And the way he pulls my mouth to his, moving with me in a dance that feels new and familiar all at once, I know this is something so much more than it was supposed to be. Then it should be.

"God, Arden, how do you always feel so incredible?" he rasps thickly, rocking my hips back and forth.

"I could say the same about you," I murmur, pushing away deeper thoughts and allowing myself to get lost in the moment.

"I can't get enough of you," he whispers, his hands roaming my body like he's trying to memorize every inch.

I almost say the words, nearly admitting that I'll never have enough of him, either. That I might *only* want him for the rest of my life.

But I don't. I shouldn't.

We both know this works because it's temporary, don't we? He doesn't have to commit, not really. Not the way he would if I told him the truth…that I've fallen in love with him despite all my carefully constructed rules.

Pushing down the doubts, the fears, and the expiring time clock, I let myself climb higher, chasing the peak of pleasure and anchoring myself to Mark. There is only us, only this, only what we've become together. And right now, it's everything.

Light filters in through the window as my eyes flutter open. Instinctively, my hand reaches for the other side of the bed, surprised when I grasp an empty blanket. With tired eyes, I toss on my favorite pajama bottoms—now conveniently back at Mark's apartment—and shuffle toward the kitchen.

I find Mark at the table, typing on his laptop, two steaming mugs of coffee already in front of him. He glances up, his gaze sweeping over me as his too-charming smile flashes. "Finally sleep, or did I just wear you out properly?"

Warmth creeps up my cheeks as I add creamer to the coffee, avoiding his playful stare. "You definitely got my mind off my wandering thoughts."

Something tender shifts in Mark's expression before he stands, shifting the topic breezily. "Hungry? I picked up some breakfast stuff on my way home yesterday since you have that exam today."

Reckless affection swells as he retrieves fruit and yogurt purchased simply because I mentioned liking them. No one else knows or cares about my food likes beyond casual preferences, yet somehow, Mark pays attention to the little details in a way that's both adorable and terrifying.

"Still spoiling me, Mark? You've already got me hooked."

"Consider it hazard pay for putting up with my middle-of-the-night study sessions." His exaggerated wink startles a surprised laugh as memories of last night's "study session" flood back. "But I can go back to offering protein sludge instead if you'd prefer." He shakes his smoothie cup temptingly my way.

I wrinkle my nose exaggeratedly. "Charmer and health foods fanatic? How'd I get so lucky?"

Mark takes a drink, smirking as he sets it back down. "I seem to recall something about my intelligence and ambition, too. You know, when you told my mother how lucky you were to find me."

I reach for my spoon with a coy grin, warmth pooling traitorously. "Hmm? Doesn't ring a bell."

Mark chuckles softly, his grin falling as he glances back at his computer. "I should warn you, my travel schedule sucks for the next two weeks."

"A few Mark-free days coming up then?" I slant a considering look in his direction. "I might finally get time to catch up with friends before the graduation chaos, then."

Mark gasps dramatically. "Ditching me already? Here I'd hoped you'd spend the time missing me."

I stir my yogurt idly, swallowing down the resurfaced need to tell him that no matter where he is these days, I'm missing him. We made rational rules early on, after all...

No falling in love or planning forever futures echoes accusingly in my head. And I wonder suddenly, with terrifying hope, whether Mark wrestles with why we set such self-preserving restrictions as much as I have lately.

But, like last night, I forcibly abandon the thought, swallowing the lump choking my throat. "It will just make our time together that much sweeter."

Mark nods, his eyes already scanning his laptop screen again. But before his professional focus fully sets in, I glimpse the anxiety in his expression—a quiet acknowledgment that this barely held-together bubble of paradise shrinks by the day.

I finish the last yogurt bites, my appetite vanishing as I think about saying goodbye. But responsibilities, like my exam, won't wait just because my emotions are a tangled mess.

I stand abruptly, needing some space to weigh the turmoil fighting inside.

"I should probably head out," I say, aiming for casual. "Class soon and all."

I lean down to kiss Mark's cheek, but his fingers catch mine before I can retreat. His eyes, warm and knowing, search my face. "Is something else still on your mind, babe?"

Damn. When did he get so good at reading me?

The words "I love you" dance on the tip of my tongue, but fear holds them hostage. Instead, I force a smile. "Just pre-exam jitters. You know how it is."

Mark's thumb traces my cheekbone, his touch achingly tender. "You've got this, Bubbles. At this point, grades don't really matter. But if you need a study break later..." He winks, a mischievous grin spreading across his face. "I know some great stress relief techniques I can show you when I finish work tonight."

I swat his shoulder even as happiness briefly chases away the gloom. "I bet you do, Hotcakes. Save it for Friday, okay?"

As I head towards campus, guilt gnaws at me. I've always prided myself on honesty, on facing challenges head-on. So why am I running from this?

In the lecture hall, I stare blankly at my notebook, the professor's words a distant buzz. My mind keeps circling back to Mark, to the future that's rushing towards us like a freight train.

What happens when I leave? Will this connection we've built survive the distance? Do I want it to? Does he?

I shake my head, trying to focus. One step at a time, Cooper. Ace this exam, then figure out how to tell Mark that he's become more than just a temporary fling.

But as I jot down notes, a small part of me wonders if I've already missed my chance to change the course of our story.

"Hey, Arden!" a voice whispers from beside me.

I glance over to see my roommate, Mandy.

"You okay? You seem a little out of it," she says softly, her brow furrowed in concern.

I force a smile. "Yeah, just tired."

Mandy nods. "Didn't see you last night. Too much time with the new beau before splitting after graduation?"

Her words only twist the knot of anxiety tighter.

Noticing my distress, Mandy places a comforting hand on my arm. "Hey, I thought Mr. Super Star was temporary?"

"Yeah, I thought so, too," I admit, my voice cracking.

"Well, if it's meant to be, you'll figure something out." She smiles, giving my arm a final squeeze before turning her attention back to the lecture.

But that's just it…I'm not sure how.

After class, I take a walk around campus, hoping the fresh air and change of scenery will help clear my head. Meandering through the familiar paths and buildings, a sense of nostalgia washes over me. So much has changed in the past four years, both in my life and in myself.

I find a quiet bench overlooking the quad and sit down, pulling out my phone. I scroll through my contacts until I find Cora's name, my thumb hovering over the call button. Taking a deep breath, I press it, holding the phone to my ear as it rings.

"Hey, sis!" Cora's cheery voice greets me. "What's up?"

"Hey, Cora," I say, my voice sounding strained even to my own ears. "Do you have a minute to talk? I need some advice."

"From me? Is everything okay?" Her tone takes on more concern and I laugh shakily, the words tumbling out of me in a rush.

"It's Mark. I...I think I'm in love with him and it's scaring the hell out of me."

There's a beat of silence on the other end of the line before Cora speaks again, her voice gentle now. "Oh, Dee. I mean, he seems to really care for you, too."

My breath catches. That's exactly the problem. Mark does care. In a way I haven't had before—or ever expected. Not when I've grown up with emotionally distant parents, been in fickle social circles, and had fleeting romances. It's why I created armor to keep myself at arm's length from everyone, determined to chart this course alone.

"But I can't stay in Chicago. What about my job? The promise I made to Mom and Dad? They're already disappointed enough in my choices."

Cora lets out a long breath like she's grappling with what advice to offer. "Maybe he'll wait for you."

But would he? And is that even fair to ask?

"I can't expect him to," I say, firmly tamping down erupting hope that he'd change for me.

Cora's soft certainty barrels through my weak excuse. "Or maybe you're afraid he would? That he'd wait and then regret it?" She huffs playfully, not sensing my spiraling thoughts at the word *regret*. "I mean, knowing you, you already have a pros and cons list charted in a notebook."

I do. And it only shows me what I don't want to see. *The right answer is Florida and letting him go.* I know I should leave it to fate. That whole "if it's meant to be, let it go" concept.

But the truth is, no list can capture the magnitude of what I stand to gain or lose, and the realization leaves me grappling for steady footing I've always taken for granted. Keeping what I found means relinquishing all control of my future. It means surrendering to this powerful, completely irrational emotion without any guarantees or safety nets in place, especially when Mark's been clear he doesn't want to wake up and regret being tied down to someone.

And I won't be someone he regrets in the end.

I let out a long breath, reeling in my emotions. I know what I have to do, what I need to do, and it's never changed. Because I can't be selfish with someone else's emotions, the same way I can't act recklessly and give up my own goals for a feeling I can't be certain about…as much as I'm starting to wish I could.

20

Mark 🏐

Now, May 1st

Staring at my phone in between sets, I can't help but pull up my text thread with Arden. Even the adrenaline rush of working out does little to curb the craving building, knowing I'll see her tonight.

After three days away for work, and the news that I have to attend a conference this weekend, I want as much time together as she'll allow. Unless...

I finish the last set of bicep curls as an idea hits me. Before I even realize it, my fingers are tapping away at the screen.

> Me: *Come by early tonight? Missing your gorgeous face.*
> Arden: *Aww, is Marky needy today?* 😊
> Me: *For you, always.*
> Arden: *Sure you can handle my pent-up sassiness after three days?*
> Me: *Bring that sass to my apartment, woman. I'll show you*
>   *EXACTLY how I plan on handling every delicious inch...*
> Arden: *Wouldn't expect anything less. Better be rested up from*
>   *your trip.*
> Me: *I'm ready to go all night long, darling!* 🏃
> Arden: *Be there in 20* 💋

I sprint back from the gym after getting unexpectedly cornered by a group wanting early baseball season projections. Barreling inside impatiently, I hear familiar laughter that has my heart racing faster than my workout. I halt, frozen, gaping as Arden materializes in the kitchen, leaning casually against the counter, mid-conversation with Jake. Her tousled ponytail hints alluringly at the visible skin I've been craving endlessly.

As though sensing my blatant stare, her eyes lock onto mine.

"You know I'm not ashamed to gawk at you publicly, so don't look surprised," I admit, letting my gaze trail her silhouette again before closing the distance between us in two eager strides.

My palms roam up and down her shoulders like a starved man suddenly restored with sustenance. *Home.* Arden laughs breathily as my mouth meets hers, unable to hold back my hungry kisses any longer. I don't think she's complaining, judging by how her fingers fist into my hair as quickly as my tongue reaches hers.

We come up gasping eventually, her husky chuckle hinting that she's enjoying this unabashed homecoming scene. "Missed me, hmm?"

I brush my nose against hers. "Think that feeling might be mutual, babe."

A subtle throat clears beside us, reminding me we still have an audience. I unwind just enough for Jake's knowing smirk to swim into focus over Arden's shoulder.

"Uh, sorry, man...you two were saying?" I manage roughly, distracted by tempting lips not nearly close enough to mine.

"Smooth," Jake laughs, heading back toward the fragrant garlic dish sizzling on the stovetop. "Just take it to the bedroom already. I'm trying to cook dinner."

If he insists.

With zero hesitation, I sweep up an entirely too willing Arden, relocating our eager reunion behind closed doors.

Arden melts deliciously as I trail wet kisses down her neck. "So...good trip, then?" she rasps, distracted.

I groan, pressing even closer, while regretfully pulling my lips from her unfairly addictive skin. "Was productive, but too damn long..."

Arden's expression dances with delight and understanding. "Sounds terrible. But you're home for a bit now, yeah?"

I huff a disappointed laugh. "Unfortunately, I was told I'm attending some training conference in Atlanta this weekend."

I watch as her emotions shift swiftly—disappointment, flaring hope, trepidation—before her mouth presses thin. "Of course, work stuff comes first. You told me you'd be traveling a lot."

Is that relief or regret pinching her tone before she pastes on a too-bright smile?

I grasp her hands tightly, pulse suddenly galloping. "Well...the conference is just during the day. Nights are still free." I entwine our fingers, daring to ask the dangerous question. "Maybe you'd want to come with me? Escape the real world for a bit."

I pray she can see the need in my expression, how much I want this final weekend together before her graduation next week.

I hold my breath anxiously as Arden chews on that damned lip before exhaling hard. "A secret weekend getaway? You sure that's a good idea?" Something bright and daring sparks behind the forced lightness, though.

"I was thinking, more like, the best idea ever." My answering kiss steals her laugh.

"Okay, then, one crazy weekend away," Arden murmurs silkily.

As our mouths meet passionately, no doubts linger about stealing these final weekends while fate allows.

I burrow eagerly into her neck, addiction already spiraling. "I need to shower, if you're in for that, too?"

She giggles indulgently, guiding my wandering palms appropriately northward. "You're completely insatiable. You know that, right?" she hisses throatily.

I grin roguishly, refusing to be deterred now. "When you're in my arms, hell yes." I trace her collarbone, voice dipping suggestively. "Especially picturing you wet and naked against me."

A strangled sound escapes Arden before she fiercely yanks my mouth back to hers. We kiss until the room spins dizzyingly.

"Do you know how tempting you are?" she eventually manages raggedly.

"Me?" Laughing, I lift her, pinning her to the mattress instead. "You know I can't get enough of you, babe."

Arden's eyes burn with desire and affection that sear to my core. Her fingers trace my cheek tenderly. "I missed you, Mark," she whispers almost shyly. "And not just for the amazing sex."

The admission sends a flood of protectiveness and longing surging everywhere. I capture her delicate hand against my pounding heart, seeing my own naked vulnerability reflected now.

I press my forehead to hers, the playful mood shifting into something profoundly intimate. "God, I missed you, too. More than makes sense, probably."

Arden makes a soft sound of empathy, palms cradling either side of my face. When her eyes shine overly bright, she blinks swiftly, rallying teasing bravado like armor.

"Guess we've got some time to make up for, then?" Her nails trail fire down my chest. "We should probably stop wasting time talking when we have plenty of better things to do, hmm?"

I bark out a helpless laugh, even as she skillfully shatters any remaining emotional defenses with her usual fiery flair. Emotions tamed for now, I happily surrender instead to Arden's insatiable demands, determined to take advantage of every moment this stunning woman gives me.

We eventually stumble into the steam-fogged shower. I soak in Arden's skin, slick against mine once more, obsessively tracing her body with heated, open-mouthed kisses that trail lower.

Arden arches into my ruthless explorations, nails scoring delicious trails down my back. "You're never allowed to leave again," she pants above the pounding water surrounding our private haven.

I lift my head briefly, emotions surging. "Never? Even if I promise this kind of homecoming every time?"

She hums as my tongue continues its relentless assault.

"Mark. Damn," she rasps, fingers grasping my hair desperately.

I still inside of her as her body writhes, seeking friction.

"That's what I thought," I tease, pressing my lips to the top of her swollen folds. With single-minded devotion, I return to eliciting those delightful whimpers until any other thought except making her come undone around me vanishes.

Eventually, we spill back into the bedroom on shaking legs, scanning for remnants of the clothes we had scattered earlier. I toss on a t-shirt and boxers, glancing up to see Arden pulling on those favorite pajama bottoms that somehow ended up back at my place.

As though reading my transparent thoughts, she stretches onto her tiptoes, a coy smile on her lips. "Easy there, insatiable one. How about dinner and a movie before round eighty-seven?"

I chuckle, nuzzling her silk-spun locks. "You joke, but I doubt any meal could be as satisfying as another taste of you."

Despite my wayward thoughts, already picturing her bent deliciously over my bed, I grasp her hands and tug her toward the living room for actual nourishment.

Arden leans close as we fill plates, whispering invitingly, "If you're extra charming tonight, maybe we can try something new later?" Her nails trace a deliberate path down my forearm, and I inhale sharply as vivid images flood my vision.

Giggling, Arden pulls me onto the couch beside her. "Food and movie first, remember?"

When we finish eating, Jake flips the lights, wrapping Arden and me in semi-dark privacy as we watch tonight's movie. The allure of her proximity has me sneaking caresses along the bare skin between her tank and pajama waistband.

Arden gasps, grabbing my wrist. "Couldn't even wait ten minutes, could you?" But she doesn't relinquish my palm, just interlaces our fingers and snuggles closer.

I nip her shoulder, eliciting another delighted laugh.

"Careful issuing empty challenges if you aren't prepared for swift follow-through, Bubbles."

I can feel her grin more than see it, and the image alone has heat coursing through my veins.

And, fuck, if I ever dreamed I could be this content holding a woman's hand on a random Tuesday night, watching a movie. Or maybe I've known it since that first night together, already aware of how perfectly this remarkable woman fits next to me. Only now, having her here doesn't scare me.

But the thought of her leaving?

That has an ache so deep forming, I can already feel the pain.

21

Arden ♥

Now, May 5ᵗʰ

I stare out the hotel window at the busy streets below, snuggled in a plush robe that I'm seriously considering smuggling home with me. I mean, it's like being enveloped in a cloud of marshmallows! On the other side of the room, Mark's soothing voice shares updates about some player's recent injury via his cell as I attempt to commit this moment to memory. Everything about the last twelve hours feels deliciously wonderful, like a storybook montage coming to life. Between the plane ride, local dinner date, and steamy night in a new bed, it's as if I'm glimpsing a possible future that's somehow better than my wildest dreams.

If my wildest dreams didn't also include the job I accepted in Tampa.

As Mark ends the call, I pivot openly admiring the shirtless vision fresh from the shower. "So, how long before you have to grace the masses with your presence?" I ask, aiming for casual but probably missing by a mile.

"Why? Got something in mind?" Mark grins, his eyes twinkling with mischief.

I saunter over, channeling the inner seductress Mark brings out in me. "Oh, I don't know. I'm sure we could find some way to pass the time."

Mark groans appreciatively as his palms grasp reflexively at my hips. "You're enjoying torturing me for once, huh, Bubbles?" His mouth descends insistently toward mine before forcing himself to step back. "Rain check for tonight? As much as I'd love a repeat performance, the first session starts in ten minutes."

Mark is turning me down? What parallel universe have I stumbled into?

But seeing his jaw clench with genuine disappointment, something clicks suddenly. Beneath his cocky facade lies an equally committed career-focused man. Part of me is thrilled to see this unexpectedly serious side, too, realizing there's so much more to him than the one-dimensional playboy perception I initially had last year.

Oblivious to my epiphanies, boyish excitement glints through Mark's feigned sternness as he gets dressed. "I'll be back as soon as the last seminar wraps up." He leans in, stealing a quick kiss. "We can grab dinner, then continue testing the soundproofing in the room."

I lob a pillow at him, which he dodges with a laugh. But as he reaches the door, he pauses, his expression softening.

"Just for the record," he says, a hint of vulnerability in his voice, "I could get used to coming home to you."

And with a wink, he's gone, leaving me to process that little bombshell.

Wait, what?

Did Mark "No Strings Attached" Bell just casually drop a hint about a future? And then leave? Talk about a cliffhanger.

For two weeks, we've been dancing around the "what comes next" conversation. I'd convinced myself this was just a fun fling. But now? I'm not so sure.

Does Mark see this—see us—as something more? And if so, why drop it so casually as he's walking out the door?

No. Surely, I'm overanalyzing again, reading too much into a passing comment. He probably just meant that he's enjoyed this trip as much as I have, that it's nice to know I'll be here when he gets back. Right?

No use continuing to play guessing games. I'll have to corner him later and demand answers. For now, though—I glance back toward the bustling city below—my initial plan of shopping and nails should be a welcome distraction to keep my lovesick mind occupied before I spiral into full-on rom-com heroine mode.

Quietly reading in the chair by the window, I nearly jump out of my skin when the door swings open, my book tumbling from my hands mid-chapter. I look up to find Mark's gaze circling me appreciatively as he continues my way.

"Hey, beautiful!" His big, warm hands find my hips, pulling me into his chest. "Hope you enjoyed the day while I missed you like crazy."

I lean into his sturdy frame, my startled heart doing a little tap dance. "Something tells me you managed to charm the room just fine without me."

Mark's grin widens, and he tugs me closer until our noses nearly touch. "You know you're the only one occupying my thoughts 24/7." He brushes his lips over my ear, his breath warm. "What if I told you I spent most of the day imagining all the fun trouble we're getting into tonight?"

"Oh yeah?" I tease, my pulse quickening. "Anything specific?"

His fingers trace the neckline of my dress, leaving goosebumps in their wake. "Let's just say last night left quite an impression. And then how I left this morning…"

I bite my lip, fighting a grin. "I aim to please."

Mark's hand slides to my waist, pulling me closer. "Speaking of pleasing," he says, his voice low and intimate, "I know we have dinner plans, but I'm thinking dessert might be in order first."

His lips find my neck, and I have to stifle a moan. Part of me knows we should talk about his comment from this morning— the whole "coming home to you" thing that's been ricocheting around my brain all day. But with Mark's hands on me, coherent thought becomes a challenge.

"We can be quick," he suggests, lips blazing fire across my collarbone as his fingers slip beneath the hem of my mid-thigh-length dress. "You wouldn't even have to get fully undressed…"

God, the sparks this man creates with just a brush of his fingertips. I've been attracted before, even seduced by skillful lovers. But never consumed so swiftly by intoxicating chemistry that short-circuits all reason until only *more, now, please* echoes through my mind.

So, I surrender to his passion, deciding heavier conversations can wait. After all, who am I to deny the man dessert?

"Well," I manage, my voice breathier than I'd like, "I have been craving something sweet."

Mark's answering grin is downright sinful. "Oh, Bubbles, I'll give you sweet."

His mouth crashes into mine, urgent and demanding. We stumble backwards until my legs hit the bed. Mark spins me around, pulling me flush against his chest, and I can feel exactly how much he wants this.

Mark grips the fabric of my thong, rolling the thin material slowly down my legs.

I catch his wicked grin as he stands, dropping his pants. *Well, hello there, Mr. Dessert. Looks like I'm in for quite the treat!*

He taps the edge of the bed, commanding, "On your knees, up here, please."

And where I like control, I utterly love it when Mark commands the bedroom. So I do as I'm told, trusting that however he's positioning me, he's doing it with both of us in mind.

His hands roughly grab my hips as his thumbs caress my dress upward.

One hand releases me, and the sound of the condom wrapper tearing makes me drip with anticipation.

His teeth sink sweetly against my flesh as his fingers trail up the inside of my thigh.

"Spread your legs further, baby," he begs.

As I shift, his hand climbs higher and higher until the firm grasp of my hip being wrenched back toward him has me stilling.

"Good. Just like that."

Mark's hand grazes over my saturated clit teasingly before I feel something bigger in its place. He guides my waist backward, filling me.

"This okay?" he asks, soothing his thumbs over my lower back at my gasp.

I hum in agreement, my mind hazy with pleasure and words failing me.

"Tell me if it's too much, baby," he urges, his movements becoming gentler.

"No. Don't stop," I breathe, bucking my hips against him.

He groans in response, starting to move back and forth, hands holding me in place as he gradually increases speed and pressure. "Fuck, Arden. You're so tight like this. I won't last long."

"Harder," I plead.

His excited whimper has me grinning, gripping the comforter to hold myself steady as each thrust hits deeper. I'm cursing his name, begging for it harder, until the pleasure and pain mix ferociously into something raw and incredible.

I cry out, convulsing as Mark holds me upright against the waves of pleasure consuming me. He thrusts harder, continuing through my orgasm until my name is tumbling from his lips, his body tensing inside and behind me when he finds his release.

He moves slowly afterward, until we both calm, letting the surges of ecstasy carry us.

As our breathing gradually steadies, I feel Mark's gentle touch trailing down my spine. He places a soft kiss against my tailbone before carefully easing out of me. My body, stretched and thoroughly satisfied, sinks into the mattress.

Mark collapses beside me, his chest still rising and falling rapidly. He peppers my skin with tender kisses, slipping his hands to the inside of my thighs and massaging gently.

I can't help but let out a contented sigh.

"Happy to give you a full rub down if you'd like, my insatiable goddess," he murmurs, a playful note in his voice.

I turn my head to meet his gaze, finding his dark eyes soft and open.

"I won't complain," I respond softly.

As I lay there, basking in the afterglow and Mark's gentle ministrations, a realization washes over me. This man, with his tender touches and caring gestures, has completely upended my carefully ordered world. For someone who claimed he couldn't handle relationships, he's doing a remarkably good job of making me crave more time with him than either of us had initially bargained for.

Who knew a self-proclaimed playboy could be so...boyfriend-y?

But I shove down the overwhelming emotions, forcing playful levity instead. "Is the massage sure to be followed by more sexual favors?"

Mark grins easily, his strong hands already working distracting patterns into my flesh. "I mean, only if you insist on indulging my primal addictions."

I smile, catching the irony in his statement. "Well, we can't have anyone thinking you've gone soft, Romeo."

Mark presses a smacking kiss to my forehead, laughing to himself. "Way too late for that, Bubbles. Seems you're stuck with me hopelessly smitten already. Prepare for a lifetime of swooning and cheesy one-liners!"

Did he just say lifetime?

Mark tugs me to my feet before I fully process his unprecedented confession. "Whoa there, still a bit wobbly, hmm?" He steadies me with a grin. "Clearly means it's time to feed you, babe."

When my legs refuse to move, Mark smiles, tapping my nose playfully. "Hey, don't act surprised. I think I've made it pretty clear, I enjoy *all* our time together...even when we're not naked and tangled up in sheets."

It's official...He's ruined me for all *future relationships.* No other guy has brought me to my knees with just a look and a smile. And I have a feeling no one else could completely wreck and rebuild me the way this man has. Because, despite fighting tooth and nail, I've fallen hopelessly and irrationally in love with this charming flirt.

I shove down the swirling emotions, aiming for casual teasing instead. "Okay, Mr. Smooth Talker, let's see if you can keep up the charm offensive at dinner."

Mark's eyes sparkle with amusement. "What's in it for me if I manage to be a perfect gentleman?"

I pretend to consider, tapping my finger against my lips. "More dessert? Or maybe I finally show you my secret talent?"

His eyebrows shoot up, intrigued. "Oh, there's a secret talent? More than what I've already seen? Let me guess... You can juggle? No, I've got it. You're secretly a world-class yodeler. You definitely have the lungs for that."

I laugh, shaking my head. "You'll have to wait and see. That is, if you can behave yourself."

"Challenge accepted," Mark grins, pulling me closer. "Though I have to warn you, being on my best behavior around you is no easy feat."

I pat his cheek playfully. "I believe in you. Just remember, hands to yourself, not on me!"

Though my exterior appears calm, in my chest, butterflies take eager flight, thinking through all the snippets of confessions that have escaped Mark's tempting lips during this trip. *Coming home to me. Enjoying all our time together.* Maybe this was a terrible idea, but right now, wrapped securely in his anchoring warmth, I'm happy simply existing in this moment, curious about what other confessions he'll reveal before our time runs out.

Mark leans back in his chair with a contented smile as we finish our meal. "That was amazing. I don't think I could eat another bite."

I laugh, sipping the last of my wine. "Me neither. I'm so full I might need to be rolled out of here."

Mark's eyes sparkle with mischief as he reaches for my hand across the table. "Well, I know the perfect way to work off all those calories. There's a great jazz club just down the street. What do you say we head over there for a few?"

I raise an eyebrow, intrigued. "Jazz, huh? I didn't peg you for a smooth jazz kind of guy."

He grins, standing and pulling me to my feet. "I'll have you know I'm very cultured. I'm full of surprises, remember?"

"Alright, hotshot," I concede, letting him pull me to my feet. "Lead the way."

The Atlanta air is warm against my skin as we step outside, the faint sound of music drifting from nearby bars. Mark's hand finds mine, our fingers intertwining as we walk.

"This is nice," I murmur, leaning into him slightly. "Just us, no distractions."

Mark presses a kiss to my temple. "See? I told you it'd be the best idea ever."

I roll my eyes, but can't suppress my smile. "Don't let it go to your head."

The jazz club is dimly lit and intimate, the soft strains of a saxophone filling the air. As we settle into a corner booth, Mark's arm draped casually over my shoulders, I'm struck by how right this feels.

"Ready for more adventure?" Mark asks, his voice low and teasing.

I look up at him, warmth blooming in my chest. "I never want this to end," I admit, the words slipping out before I can stop them.

Mark's eyes soften, and I see understanding flicker across his face. For a moment, I let myself believe that maybe, just maybe, this perfection could last. But the rational part of my brain kicks in, reminding me that we're still in the honeymoon phase. That next week is looming, ready to burst this beautiful bubble we've created.

Still, as Mark pulls me closer and the music washes over us, I decide to push those thoughts aside. For now, I'll let myself enjoy this moment, this weekend of bliss we've created.

The mellow tunes and steady stream of drinks create a comfortable atmosphere for Mark to open up about his career. There's an unmistakable passion in his voice as he outlines a new rehab strategy he's crafting. Curious, I dig deeper, and he shares how a personal setback—an injury in his final year of college— sparked his mission to help other athletes bounce back stronger.

I make a thoughtful sound. "You must be pretty knowledgeable about sports medicine, physical therapy, and all that, then."

Mark shrugs, almost bashful. "I've always been passionate about sports. And I feel useful, validated, I guess."

I start to respond, pausing when two enthusiastic strangers appear at our table.

"Well, well, if it isn't the famous Mark Bell," the stockier man announces. He grins at me conspiratorially. "See you still have natural talents with the ladies, too."

I bristle, but Mark just laughs, unfazed by the bold ribbing. "Arden, meet Reggie and Clark. We met last year at a conference and chatted about former glory days of playing baseball in college." He nudges me playfully. "They like to give me crap." Sobering slightly, he adds more genuinely, "But they're really the best in the business."

I relax as pleasantries are exchanged.

Reggie leans eagerly across the table. "So, Bell, are you going to share your secrets for taming all those unruly pros yet? I swear you've got some magic touch the way you get even the surliest athletes smiling through rehab."

Mark chuckles, though I sense a hint of bashfulness at the blunt praise. "Please. I just use basic empathy and psychology. Anyone could do it."

"Oh c'mon," Clark interjects wryly. "Just last month, you single-handedly prevented a shutdown ace from getting Tommy John surgery. That's not nothing."

As they continue debating sports medicine, I find myself captivated by this driven, intellectually curious side of Mark I'm uncovering. The man who creatively solves problems and forges trusting bonds with temperamental players. Gone is the cocky playboy front—instead, I see someone ambitious using his talents to make a real difference.

And I'm struck by how much I love this version of him, too. It's like discovering a hidden superpower—the ability to make my heart race with just a flash of his brilliant mind.

After his friends say goodbye, fondness swells as I trace a finger down Mark's jaw. "Well, you certainly impressed them, Mr. Rising Star. Though, I should admit how turned on I was seeing you exercise that brain of yours."

Mark raises an eyebrow, a mischievous grin playing on his lips. "Oh, you like it when I talk nerdy to you, huh? Well, let me tell you about the fascinating world of muscle recovery and rehabilitation techniques..."

I laugh, swatting his chest playfully. "Stop it, you tease! You know I can't resist your intellectual charm. Keep talking like that, and we might not make it out of this bar."

He leans in, his voice lowering to a husky whisper. "You know I don't back down from a challenge, Bubbles."

I feel my cheeks heating up, but I refuse to concede defeat. "Depends on how impressive your nerdy talk is, hotshot. Why don't you tell me more about this passion of yours? What's your ultimate goal in the world of sports medicine?"

Mark's expression shifts, a gleam of sincerity in his eyes. "Honestly? I'd like to open my own elite sports medicine clinic one day. A place where athletes can receive the best care possible, with state-of-the-art facilities and a team of top-notch therapists."

"Look at you, Mr. Ambition," I tease, but I can't hide the admiration in my voice. "So, what's the five-year plan to make this dream a reality?"

"Five year, plan, huh?" He leans back, his enthusiasm growing. "Well, first, I need to gain more experience and build my reputation in the field. I'm thinking about pursuing some advanced certifications and maybe even a master's degree. Then, I'll start scouting locations and gathering a team of brilliant minds to join me in this venture."

As he continues outlining his plan, detailing the mentorship program he wants to create and the cutting-edge techniques he hopes to implement, I find myself both captivated and conflicted. His passion is undeniably attractive, but it also reminds me that our paths may diverge sooner than I'd like. Because I know driven Mark likely won't abandon his ascending career simply to follow me anywhere. It's like realizing we're two shooting stars destined to burn brightly together before our paths diverge.

I push down the bittersweet feeling, focusing on the present. "I'm impressed."

"What can I say, all your future planning has inspired me." Mark reaches for my hand, expression sobering. "I know we agreed not to make any promises, Arden. And I'm not asking for forever. But I need you to know that whatever happens, you've changed me. You've given me the courage to dream bigger and the strength to chase those dreams."

I nod, blinking back the tears that threaten to fall. "You've changed me, too, Mark. In ways I never expected."

We sit there for a long moment, our hands clasped tightly, the weight of our words hanging in the air between us. Outside, the world keeps moving, oblivious to the quiet revolution taking place in our hearts.

Mark's wandering lips graze my shoulder, pausing as emotion thickens the air between us. His dark eyes search mine, displaying equal parts adoration and anguish, like he's reading my mind.

"Where did I lose you to just now, baby?"

I shake my head almost shyly at his tender tone, grappling to conceal the painful epiphany striking without warning—no passion will ever eclipse what we've discovered together. Yet, the careers and dreams pulling us in opposite directions seem like equally unmovable forces.

"Just wishing I'd appreciated this beautiful brain of yours sooner," I hedge instead, offering a wavery smile.

Mark searches my expression, thumb tracing my cheek. Then he tilts my chin up indulgently, without pushing further.

As his mouth finds mine in a devastatingly tender kiss, I cling tighter, soaking up his warmth and electrifying nearness. And as his muscular arms enfold me now, I accept that however deeply he's come to mean, fate always intended an expiration date for us. Even if surrendering feels like tearing out shards of my own heart.

22

Mark

Now, May 9ᵗʰ

I stare as Arden finishes her wine, another memory to photograph in my mind before she withdraws further. Because, like clockwork, three days post-Atlanta, inevitable distance unfolds. Brick by brick, I've watched her gradually retreat, rebuilding the walls that so fiercely guarded her heart before she let me in. And having glimpsed the other side, I'm not sure I can go back.

I clench my fist painfully, wishing I could freeze time.

Not like I actually stood a chance at convincing her to stay anyway, being caged to a man who's afraid he'll wake up one day and regret her. She's destined for more. A future she's worked so hard to craft. No. I have to let her go, never telling her that, despite our best intentions, I've fallen completely in love with her.

"You okay over there, Mr. Deep-in-Thought?" she teases lightly.

The lump in my throat aches to escape. *Just tell her you love her.* But I can't. I promised. So, I lock those words away, forcing an easy grin. "Learned it from the best, babe." I stand, reaching out my hand. "But thinking it might be fun to head over to Sadie's, if you're good for a few more hours of hanging out. The Rhoades are playing there again."

"Definitely game." A genuine smile flashes across her expression as she folds into my arms, adding, "Still itching for a do-over from the last time we saw them play?"

I laugh, forcing my still-wandering mind to remain present. Especially at the memory of *that* night. "Can't say I didn't enjoy the charged flirting. Just wish you'd have ditched whatever-his-name-was and spent the night with me instead."

Her lips quirk in playful torment as the spring air greets us. "Like you can talk, Mr. Supermodel-for-a-date?"

I frown at her teasing insinuation. "I think she was gone the moment I tried to kiss you on the dance floor."

She hums gently, melting into my side as we walk the few blocks to the bar. But our stroll is interrupted midway by a violent buzzing from her purse.

Arden quickly reaches for it, her lips falling into a puzzled frown as she clicks the flashing screen. "Hey, Mom." She blinks rapidly, replying in a strained tone, "Oh wow, that's great! …Yeah, no, I'm excited, too."

She chews her lip distractedly, avoiding my searching look. "Of course, but are you sure that's enough time? …Yeah, no, I understand… Uh-huh, can't wait." More muffled chatter filters through before she exhales shakily. "Yup, talk more tomorrow. Bye."

The call ends, leaving an uneasy silence as she picks up her pace and shuffles forward. I grasp her hand, tugging her back close.

"Hey, what's going on? Everything okay?"

Arden forces a wafer-thin smile. "What? Oh, yep, all good…just a change in plans for the next few days." Her gaze scurries away from mine, mind turning a mile a minute.

I tilt her chin up gently, heartbeat quickening with uneasy premonition. "Change of plans, how?"

Rubbing her hand over mine, she lets out a deep breath. "My parents got back from Europe early, so now, they can make my graduation ceremony tomorrow."

Not understanding the issue, I stare at her. "That's great, Arden. Graduating is an amazing accomplishment, and they should be here to support you." My mind adding, *even my parents showed up for graduation, playing the proud parent role and all.*

"It is…" she answers, pausing as if to think through how to say the rest. "It's just…Now they're flying in tomorrow morning. They scheduled dinner with some local family members tomorrow to celebrate while they're in town, and they rearranged my flight back to be with theirs on Friday night instead of Saturday morning."

Pretending like I didn't just get hit by a bus at the unexpected loss of one final night together, I plaster on a neutral expression. I know I'm failing when my shoulder dips as I speak. "Okay…I, uh, guess that makes sense."

Makes sense? It makes no sense. It's upending every plan she's already made for the next two days. And Arden doesn't make plans lightly, proven by her meticulous calendar and inability to be late. Ever.

Arden bites her lip, hesitantly opening and closing her mouth before words finally emerge. "About tomorrow…Maybe you'd want to join us for dinner?" She rushes on, making me concerned for whatever my expression told her. Did it sink as low as my stomach? "You know what, never mind. Pretend I didn't ask. We can meet up after the farewell party like we planned."

I drag a hand through my hair, fears of the last week rearing their ugly heads. How do I meet her parents and then say goodbye twenty-four hours later? Obviously, she hasn't thought this through, or she wouldn't be asking. Meeting Mom and Dad Cooper signals commitment and the potential for a future. Not to mention somebody else to remind me I'm not marriage material.

"Babe, I'm touched and want as much time with you as you'll give me. But I have that home game I'll be at for work, and even if I could get back in time, won't having some mystery plus-one raise eyebrows?" I dodge her stare as my heart clenches painfully in my chest. *Mystery plus-one?* Not wanting to sound like a complete asshole, I add, "You've just mentioned how critical they can be. I don't want to be something else they'll question your choices about."

Her face falls almost imperceptibly before she covers her disappointment with a delicate shrug. "You're probably right…less potential drama with keeping it simple."

I'm not sure she realizes how well I can read her once-disguised poker faces. The one right now is telling me she's completely heartbroken despite her parents actually making an effort. No matter how much she's attempting to distance herself from me, she still wants as many of the moments left together as I do, and I just shut her down for what? To protect her? Or me?

I stare wordlessly, grappling against the urge to blurt impossible promises that I'll upend everything in my life for her. But it's a promise I can't be sure about…because I have no idea if, a year from now, I'll wake up and break her heart further. So, instead, I fake another grin, shutting down the confession.

"Let's just enjoy tonight, okay? Not let this ruin it," I chance lightly.

She nods, and I softly kiss her lips, a silent reminder that I'm still here, that the fragile bubble we've built these last six weeks is still intact for two more days.

The pulse of music washes over us as I steer Arden into the familiar neon glow of Sadie's Bar. Jake briefly meets my eyes from the stage, his enthusiastic grin faltering as he notices the tension visible in our expressions.

I offer a subtle head shake toward him—*we're working on it*—before focusing only on the alluring woman still pressed close to my chest.

As Jake kicks off the words to a sultry R&B song, I lean even closer, letting my nose graze Arden's silky hair. "I know you think my dancing is questionable, but humor me?"

Arden smiles softly. "Absolutely."

I lead her toward the dance floor, tugging her irresistible curves flush to me. Arden releases a surprised gasp at the force, hands fluttering to grip my shoulders before we mold seamlessly together.

I tune out everything but how Arden feels pressed up against me. We might as well be alone in here. The way she's touching me, moving with me... I still can't wrap my head around the fact that this incredible girl is with me, even if it's only for a few more days.

A couple songs later, we're both grinning and sweaty. I catch Arden's eye and nod towards the bar. She gets it immediately, flashing me that smile that makes my stomach do backflips.

We weave through the crowd, my hand on the small of her back. Just before we reach the bar, I can't help myself. I spin her around and pull her in for a kiss that's definitely crossing into not-safe-for-public territory.

I'm so caught up in Arden that I almost miss the voice cutting through the noise. Almost.

"Mark freaking Bell, is that you?!"

Shit. I know that voice.

I break away from Arden, my head snapping up to see Lanie, my ex from high school—and the girl I turned down not too long ago—suddenly right there next to us.

"I had no idea this is where the Rhoades played," Lanie coos, leaning in way too close. "I would've come out ages ago if I'd known."

Before I can back away, she plants a kiss dangerously near my lips.

You're fucking kidding me. Tonight? Now?

"Uh...hey Lanie." I shift awkwardly, catching Arden's wide-eyed look. I pry Lanie's hands off my belt loops, trying to keep my cool. "Didn't expect to see you out this way."

Or ever again after the scene at my parents' house.

"Just out with some friends." Lanie's eyes slide to Arden, all faux innocence. "And who's this?"

I bristle at the condescension in her tone, my arm tightening around Arden's waist. "This is Arden, my girlfriend."

For the next two days, anyway. But I'll be damned if Arden thinks anyone else can hold my attention, no matter the countdown.

Lanie's eyebrows shoot up, her look speaking volumes. "Well, isn't that... interesting."

Shit. She's gonna ruin this.

She turns to Arden with a plastic smile. "It's so nice to meet you, Arden. You know, Mark and I go way back. I'd be happy to share some stories... give you the inside scoop, so to speak."

Is she for real right now?

Before I can intervene, Lanie continues, her tone sickeningly sweet. "Just don't get too comfortable. Mark's always been more of a 'fun and games' kind of guy. Not exactly the settling down type, if you know what I mean."

Arden's grip tightens, and I can practically hear the gears turning in her head, all those doubts creeping back in. I want to tell her Lanie means nothing, that I'd follow her to Tampa if she asked. But there's this nagging voice wondering if Lanie's right. If I'm cut out for the real deal. If Arden and I only work because there's no pressure.

I shake my head, trying to clear the thoughts. "Lanie—"

"Oh, I know exactly what you mean," Arden says, cutting me off. Her voice is calm but has an edge of steel. She turns to me, her fingers trailing down my chest in a move that's both possessive and challenging. "It's funny, actually. I originally asked for something casual, no strings attached. But Mark? He wanted more. Said he was ready for something real."

Her eyes meet mine, and I see a mix of emotions there–love, trust, but also a hint of sadness that makes my heart clench. Because no matter how much I've come to mean, she can't stay. Even though I've known it all along, seeing it there, plainly written in her expression, hurts more than I'm prepared for.

I push away the thought. It's a conversation for another time.

Instead, I wrap my arms around Arden, meeting Lanie's smug look over Arden's shoulder in a silent dare: *Try to ruin this...it's impenetrable by outside forces. The only thing capable of destroying what we've built is time.*

"So, Lanie," I say, my tone light but firm, "was there something specific you wanted to tell my girlfriend?"

Lanie's smile falters, a flash of uncertainty crossing her face. But she recovers quickly, shrugging carelessly. "Whatever. Enjoy playing house with the flavor of the month. I'll see you around. Just like always."

With that parting shot, she turns on her heel and saunters away.

I hold Arden closer, breathing in her familiar scent. How has it only been three months that we've known each other? Because breathing without her now feels somehow impossible.

"I'm sorry about that," I whisper apologetically. "Please don't let that mess up our night."

Arden spins, hurt flashing in her expression, even as she covers it with a breezy smile. "Thought you didn't do 'again'? No more than four weeks...or something like that?"

I laugh without humor. "Always no strings attached until you, apparently." I guide Arden toward the exit, needing a quieter place to talk, really talk for once.

When we're finally outside in the moonlight, I brush a stray piece of hair behind her ears, meeting her coffee-colored gaze. "You know no one else has ever held the same place in my heart as you do, right?"

Arden's eyes shine as they look up to mine. "That's what makes this all so complicated, Mark. I never meant to fall…" She stops, biting her lip. "We made those rules for a reason. To make this less messy."

I cup her face in my hands. "I love the messiness of it, Arden."

Her expression softens, that deep, unspoken feeling passing between us before she closes her eyes and exhales. "But we can't. I can't."

"Why?" The word tumbles out of my mouth, even though I know the answer.

Her plan. Her life. My job. My goals. They don't line up.

"I told you I wasn't that girl," she whispers, imploring me to understand. "I'm not impulsive and irrational. And as much as I've loved every part of the last six weeks, I can't give up on the goals I've worked so hard for."

I pull her against me, forcing down the lump in my throat and press a kiss to her head. "I know, baby. I don't expect that. I just…I don't want to lose you."

"I don't want to lose you either, Mark," she murmurs against my shoulder. "But we both knew this was coming. I can't ask you to give up your career, your life here, just like you can't ask me to give up mine."

I swallow hard, knowing she's right but hating it all the same. "So, what do we do?"

Arden takes a deep breath, pulling back to meet my gaze. "There's something else I never told you. It's not just that I want this job in Tampa. It's that it checks every box for me. It's experience, a rotational program that places you into the right role after six months, but it also allows me to fulfill an obligation to my parents."

I blink, surprised. "What obligation?"

"After graduation, I...I committed to staying with them. For six months, at least. It was the only way they'd agree to let me turn down law school. The only way to get them off my back." She looks away briefly, and I can see the tears building in her eyes. "They threatened to make me pay back all my loans if I didn't. But that wasn't the only reason I agreed. It's proving that I'm serious about what I want. And I guess, more than anything, I want to show them that it makes me happy. That maybe, they'll approve of my choice. If that even makes sense."

I close my eyes, letting her words sink in, understanding her hesitation. The way she's been pulling away, rebuilding her walls. She's not just choosing her career over me. She's honoring an impossible compromise. One that leaves no room for a brand-new relationship.

"Okay," I whisper, my throat tight. "I get it, Arden. I do."

"I've thought about it so many ways, Mark," she says softly, pressing her forehead to mine. "Asking you to try. To make it work. But the distance will only destroy this, destroy us slowly, no matter what promises we make now. I can't...I don't want us to end like that."

Lanie's words from earlier resurface, leaving me questioning if I'm cut out for real commitment.

But then I think about everything we've been through together. The way Arden sees past my bullshit, the way she challenges me to be better. The way she makes me feel alive and hopeful and terrified in the best possible ways. And I want to tell her that we can figure it out. That I'll wait for her, that I'll come to her, that we'll find a way. But I know that's not what she needs from me right now.

She needs my support, my understanding. Even if it breaks my fucking heart.

So, instead, I hold her tighter, memorizing every detail.

"Just promise me one thing," I murmur, my voice cracking. "Promise me this isn't the end."

Arden glances up. Her eyes are fierce and bright, stealing my breath. "I promise, Mark. But I don't want to hold you back from living your life. That's always what these rules were for. What I wanted for you."

I nod, blinking back the burning in my eyes as words stick in my throat. *Being with you is all I want. You're the best thing that's ever happened to me.* But that admission will only make this harder for her.

As we stand together in the cool night air, both of us sensing the time slipping like sand in an hourglass, a lone star shoots across the sky, and I make a silent vow. No matter what the future holds or how far apart our paths may take us, I will never stop striving to be the man she sees in me. The man she has inspired me to become. And maybe, if I can prove I'm worthy of her love, fate will be kind enough to bring us back together someday.

Because come Friday, I know I'll have to let her go.

23

Arden ♥

Now, May 10th

I raise the champagne flute to my lips, the bubbles dancing on my tongue, but the usual celebratory sweetness is tainted by a bittersweet aftertaste. Graduation, the day I've been working towards for the past four years, is finally here. Yet, instead of joy and excitement, a sense of melancholy clings to me like a stubborn shadow.

It's not hard to pinpoint the reason for my conflicted emotions. Last night's conversation with Mark, the painful acknowledgment that our time together is coming to an end, weighs heavily on my mind. The memory of his face, the way his eyes dimmed with a sad understanding as I explained why I had to leave, is seared into my brain.

I know I made the right choice, the logical choice. I've worked too hard, sacrificed too much, to throw it all away now, even for something as incredible as what Mark and I share. But that doesn't make it any easier to say goodbye, to walk away from the man who's captured my heart so completely, especially after how the rest of the night went. Because, for the first time, we made love knowing it could be the last time.

And damn if it wasn't spectacular and heartbreaking, the way he kissed me, the words he whispered in the dark, the emotions his body displayed without a single word leaving his mouth. I knew it, then. Knew without a doubt that he'd fallen in love with me, too.

It's partly why today stings so bad, why I haven't been able to answer his texts since I left his apartment this morning to finish packing. My future is waiting for me in Florida, in the job I've worked hard to secure and the goals I've set for myself. And as much as it hurts, I know I can't ask Mark to put his life on hold for me, just like he can't ask me to give up on my dreams.

The arrival of my parents pulls me from my thoughts, and I force a smile, hoping they can't see the cracks in my carefully crafted facade. They beam with pride, their congratulations and well-wishes washing over me, but all I can think about is how much I wish Mark were here beside me. With his hand in mine, he'd be a steadying force amid all this change.

I pass the champagne flute between my hands, nodding along absently as my parents recap their European trip for the tenth time. The buzzing phone in my clutch goes ignored yet again. No doubt another message from Mark checking on my post-ceremony plans.

I spot Cora waving enthusiastically from across the room, standing next to my former roommate. Excusing myself, I weave through the crowd to join them.

As soon as I'm within earshot, Cora leans in, concern etched on her face. "Everything okay? You look a million miles away."

I glance around, then gently tug her arm. "Can we talk somewhere a bit more private?"

Once we're away from prying eyes, I let out a heavy sigh. "I'm torn about seeing Mark again before I leave tomorrow. I think it just sets me up for more heartache."

Cora's eyes soften with understanding. Then, a mischievous grin spreads across her face. "You know what this calls for? Stronger drinks and less overthinking."

I can't help but laugh, raising my glass in agreement. "Cheers to that. Let's give this chapter a proper send-off." *And maybe numb these conflicting feelings about a certain charming athletic trainer in the process.*

Another hour passes in a blur of polite smiles and small talk with well-meaning relatives and friends. Finally, I manage to extract myself, citing the need to finish packing before the movers arrive in the morning. Cora and I make our escape, heading toward my nearly empty apartment.

On the way, we stop at a liquor store. While Cora browses the shelves, I finally gather the courage to check my messages from Mark.

> Mark: *Hey. Miss you. Congrats on your graduation! Hope dinner was great.*
> Mark: *Surviving the family small talk?*
> Mark: *I know today's probably crazy for you, but let me know if you still want to meet up. Just leaving the ballpark.*
> Mark: *Where can I meet you?*
> Mark: *Getting a little worried here. Everything okay?*

I stare at the screen, my thumb hovering uncertainly over the keyboard. The urge to see him one last time wars with the fear of making this goodbye even harder.

Still, just thinking about his voice, his touch, has a shiver running down my spine. What if he suggests long distance? Or worse, what if I'm tempted to throw away everything I've worked for? If one kiss from Mark is enough to make me re-think my carefully constructed plans, what would happen if he asked me to stay? Would I have the strength to say no?

I sigh harshly, pushing a hand through my hair, trying to rationalize all the reasons I shouldn't see him tonight. But the thought has tears burning unexpectedly. Somehow, despite our expiration date, Mark feels intrinsic, like a piece of my soul I'm not ready to relinquish just yet.

I slide the phone back into my clutch, forcing myself to be realistic. We're so young. It's only been a few weeks. We haven't faced any real challenges yet. These intense feelings could vanish at any moment—with his next admirer, a work trip temptation, or when he realizes relationships require more effort than he's willing to give.

No. This was amazing, but it was always meant to end. We both need it to. Maybe someday, when our dreams align instead of conflict, fate will surprise us. But for now, as Mark said that first night at the bar, we have terrible fucking timing.

I push open my apartment door, faltering at the sight of stacked boxes and bare walls. The once cozy living room feels cold and sterile, a stark reminder of the life I'm leaving behind. A memory of the first night Mark spent here, curled up on the couch, opening up to me, flashes through my mind, leaving a bittersweet ache in my chest.

Sensing my spiraling thoughts, Cora chirps brightly, "Want me to pour us some drinks? Then you can spill what's really on your mind."

I give her a weak smile. "Oh, sis, we donated all the kitchenware. We're drinking out of the bottle tonight."

Cora grins mischievously. "Well, in that case, let's get this party started!"

We settle on a blanket spread across the empty floor, passing the bottle back and forth. As the night progresses and the alcohol flows, our laughter fills the room. We share stories about the challenges of adulthood, giggling like carefree schoolgirls, and for a brief moment, it's like everything else doesn't exist.

Just as we're about to open the second bottle, a sharp knock shatters our bubble. My heart leaps into my throat because there's only one person who would show up unannounced at this hour.

Mark's deep eyes meet mine as I open the door. Whatever he planned to say evaporates as he wordlessly pulls me into a fierce embrace. I melt against his solid chest, inhaling the intoxicating scent that is purely him—a tantalizing blend of citrus, sandalwood, and happiness.

"You came," I whisper, surprised by the tears already forming. "How'd you know where to find me?"

Mark's arms tighten around me. "I tried a few other places first. I had to see you, Arden. Don't push me away yet. I'm not ready to let go of the woman who stole my heart."

I pull back, searching his face. "I'm sorry... I should've responded. It's just..."

It's just that I love you too much to make you wait for me.

Sensing my unease, he guides us further inside, freezing when he notices Cora for the first time. "Oh, I...I didn't know your sister was here. I shouldn't have...I can go."

"No. You should stay," Cora interjects quickly. "I can go back to the hotel."

Be alone with Mark? I don't think my heart can handle that right now.

"No, Cora. It's fine. We can all hang out." I attempt a light tone, but my trembling hands betray me as I reach for the wine. "Mark can help us finish the next bottle off."

He reaches out, stilling my restless hands with his steady warmth. "Something tells me you don't need me for that, Bubbles."

"No?"

He smirks, seeing straight through my wafer-thin composure, as he pulls me to his chest. "I know every tell behind this polite mask, baby. The way your fingers twist together when emotions run too hot. The way your lips press thin so you don't let your emotional reaction slip before you have time to think it through."

His thumb traces my cheek with infinite patience. "But tonight, you're wanting to forget…so there's not a bottle of wine you won't drink if you think it'll give you momentary amnesia."

I still, pulse hammering wildly, because this man reads even my deepest layered armor as though it were glass. Choked by emotion, I manage lightly, "Well then, do you want to forget with me and Cora?"

He slides the bottle from my fingers, the other hand gripping my hip to keep me close. "No, Arden. I don't plan on forgetting anything, especially not a single moment spent with you."

Mark's tender gaze holds mine as my fractured pieces realign in his sheltering arms.

Eventually, I find my voice again. "Thank you for coming tonight," I say thickly. Unable to resist, I trace the lines of his handsome face, awe swelling dangerously. "Somehow, you always know precisely what I need, even when I'm too stubborn to admit it."

Mark presses his forehead to mine, his scent washing comfortingly over me. "And I'll be here giving it whenever you let me back in," he vows gently.

Our charged bubble lingers until subtle movement stirs. Cora offers a tentative smile from the living room as Mark clears his throat.

Sensing my fragile poise, he keeps his tone playful. "So, uh, I don't suppose proper glasses are anywhere in this packing chaos?"

When Cora shakes her head, mischief glints through his lasting emotion. "Okay, then, looks like we're playing pass the bottle."

I raise an eyebrow, a smirk tugging at my lips. "Oh, really? And here I thought you were more of a 'sip from the finest crystal' kind of guy."

Mark chuckles, his eyes sparkling with amusement. "What can I say? You bring out my wild side, Bubbles."

I grin as a silent promise passes between Mark and me. "Well, if we're going to be wild, maybe we should have a pillow fight after?"

Fall with me, Mark. One final time.

Not missing a beat, Mark twists the top of the wine off, winking subtly. "Only if we can play seven minutes in heaven next. I call dibs on getting stuck in the closet with you, Juliet."

I smile, my heart melting into a puddle. "In your dreams, Romeo."

Cora perks up tipsily, her eyes darting between us with a knowing smile. "Ooh, how about truth or dare?"

I groan, shooting Mark a pointed look. "See what you've started?"

He grins unapologetically, slinging an arm around my shoulders. "Hey, I'm just here to make sure you have the best last night possible. And if that means enduring drunken dares, I'm in."

His heated look hints at intimate revelations he's willing to voice if I dare ask. And as his lips graze my cheek, warmth pools deliciously. Because, somehow, I know that before this night ends, more of me will belong irrevocably to this man.

"Game on, then," I arch a brow. "You can even ask first, Hotcakes."

Whatever comes next can't erase this. So, with one night left, I bravely turn the page toward lighter moments, trusting he'll catch me if I stumble.

As we settle into the living room, Mark holds up the bottle ceremoniously. His knee presses subtly closer to mine, but to my surprise, he selects Cora.

"Truth or dare?"

The mischief glinting in Cora's expression is clear. She plans to take us both down, whatever it takes.

"Dare," Cora announces proudly.

Tapping a finger to his chin and taking another swig of the shared wine bottle, he grins before daring her to run down the halls of the complex, singing her favorite song.

Way to go easy on her.

Mark and I laugh as we watch her run from one end of the hall to the other, singing her ballad and probably waking our sleeping neighbors.

When Cora returns, a sly smile spreads as her gaze settles on me. "All right, sis. Truth or dare?"

I hesitate, the wine already clouding my judgment. But I've never been one to back down from a challenge, especially in front of Mark. I straighten my shoulders, selecting "dare," not ready for the truth question I know would come my way from my cunning little sister.

Cora's grin turns devious. "I dare you to recreate our epic dance choreography to Britney Spears's 'Baby One More Time.' The one you spent weeks forcing me to practice when I was ten."

The color drains from my face as Mark erupts into laughter.

"You can't be serious?" I ask, my heart doing a tiny flip, seeing the genuine smile—void of all masks—on Mark's face. When Cora crosses her arms defiantly, I huff out a breath. "Ugh, fine."

I flip on the song, my cheeks flaming red as Mark's dark eyes track me eagerly. Under their expectant stares, muscle memory kicks in, recalling every dramatic hair flip and silly body roll from hours of practice as a teenager.

By the chorus, Mark's laying on the floor holding his stomach, eyes streaming with laughter. "Oh my God, please never stop being this adorable," he manages between gulping breaths.

Mortified by the time the song ends, I collapse onto the floor, unable to hide my burning face as I grasp for any remaining dignity.

Eventually, their laughter slows. I notice Mark, wiping his eyes, sprawled casually with one hand propping up his perfect torso. The top buttons of his shirt hang open alluringly. With liquid courage still thrumming through my veins, impulse has me shifting closer.

"Okay, hotcakes, truth or dare?"

Mark's full lips quirk cockily, clearly expecting an easy victory here. But then he surprises me, hooded eyes turning smoldering. "Truth."

My mouth runs dry, dizzy with tempting possibilities. But terrifying question options stick in my throat—like asking him if he loves me hours before leaving indefinitely.

Sensing my spiraling hesitation, Mark adds throatily, "Anything you want. I'm an open book tonight, baby."

Before fully thinking it through, my tipsy mouth's already asking, "Why didn't you tell me it was your birthday during our first dinner together?"

A slow smile spreads across Mark's face. "Jake told you, huh?"

I shrug. "I might have coaxed it out of him one night when you were traveling. Promise I did it only for the intent of figuring you out."

"And did you? Figure me out?" he asks curiously.

I bite back a grin. "This was your truth, not mine."

"Fair enough. Guess it was my ace in the hole if things went poorly. That you had to stay and humor me." Mark's expression shifts to naked honesty. "But it didn't. It was perfect, and I didn't want to ruin the moment by making you feel obligated to make it more special. It was already what I would've wished for. Minus the goodnight kiss."

Lost in each other's gaze, I barely notice Cora rise with an exaggerated yawn. "You know what? I should probably call it a night. Let you two talk."

I glance up, catching her wink, likely from the sudden shift in conversation.

"I'll see you in the morning, guys."

I mouth a silent "thank you" as she disappears into the bedroom before returning to Mark's searching eyes.

"It was perfect," I whisper.

"Come here, baby." Mark pulls me into his chest, cradling me as he kisses the top of my head. "I know I already told you how much you terrified me that first night in my room. But I might've made a promise afterward to Jake, that if fate somehow brought you back to me, I wouldn't screw it up again."

So that's why he was so kind at the hospital?

Wait. He was talking to Jake about me even back *then*?

Mark turns my palm over, brushing fervent kisses as his dark eyes bore into mine. "Don't leave tomorrow thinking you were ever a game, or some fling, Arden. You know you're more. So much more than I ever expected."

So many emotions stir, but right now, I can only anchor on his name.

"Mark…"

"I know goodbye is gonna suck." He pulls my face closer to him, his forehead resting on mine. "But you tell me what you need from me…what'll make this easiest on you, okay?"

I nod slowly, regret dropping like a lead weight in my gut. As much as I want to hope for something long-term or long-distance with Mark, I already know what it'll look like. And I think deep down, he does, too.

"What time are the movers here tomorrow?" he asks, brushing a soft kiss to my forehead.

"Nine," I manage weakly, clinging to him tightly. As the bittersweet finality of our situation sinks in, I whisper half-heartedly, "We should probably get some sleep, huh?"

Mark nods reluctantly. "Yeah, probably."

But neither of us moves. We stay curled together, our gazes locked and our hands intertwined. In that instant, I'm struck by the overwhelming urge to memorize every detail of him—the flecks of gold in his warm brown eyes, the dimple in his left cheek, the way his lips quirk up at the corners when he's truly happy.

I want to bottle this feeling, to carry it with me wherever I go. Because even though I'm leaving, even though our future is uncertain, I know that loving Mark has changed me in ways I'm only beginning to understand.

The last thing I hear as I let Mark's warmth carry me into a blissful dream world is his ragged plea against my ear. "Stay, baby. Right here, always."

And for tonight, wrapped in the memories we've shared and the love we've found, I'll believe that anything is possible.

24

Mark 🌑

Now, May 11th

I slowly peel open my eyes, blinking at the unfamiliar daylight flooding the bare living room. The empty wine bottles explain the faint headache pulsating as I stretch stiff limbs, trying not to wake the sleeping beauty on my left shoulder. Warmth floods my chest, remembering the laughter and teasing confessions last night, at least until the reality sets in that this is it. The brutal farewell I've been dreading since kissing her again six weeks ago.

Time to get used to the word *friend* when it comes to Arden Cooper.

I trace the collarbone peeking alluringly from Arden's oversized tee, picturing what fun we could have had with this privacy if last night's laughter had led down more scandalous paths, instead of the emotional ones we both knew were inevitable.

I sweep tangled strands off her cheek, pulse already pounding as I lean close to whisper, "Babe, time to get up. Movers will be here soon. Lots of chaos to tackle."

"Chaos, huh?" Arden yawns exaggeratedly, adorable even with mascara smudges and bedhead.

"Something like that." Sensing the quick shift of her expression as she takes in the empty room, I tilt her chin to mine. "Tell me how to help today, Arden. What'll make this easier?"

She glances up at me, eyes caked in rare emotion. "Coffee? Xanax? Turn back time and pretend I'm not Cinderella at the ball, and the clock's not about to strike midnight."

My easy laugh coaxes a genuine smile, one I'd like to imprint in my brain forever. "You'll always be Cinderella. Can't say I'd make a good Prince Charming."

"Don't sell yourself short. You can be my Prine Charming anytime."

"Might take you up on that." We laugh as I pull us both to our feet, sobering when we take in the harsh truth, evident by the boxes stacked against the wall.

I paste on a cheerful facade, determined to keep things light. "Can't turn back time, but I can fetch breakfast." I place a gentle kiss on Arden's forehead. "Maybe when I get back, we can play another sleepover game? Really liked the seven minutes in heaven idea."

I tickle Arden's midsection until she dissolves into giggles, practically pushing me out the door. "Hurry back with caffeine. Please."

When I return twenty minutes later with breakfast, Arden's wrapped in a blanket on the floor, chatting with Cora, and the movers are making swift work of the apartment.

Before desolation hits, I settle beside Arden, determined to maintain a smile.

"So, what stories should I tell to lighten the mood?"

Cora perks up, grinning. "Ooh, tell me something embarrassing about my sister!"

Arden shoots her a glare, simultaneously elbowing me playfully. "Please ignore her, Mark." She glances upward, flashing me a bright grin. "But maybe something cheerful, like your favorite memory from childhood."

"Easy. Baseball." I wrap my arm around Arden as a wistful smile spreads across her face.

"And not just the sport itself," I continue. "I enjoyed playing, but it was also one of the few times my parents were together when I knew they were there for me. Proud of me."

Arden reaches out, tracing the line of my jaw with gentle fingers. "They are proud of you, Mark. I am, too."

I swallow past the lump in my throat, determined not to get too emotional. "What about you guys?"

As Arden and Cora share happy stories of their childhood—Arden's valedictorian award, trips they've taken, even some disastrous dates they've had—laughter fills the room.

But too quickly, footsteps at the door signal the reality waiting.

"Sorry to interrupt..." The mover's apologetic look slices through the cozy intimacy now that their task is complete. "Just finished loading the last item, ma'am. All set here."

Arden nods tightly as his boots retreat down the corridor, feet echoing with appalling finality. This borrowed oasis has reached its conclusion. And however we pretend, there's no shielding our fragile hearts from the next brutal goodbye.

Sensing the shifting mood, Cora offers Arden a bolstering hug. "I'll head to the hotel. See you there in a bit?"

We walk Cora to the door, the resounding thud of it shutting as she departs almost deafening.

Now what?

Opting for tenderness to start this crucial conversation, I lift Arden onto the counter in front of me. "Tell me what's going on in that big brain of yours, beautiful." I smooth both hands down her arms coaxingly as I struggle to meet her forlorn eyes.

Arden burrows into my embrace as though she's imprinting herself there. "I wish I could bottle your stubborn strength for when I'm questioning my decisions alone."

"*My* stubborn strength, babe? You've got enough fiery will to conquer the world single-handedly if you wanted to." I gently stroke her chestnut strands, realizing how perfectly her temple fits tucked beneath my jaw. "Just don't forget me in the process."

"I'm not sure amnesia could make me forget you, Mark."

Her heavy exhale punctuates the silence until she meets my longing stare. Even with shadows beneath her melted chocolate eyes, she effortlessly unravels my battered heart. I seal my lips over hers, pride and devotion swelling dangerously.

I hold her, holding back promises that this affection could outlast distance and time. I told myself I wouldn't do that, wouldn't make this worse. "I'll be your biggest cheerleader anytime you need me, okay?" I vow instead, tracing her delicate knuckles. "Call whenever you want. I'll show up on the next flight...in whatever capacity you want or need me."

Arden rallies a wavery grin. "Not sure what happened to my cocky playboy, but I kinda like this serious side of you."

I huff a brittle laugh, cradling her smooth cheek. "You happened, babe."

Arden curls into me, smiling against my chest as she whispers, "I like that line...feel free to use it whenever you want."

I hold her tightly, wishing she wasn't about to be ripped from my arms.

When our shaky breaths slow in unison, I finally summon the courage to ask, "Ready to go?"

Her cheek presses desperately to my racing heart. "Just a little while longer..."

I smooth her hair, tamping down my own dread. "I could drive you over there. We can sit in the car as long as you'd like, okay?"

She hums, allowing me to guide her outside toward my car.

As we sit in the car in front of her parents' hotel, the weight of our impending goodbye hangs heavy in the air. I can feel Arden's eyes on me, searching my face for some sign of what to do next. But the truth is, I'm just as lost as she is.

How do you say goodbye to the person who's become your whole world? How do you let go of the one thing that makes you feel alive and complete?

I reach for her hand, twining our fingers together and holding on like a lifeline. "Arden, I..." My voice cracks, and I have to swallow past the lump in my throat. "I don't know how to do this."

She squeezes my hand, her own eyes shimmering with unshed tears. "Neither do I," she whispers. "But we have to try, right? We have to be strong for each other."

I nod, wishing this wasn't our reality. "I'm going to miss you so much," I manage, my vision blurring. "I don't know how I'm going to get through each day without seeing your face or hearing your voice."

Arden leans in, resting her forehead against mine. "I'm going to miss you, too, Mark. More than you could ever know." Her breath hitches, and a single tear escapes down her cheek. "But this isn't forever. We'll find a way to make it work. After my training, maybe?"

"I'd love that," I say softly, my eyes closing as I breathe in her scent one final time. "I never thought I'd have a relationship this long. Until you. If you need six months to get settled, I'll figure out how to give you that."

She smiles then, a watery, trembling thing that breaks my heart and puts it back together all at once. "No expectations. No rules. I don't want you to regret waiting."

I don't respond. Can't respond. So, I close the distance between us, capturing her lips in a kiss that says everything I can't put into words. It's a kiss of love and longing, of promise and possibility. A kiss that will have to sustain us through the lonely nights and the endless miles.

And when we finally pull apart, breathless and aching, I have to believe that this is just the beginning of our story, not the end.

25

Arden ♥

Almost Three Months Later, August 3rd

I stare glumly into my wine glass as Jada chitchats brightly about
Paul's "thriving" fishing charter business across the dim
restaurant table. Somehow, she roped me into a surprise double
date under the guise of a girls' night. I don't know what the
bigger shock was, her attempting to set me up with the guy who
overtly hit on my nineteen-year-old sister earlier this summer, or
that she's managed to date Dax for all of three weeks. But despite
this strange situation, Jada's invitation for a night out was a
welcome distraction from career responsibilities and the ex I can't
seem to move past.

As I take a sip, I can't help but think about the past three
months. I've felt Mark's absence every day since leaving Chicago
like a physical ache. I've thrown myself into my new job,
desperate for anything to keep my mind from replaying our final
moments together. But in the quiet moments, when the
distractions fade away, I reach for my phone, hoping to see his
name light up the screen. Hoping that maybe, just maybe, he
misses me as much as I miss him.

The last time we spoke, more than two weeks ago, Mark sounded tired. His voice was strained as he told me about his hectic work schedule. I listened, offering encouragement, but the ease that had once flowed between us had been replaced by a palpable tension, awkward pauses, and forced small talk. It was as if we were both holding back, afraid to say the things that really mattered, afraid to acknowledge the growing chasm between us.

I can't pretend it was all him pulling away, though. The doubts started creeping in a few weeks after I moved down here when a party photo lit up my social media feed. There was Mark, his arm slung around a pretty blonde with a carefree smile. I know it was irrational. I know I told him to let me go. But seeing him so happy, so unaffected by our separation, made something twist painfully in my chest. I started backing off, stopped reaching out because I've been too afraid to face the reality that maybe he was moving on without me.

"So, Arden, Jada tells me your parents have a place nearby on the beach," Paul remarks casually, leaning closer than I'd prefer. "I imagine waking up to the ocean is stunning."

I stir my salad, tamping down irritation at his obvious setup line. *I bet he'd love to see it, too, huh?* But before I form a polite letdown, my phone buzzes angrily on the table, and my lungs constrict as I see the name. *Mark.*

My wine glass pauses midair, disbelief and yearning hitting concurrently. *Is he thinking about me, too?* I click to open the message, my pulse already tripping.

> Mark: *Finally have a free night. Caught the guys playing a set and couldn't help thinking of you...*

Below the casual text is a photo of Mark grinning with Jake and Owen at Sadie's bar, setting off bittersweet nostalgia. And damn him, those unfairly tempting top buttons being undone hint at memories of what's waiting beneath.

I slide the phone discreetly away, avoiding Jada's poorly concealed annoyance at my distraction.

"Ex issues again?" she questions pointedly, lips pursing over her refilled wine glass.

I smooth my expression into polite pleasantness. "Just a friend from Chicago telling me about a concert." But even the platonic label sounds unnatural attached to the man who still effortlessly quickens my pulse.

Jada arches one skeptical brow but redirects breezily, "They any good, at least? You lit up like downtown just now."

"They're amazing." Without thinking twice, I cue up the video of their performance I took on my birthday last February. But replaying moments from that night, my thoughts stray to Mark. The look in his eyes when I first saw him, his grin when I joined him in the VIP section, his lips dangerously close to mine on the dance floor, and the glimpse of the beautiful man behind the Playboy mask.

Damn it.

The clip ends with enthusiastic compliments from the table. However, I'm still in a daydream where a certain dazzling smile is reserved only for me. As the server appears to collect plates, Paul's heavy palm lands uninvited on my forearm.

"Well, if that gloomy gaze means Chicago didn't work out, no need to look backward..." His thumb trails distracting circles and any further appetite vanishes. "I know some excellent ways to help forget old flames. Maybe after dinner, you and I—"

"Oh wow, I just realized how late it got," I interject too brightly, shrugging subtly from Paul's clinging touch. "I should head home."

Ignoring Jada's wordless disappointment, I drop cash on the table hastily. I won't be sticking around to humor Paul's presumptuous pawing or offers for a later rendezvous.

As I head into the sultry night alone, recollections stir unbidden—Mark's searing stare heating my skin, his possessive grip branding my hips as we swayed recklessly on crowded dance floors, his warm exhales teasing delightfully scandalous promises as midnight dwindled.

I bite my lip as dangerous need pierces through. Resist as I might, if Mark dares to illuminate my phone screen later, nostalgia will override any logical protests, and I'll be helpless but to indulge in reckless dreams where Chicago's most magnetic playboy still whispers forbidden temptations meant only for me.

I slip inside the quiet condo, unsurprised to find Cora curled up with a novel among the boxes packed for her sophomore move-in weekend. She glances up sheepishly from a creased paperback, color rising.

"Hey! You're back early." She hastily shoves the book's photo cover, which depicts a shirtless, muscle-bound model, out of sight. "The date was a total bust, I take it?"

I blow out an exhausted breath, collapsing beside her on the bed. "Boring at best, borderline harassment at worst." With a significant look at her stash, I nudge her shoulder playfully. "But it seems I'm not the only one seeking a fictional escape tonight?"

Cora sticks her tongue out, grin returning. "Maybe we both need a little romantic fantasy after recent flops." Her eyes turn thoughtful as she studies me. "Are you still thinking of cutting ties completely with Mr. Baseball Trainer?"

I gnaw my lip raw, the unsent response I typed on the walk home practically glaring at me from the lock screen. Ignoring him tonight leaves my whole being unbearably hollow, our story somehow feeling unfinished.

"I don't know what's left to cling to, really..."

Cora makes a sympathetic sound, glancing speculatively between an explicit cover promising *Bound by Passion* and my conflicted expression.

A slow smile curls on her lips as she slides the paperback onto my lap. "Well, sis, maybe enjoy some steamy wish fulfillment before deciding." She winks exaggeratedly. "Sounds like you need the distraction nearly as much as me."

"Or a few more drinks," I respond, eyeing the wine bottles in the hallway.

Cora's answering grin has me retrieving a bottle opener and two glasses.

A few glasses and an hour of precious sister talk before Cora leaves next week has me pleasantly buzzed. But instead of heading to my room and calling it a night, I find myself heading out the back door, letting the cool breeze and crashing waves sort out my restless thoughts.

My phone screen blinks accusingly until I finally click the familiar contact, the wine eclipsing any remaining hesitance. Because here, alone at midnight, without distraction or judgment, the undeniable truth gnaws at me—I miss my best friend.

I pace restlessly in the sand as the dial tone drags painfully. And when the line connects, I pray whatever words spill out of my mouth might start mending this frayed lifeline I still crave.

"Arden?" Mark's surprised voice cuts through the background noise before I hear a mumbled "Give me one sec," clearly not meant for me. I feel a rock drop in my gut, wondering who is there with him.

When the music fades, Mark's concerned tone pulls me back. "Hey. It's late. Is everything okay?"

I chew on my bottom lip as words tumble freely in my tipsy state. "Yeah, sorry. I just…missed your voice." My vulnerable admission hangs heavily until Mark's voice fills the gap.

"Have you been drinking, babe?" He clears his throat before gently adding, "Not judging if so. I just hope I didn't upset you earlier…with the text I sent."

Tears threaten to fall unexpectedly, simply hearing the care in his tone. "Guess the photo made me sentimental for last spring. Though I will admit, I've had more than a few glasses of wine tonight." I force a breezy laugh, settling into the sand. "But enough about me. How's life in the big city treating you these days? Breaking hearts left and right, I'm sure."

Mark chuckles, the sound warm and familiar. "Please, you know you're the only one who ever had a hold on mine." He pauses, and I can almost see the mischievous glint in his eye. "Unless you count me breaking Jake's heart, being gone most of the summer for work?"

Longing pierces so sharply I pull my knees to my chest. "Don't suppose you're in Florida anytime soon…?"

"Trust me, if I were, you'd be my first call, Arden." Sensing my spiraling overanalysis, Mark redirects gently. "Tell me about the job. I bet you're already running the place."

I laugh, grateful for the change in subject. "Oh, you know, just whipping everyone into shape with my dazzling wit and charm."

"That's my girl," Mark says, pride evident in his voice. "But, seriously, how's it going? Is it everything you hoped for?"

I hesitate, wondering how honest I should be. "It's…good. Great, actually. I love the work, and the people are amazing. It's just…" I trail off, unsure how to put the ache in my chest into words.

"Just what, babe?" Mark prompts gently.

I don't even know who I'm protecting anymore, keeping the truth inside.

I take a deep breath. Time to lay my cards on the table. "It's just not the same without you."

Mark's quiet for a moment, and I hear him take a shaky breath. "I know exactly what you mean. Being here tonight, I swear I can almost hear your laugh over the music. It's like you're haunting me in the best possible way."

I swallow past the lump in my throat. "Who knew the infamous Mark Bell was such a sap?"

He chuckles, but there's no humor in it. "Only for you, Bubbles. Only for you."

We lapse into a comfortable silence, the distant sounds of the ocean and the bar in the background filling the space between us. It's almost like we're together again, sharing a quiet moment under the stars.

Finally, Mark breaks the spell. "I hate to cut this short, but I should get back to Jake. He's having a rough night. A story for another day, perhaps." He pauses, exhaling a long breath against the receiver. "But, Arden?"

"Yeah?"

"Don't be a stranger, okay? I'm always here for you, no matter what."

I smile, my heart full to bursting. "I know. The same goes for you, Trouble. Always."

"Sweet dreams, beautiful."

"Goodnight, Mark."

As the call disconnects, I hug my knees closer to my chest, feeling lighter than I have in months. Maybe we can't be together right now, but knowing that Mark still cares and misses me just as much as I miss him is enough to keep me going. So, I'll cherish these precious glimpses into the heart of the man I can't let go fully, praying that one day, there might be an opportunity for something more.

26

Mark

A Week Later, August 10th

The key turns in the lock, the sound echoing through the empty apartment as I stumble inside. Another day of whiny athletes and bruised egos after a long string of road games.

I toss my bags aside, not bothering to unpack. What's the point? I'll be back on the road in a few days anyway. It's been like this for months now, ever since...

I shake my head, trying to dislodge the thoughts that always creep in during these quiet moments. Thoughts of her. Arden.

It's been three months since she left for Tampa, three months since I watched her walk away from me and into her new life. We promised to stay in touch, to make things work despite the distance. And at first, we did. Daily texts, weekly phone calls, even the occasional FaceTime session when our schedules aligned.

But as weeks turned into months, the communication grew more sporadic. Arden was throwing herself into her new job, determined to make a name for herself in the consulting world. And I was bouncing from city to city, working long hours and trying to prove my worth to the organization.

Somewhere along the way, the texts became fewer and farther between.

I collapse onto the couch, my head falling back against the cushions. I should be used to this by now, the loneliness. It's not like I haven't gone through dry spells before. But this feels different. Heavier, somehow.

I think back to Fourth of July, that night at Trevor's party. I hadn't even wanted to go, but he came and picked me up, insisting that I needed to "get back out there." And like an idiot, I'd listened, desperate to feel something aside from empty.

The party was a blur of too-loud music and too-strong drinks. I remember flirting with some girl, letting her pull me in for a kiss. But as soon as her lips touched mine, I recoiled like I'd been burned. It felt wrong, like a betrayal, even though Arden and I established we weren't together.

I'd mumbled some excuse and bolted, leaving a confused Travor in my wake. And the next day, when I saw the picture of me and that girl splashed across social media, the only thought that crossed my mind was wanting Arden to see it. I wanted her to care enough to call me out on it and demand an explanation. At least then, I'd have known I meant something, seen a spark of jealousy that showed me she still wanted more with me.

But she didn't. And that silence was more deafening than any accusation could have been.

I drag a hand down my face, feeling the stubble that's accumulated over the past few days. I need to pull myself together, to focus on my job and my own life. I can't keep pining over a girl who's states away, who made it clear right now didn't work between the two of us.

Maybe I shouldn't have messaged her spontaneously last week. But being back at Sadie's, and dealing with Jake's spiral after his blowout fight with Tessa earlier this week, had me craving her steadfast support…craving any piece of her.

234 | Nicole Crystal

So, yeah, fueled with liquid courage and desperation, I'd reached out. And to my surprise, she actually returned the favor.

When she called me back at midnight, I was still at the bar with Jake, but nothing could stop me from answering. And now, I keep replaying that conversation in my head, trying to read between the lines.

Instinctively, my fingers reach for my phone. But before I can flip to her contact, I notice the message from Jake. The reminder about the barbecue at his parents' house this evening, the one to welcome Thomas home after returning from the East Coast. And even though I want to veg out, I know I can't bail.

Not on him. Not when I promised I'd be there.

With a resigned sigh, I change into fresh clothes before navigating the familiar stretch toward my childhood hometown.

Here's to hoping my parents are miraculously out of town.

Mrs. Rhoades pulls me into a big hug when I arrive. Her enthusiasm about next month's anniversary party is infectious as she coaxes promises of attendance. *Damn me and my and my promises.* Across the yard, Jake offers an approving grin, no doubt excited to see me push beyond my hermit tendencies.

But the warmth comes to a screeching halt when I see her. My mother, holding court near the drink table, her perfectly styled hair and designer sundress standing out among the casual crowd.

Always the center of attention.

She catches my eye and waves me over, her smile a little too bright, a little too practiced. I know that look. It's the same one she uses when she's about to meddle in my life.

I grab a beer from the cooler, steeling myself for the inevitable interrogation. "Hey, Mom. Quite the turnout today."

"Mark, darling!" She loops her arm through mine, her perfectly manicured nails digging into my skin. "I was just telling everyone about your busy summer, all that traveling with the team. You're making quite the name for yourself, aren't you?"

I force a smile, trying not to wince at her tight grip. "Just doing my job, Mom. Nothing special."

She tuts, shaking her head. "Don't be so modest, dear. It's unbecoming." She steers me towards a group of her friends, their curious gazes raking over me like I'm a prize stallion at auction. "Now, I know you've been a bit down since that girl of yours left, but I have the perfect solution. Miranda's daughter is back in town tonight, and she's been asking about you."

I feel my jaw tighten, anger simmering in my gut. Of course she'd bring up Arden and twist the knife a little deeper. And, of course, she'd have some random girl waiting in the wings, ready to pawn me off like a consolation prize.

"I'm doing just fine on my own, Mom," I grit out, my fingers tightening around my beer bottle.

She arches a perfectly plucked eyebrow, her gaze assessing. "Are you, though? You look like you haven't slept in weeks. And that beard…" She wrinkles her nose as if the mere sight of my facial hair offends her.

I run a hand over my chin, the rough stubble a reminder of just how long it's been since I've had a reason to care about my appearance. About three months.

I glance at the women surrounding us, their eager faces waiting for my response. Waiting for me to play the role of the charming, eligible bachelor. But I'm so damn tired of pretending.

"Maybe there's more to life than just getting laid," I say, my voice low and tight. "Not that I'd expect you to understand."

My mother flinches, just for a second, before smoothing her features back into that perfect, plastic smile. "Oh, honey. Don't take your anger out on me just because that girl left you high and dry. I warned you she'd get bored and move on to the next shiny thing. I'm just trying to be supportive."

Her words hit their mark, each one a tiny dagger straight to the heart. Because as much as I hate to admit it, a small part of me wonders if she's right. If Arden did get bored of me, of us. If she found someone else to make her laugh, to hold her at night.

I down the rest of my beer in one long gulp, the bitter liquid doing little to dull the ache in my chest. "You know what? I think I'm gonna head inside. Need something stronger today."

I'm done playing her games, done being the dutiful son.

I stalk towards the house and into the kitchen, bracing myself against the counter.

Maybe I should've thought more about that promotion to Arizona. At least then, I wouldn't be forced to deal with run-ins like this.

I grab the bottle of whiskey from the cabinet above the fridge and pour a glass.

"Hitting it a little hard, huh?"

I set the drink down, glimpsing my father entering the kitchen. *Great, just what I need. Another lecture on how I'm screwing up my life.*

But instead of disapproval, I find something like understanding in his eyes. He reaches for the bottle of whiskey, pouring another glass and settling onto a barstool.

Maybe it was the run-in with Mom, or the fact that I no longer care about their approval, but I slide next to him and finally ask the question that's been on my mind for years.

"Why are you still with her? Not like you make each happy." My voice comes out tentative, gaining confidence as it all spills out. "I heard you both that first night. The day you realized what she was doing, that she was cheating. I thought you'd leave her. Thought maybe you and I could…I don't know, get away?"

I turn as my dad runs a shaky hand down his face, hints of shame teasing his features. "Not everyone can see the future, son. Know how things are gonna turn out. At the time, your mother and I…well, we thought you needed to have us both by your side. Then you got older. Got into sports. Guess we assumed you wouldn't even notice what was happening at home."

I snort, taking another swig. "Notice? She flaunted it. Met up with coaches, teachers, hell, friends of mine. And then you…you just joined in."

I stare unblinking as he falters, a foreign crack visible behind his defenses. Swallowing hard, Dad meets my stare with more openness than I can recall. "I wanted to leave her at first."

"What changed?" I wince into my drink. *Do I actually want this answer? Will I just see myself as more of a disappointment in their eyes? The reason their lives got screwed up.*

He takes a long drink, meeting my glare wearily. "Before I met your mother, I was dating a girl for a long time. She and I were only sixteen when we met, but damn was I head over heels for her. We were so young…too young for that kind of love. Bound to fuck up. Not sure what exactly happened, but we parted ways, and it tore my heart to shreds." He pauses, giving me an assessing stare. "Then I met your mom a few months later."

Mom was his rebound. God, why does that make it all ten times worse?

Dad looks back at his drink, lost in memory. "Your mom and I had only gone out a few times when she found out she was pregnant with you. We were scared. Didn't know what to do. And I may not have loved her then, but I cared enough for her not to leave her alone."

"Some love story, Dad," I mock, raising my glass before tipping it back again. "You ruined your life because I came along."

He shakes his head, placing a hand on my shoulder. "That's exactly why I haven't shared this before, Mark. But you need to know that what happened with your mom and I…it wasn't you." Meeting my stare, he continues. "You've always been the best part of what happened between us. Our relationship…well, I thought love would come in time. I made a promise to her, to you. And damn, I tried. I was working all the time to pay the bills, constantly stressed. She didn't make it easy by making me feel like I trapped her. When I finally found out she was cheating, you wanna know what I felt?"

His expression shows years of regret as his gaze bores into me. "Relief. I felt fucking relieved. How pathetic is that?" This time, he tips his drink to mine. "I was ready to walk out and start fresh, to go back to who I was before we'd gotten together. I looked up the girl from high school. The one I'd never gotten over. She was still in town, and I thought it was some sign."

He takes a long swig, not breaking our eye contact as I start to understand my father more than I ever have. "It had been seven years. And the moment I saw her again, that same rush came rolling right back, lighting up my chest like a firework…at least until I found out she was getting married. She'd found someone else." He sighs, glancing into the amber liquid in his glass. "So I came back home. Figured if I couldn't have my one true love, it didn't really matter if I was married or divorced. I had you. Your mom and I had our good days. On our bad ones, we'd stay away from one another. It worked for us, but it was never love, never the can't-breathe-without-you feeling I had once."

"That was my biggest regret, Mark." His eyes tick back up to mine. "It wasn't having you. It wasn't marrying your mom. It was being too naïve to do whatever it took to keep the woman I couldn't see the world the same without. I'd found it and let it go."

I stare at my father, my heart pounding in my chest as his words sink in. *He never regretted marrying my mother or having me. He only regretted losing his true love.*

The revelation hits me like a punch to the gut, leaving me breathless and reeling. Everything I thought as gospel my entire life turns to ash instantly. All these years, I'd built up this image of my father, of marriage and kids, as settling for a life of misery. But now, I see him in a different light—a man who made difficult choices, who stuck by them, and lived with the consequences of his actions—someone who loved me despite it all.

I swallow past the lump in my throat, my voice rough with emotion. "Dad, I...I had no idea."

He shakes his head, a sad smile playing on his lips. "I never wanted you to know, son. I didn't want you to think that you were a mistake or a burden."

Tears prick at the corners of my eyes, and I blink them back furiously. I can't remember the last time my father spoke to me with such raw honesty and vulnerability.

"But why didn't you fight for her? The girl from high school?" I ask, my voice barely above a whisper.

My father sighs, his shoulders slumping as if the weight of the world rests upon them. "I was young and stupid, Mark. I thought I could move on, that I could learn to love your mother the way I loved *her.*"

He takes a shuddering breath, his eyes distant. "And maybe there's truth when they say there's only one soulmate out there. At least for me. Because Elyse is still happily married with her own family, and I'm still hopelessly wondering what might have been if I'd taken a chance sooner."

I nod, thinking of Arden. Of the way she makes my heart race and my palms sweat, the way she challenges me and supports me in equal measure. The way I can't imagine my future without her in it.

Does that make her my soulmate? Do I believe in soulmates?

"What if I found *the one*?" My voice cracks, saying it out loud finally. "What if I don't know how to get her back?"

My father's eyes snap back to mine. "Then go after her. Find a way to show her how much she means to you. Don't let pride or fear or anything else stand in your way."

A sense of determination settles over me like a cloak. I think of the future I want with Arden, the life I want to build with her by my side. To hell with everything else.

"Thanks, Dad. For sharing that story, for giving me a different perspective."

My father smiles, a real smile this time, one that reaches his eyes and crinkles the corners. "Glad I can offer some good advice these days. Now go on, enjoy the party. And if your mother tries to set you up with any more of her 'prospects,' just send them my way."

I laugh, feeling lighter than I have in weeks. As I make my way back outside, I know something inside me changed. The recognition hitting that I've had it wrong for so long. Because if I spent the next 100 years with Arden, I know I wouldn't regret a single day.

She's it.

And I'm ready to do whatever it takes to have her back.

Stepping to the side of the house, I pull out my phone and click call.

"Mark?" Her voice, warm and familiar, sends a jolt through me.

"Hey, you." I lean against the brick, trying to play it cool despite the way my heart is racing. "I was just thinking about you."

"Oh, really? What about?" I can hear the smile in her voice, the teasing lilt that never fails to make me grin like an idiot.

I chuckle, running a hand through my hair. "Well, when I was driving out to the Rhoades' house this afternoon, I passed our epic mini-golf date spot. Made me think of that hole-in-one you shot."

"Epic?" Arden laughs. "Didn't we get kicked out for your 'inappropriate behavior' behind the castle?"

"Our. And I was just trying to properly celebrate your victory," I protest, feeling my face heat up at the memory of exactly how I'd 'celebrated. "Not my fault your put stance is irresistible."

She hums. "Next time we'll have to see if you can control yourself long enough to actually finish a game."

"Next time?"

There's a beat of comfortable silence, and then Arden clears her throat. "Actually…" She trails off momentarily, and I'm pretty sure I stop breathing. "In a shocking turn of events that surprised no one, my parents bailed on helping Cora move into her dorm tomorrow. They decided to ship all her stuff instead. So, guess who's hopping on a plane to make sure her little sis doesn't have to be alone for move-in day?"

My brain short-circuits for a second, trying to process her words. Arden. Nearby. Tomorrow.

"Wait, seriously? You're going to Champaign?" I ask, my voice rising with barely contained excitement.

"Yep!" she confirms, and I can picture the way her eyes must be sparkling. "I know it's a few hours away and it's only until Sunday…"

"Arden, that's…wow. Yes." I exhale, a giddy laugh bubbling up in my chest. "Do you need a ride from the airport? I can pick you guys up. Help carry boxes. Whatever you want."

"Really? You're not too busy with work or anything?"

"Are you kidding? I'd cancel the World Series if it meant getting to see you." The words are out of my mouth before I can stop them, but I don't regret them. Not even a little.

There's a pause, and I swear I can hear Arden's breath catch. "I've missed you too, Mark."

My heart feels like it might burst out of my chest. "Then let me be there, Arden. Let me help with Cora, and then...maybe we can talk? About us?"

"I'd like that," she says softly. "I'll text you our flight details."

"Please. And Arden?"

"Yeah?"

"Just so you know, I'm going to hug the crap out of you when I see you. So, be prepared."

She laughs, bright and beautiful. "I think I can handle that. Tell Jake and the boys I said hello, and I'll see you soon, then."

"Not soon enough," I mutter, hitting the end button before I say something truly sappy.

I stare at the phone in my hand, a goofy grin spreading across my face. I'll see Arden. Tomorrow. And yeah, it's just a short time, but it's a chance. A chance to hold her, to kiss her, to tell her all the things I've been too afraid to say.

A chance to fight for what we have, no matter what it takes.

I slip the phone back into my pocket, my mind already racing with ideas. I need to make this weekend count. Need to show Arden that what we have is real, that it's worth taking a risk on.

And I think I know just where to start.

I glance at the crowd in the backyard, spotting my high school baseball coach and biggest mentor, Drew.

With a newfound spring in my step, I head toward the party, counting down the hours until I can see my girl again. Because that's what she is, what she's always been.

Mine. And this time, I'm not letting go.

27

Arden ♥

Now, August 11ᵗʰ

My heel bounces anxiously against the worn carpet as our plane taxis to the gate. Three endless months apart have boiled down to this moment…seeing Mark again.

The seatbelt sign dings off, and Cora glances my way, no doubt reading my transparent nerves as I smooth imaginary wrinkles from my romper. She offers an encouraging smile as we gather our bags.

"Promise I'll try not to make this too awkward," I manage, hoping levity might steady my hammering pulse. "And I appreciate how cool you've been about the last-minute change of plans."

Cora laughs, looping her arm supportively through mine. "Oh, trust me, watching you two reunite will be payment enough after seeing you miserable all summer." Her playful grin softens. "Just follow your heart this weekend, okay, Dee? No overanalyzing."

"Who are you, and what did you do with my baby sister?"

She giggles, but it does little to suppress the panic washing over me as we weave through the terminal. What if I see him and never want to go back? What if whatever spark that existed between us dimmed?

Cora glances at me, concern etched on her face. "Hey, you've got this," she whispers, giving me a reassuring squeeze.

I take a deep breath, trying to steady my nerves. Yesterday's phone call proved our connection still burns red-hot, but I can't let my guard down. Not when my heart's a ticking time bomb of emotions, ready to explode at any second.

My eyes dart around the space, skimming over unfamiliar faces until they lock onto a pair of warm brown eyes that I'd know anywhere. They're the eyes that have been living rent-free in my head since the day we met, able to turn my knees to jelly with just one look. This look to be precise. The one staring right at me as if I'm the only person in the room, devouring me and accepting me all at the same time.

Mark flashes that trademark grin of his from across the lobby, and then he's moving toward me, parting the crowd like a modern-day Moses. Before I can even process what's happening, I'm engulfed in his arms, pressed against his chest like it's where I've always belonged. Like every piece of me that's been MIA these past few months just came rushing back home.

His palm cradles the back of my head, nose burrowing into the crook of my neck intoxicatingly. "Fuck, I missed you. Three months was way too long, baby."

Emotion chokes me, feeling him solid and real after so long. I finally peel back enough to cradle his stubbled jaw, getting lost for a breathless moment in those dark eyes sparking with wonderstruck joy.

A discreet throat clears behind us. We both turn to see Cora grinning indulgently.

"Not that I want to interrupt this beautiful reunion, but remind me, who's taking me to get my car?"

"Shit. Sorry." Mark's flushed laugh rumbles under my cheek as his grip reluctantly loosens, but his palm stays anchored possessively at my lower back. He holds out a hand to shake Cora's enthusiastically. "Chauffeur at your service."

"Great. We'll make use of those muscles with all the boxes we have to pick up," Cora replies indulgently, spinning on her heels and motioning for Mark to lead the way.

The fifteen-minute ride to where Cora's car and dorm items were shipped feels like seconds as conversations flow animatedly. Mark's fingers stay woven with mine over the center console as he shares charming quips about the recent mishaps of his injury-prone clients.

But when Cora slides into her overstuffed SUV, palpable awareness charges the small space suddenly separating Mark and me. *We're alone.* His shy smile hits me like a gut punch before he draws me urgently closer, my world narrowing only to the press of his perfect mouth on mine.

The short blare of Cora's horn finally breaks us apart, and I wonder how long we were kissing.

Mark rests his forehead on mine, a lop-sided grin spreading across his face. "Wow, I forgot how much I love kissing you," he whispers fervently, voice thick with promise and an unfamiliar vulnerability. "I would've driven to the moon and back just for that."

I can't stop the giggle that bursts from my chest. "The moon, huh? And here I thought you just missed my witty banter."

Mark chuckles, his eyes crinkling at the corners. "Oh, I missed everything about you, Bubbles. The banter, the sass, the way you make my heart race like a lovesick teenager."

Silence hangs between us after the unexpected confession, and Mark shifts the car into drive.

Glancing at my fingers twisting recklessly together, he leans closer, his tone teasing. "Uh-oh, I know that look. What's going on in that pretty head of yours?"

I look up at his brief, assessing gaze before he turns back to the road. "I should've told you I was coming here before you reached out yesterday," I admit softly. "I booked the flight on Wednesday. I just…I wasn't sure I could handle seeing you again."

Mark's expression remains maddeningly neutral, though I sense a flicker of nervousness in his eyes. "And now that I'm here…?"

"It's complicated." I swallow, summoning courage. "I can't move back yet, but being with you again, it's like…like…"

"Like what?" Mark prompts, his voice soft.

"Like oxygen," I admit, my cheeks flushing. "Like I can finally breathe again."

Mark's grin outshines the city lights as he replies, "I know exactly what you mean, babe. It's like the world makes sense when we're together."

His fingers intertwine with mine, maintaining that connection until we pull into the parking lot. As he shifts the car into park, I'm already anticipating our next touch.

How quickly can we unload Cora's car? I wonder, craving the opportunity to be back in his arms, back in his undivided attention.

We spill into the crowded corridor, naturally gravitating towards each other amidst the chaos. Mark proves to be an indispensable anchor, his muscular arms effortlessly hefting awkward boxes up to Cora's new dorm.

When we're finally grabbing the last box, my hand brushes against Mark's, sending a spark of need through my body. *Almost there, Arden.*

Mark looks up, a playful grin tugging at his lips. "Careful there, Bubbles. Wouldn't want you to strain something."

I roll my eyes, my smile betraying me. "Worst case, I have my own personal trainer on hand if needed."

His gaze darkens, voice dropping to a whisper. "Always happy to rub out any issues." He flashes a secret smile, filled with meaning meant only for me.

I'd forgotten how quickly this man unravels me.

The subtle touches and glances continue as we finish unpacking Cora's belongings in her dorm room. As she chats brightly about plans, the realization hits me that despite walking away months ago, Mark still effortlessly possesses my heart. And I'm left asking the question why I'm trying to fight it, when my entire body is screaming for me to give in.

Finally, Cora surveys her finished room, beaming. "It's absolutely perfect! I can't thank you both enough for being here." Her grin turns mischievous as she starts ushering us towards the door. "But now, you two should make the most of tonight. Go on, I'm totally fine on my own."

Despite our laughing protests, we find ourselves gently pushed into the hallway, the door closing behind us with a decisive click.

"So, my place, then?" Mark murmurs silkily, already drawing me closer.

"Yeah." I melt into his embrace as he leads me toward his car. "I still can't believe you came to help with this. You're pretty incredible."

His expression softens, his eyes filled with warmth. "Arden, I'd do anything for you. Don't you know that by now?"

I lean over, pressing a lingering kiss to his cheek. "I'm starting to."

Mark swiftly guides us out of the parking lot, reaching for my hand and intertwining our fingers. "Part of me wants to drive straight to my apartment and spend the rest of the day showing you how much I've missed you," he confesses, his voice low and rough. "But another part of me wants to take this slow, to savor every moment."

I squeeze his hand, touched by his consideration. "Well, you have me for about fourteen hours, but after… Let's just say I don't plan to wait so long to see you again."

He brings our joined hands to his lips, kissing my knuckles softly. "I like that plan."

As we merge onto the highway, Mark's hand drifts to my thigh, his touch igniting sparks beneath my skin. "You know, I might've underestimated how hard it would be to take things slow. Because right now, all I can think about is how much I want you."

I feel a blush creeping up my neck. "Oh really? And what do you propose we do about that?"

He grins, his voice dropping to a husky whisper. "Well, there's a rest stop about fifteen minutes from here. We could always...take a little detour."

I bite my lip, trying to hide my smile. "A detour, huh? I suppose I could be persuaded."

Mark's hand inches higher, his fingers toying with the hem of my romper. "I'll make it worth your while, I promise."

I trail my fingers along his arm, working my way towards his belt. "You know, not every guy would give up their day off to help move their...pseudo-girlfriend's sister?"

"Pseudo, huh?" He raises an eyebrow, squeezing my thigh playfully. "Maybe we can talk about that after we discuss the creative ways you can pay me back."

I laugh, delight and desire swirling dangerously. "Oh? And what kind of payback did you have in mind?"

His grin turns wolfish. "Let's just say it involves the next fourteen hours and very little sleep."

As images flood my mind—back seats, tangled sheets, breathless moments—I realize we're definitely on the same page when it comes to "payback."

Mark pulls into the secluded rest stop, quickly unbuckling his seatbelt. He grips the steering wheel, glancing around before turning to face me, eyes already dark with want.

"You sure you're okay with this, baby?" he breathes, his hand cupping my cheek.

I lean into his touch, marveling at the surreal wonder of being here with him, like this, after so many months apart. It's almost too good to be true, like a dream I never want to wake up from.

"Couldn't talk me out of it now if you tried," I reply. My fingers tangle into his hair as I pull him closer until our lips meet.

"Rule breaker Arden...I like her," he hums.

As I nip at his bottom lip, Mark groans, his tongue sliding against mine with a desperate hunger that mirrors my own.

We break apart, panting, our foreheads pressed together.

"Back seat," I rasp. It's not a question, but a statement.

"Finally giving me that seven minutes in heaven?" he teases with a wink.

"Only seven minutes?"

He grins, tugging me out of my seat. "Oh, baby, I'm just getting started."

As we crash into the backseat like two teenagers sneaking around after curfew, I can't help but giggle at the absurdity of it all. Here we are, two supposedly mature adults, pawing at each other like we've just discovered what hands are for.

"Why'd you have to wear Fort Knox today?" Mark grumbles, waging war with my rompers zipper.

"Oh, I'm sorry," I quip back, tugging at the garment. "Next time I'll just show up in a handy tear-away outfit."

Mark's eyes light up at that, a devilish grin spreading across his face. "Now there's an idea I can get behind. I'll keep that in mind for Christmas."

As I wiggle out of my romper in the confined space, I'm suddenly very aware that this backseat was definitely not designed with adult activities in mind. My elbow connects with something hard—the door handle, maybe?—and I let out a yelp.

"You okay there, Houdini?" Mark asks, pausing in his own clothes-shedding mission.

"Just peachy," I grumble, rubbing my elbow. "Remind me again why we thought this was a good idea?"

But then Mark's hands are on my bare skin, his touch gentle yet electrifying.

"Oh," I breathe, "That's why."

He chuckles, the sound low and intoxicating. "Still think we should've waited till we got home?"

I pretend to consider it for a moment, then pull him closer. "Nah, I think I can suffer through a few bruises for this."

And with that, his lips are on mine and he's lowering me onto the seat.

"God, Arden, you're so beautiful," he murmurs, his lips trailing hot kisses down my chest. "I've dreamed of this moment every night since you left."

I arch into his touch, my nails raking down his back. "Every single night."

His hand slides between our bodies, his fingers dipping beneath the lace of my underwear. I gasp, my hips bucking against his touch.

"So responsive," he growls, his teeth grazing my earlobe. "So perfect."

I reach between us, palming his hardness through his boxers. He hisses, his eyes slamming shut. "Arden, fuck..."

"I need you inside me, Mark," I pant, hooking my fingers in the waistband of his boxers. "Please."

He doesn't need to be told twice. In one swift motion, he rids us of our remaining clothing, his naked body pressing deliciously against mine.

"Tell me you want this," he demands, his voice rough with need. "Tell me you need me as much as I need you."

"I want this," I assure him, my legs wrapping around his waist. "I need this. I need you, Mark. Only you."

He reaches into the pocket of his jeans, quickly ripping open a condom as his mouth continues to explore mine. Then, with a groan of surrender, he thrusts into me, filling me, completing me. I cry out, my head falling back against the seat, my fingers digging into his shoulders as months of need are finally fulfilled.

He stills for a moment, his forehead resting against mine, his breath mingling with my own. "This feeling, baby," he rasps against my lips. "How'd I survive without you?"

My heart swells with joy and love and overwhelming emotions I can't put into words. "We didn't. Not in a way that mattered."

He smiles, running a thumb over my bottom lip. And then he's moving, his hips rocking against mine as his mouth claims mine in a kiss that sets my soul on fire.

"Arden…needed this…need you."

When his tongue explores my exposed chest, jumbled words and pleas slip from my mouth. Mark only thrusts harder, rough groans escaping the louder I get.

My breathy tone mingles with the heavy panting filling the car, my body aching—begging for more.

As if reading my thoughts, Mark grunts out a lust-drenched "Fuck, yes, baby."

Our need turns urgent and desperate—a desire to feel connected again after so long without each other, to bring each other to the point of ecstasy. Sweat glistens as our bodies tangle and grind together, lost in a world where time stands still.

Above me, Mark slows, eyes seeking mine. "Be mine, Arden."

I nod feverishly as he moves deliberately in and out. "Always, Mark."

The desire pooling between us—something beautifully raw and perfect—has every part of my body unraveling. We keep moving together, but slower now, savoring every touch and taste of each other's skin. Mark traces his fingers down my stomach, teasing my clit with his thumb, causing skyrocketing pleasure I can't hold back. Each wave hits harder as my muscles clench, gripping Mark tighter as he lets go, too. His name tumbles free in rasped prayer before his mouth swallows mine in reverent appreciation.

Our breathing finally slows, hearts still racing from the thrill of being together and the risk of getting caught.

Mark presses his forehead to mine, his breath still coming in quick puffs. "I had this whole romantic reunion planned. Candles, rose petals, the works. Instead, we christened my car like a couple of horny sixteen-year-olds."

I smile, running my fingers through his damp hair. "Are you kidding? This is way better. Plus, think of all the truckers we've entertained. We're basically public servants at this point."

He laughs, his eyes crinkling in that way that makes my heart do somersaults. "Arden Cooper, saving the world one scandalous rest stop at a time."

We gaze at each other, goofy grins plastered on our faces. Mark sighs contentedly, "You know, I'm starting to see the appeal of staying here forever. Just you, me, and this not-so-accommodating backseat."

"As tempting as that sounds," I tease, poking his chest, "I don't think 'lives in a car' is the career upgrade my parents were hoping for. Besides, didn't someone promise me a proper bed for round two?"

Mark presses a quick kiss to my lips. "You're right. We should probably make ourselves presentable and hit the road." He pauses, eyeing my disheveled state. "Though I have to say, the 'just thoroughly ravished' look really suits you."

I swat his arm, laughing. "Flatterer. You're not looking too put-together yourself, hotcakes."

As we reluctantly disentangle and start redressing, I can't resist a playful jab. "I've got to hand it to you, Mark. That was quite the impressive display of...flexibility. Though something tells me this isn't your first rodeo in this backseat."

Mark tosses me an exaggerated scowl. "I'll have you know, Bubbles, that my car and I have been saving ourselves for someone special." His expression softens, eyes twinkling. "Turns out, she was worth the wait."

I feel a blush creeping up my cheeks. "I can see that," I mumble, unable to hide my smile.

We settle back into the front seats and Mark reaches for my hand, intertwining our fingers. "So, about that title thing we need to discuss..."

28

Mark

Now, August 12th

Waking up with Arden wrapped in my arms again, her soft curves pressed against me, is hands down the best way to start a day. The gentle sunlight filtering through the curtains makes her skin glow. I can't resist trailing my fingers along her bare shoulder, marveling at how she fits so perfectly against me.

Last night was...intense, to say the least. I'm pretty sure the neighbors will be giving me knowing looks for weeks after the way Arden screamed my name. Not that I'm complaining. Making her come undone beneath me, watching her eyes roll back in pleasure? Yeah, that'll never get old.

I press a kiss to her temple, grinning as she stirs, her nose scrunching adorably. "Well, someone clearly woke up ready to continue last night's adventures," she mumbles, her voice husky with sleep.

"What can I say? Waking up next to you is like Christmas morning. I just want to unwrap my present over and over again," I tease, grazing her ear.

Arden laughs, toying with the handcuffs still hanging from the headboard. "Think you made that perfectly clear last night."

I smile as flashbacks fill my vision. "Happy to remind you again."

She twists in my arms, her eyes finding mine, and the playfulness between us shifts into something deeper.

I brush a strand of hair from her face, my thumb grazing her cheekbone. "I've missed this. Missed you. These past few months were hell," I confess, my voice rough and emotional. "I tried to move on, to fill the void with work and friends, but I'm helplessly addicted to your fireworks, ruined for anyone but you now."

Arden searches my expression desperately. "I know what you mean."

"Do you, baby?" I run my thumb over her parted lips as nerves threaten to choke my cracked whisper. "I know we touched on it yesterday, but I want *you*. I want to rewrite the rules, be more than scattered texts or tipsy two a.m. calls with no expectations. I want it all, can't stand the thought of you being anyone else's but mine.

"I know I'm not the best at relationships, but I'm willing to try and learn. And if that means only phone calls and stealing weekends until your job placement happens, then so be it." Seeing lingering doubts swirling in Arden's eyes, I backtrack, wondering if I'm asking too much. "Or maybe—"

Arden silences me with a quick kiss. "Don't take it back." Her voice catches as she threads her fingers into mine desperately. "Last spring, I...I thought asking you to do long distance was selfish. You told me you didn't do commitment, and I didn't want to be something you'd wake up one day and regret. I thought I was protecting both of us, but now...I'm not sure I was protecting us at all. Because somehow, in a few short months, you became the best part of me. A part I don't want to lose again."

"So that's a yes?" I dare to ask.

"I want to rewrite the rules, too." She surges forward, capturing my lips in a desperate kiss that steals the air from my lungs.

I return her embrace with the same emotion, my hands roaming her bare skin, desperate to touch, to claim, to cherish.

When we finally break apart, we're both panting, our chests heaving.

Arden rests her forehead against mine, a smile playing at the corners of her mouth. "I guess this means you're officially off the market. No more playing the field."

I grin, pulling her closer. "Baby, the only field I want to play on is the one with you cheering me on from the stands."

Arden groans, rolling her eyes even as a laugh bubbles up from her throat. "Are we becoming that cheesy couple that uses sports metaphors to talk about our relationship?"

"I don't know. Does it turn you on the same way it does me? If so, swing away." I add an exaggerated wink just for fun.

She shakes her head, laughing. "You're ridiculous, you know that?"

"Yeah, but you love me anyway."

The words slip out before I can stop them, and for a moment, I panic, wondering if I've pushed too far, too fast.

But then Arden's expression softens, her hand coming up to cradle my cheek. "Yeah, I do. God help me, but I really do."

I huff a surprised laugh at her determined verdict, relief and euphoria crashing through me. I flip our positions in one smooth movement until I'm hovering above her. "So then, girlfriend who loves me...what trouble can we get into before I drive you to the airport?"

Arden grins, nails already roaming my skin. "Why do I get the feeling your idea of trouble involves significantly less clothing?"

Leaning closer to her ear, I stage whisper, "As much as I'd love to stay in this bed until the minute we have to leave, worshipping every inch of your body, I didn't just ask for a long-distance relationship for the sex."

With a quick kiss on her cheek, I push myself off the bed and grab her hand as she watches me, stunned. "C'mon. Jake stayed at Tessa's last night. Let's start with breakfast."

Arden smirks, letting me pull her to her feet. "Breakfast?"

"Breakfast," I confirm, my wandering hands reluctantly stilling. "This time, let's make a mess of the kitchen."

Laughing, she pulls on a pair of shorts and dances toward the kitchen. I grin, tugging on a pair of sweatpants before following.

Arden's eyes sparkle as she pulls out mixing bowls. "How messy are we talking?"

"Hmm, let's not get too complicated. I'm no chef, Miss Quiche Baker." I wrap both arms snugly around her waist from behind, nuzzling her silken hair. "I'd prefer putting my efforts into the gorgeous company."

Arden hums indulgently, leaning into me as she cracks eggs. I perch my chin on her shoulder, shamelessly determined to "help" however I can with our bodies so distractingly close.

Our playful touches make quick work of the kitchen. Between the stolen floury kisses and smeared batter over skin, our laughter echoes giddily as we "attempt" to cook.

Eventually, I haul a flour-dusted Arden onto the cramped balcony, two plates piled high with lopsided creations. Sunshine glows against her smooth skin as she chatters animatedly about her job and summer stories involving her sister. My fingers trace lazy patterns up her arm, marveling how even this mundane moment feels sacred with her.

As our conversation fades to a comfortable silence, Arden rests her cheek against my shoulder with a tiny sigh that mirrors my own wistful thoughts.

"Are we crazy thinking this could work? That someday this could be an ordinary Sunday?"

I lean my head against hers. "I hope it never feels ordinary. But, yeah. I know it won't be easy. And you have what? Three more months of your rotation before you're placed somewhere?"

258 | Nicole Crystal

Arden nods subtly. "Then we figure out next steps?"

I hear the slight hesitance in her voice. I know it's the rational part of her brain...the piece still trying to grapple with the details, knowing one of us might have to give up something.

I shift, tilting her chin to face me. "I *promise* you, we will find a way, Arden. However long, whatever it takes." I emphasize the word promise, hoping she knows the extent of what I'm saying. I don't make promises I don't intend to keep.

Arden rests her forehead against mine, her whispered words soothing my soul. "I trust you, Mark."

With renewed determination, we gather the breakfast dishes and head inside, ready to face whatever the future holds.

Together.

29

Arden ♥

Four Weeks Later, September 13th

The late Florida sun sets relentlessly in the picture window, its beauty begging to be shared with someone.

Instead, I push the glazed carrots aimlessly around my plate, my appetite vanishing as my parents monopolize the dinner conversation by rehashing office politics and upcoming vacations. Their thinly veiled scrutiny will no doubt lead to another nighttime migraine. I brace for the inevitable critique about to crash over my shrinking shoulders now that it's just the three of us.

Right on cue, my mother delicately pats her mouth with the linen napkin, spearing me with an assessing look. "It's been a while since we've all had dinner together, wouldn't you say, Arden? How are things? It seems like you've been pretty busy."

I resist the urge to roll my eyes and remind her that it's not just my schedule preventing family time. Their new business venture takes their attention most evenings, not that I'm complaining.

"You know, late hours and networking mixers. Just trying to take this whole career concept seriously." I keep my tone purposefully light despite an increased defensiveness.

"Well, I'm sure with enough dedication and schmoozing the right executives, you'll escape the entry-level grind soon enough," my dad remarks distractedly, attention absorbed, replying to emails under the table.

I grit my teeth against the irritation of his patronizing assumption that connections alone can fuel professional advancement.

Before I find the right diplomatic words, my mother adds, "We're just concerned this consulting firm wasn't quite the fast-paced environment you thought it'd be. There's still time to interview for attorney roles here..." she trails off leadingly.

I set down my fork slowly, my pulse already elevating. Contrary to their belief, I love my job. It's the weight on my shoulders of what's in Chicago that has me returning home somewhat moody most days.

"I'm adjusting to the learning curve of this current project. But I'm enjoying the corporate analysis work," I respond, meeting her skeptical gaze. "I'm not abandoning it yet to resurrect the law school plan, if that's what you're suggesting."

As I sit there, defending my career choices to my parents, I can't help but feel a surge of pride for the work I'm doing. Just last week, I led a team in developing a strategy that saved our client millions in operational costs. The thrill of solving complex problems and making a real impact is what drives me, even if my parents can't see beyond the prestige of a law firm.

My mother exchanges a loaded glance with my stone-faced father. "We want you to achieve your full potential instead of languishing somewhere unchallenged."

I clench my napkin tightly, frustration boiling over. Why can't they express pride in my accomplishments instead of focusing on the next ladder rung?

I glance at my phone, wishing Mark knew precisely when to text me. Right now would be perfect! He's the one steady anchor, even states away.

"Something the matter?" my mother asks curiously.

"Just checking on the plans with Jada for this weekend," I answer lightly, scanning the calendar. How many more days until baseball season's over? Realizing Mom's assessing me, I add flippantly, "Unless you two care to join twenty-somethings club-hopping?"

Surprisingly, Mom offers a gentle smile. "That reminds me, dear. A former attorney friend of mine mentioned her son was moving down here. I thought maybe you could show him around."

I nearly inhale wine at her transparent matchmaking. Tempering my irritation, I volley lightly, "I didn't realize my social calendar warranted parental meddling suddenly." At their loaded glance exchange, surprising honesty slips out. "Especially since I'm quite happily seeing someone already."

Mom blinks rapidly as Dad chimes in, still glancing at his phone. "Dating someone, huh? Did you meet him at work?"

"Chicago. Which I'm sure won't score me any approval points." I maintain casualness despite the fluttering nerves and exhilaration coursing through my body at the admission.

At their skeptical stares, I straighten in my chair. "Yes, it's a long-distance relationship." Affection touches my voice, staunchly defending him. Defending us. "And I'm hoping you'll accept my decision, not question it."

They exchange more loaded glances across the table before Mom turns toward me. "Well, if you're happy…" she says, reaching to pat my hand in a conciliatory gesture despite the steel glinting behind her eyes.

Is she actually being supportive? Or does she think this is temporary, so she isn't concerned?

Either way, I'll take it as a small step forward.

Post dinner, I head up to my room, clicking the speaker button as Jada's voice fills the room. "Any big plans this weekend, girl?"

I contemplate my unexciting schedule—work projects, reading, and missing my boyfriend from afar. "Oh, you know, wild parties every night," I joke wryly.

Jada laughs. "Well, Paul's trying to get a group together for drinks tomorrow if you're free?"

"Still trying to set me up, Jada? How many times have I told you I'm dating Mark now?"

"Right, the mystery hunk from college," Jada replies. I can practically hear her eye roll through the receiver. "C'mon, it's just a fun night out. Promise no ulterior motives this time."

Before I respond, the phone beeps with an incoming call.

I light up when I see Mark's handsome face flash on the screen. "I'll think about it, 'kay. But I've got another call. My 'mystery long-distance boyfriend' is checking in."

Jada huffs indulgently. "Fine, but I'm telling him you'll be there tomorrow. Have fun chatting with the imaginary dreamboat."

I accept Mark's call with a delighted grin. "Hey, you! How was the flight?"

Mark sighs wryly. "Long and crowded. But it makes it all better to hear your voice." He pauses before asking, "How was your day? Did you still end up having dinner with the parents?"

"Yep!" I fall onto the mattress, my smile growing by the second. "I might've mentioned I was in a relationship."

"Oh, really? How'd that go over?" Mark's pleased grin is audible through the line.

"Surprisingly…okay."

"Good. They won't be too shocked when I finally meet them and charm their socks off."

My grin turns foolishly smitten. "So confident, hotshot?"

"Don't pretend to be shocked, babe." There's a quick pause before he adds, "Speaking of family, did you think any more about the Rhoades' anniversary party in two weeks?"

"Unfortunately, I'm not sure it'll work out. I'm still trying, though. I hate the thought of you facing your family without me." I perch cross-legged on my bed, disappointed in his crazy family dynamics. They make mine trivial by comparison.

Mark makes a dissenting noise. "It'll be fine either way. I knew it'd be a long shot. There's hope, though. I think my dad and I are finally on the same page."

Warmth floods my chest at the sincerity in his tone.

"That's great, hon. One down. One to go."

He chuckles before adding softly, "Someday, all this will be easier. Our parents will realize how amazing their children are."

Can't wait for that day.

We drift into lighter topics before we reluctantly say goodnight. No matter the miles, though, just hearing Mark's playful laughter helps soothe the remaining insecurities of dealing with critical parents and doubtful friends.

Why'd I ever doubt this? Doubt him?

Before bed, I scroll through a few emails that came in after hours. My eyes catch on one as my stomach drops, reading the subject line. "Urgent: Changes to Associate Program."

I open the email, a sense of foreboding washing over me. As I scan the contents, my chest clenches. Maybe the comfortable future I've been envisioning might not be so certain after all.

30

Mark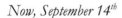

Now, September 14th

Another day, another chance to whip some pro athlete into shape. I mean, who wouldn't want to spend their Friday morning watching grown men grunt and sweat while I put them through their paces?

I'm in the middle of guiding my star rookie through a series of resistance band exercises when my phone buzzes with a new text. A grin tugs at my lips as I see Arden's name light up the screen.

> Arden: *Any words of wisdom before heading into this meeting?*
> Me: *You don't need any more wisdom. You'll kill it… Unlike my current exercise lessons here…* 💪 👆
> Arden: *Oh, I don't know. Pretty sure most people would pay good money to watch your workout demonstrations instead…* 👀

I bite back a groan, images of Arden watching me work out flooding my mind. Damn, I miss that woman. The way she keeps me on my toes, challenges me, makes me want to be a better man.

"Alright, Stevens, let's take five," I call out, tearing my gaze away from my phone. "Then we'll get you game-ready. Can't have you slacking off just because I'm distracted today."

Stevens chuckles, shaking his head as he towels off. "Must be some girl, huh, Bell?"

"You have no idea," I mutter, a stupid grin spreading across my face.

I'm about to fire off another flirty text when an unfamiliar number flashes across my screen. Frowning, I hit accept, bringing the phone to my ear.

"This is Mark Bell."

"Mark! Oh, thank God. I didn't know who else to call in the middle of this crisis!" The voice on the other end is frantic, immediately setting me on edge.

"Whoa, slow down. Who is this?" I ask, my brow furrowing as I try to place the caller.

"Sorry, it's Paige. I'm in Tampa. Your boss gave me your number."

Tampa? Why the hell is someone from Tampa calling me?

"Listen, I wouldn't normally bother you, but we've got a situation here. Javier pulled a quad. Might be worse. Our lead trainer just left without notice, and with playoffs coming up, we need him back on the field ASAP."

Javier...? The name clicks into place. Right, the catcher I worked with at the beginning of the season before he got traded.

"Okay, and what does that have to do with me?" I ask, even as a flicker of anticipation builds in my gut.

"He's asking for you, Mark. Says you're the only one he trusts to get him back in playing shape. We talked to your boss, and he's agreed to send you out here for the weekend. We'll cover all expenses, plus a nice bonus. We just need you here for the next two home games."

The weekend. In Tampa. Where Arden is.

I'm barely listening as Paige rattles off the details, my mind spinning with possibilities. *A chance to see my girl, to hold her in my arms again, even if it's just for a little while.*

"Mark? You still there?"

I blink, snapping back to the present. "Yeah, yeah, I'm here. Email me everything I need to know. I'll be on the next flight out."

As I hang up, I can't stop the giddy laugh that bubbles up in my chest. I'm going to see Arden. After weeks of stolen phone calls and aching to touch her, I'm finally going to be in the same city as the woman who's completely turned my world upside down.

The flight to Tampa feels like an eternity, every minute stretching out like an hour. My fingers drum against the armrest as I picture Arden's face when she sees me. Will she be surprised? Happy? Maybe a little annoyed that I didn't give her a heads up? She does hate changes to her plans…

Whatever. It's worth the risk.

I pull out my phone, grinning at our text exchange from earlier.

> Me: *Please tell me your hot Friday night plans involve missing your favorite handsome BF.* 😀
>
> Arden: *Aren't we confident…* 😏
>
> Me: *Hey now, just preemptively pining over here*
>
> Arden: *Uh-huh. Jada's dragging me out, but don't worry. I'm always missing you.*
>
> Me: *Anywhere interesting?*
>
> Arden: *Beachside. The place Cora worked this summer, just down the beach from my parents.*

Me: *If anyone tries stealing you away, remember I've got exclusive rights to all that chaos...*

Arden: *Might need a reminder later of just how thorough those "rights" get*

The cab driver clears his throat, giving me a knowing look in the rearview mirror. "We're here, man."

I glance up, the imposing stadium looming outside my window. Right. Time to focus on the job at hand before I can play out all the fantasies running through my head.

The next few hours are a blur of assessments, consultations, and rehab plans. By the time I finally escape the stadium, the sun has long since set, the muggy Florida air clinging to my skin. I barely remember to check into my hotel before I rush back out, hailing a cab to Beachside.

As I step inside the crowded bar, the nerves I've been keeping at bay come rushing back in full force. The air is thick with the scent of spilled beer and sweat, the music's bass thrumming through the soles of my shoes. Laughter and chatter mix with the clinking of glasses and the occasional whoop of excitement from the dance floor. The heat of the packed bodies is almost overwhelming, but I push through, my eyes scanning the crowd for the one face I'm desperate to see.

And then, like a beacon in the night, I spot her. Arden—my Arden—laughing with her friends, her head thrown back in carefree abandon. She's a vision, showcasing her lethal curves draped in short black fabric that should be illegal in all fifty states...outside of my bedroom.

I'm about to make my move when some Ken doll wannabe sidles up to her, his hand sliding possessively over her back. I see red, my fists clenching at my sides as I watch him lean in close, his lips brushing against her ear.

But before I can storm over and introduce his face to my fist, Arden steps smoothly away, her smile polite but distant as she removes his hand from her body. That's my girl. Cool, collected, and not taking shit from anyone.

Pride swells in my chest as I close the distance between us, my eyes locked on her. I slide my arms around her waist from behind, my lips finding the shell of her ear.

"Excuse me? Do you happen to have a Band-Aid?" I murmur lightly. "I think I scraped my knees falling for you."

Arden spins in my arms, her eyes wide with shock as she takes me in. "Mark?! What are you...? How did you...?"

But then she's launching herself at me, her arms wrapping around my neck as she crushes her body to mine. I bury my face in her hair, inhaling the sweet scent of her shampoo, the feeling of her in my arms better than any drug.

Dimly, I'm aware of her friends gaping at us, Ken doll seeming more agitated than shocked like the other two. But I focus on Arden, the way she feels, the way she smells, the way she makes my heart race like nothing else.

The sound of an awkward throat-clearing filters through our euphoria.

Arden pulls back first, glancing at her wide-eyed friends. "Oh! Um..." Flustered pink stains her skin, but joy glimmers irrepressibly. "Everyone, this is Mark."

The three individuals at the table eye me with varying degrees of attentiveness. The two women raise eyebrows while the man—who had his claws on my girl—feigns no interest at all.

"*The* Mark?" one of the women asks, jaw agape.

They've heard of me. She's told them about me.

"The one," Arden answers casually, tapping at my chest. "But, um, I think I need a raincheck on tonight. I have to...I'm gonna go and catch up." Without awaiting responses, she firmly steers us toward the shadowed patio.

The chilled oceanfront air clashes exhilaratingly with the scorching heat this tenacious woman ignites simply being near me. And when Arden fists both hands into my shirt as leverage to yank my mouth urgently to hers, I lose any remaining restraint. I lift her effortlessly until her legs lock around my waist, our tongues already dueling fiercely. My greedy hands smooth up her bare skin, now appreciating her too-short dress. I kiss down her throat, groaning playfully against the supple flesh I've relentlessly craved the last few weeks.

"Damn, I missed your fireworks down to molecules, baby," I whisper raggedly.

Arden arches sharply as my fingers trace her lace panty lines. "I missed you, too. But how...?"

With her helplessly soft plea, my grasp flexes on her lush curves. "It's a long story. One that can wait until we've properly reunited."

Somehow, her throaty laugh breaks through the desire-laced fog enveloping us. "As tempting as semi-public hookups are with you, security watches this building. Not to mention, my parents could walk by at any moment."

I huff regretfully, glancing at the moonlit beach as my grip gentles to something more publicly decent. Not that anything could douse the volatile thoughts now flooding my brain. "Suppose we could find somewhere a little more private. I've got a hotel room down the street and could call for a ride."

She glints with mischievous glee as she pulls me toward the beach. "I've got a better idea. You're sober enough to drive, right?" At my confused nod, she removes her heels and rushes down the shore ahead of me. "Good."

Slipping off my shoes, I chase after her, my heart pounding in time with her giggling as she zigzags across the sand.

God, I love her laugh.

She stops, breathless and beautiful, outside a row of multi-unit condos. I cage her gently against the crumbling stucco alcove, drinking in her flushed cheeks and fiery eyes.

I love her.

"I'll grab a few things and the keys," she says temptingly, her fingers toying with the collar of my shirt. "Meet you out here in five, and you can tell me what the heck you're doing here."

"What? A guy can't just surprise his gorgeous girlfriend?" I grin.

Arden rolls her eyes, but I catch the smile tugging at her lips as she disappears inside.

Damn, this woman…

When she emerges a few minutes later, I'm leaning against the fence, trying to look casual and failing miserably. My jaw drops when I see her, all long legs and windswept hair, a duffel bag slung over her shoulder.

She shakes her head, tugging me toward the front of the building. "C'mon, hotshot. We'll take my car."

I pause, staring at the four-wheel drive vehicle in front of me as she hands over the keys.

"Never would've pegged you for a Jeep girl."

Arden's throaty laugh lances straight through me. "What? Can't handle it, Mr. Sports Car?"

Challenge accepted.

I catch her around the waist, pulling her flush against me. "Baby, I'll tame you and this beast of a car. Just you watch."

Her nails score wickedly up my bicep, and I flex reflexively, my grip tightening on her hips. *The things this woman does to me.*

"Not here," Arden murmurs, her lashes lowering in a sultry promise that has me ready to combust. "We should go."

She disentangles herself from my arms and climbs into the passenger seat with a coy smile. I take a moment to adjust myself before hopping behind the wheel.

Starting the engine, I glance over at the goddess beside me. Her hair cascades flawlessly across her golden shoulders, the already-short hemline of her black dress riding up to reveal tempting glimpses of her inner thighs.

Four weeks away from her is way the fuck too long.

"Stop gawking and drive, babe," Arden teases, though her flushed cheeks betray her enjoyment of my blatant admiration.

"Sorry, can't help it when you look so damn sexy," I mumble, scrubbing a hand over my face in a vain attempt to focus. "Here, navigate for me, will you? I have no idea where the hell I'm going."

I toss her my phone, grinning as she inputs the hotel's address. "How about you spill why you're here as we go," she suggests, her eyes sparkling with curiosity. "Fewer questions for later."

Smirking, I rehash the day's events as I drive, though my gaze constantly slips to other areas of her body.

Arden shoves me playfully, laughing as she catches me staring for the hundredth time. "Eyes on the road, babe. So, you're here through midday Sunday? How'd I get so lucky?"

I catch a rogue curl, tugging it as I pull into the parking lot. "Oh, you're about to get really lucky."

My hand rests possessively on the small of Arden's back as I guide her out of the Jeep and through the lobby. The ten-minute drive here already making me harder than granite, just thinking about having her all to myself.

We barely make it inside my room before I have her pinned against the door, my mouth claiming hers in a bruising kiss. Arden melts into me instantly, her sultry moan igniting a primal hunger.

Clothes become collateral damage as we tear at each other desperately, needing to eliminate any barriers between us. I worship every inch of newly exposed skin with greedy hands and lips, relishing her breathy gasps and the way she arches into my touch, silently begging for more.

She shoves me onto the bed, her eyes dark with hunger as she crawls over me like a predator stalking her prey. My cock throbs as she grinds against it, her dripping pussy driving me insane with need.

I groan, my hands gripping her hips hard enough to bruise. "Damn, baby. You're so wet."

"It's been a month. Think I didn't miss you?" she pants, teasing my tip against her swollen clit.

A growl rips from my throat at her words, love, lust, and desperation threatening to consume me. I cup her face, pulling her in for a kiss that shifts the mood from desperation to something deeper.

"I missed you," I breathe against her lips. "So much."

Her eyes soften as she blinks down at me.

I drink in the sight of her—flushed, smiling, still utterly wrecked with desire. "I want to feel all of you, Arden," I murmur, my thumb tracing her jawline as I dare to ask, "Bare, if you'll let me."

She studies me, her breath coming in quick pants. "Are you... I mean, have you ever...?"

I shake my head. "Never. Too afraid of…repercussions. But I'm clean, I swear."

"You're not worried now?" she questions softly, quickly adding, "I mean, I'm protected, but…"

"Arden," I cut her off gently, meeting her gaze. "Nothing about you scares me. I'm all in here. Have been since before that night at the bar, if I'm being honest."

Her breath hitches, eyes shining with emotion. "I love you, Mark."

"I love you too, baby," I reply, my voice rough with emotion. "More than I ever thought possible."

I lean in to kiss her again, my hands sliding down Arden's sides, coming to rest on her hips. She moves slightly against me, a soft gasp escaping her throat.

Then she's sinking down on me, and I nearly black out from sheer bliss. Velvet heat grips me like a vice as she takes in every inch, our bodies fitting together like we were made for this.

"God, you feel incredible," I grit out, fighting the urge to blow immediately.

Arden sets a punishing pace, riding me with abandon, nails raking angry red lines down my chest. The sting only heightens every sensation, pushing me closer to the edge.

"That's it, use me," I growl as she chases her high. "Take exactly what you need. I'm all yours."

She comes with a scream of my name and I follow instantly, vision whiting out as I empty myself inside her. Wave after wave of euphoria crashes through me, more intense than anything I've ever felt.

I wrap myself around Arden's quivering form as we gradually float back down, sweat-slicked skin sliding deliciously. Threading my fingers through damp tangles of hair, I pepper kisses across her face, overwhelmed with tender awe. Making love to this woman, being one with her so completely—nothing else compares.

"So that's what heaven feels like," I murmur against her temple.

Arden hums, a little smile on her well-kissed lips. "You enjoyed it?"

"Understatement of the century," I laugh, still catching my breath. I trace her face with my fingertips. "I loved it. Love you. This past month... I never want to be apart that long again."

Something in my tone must give me away because Arden pulls back slightly, her eyes searching mine. "Getting sentimental on me?"

I think about the ring I ordered last month, curious when it'll be in. Because right now, I see it all. Marriage, kids, a white picket fence. Anything and everything this beautiful woman wants.

"Maybe a little," I admit, trying to play it cool. "Is that okay?"

Arden's smile is soft and warm. "More than okay," she says, leaning in for a kiss.

As our lips meet, I'm struck by how right this feels. Not just the physical connection, but everything—the easy banter, the way she sees right through me, the future I can imagine with her by my side.

But I'm not scared. Not even a little. I'm excited.

When I get back from this trip, I'll call Coach Drew. I'll finish putting a plan in place.

For now, though, I just hold Arden tighter and let myself drift off, feeling like the luckiest bastard alive.

31

Arden ♥

Now, September 15ᵗʰ

The sound of the doorbell sends my heart racing before I even reach for the handle. I swing it open, seeing Mark in all his handsome glory, his dark eyes lighting up the moment they land on me.

"Hey, beautiful," he murmurs, pulling me into his arms and burying his face in my hair. "Missed you."

I giggle, snuggling into his embrace as memories of our incredible weekend together flood back. Two nights of pure bliss in a hotel room, spending every waking moment together when he wasn't at the baseball field. It's been more like a dream world than reality.

Now, joining him for the game today? Seeing him in work mode? I couldn't resist.

"It's only been four hours since you saw me," I tease, but I'm grinning like a fool.

"Four hours too long," he counters, pulling back to flash me that heart-stopping smile.

His gaze rakes over my body appreciatively, lingering on my jersey. "I can't tell you how happy I am that you decided to come with. I've been dying to see you dressed for the ballpark. And, damn, you did not disappoint."

His fingers glide over the brim of my baseball cap, and I fight a smile. "Always a charmer, huh?"

"With you in this getup?" He grips my waist, pulling me into him. "I'm not sure I'll be able to focus on anything else."

I roll my eyes, even as tingles pulse everywhere he touches. "I thought you said I wouldn't be a distraction."

Mark smirks, his eyes glinting with mischief. "Yeah, I might have stretched the truth a bit to get you by my side for a few extra hours."

"Mark," I plead as he leans closer, glancing around the empty room before his lips graze mine.

My hands come up to rest on his chest, feeling the steady thrum of his heartbeat beneath my palm. "I won't get you in trouble or anything, will I?"

"Nah," he assures me, his voice a low rumble against my skin. "I don't even work for the team, remember? I'll have my phone. Check-in between innings. It'll be fine."

I let out a shaky breath, my fingers curling into the soft fabric of his shirt. "Then I guess we better go before I make you late, too."

"Javier was warming up when I left. We're good for a few more minutes." He presses a quick kiss to my cheek before pulling back, his expression turning adorably sheepish as he rubs the back of his neck. "I was curious if your parents were around."

My eyes widen, surprise and a hint of panic welling up in my chest. "My parents? Why? You want to meet them?"

Mark takes my hand, his fingers lacing through mine. "I just thought it might be nice, you know? To introduce myself while I was in town."

I search his face, taking in the earnest expression in his dark eyes and the hopeful quirk of his lips. He's putting himself out there, I realize, making an effort to be a part of my life in a way that matters.

"Okay. They're out back," I finally manage.

Mark's answering grin is blinding. "Yeah?"

I nod, guiding him through the house toward the back porch. "Fair warning, though, they can be a bit...intense."

He doesn't have time to answer before we're out the door, glimpsing my parents in typical Sunday afternoon routines—computers at the ready. They both glance up as we approach, identical expressions of surprise on their faces.

Here goes nothing.

"Mom, Dad," I begin, my voice surprisingly steady despite the butterflies in my stomach, "You remember how I said I was heading to a baseball game this afternoon? Well, this is Mark. The guy I'm going with. My boyfriend."

Wow, it feels good to say that. Boyfriend. The man I love. One who loves me back.

Mark extends his hand, his most charming smile in place. "Mr. and Mrs. Cooper, it's a pleasure to meet you. Arden's told me so much about you both."

My father stands, shaking Mark's hand briefly before giving him an assessing look. "Mark, was it? I don't believe we've heard much about you at all."

I wince at his blunt statement, but Mark takes it in stride. "Well, sir, that's probably because Arden and I have been focused on our respective careers. But I care about your daughter very much, and I wanted to take the opportunity to introduce myself while I was in town."

My mother's sharp gaze darts between us, her lips pursed. "And what exactly do you do, Mark? Arden mentioned you're in Chicago?"

"I'm an athletic trainer," he replies smoothly. "I work with professional athletes on injury prevention and rehabilitation. Baseball is my passion. I came down to help a former client who plays for your Tampa team, and Arden's humoring me by joining today."

278 | Nicole Crystal

"Interesting," my father remarks, his tone skeptical. "And you think this...arrangement with Arden is sustainable? With her career here and yours up north?"

Thanks, Dad. Nothing like getting straight to the point.

Mark meets his gaze steadily. "I have faith in us. And who knows where we both end up longer term. Athletic trainers are needed everywhere."

Mark's tender glance, combined with that sentence, echoes in my brain deafeningly. Is he suggesting...?

The flutters in my stomach pause as my mother scoffs, her eyes narrowing. "Faith? That's a bit naïve, don't you think? Relationships take more than just faith, especially when there's distance involved."

I bristle at her condescending tone, but before I can speak, Mark's hand squeezes mine. "With all due respect, Mrs. Cooper, I know that relationships take work. But I'm not one who backs away from a challenge, especially when I know Arden's someone worth fighting for."

My father clears his throat, looking slightly taken aback by Mark's determined response. "Well, I suppose we'll have to trust Arden's judgment on this."

It's not exactly a ringing endorsement, but it's a start. As we say our goodbyes and head toward the car, I can't help but feel a swell of pride and affection for the man beside me. He stood up for us, for our love, without hesitation. That gives me hope that we can find a way to make this work, no matter what obstacles come our way.

"I can't believe you said that," I whisper when we reach my Jeep.

He looks down at me, his expression soft. "Said what? That you're worth fighting for, or that'd I move for you?"

I bite my lip. "Both. But more the latter. You love your job. Chicago. The Rhoades. Giving it all up...there are so many unknowns."

Mark's thumb brushes my cheek. "You overthink things, baby. But not this." His heated exhale fans my lips as he holds my searching stare. "Because I can't breathe without you now. Can't sleep without imagining your body against mine. Can't picture walking on this earth if I'm not beside my best friend."

He runs his finger down my parted lips. "I'll wait however long you want me to, but say the word, and I'll be here. Wherever 'here' is for you."

Could I really do that? Force him to give up everything for me when I couldn't give it all up for him?

I rise up on my toes to brush my lips against his. "I will. Give me some more time, okay? Let me figure out the right long-term plan that works for both of us?"

"Of course." Mark smiles against my mouth, his arms banding around me and pulling me flush against him.

We stay like that for a long moment, lost in each other until the distant sound of a car horn reminds us where we're supposed to be. The game he's in town for.

"To be continued," Mark murmurs, his eyes sparkling with promise as he opens the passenger door for me.

As we drive towards the ballpark, his hand resting possessively on my thigh, giddiness fills me. Because maybe someday, this could be my everyday life, even if it might not happen as soon as I hoped.

The energy of the ballpark is electric as we find our seats, the buzz of the crowd, and the smell of popcorn and hot dogs filling the air. I grin, taking it all in, caught up in the excitement.

"I probably should've asked, but have you ever watched a full baseball game before?" Mark questions, catching me craning my neck to see everything.

I roll my eyes, but can't hide my smile. "I've seen games before. I just...maybe haven't paid this much attention."

"Ah, so you're here for the charming company. Got it."

I elbow him playfully. "Speaking of baseball, what position did you play? Before?"

Mark grins, taking my hand and pointing towards the field. "Shortstop. Right there, between second and third. It's all about quick reflexes and a strong arm. You're basically the field general for the left side."

"Sounds important," I muse. "I bet you were pretty good."

His eyes light up with that familiar cockiness. "Oh, I was spectacular. Still am, just in...different ways now."

I feel my cheeks heat up, memories of just how "spectacular" he can be flashing through my mind. "At the risk of inflating your ego, yes, they're pretty impressive. Though, I could use some more one-on-one lessons just to be sure."

Mark chuckles, his hand finding mine and interlacing our fingers. "This is gonna be a long game."

As the players take the field, I can practically feel Mark's focus shift, his gaze sharpening as he assesses their movements. It's fascinating to watch him work, to see the gears turning in his head as he analyzes each athlete.

"See something interesting, or just admiring the view?" I joke, nudging him with my shoulder.

Mark grins, his eyes never leaving the field. "Can't it be both? But in this case, I'm checking Javier's mobility. He looks good, but I want to keep an eye on that quad."

As if on cue, one of the coaches jogs over to our section, waving to get Mark's attention. "Duty calls," Mark sighs, kissing my cheek. "Be right back."

I watch as he makes his way down to the field, huddling with the coach and the player in question. Even from a distance, I can see the respect and camaraderie between them, the way they listen intently to whatever Mark's saying.

It's a side of Mark I've never witnessed before, and it only makes me fall for him harder.

Before long, he's jogging back up the steps, a boyish grin on his face as he plops down next to me. "Miss me?"

"Terribly," I deadpan, fighting back a smile. "Though, I need my coach close for all these lessons you promised."

He laughs, slinging an arm around my shoulder. "Patience, beautiful."

As the game continues, Mark peppers me with tidbits of baseball trivia and strategy between checking on Javier. I'm fascinated by the knowledge and passion that shines through with every word.

"You know, you're pretty sexy when you talk sports," I tease, trailing a finger down his chest. "All that intensity and focus...it's doing things to me."

Mark's eyes darken, his hand tightening on my thigh. "Careful. Keep talking like that and I might have to find a dark corner to drag you off to."

I grin, heat simmering under my skin at the thought. "Don't make promises you can't keep, Hotshot."

"Never do," he growls in response.

And boy do I know the truth in those words… Promises and rules from last spring ring piercingly.

Somewhere around the seventh inning, Tampa takes a commanding lead, and they pull Javier "to rest," or so Mark says.

"Does that mean you're no longer in work mode? No more trips to check on the catcher between innings?" I ask, drawing distracting patterns down Mark's forearm.

He flashes a wicked grin. "I have to stay close, but nothing keeps us in these seats."

"About that promise—"

I don't even get the rest of the sentence out before Mark's on his feet, tugging me behind him.

I laugh at his eagerness. "Where are you taking me?"

There's a mischievous glint in Mark's eye as he guides me through the labyrinth of hallways beneath the stadium. "Just trust me."

We pass a guard post, and Mark flashes a badge, dropping a few names to ensure no one raises an alarm despite the game being almost over.

Walking a few feet further, Mark turns us toward a shadowy corner, backing me against a locked office door, his mouth trailing hungry kisses from my lips down to the button of my jersey.

"Damn, girl," he mumbles against my skin, setting me ablaze with his touch. "What are you doing to me? Getting me to sneak around just for a better taste of you?"

I gasp dramatically, playing along. "Me? I seem to remember someone talking about 'talents' and making me all hot and bothered."

Mark chuckles, the sound vibrating against my throat. "Fair enough. But what do you expect? You're driving me crazy in this outfit." He scoops me into his arms, carrying me further down the hallway and into a private room.

Yeah, this man doesn't break promises. And it has desire pooling desperately now.

Mark flips on the lights as we stumble into the small medical room, his hands steady as he lifts me onto the exam table. I glance at the clock, my heart racing. "Think we have time for a full assessment, Coach?"

His eyes darken, a mischievous grin spreading across his face. "For you? Always." He pulls off his shirt in one smooth motion. "But we might have to make it a crash course."

I stare, my fingers itching to roam across his toned chest. "Then what are you waiting for? Show me some of these one-on-one lessons."

Mark steps between my legs, his hands sliding up my thighs. "Careful what you ask for, baby."

I roll my eyes, but can't suppress a shiver at his touch. "Less talking, more action, hotshot."

Our lips crash together, the kiss deep and desperate. I moan into his mouth, my hips arching off the table as his fingers find the waistband of my shorts.

I tug at his belt, impatient. "These need to go," I mumble against his mouth.

Mark chuckles, his breath warm on my skin. "Yes ma'am."

In a flurry of movement, we shed our remaining clothes. Then he's back, his body covering mine, the delicious friction making me gasp.

"Ready for me already, Bubbles?" he teases, his kisses inching lower on my chest.

"Been ready since we got here," I breathe, pulling him closer. "Can't seem to get enough of you either."

"Glad we're on the same page," he murmurs into my skin.

He doesn't waste any more time, sinking into me. I cry out, hands gripping the edge of the table as the sensation of him, fully bare and deep, overwhelms me in the best possible way.

My head falls against his shoulder as he moves in a tantalizing rhythm, shifting us, moving until he finds just the right angle and my eyes roll back into my head.

With each thrust, I focus on breathing, but when my hips raise to meet his, everything else fades away.

I can only feel. Be. Trust. Fall with this incredible man.

My nails press into his skin as I start to lose myself.

"Look at me," Mark commands, his hand cupping my cheek. "I want to see you."

I force my eyes open, meeting his heated gaze. The intensity of his stare, the depth of emotion swirling in those dark depths, pushes me over the edge. I shatter around him, his name falling from my lips like a prayer and a curse.

Mark follows right behind, burying his face in my neck as he finds his release. We cling to each other, chests heaving, hearts pounding in sync.

"That was..." I trail off, my mind still hazy with pleasure.

"Scandalous? Spectacular?" Mark offers softly, pressing a soft kiss to my lips. "I'm not sure I give *your* talents enough credit. And those screams, baby..."

Somewhere in the distance, cheers erupt reminding me exactly where we are.

I scrunch my face together. "Yeah. I got a bit loud, huh?"

"My fault. Too much hands-on training," he responds, giving me another peck before peeling himself off me. "But for the record? Best crash course I've ever given."

I roll my eyes as he holds out his hand.

"Come on. Let's get you dressed. I probably need to check in with the medical team by now."

After we hastily redress in the cramped clubhouse room, giddiness keeps sneaking out. We steal more secret kisses, not ready to part from one another.

Finally, Mark releases me, promising to meet me by the car when he finishes his post-game assessment.

I stroll toward the parking lot, my mind still spinning with excitement from our surprise weekend together. And hope erupts at the thought of more weekends like this, the possibility of a future where we can be truly together, and all of this time apart can be a distant memory.

I lean against my Jeep, adjusting my ball cap to a playful angle as I wait for Mark. The late afternoon sun blazes bright, but it's nothing compared to the warmth that surges when I finally spot him heading towards me.

"All good?" I ask breezily, hopping into the driver's seat and maneuvering us out of the parking lot.

Mark frowns, his hand finding my knee. "Unfortunately, yeah."

Right. The end of our time together.

Mark forces a smile, adding, "And nothing's changed about the anniversary party?"

I bite my lip, mentally flipping through my calendar. "It's the twenty-eighth, right?" When Mark nods, I blink away my own disappointment. "I still don't think it's an option. My client pitch is the Monday after. But if by some miracle it can work out, I'll let you know."

The disappointment in Mark's eyes mirror mine, and I hate that I can't promise I'll be there when he wants me to be, maybe even needs me to be... But I shouldn't commit to something I'm not confident I can make. That disappointment would be worse.

We reach the airport too quickly, my heart feeling like it's being squeezed in a vice. I turn to Mark, trying to memorize every detail–the way his hair falls across his forehead, the curve of his jaw, the warmth of his hand in mine.

"See you soon, hopefully?"

"Soon," he repeats, leaning in to trace his lips across my collarbone. "Wish this long-distance thing came with a fast-forward option built in."

I laugh, but it comes out more like a sob. "I suppose I should be proud that Chicago can't function properly without you for a few more days."

Mark cups my face, his eyes searching mine. "Hey, October's almost here. If the party doesn't work out, maybe I can plan more time down here."

October. Why does that sound so far away?

"That'd be nice, Mark."

How can he be so patient? So perfect? Why aren't I as confident?

My expression falls before I rally myself. "C'mon, Romeo, we'll end up sitting in here all night if you don't leave now."

He flashes an adorable puppy dog pout. "Why do you always have to be so logical?"

His tone tells me he's joking, but his words hint at a deeper question I've been asking myself lately, especially after Mark so effortlessly offered to move across the country to be with me.

But before I can think too deeply, Mark tips my chin to his, pressing his lips to mine in a deep and desperate kiss. I cling to him, my fingers digging into his shoulders, wishing I could freeze time and stay in his perfect embrace forever.

"Love your fireworks, Bubbles," he mutters softly.

"Love you, Trouble." I brush my nose against his. "Travel safe and call when you land, please."

His answering smile has me melting into a puddle. "I'll be annoying you nonstop with calls and texts, Juliet."

I watch him walk away, my heart feeling like it's splitting in two: One half leaving with him, and the other still the girl dreaming about breaking glass ceilings and crafting her own success.

How can I choose between something I've always wanted and what I'm starting to realize I can't live without?

32

Arden ♥

Two Weeks Later, September 28th

I stare at my computer screen, relentlessly finishing the presentation for Monday. Despite my mind circling to Mark and the party this evening, I attempt to concentrate.

But I can't.

Taking a quick minute to calm my restless energy, I pull out my phone to message the one person always on my mind.

> Me: *Wishing I could be there tonight. Thinking of you.*
> Mark: *Picking up tuxes with Jake. Gonna need your soothing voice as a lifeline if this crashes badly.*
> Me: *You know I'm always here, babe. Miss you.*
> Mark: *Miss you, too.*

I know how nervous he gets being around his mother, and I'm disappointed I can't be there to steady him. But I couldn't ask for time away—not without reviewing this pitch with my boss first.

"Arden, got a minute?" My boss's voice floats over my cubicle wall. I look up to see him gesturing towards his office, his expression unreadable. "Need to discuss some updates with you."

My stomach does a little flip as I follow him. "Sure, of course."

We chat about current projects for a few minutes, the usual Friday morning rundown. When I mention sending over pages for Monday's presentation by the end of the day, he waves it off. "No rush. This weekend is fine."

His tone has my impatient curiosity pricking. *Should I be worried?*

Finally, he leans back in his chair, a hint of a smile playing on his lips. "I'm sure you're wondering why I called you in here."

I nod, probably a bit too eagerly. "The thought had crossed my mind."

He chuckles. "Alright, I'll cut to the chase. Remember that email about restructuring the associate program?" At my nod, he continues. "Well, there's more to it. We're finalizing some structural changes with the goal of better serving our East Coast clients. There will be a new satellite office launching in New York next month."

East Coast? New York?

"During our leadership meeting, your name came up as part of the new team up there."

My jaw drops. *Is he saying what I think he's saying?*

"I know it's a lot to take in," he says, his tone gentle. "We'd love to keep you here in Tampa, but sometimes the best opportunities for growth are in new ventures."

He pauses, giving me a chance to process. "So, what are your thoughts?"

What do I think? I think New York is even further from where I want to be. I think I'm more confused about my priorities than ever. And I think... I think I might need to take a leap of faith on something–someone–I never expected.

"I...wow. Thank you for considering me," I manage, my mind still reeling. "This is...a lot to process. Could I have some time to think it over?"

"Of course," he responds kindly. "I know you're scheduled to come in this weekend, but why don't you take the weekend and think about it? Send me the presentation and we can review it on Monday morning instead."

I nod numbly, not sure what else to say. My thoughts stray to two weeks ago, to Mark's bold declaration that he'd go anywhere if I asked. Am I willing to do the same?

As he gathers papers, preparing to dismiss me, impulse has words bursting out unexpectedly. "Actually, no. I know my answer. I don't want to go to New York."

My boss settles back into his chair, giving me his full attention again. "No? Based on what we've discussed, I thought you'd be thrilled for the opportunity."

"It's an amazing opportunity, sir." I fidget anxiously for a moment under the sharp scrutiny before finding my courage. "I believe my work performance speaks for itself over these past few months. And I sincerely love the opportunities and growth potential with this firm." I hesitate only briefly, my heartbeat thundering at the thought of veering onto personal grounds with my imposing supervisor. Still, I press forward with atypical candor. "And while New York likely has the brightest fast-track prospects, I think it's best for me to be in Chicago, with or without this firm."

"Chicago?"

"Correct." I hold his assessing gaze, refusing to break eye contact or backpedal despite the anxiety threatening to choke my nerves.

My boss leans forward, his brow furrowed. "I have to say, Arden, this is quite a curveball. I thought you were all in on the corporate fast track."

I take a deep breath, willing my voice to stay steady. "I was. I am. But... I've realized there's something else. Someone else. And I can't ignore that anymore."

My boss studies me for a long moment, and I fight the urge to squirm.

"Well," he finally says, his tone carefully neutral, "this certainly changes things."

My heart hammers as I wait. *Is he upset? Will he dismiss me? Call me out on my bold comment about getting there* with or without *this firm?*

But then, to my shock, a slow smile crinkles the edges of his eyes. "I admire your honesty and courage. It's not easy to stand up for what you want, especially when it deviates from the expected path."

Relief floods, followed by a surge of gratitude. "Thank you, sir. I know it's unorthodox, but I truly believe I can excel in both my professional and personal life in Chicago."

He nods, tapping his pen thoughtfully against the desk. "We had someone else in mind for the Chicago position, but... let me make a call. No promises, and it might not be quite as glamorous, but I'll see what I can do."

"I greatly appreciate your understanding and flexibility," I offer, unable to stop grinning like a love-sick fool.

"Don't thank me yet," he says, but there's a twinkle in his eye. "Just promise me one thing, Arden. Whatever you're chasing in Chicago—career, relationship, whatever—give it your all. No holding back."

A surge of determination rises in my chest. "I promise, sir. I won't let you down. Or myself."

As I leave his office, I feel lighter than I have in months. It's terrifying, this leap I'm about to take. But for the first time in a long time, I'm excited about the future—all of it.

After the life-changing meeting, I step onto the sun-drenched sidewalk, my heart racing with a dizzying realization. I just turned down a promotion to New York and declared my intention to move to Chicago instead. I chose love over career ambition. Choose Mark.

A giddy laugh bubbles up from my chest. I'm really doing this.

I think back to all the moments that led me here: the instant spark when we first met, the way he challenged me, the moment at the hospital when he showed me he could be caring, the bar on my birthday when we reunited, the nights of movies at his apartment where we fell in love, and the conversation six weeks ago when we stopped fighting this inevitable soul-deep connection.

I've been arguing the unavoidable, trying to protect myself from the terrifying intensity of my feelings for Mark. But in that office, faced with the choice between a glittering career opportunity and a chance at real, heart-stopping love, I finally found the courage to leap into the unknown. And isn't that what love is? What I told Mark so many months ago? True love should be all-consuming. The kind of passion that defies logic and reason.

My phone buzzes, startling me from my trance. It's my boss. I click open the email with shaking fingers, hardly daring to breathe.

Arden, I have some good news. I spoke with leadership. They're going to entertain your idea of transferring to Chicago. Consider it tentatively approved. Let's chat the details more next week.

It's not the resounding "yes" I'd hoped for, but it's a "maybe"—and that's enough. Even if it turns into a "no," my mind is made up. I'm going.

The weight of my decision settles over me like a warm blanket. I'm about to turn my life upside down, potentially leaving my job, definitely leaving Tampa. I'm diving headfirst into the unknown, and for once, the thought doesn't terrify me. It exhilarates me.

For years, I've lived by spreadsheets and five-year plans. I've chosen the safe route, the logical path. But now? I'm choosing love. I'm choosing Mark. And somehow, it feels like I'm finally choosing myself.

This isn't about giving up my career ambitions. It's about realizing I can have both—a fulfilling career and a life with the man I love. It's about understanding that sometimes, the biggest risks bring the greatest rewards.

My fingers fly over my phone screen as I book the next flight to Chicago. My heart races, imagining Mark's face when he sees me, the feeling of being in his arms after weeks apart.

I know it won't be easy. There will be conversations with my family, moments of doubt, challenges to overcome. But for the first time in my life, I'm certain that it's all worth it. He's worth it.

As I rush home to pack, a grin spreads across my face. Sensible, predictable Arden Cooper is throwing caution to the wind, chasing her own version of happily ever after.

And you know what? It feels pretty damn good.

When the plane touches down in Chicago, panic overtakes any sense of destiny and romantic gestures. *The party.* I have no idea where it is, and with how quickly I packed, I didn't grab anything more fancy than a casual sundress. *Didn't Mark mention tuxes?* This impulsive act seems more absurdly ill-planned by the second...

During the agonizingly slow taxi to the gate, I repeatedly try Mark's phone, my nerves skyrocketing as each attempt rings endlessly into voicemail. My voice shakes slightly as I leave a vague message, saying I'm just checking in.

He'll probably freak out when he sees the multiple missed calls and assume something drastic. Knowing Mark, he'll start calling the hospitals in the area if he can't reach me.

Desperation—and a new idea—has me pulling up Jake's contact info. The background noise nearly drowns Jake out as he answers on the second ring, confirming the event is already well underway. I rush to explain the spontaneous travel whim before he gets distracted, pleading for the party details.

Miraculously, Jake doesn't even question the last-minute scheme. He's excited about it. He promises to text me the address. I clutch the phone tighter, heart in my throat, daring to make one last vulnerable request before courage fails me.

"Is there any chance you could hold off mentioning to Mark that I'll be crashing? I'd love to surprise him if possible." I hold my breath, praying I don't sound completely unhinged. Because, let's face it, who in their right mind would fly across the country on a whim to crash their boyfriend's family party?

But Jake just laughs good-naturedly. "Sure thing! Get over here soon, though I, uh…" he pauses awkwardly. "He needs you, Arden. You balance him."

We balance each other, I mentally correct as my heart throbs, picturing Mark at the anniversary party with his parents.

"I'm on my way," I reply, glancing down at my outfit. As soon as I find something that screams, *I'm not a complete disaster, please love me.*

"Sending the address now, Arden. See you soon."

I exhale as the call ends. This can still work.

Months ago, I'd never have dreamed of such a spontaneous, romantic gesture. But now? I'm ready to take a chance on love, even if it means stepping out of my comfort zone.

Entering a nearby store, I imagine what Mark's reaction will be when he sees me. Will he be shocked? Thrilled? Maybe a little bit of both? I picture him in a tux, his dark eyes widening in surprise before a grin spreads across his handsome face. The thought sends a flutter of anticipation through my stomach.

But as I browse the racks of dresses, a flicker of doubt creeps in. What if I'm overdressed? Underdressed? What if Mark's family thinks I'm crazy for showing up uninvited?

No.

I know better.

I'm confident. I'm in love. And I'm not just doing this for Mark. I'm doing it for me, too. I'm choosing to be bold, to take risks, to follow my heart. And that's something the old Arden would never have done.

Just as the thought filters in, my eyes catch on an emerald dress nestled between a sea of black and navy. It's elegant yet daring, with a plunging neckline and a thigh-high slit.

I slip into the dress, marveling at the way it transforms me. I look like a woman ready to take on the world and fight for what she wants. And what I want is a future with Mark, no matter how unconventional or unexpected it may be.

With a renewed sense of purpose (and a silent prayer for grace in heels), I pay for the dress and head out to hail a cab. My heart is pounding, my palms are sweaty, but I've never felt more alive. Because today, I bet on myself, and the prize: The career *and* the man I love.

33

Mark

Now, September 28ᵗʰ

Laughter spills from the reserved party room as I fidget with my bow tie, the fabric suddenly more restricting than it was on the drive over, or during the quick stop at the jewelry store. I was tempted to drive out Thursday when Coach Drew, also the owner of Drew Jewelers, let me know my order had arrived. But with Arden not coming, I didn't see the point of a special trip to the suburbs. Not when I'd be in town a few days later.

Now, with a ring in my pocket, at an anniversary party for my "second" family, I feel strangely nervous.

I scan the crowded space, familiar faces all blending together—old neighbors, former teachers, and even a few exes lingering near the bar. My shoulders tense, bracing against the impending small talk and prying questions from more than just my mother.

Most knew me either as the high school baseball star or the serial heartbreaker who never stayed with a girl longer than it took milk to expire. The name whispered behind hands if I approached an attractive former classmate, the warning given by wary fathers if I lingered too long catching up with their daughters home from college.

296 | Nicole Crystal

Their assumptions used to amuse my reckless ego. Now, with Arden in my life, they only highlight the empty space beside me where she should be. My fingers twitch for my phone, picturing one particular smile who showed me I was capable of more than fleeting hookups. *Damn, I wish she was here.* But maybe it's better she doesn't have to witness so much of my past on full display.

Mrs. Rhoades spots me near the entrance, her face lighting up as she pulls me into a warm hug. "Mark! I'm so glad you could make it." She assesses me with a knowing look. "I'm disappointed Arden couldn't be here, too."

I laugh, shaking my head. "Jake told you, huh?"

"He keeps me updated on all my boys," she says with a wink. "Don't worry, Mark. Have some faith. Absence makes the heart grow fonder."

"I just wish she could be here, growing fonder with me," I admit, surprising myself with the vulnerability.

Mrs. Rhoades pats my arm, her eyes filled with understanding. "She seems like someone really special to you."

My hand drifts to my pocket, feeling the weight of the small box inside. *Someone special, indeed.*

As Mrs. Rhoades returns to the party, I crack my neck as renewed purpose settles in. Time to embrace the man I'm becoming, the one Arden has helped me discover.

I make my way through the room, snagging a drink to steel my nerves for the inevitable confrontation with my parents. My mother's artificial laughter grates on my ears as I approach their table. My father acknowledges me with a cursory nod, though his attention is already absorbed in some sports recap on the device in his hands.

Glancing around the table set for eight, I wince.

Shit.

We're seated with Lanie and her family. Mrs. Rhoades probably thought she was doing us a favor, not realizing the history there, since Lanie's mom and mine have become best friends.

Lanie greets me with a flirty smile, her eyes darting around in search of my date. I can practically see the wheels turning in her head when she realizes I'm alone.

I grit my teeth, reminding myself that her opinion doesn't matter. I know why Arden isn't here, and that's all that counts.

"So wonderful to see you dragged yourself away from the cocktails, dear," my mother greets.

I offer a tight smile. "Nice to see you again, too, Mom."

"Yes! Mark, great to see you," Lanie's mother adds. "Heard you're traveling for some fancy new career now."

Work. Maybe there's hope for casual dinner conversation after all.

As we chat about my job rather than my love life, I relax, sharing stories from my summer travels. The table listens intently to my thoughts on pre-game warm-ups and season workout regimens. I even catch the pride on my father's face as I share some of the recent work I did in Arizona. *Partly why they wanted to hire me a few months back*, I think, rather than say out loud. Because no one needs to know why I turned it down. Though I'm sure they could guess.

Eventually, the ladies shift to other topics, and my dad and I discuss baseball playoff predictions.

I'm halfway through my dessert when I feel it - Mom's laser-focused stare boring into me. Her lips curl into that smile I know all too well, the one that says she's about to go for the jugular.

Here we go. I knew making it through dinner drama-free was too much to hope for.

"So, Mark," she drawls, topping off her wine glass with exaggerated slowness. "I couldn't help but notice you haven't mentioned that girl you're back together with. Arden, was it? Any particular reason she's not here tonight?"

I meet her gaze head-on, keeping my voice steady. "Arden's got a work thing in Florida this weekend."

"Ah, yes. Florida." Mom's lips thin as she glances at Lanie's mother. "Long distance must be so... challenging. Remind us, dear, what is it she does down there?"

I sit up straighter, refusing to let her condescension get to me. "She's a consultant. And she's brilliant at what she does."

I catch Lanie's eye across the table. "And yes, it's long-distance. Not just a flavor of the month."

Lanie's smile falls, no doubt recalling her words our last run-in.

Dad clears his throat, surprising me by jumping in. "Alright, let's ease up on the interrogation. The boy's clearly happy."

I shoot him a grateful look, still getting used to this newfound understanding between us.

Mom's eyes narrow, but she plasters on a smile. "Of course, I'm just looking out for our son's best interests. Can't wait until he brings that little pearl around again."

"Thanks for the concern, Mom," I say, lifting my glass in a mock toast. "But at twenty-four, I think I know what's best for me."

The Mark who craved her fickle approval would've flinched at the malice in her tone. But I'm not the kid who requires her attention any longer, the one who needs to be seen as more than a disappointment.

Lanie leans forward, her voice saccharine sweet. "Well, I think it's great that you're trying something new, Mark. But if things don't work out with your long-distance girl, know you've always got a friend here."

I bite back a sharp retort, offering a polite smile. "Thanks, Lanie, but she's it for me."

Dad nods, and I see a flash of that pride I've been chasing for years. "Glad you found someone special, son. Hold on tight to her."

His words hit home, reminding me of the regrets he carries. And suddenly, I'm overwhelmed with gratitude—for his support, for Arden, for the man I'm becoming.

As the conversation shifts, I can't help but think about Arden. God, I wish she was here. But even across the miles, her influence is clear. She's made me stronger, more sure of myself. And that's worth more than any approval I could get from this table.

With dinner concluding I make an excuse to bolt and head straight for the Rhoades brothers, who are holding court near the dance floor. Their familiar banter and good-natured ribbing are a welcome distraction from my mother and the Arden-shaped hole at my side.

At one point, Jake breaks away from the group, his phone pressed to his ear. He's talking in hushed tones, his eyes darting to me every few seconds. I raise my brow as he returns, but Tessa beats me to the interrogation.

"What was that about?"

Jake's cheeks go crimson. "Nothing important. Work stuff."

I watch them bicker, remembering the drama from last month. It hits me then—am I crazy for thinking about proposing to Arden already?

If these two can't get past one fight after two years together, what chance do Arden and I have after a measly twelve weeks?

A hand on my shoulder pulls me from my thoughts. I turn to find Coach Drew, his familiar grin a welcome sight.

"Bell, I had a feeling I'd see you here," he says, his voice dropping to a conspiratorial whisper. "Did you make it to the shop? Pick up that special something?"

I nod, patting my pocket where the small box sits, its weight both comforting and terrifying. The idea of having something as ridiculous as engagement ring on me still feels surreal. If someone had told me a year ago that I'd be considering marriage, I would've laughed in their face.

Coach Drew's grin widens, his eyes twinkling with understanding. "I'm glad you came to me last month. It was great catching up, and even better hearing about this girl who's got you ready to settle down."

I let out a small laugh. "Settle down? Coach, trust me, Arden's going to keep me on my toes more than settle anything."

"They always do, son," he chuckles, a fond look crossing his face as he glances at his wife across the room. After a moment, he turns back to me. "Have you given any more thought to that coaching offer? We're still looking for someone with your expertise."

The idea of coaching, of stepping away from the high-pressure world of professional sports medicine, is still a new one. It rolls around in my mind, tempting and terrifying all at once.

"I'm not looking to switch gears just yet," I admit. "But who knows what the future holds, right?"

Coach nods, understanding in his eyes. "Well, when the travel starts to wear on you, my number hasn't changed. You might surprise yourself with how much you enjoy the suburban life someday."

I shake my head, but don't hide my smile. Coach leans in closer, his voice low. "Any idea when you might pop the question?"

"Not yet," I confess, the uncertainty of our future weighing on me. "We're still figuring some stuff out. I guess I'll know when it feels right."

Like where we're going to be living and if she even wants me to consider giving up my job.

"Keep me posted," he says, patting my arm before disappearing into the crowd.

I rejoin the guys, letting myself get lost as we catch up with old friends and listen to people gush about the Rhoades' forty years together.

As the music grows in volume, I spot Jake pulling Tessa to the dance floor. They look happy, like they're finally getting over whatever happened between them. Maybe they'll be okay after all. Jake catches my eye across the space, giving me a nod and mouthing something that looks suspiciously like "Good luck."

Good luck? What the hell is that supposed to mean?

Before I can question it further, something catches my eye and the rest of the room disappears. I trace the path of chestnut waves falling over an emerald green dress, not daring to believe it.

It can't be...

I blink hard, thinking the whiskey's messing with me. But as she gets closer, her face coming into focus under the fancy chandeliers, I know I'm not hallucinating.

It's her. It's Arden.

34

Arden ♥

Now, September 28th

My heart races as I navigate through the unfamiliar faces, my eyes scanning the crowd for the one person I flew across the country to see. The dazzling lights and elegant décor barely register as I search the room for Mark, my mind focused solely on him.

As I weave through the guests, I feel a prickle of awareness, like a magnetic pull guiding me to him. And then, as if the universe is aligning in our favor, the crowd parts. There he is, standing in the center of the room, his gaze locked on mine.

Mark's eyes widen with disbelief as he takes me in, his lips parting in surprise. I drink in the sight of him, looking devastatingly handsome in his fitted tuxedo, and a giddy laugh bubbles up from my chest.

In two strides, he's in front of me, reaching for my hands and tugging me closer. "Arden? What are you doing here? I thought you couldn't make it."

"I couldn't miss the chance to see you so dressed up, could I?" I tease, my hands framing his face as I smile up at him.

"You planned to come?" His voice is thick with emotion, his eyes searching mine for answers.

I fall against him, my body melting into his embrace. "To be honest, it was sort of a spur-of-the-moment decision. But it's one I should have made sooner."

Mark grins, his body swaying to the beat of the music as he holds me close. "You don't do 'spur-of-the-moment,' baby."

"Apparently I do for you," I whisper, inhaling his familiar scent that smells like home now. "You wanted me to be here, and I told you no. I'm sorry it took me so long to realize my mistake."

He pulls back, concern etched in his handsome features. "What about your presentation? Your work this weekend?"

I draw his lips to mine, kissing him softly before asking, "Can we find somewhere to talk?"

"Is everything okay?" There's confusion and concern in his tone now.

I glance to my side, catching a grinning Jake watching us like a proud brother, and the joy inside me fizzes like the champagne he's holding. "Everything's perfect, actually."

Before he can question me further, I lace my fingers through his and lead him toward the exit, seeking a quieter place to share my news.

As we're about to leave the ballroom, a familiar figure steps into our path, her sequined dress catching the light. Mark's mother stands before us, her lips curved into a sugary smile that doesn't quite reach her eyes as she assesses our intertwined hands.

Mark's stride falters, his body tensing as if preparing for battle, but I pull him back, my fingers squeezing his. *We can handle this.*

"Arden, darling," his mother coos, her saccharine tone dripping with insincerity. "What a lovely surprise to see you here. Mark said you weren't coming. Ironically, we were just talking about how important communication is in a relationship. Especially a long-distance one."

Mark's jaw clenches, and I can feel him struggling to hold back a sharp retort. I catch his gaze, attempting to reassure him. *Nothing can touch us tonight.*

Taking a deep breath, I face his mother with a dazzling smile and a lifted chin. "You're absolutely right, Diane. Communication is key. That's why I wanted to surprise Mark tonight." I pause for effect, savoring the flicker of uncertainty in her eyes. "I have some incredible news to tell him, and I wanted to see his reaction in person."

"News?" Mark asks softly, turning to me with a puzzled expression.

I nod, no longer able to contain my excitement. "I requested a transfer. Here. In Chicago."

Mark's eyes blow wide, his mouth falling open in disbelief. "Wait, what? When? How?"

Tears threaten to spill over as the reality of my decision hits me. "I talked with my boss about it earlier today. He thought it could work out. I don't have all the details yet, but—"

Mark's arms engulf me, cutting off my words as he lifts me off the ground and spins me around, his laughter ringing through the ballroom. "This is incredible! You're incredible!"

Why didn't I do this sooner? Why'd I doubt how he'd react?

When he sets me down, his eyes search mine, a hint of concern in his voice. "You're not giving up anything, right? You didn't change your career plans?"

"No," I assure him, my smile stretching from ear to ear. "I get to keep my job *and* be with you. But even if it doesn't work the way I want it to, it doesn't change what I want Mark."

I watch as my statement fully sinks in.

His eyes soften, like a chocolate bar left in the sun. He reels me in for a kiss that makes my toes curl and my brain short-circuit. And when we come up for air, he's sporting a grin wider than the Grand Canyon.

"You brilliant, unbelievable woman," he chuckles, his forehead pressed to mine. "Here I was, thinking I was being all smooth, and you've already got our future mapped out."

I can't help but smirk. "Future, huh? Bold of you to assume I haven't already picked out our kids' names."

A pointed cough shatters our little bubble of bliss, and we break apart to find his mother watching us, her expression a perfect cocktail of shock and confusion. "Well, isn't this...development...just lovely," she manages, her smile razor-sharp.

Mark keeps his arm firmly around my waist, turning to face his mom with an air of confidence I've never seen. "You're absolutely right, Mom. We should celebrate!" He glances back at me with a roguish wink. "And if you'd like to join the party, you might want to get used to Arden being around. She's kind of my favorite person."

Diane's features soften as she stares at her son. "Oh, Mark. I know that's how you feel now. It's just...I don't want to see you regret your choices. End up in a situation you didn't ask for..."

Mark pulls me closer, as if I might disappear if he lets go. "Mom, this isn't your life. This isn't your story. We're not seventeen and panicking. Arden and I... I love her, can't imagine my life without her. My only regret would be letting this amazing woman slip away because I was too scared to grab happiness with both hands." He pauses for dramatic effect. "So, it's up to you if you want to support us, if you want to be a part of your future grandchildren's lives."

"Grandchildren?!" Diane and I squeak in perfect harmony, our eyes wider than dinner plates.

Mark shrugs, his grin more mischievous than ever. "Well, not right away. I figured we'd start with a goldfish and work our way up. You know, test the waters."

His mother clasps her heart, letting out a relieved breath. "Thank goodness, Mark. You just about gave me a panic attack."

But Mark's attention is all on me, his eyes sparkling with barely contained laughter. He leans in close, his whisper tickling my ear. "Just roll with it, okay? We can discuss the whole mini-Bell-Cooper's later."

Without missing a beat, I press my lips to his ear, fighting back a giggle. "You know, someday you'll make an amazing father. I mean, just look at how well you handle your mother. Our future goldfish is going to thrive."

Mark chuckles, lacing his fingers through mine and tugging me away from his open-mouthed mother. "Come with me, beautiful. There's something else I need to ask you."

Curiosity and anticipation buzz through my veins as Mark leads me toward the DJ booth. "What are you doing, Mark?"

He gives me a small, secretive smile. "Do you trust me, Arden?"

"Yes, but…"

I trail off as Mark taps the microphone, drawing the attention of the entire room. He looks out at the sea of faces, his expression nervous but determined.

"Excuse me, everyone. I know you're probably sick of speeches by now, but I was wondering if I could have your attention for a moment."

As the room quiets, Mark motions toward Mr. and Mrs. Rhoades. "We're here today celebrating Ruth and John's forty years of marriage. And for the last nineteen years, I've had the privilege of living next door, of watching them through the eyes of a child and teenager, recognizing the way they love and support each other and their three boys."

Mrs. Rhoades reaches for her husband's hand, squeezing gently.

"And I know a lot of you are thinking, 'Since when does Mark know anything about love?'" Quiet laughter sounds throughout the room at his purposeful pause. "But the truth is, it's these two who really showcase what it means to encourage each other, to seek compromise, and to always put the other's needs above your own."

Mark turns to me, his gaze intense and filled with a love so profound it steals my breath. "I never knew what that was like. To want to put someone else's needs above your own, to constantly strive to be someone better and more deserving, to feel like you can't breathe without the other...until I met you, Arden."

Is this really happening? After all the rules, the doubts, the obstacles, could he be saying what I think he's saying?

"Arden Cooper, you are the most incredible, passionate, and beautiful woman I have ever known. You walked into my life and turned my world upside down in the best possible way. You showed me what it means to love deeply, to fight for what you want, and to never settle for anything less than extraordinary."

Tears spring to my eyes as Mark reaches into his pocket and drops to one knee, revealing a stunning diamond ring that glitters under the chandeliers.

A ring? Is he proposing? I thought he was just going to say something about my move to Chicago!

But he wants forever. With me.

How is it possible that this man, this wonderful, infuriating, perfect man, loves me with such depth and intensity?

"I once told you that I didn't believe in forever," Mark says softly, his voice trembling. "But I was wrong. Because when I'm with you, forever doesn't seem long enough. I want it all with you, Arden. The house, the kids, the forever. I want to grow old with you by my side, face every challenge and celebrate every joy together."

He pauses, a playful twinkle in his eye. "And just to be clear, I know you have a career and dreams, so when I say kids, we're completely on your timeline. But I'm just putting it out there that I'm open to a whole basketball team. Maybe even a baseball team if you're feeling ambitious."

Laughter ripples through the room, and I can't help but giggle, even as happy tears stream down my face.

"Of course, Jake might need to move out before we get started," he adds, glancing back at a grinning Jake in the crowd.

Mark's expression softens when he faces me again. "If you haven't figured it out yet, what I'm trying to ask, Arden Cooper, is will you marry me?"

As I stare down at him, a thousand memories flash through my mind. The first time we met, the spark of attraction that ignited between us. The pain of his rejection, the tentative hope he offered at the hospital. The laughter, the passion, the quiet moments of understanding that brought us closer together. And through it all, the undeniable, unshakable love that has grown and flourished, rooting itself so deeply in my heart that I can't imagine my life without him.

"Yes," I whisper, my voice wavering with the force of my emotions. "A million times, yes!"

The room erupts in cheers and applause as Mark slides the ring onto my finger, but I barely hear them. All I can see is him, his eyes glistening with unshed tears, his smile brighter than the sun. He surges to his feet, pulling me into a kiss that sets my soul on fire.

In this perfect, shining moment, I feel a sense of completeness that I never knew was possible. This man, this love, is everything I never knew I needed, everything I never dared to dream of. And now, with the promise of forever stretching out before us, I know that together, we can overcome anything.

Even a whole baseball team of kids, I think with a giddy smile.

When we finally pull back, Mark's eyes shine with emotion. "I love you, Arden," he whispers, his voice barely audible above the noise throughout the room. "I know this is fast, and I promise, from here on out, we can take our time with everything else. I don't care if you wait five years to marry me. I just needed you to know how much you mean to me."

"I love you, too," I breathe, my heart so full it feels like it might burst. "Was this the plan? If I came tonight?"

Mark shrugs, pressing a quick kiss to my lips. "I picked up the ring earlier today. Told myself I'd wait for the perfect time. And right now seemed perfect."

"When did you decide this? That you were buying a ring?" I ask, still bubbling with happiness.

That boyish smile spreads across Mark's face. "The day I called you from the Rhoades' house."

He already knew then?

"But, Mark…" I trail off, warmth flooding through me. "You hadn't even seen me again after…"

He knew then, and I was still questioning if our spark would be the same.

"Like I said earlier, Arden, you turned my world upside down. I may not have known I'd ask tonight, but I knew that day, hearing your voice, there was no one else for me."

How do I even deserve this man?

"Mark…" I tug him through the party, and the murmurs of congratulations and quick hugs until we're outside alone. Then, I pull him close and kiss him like it's that first time all over again. Like he's my favorite taste, the one I never knew I loved so much until the first time I tried it. Like he's the oxygen I need to breathe.

And maybe he is.

After all, I'm not sure I was fully alive until this man showed up in my life.

"You're my forever, too, Mark," I breathe against his lips.

"Mmm. Should've known it from the beginning, Widow Maker."

I giggle at the nickname. Who'd have known that girl looking for a distraction in that playboy's bedroom would end up here, engaged, not even two years later.

Now, standing here, curled in his arms, kissing him, I realize this future is a million times better than anything I could have imagined then. Mark's better than anything I could have imagined.

I know it won't always be this easy, but there's no one I'd rather break all the rules with for the rest of my life than this sweet, sexy, supportive man.

Game on, life. We're ready to play.

Epilogue

Arden ♥

Five Years Later, November

We perch tensely on the edge of the rumpled bed, silence heavy as we await fate's verdict. Mark's thumb traces restless patterns over my knuckles, and I get lost in their movement, trying to distract my nerves from the alarm that's about to sound.

I think about how far we've come since that first night I fell into his bed at the Christmas party six years ago, the guarded and skeptical-of-love girl I was. Then again, I never would have imagined that the cocky, commitment-phobic boy I'd met would become the rock I lean on, the person who taught me to take risks and embrace the messy, beautiful chaos of life, the man who has stood by my side as my husband for nearly four years.

Our journey hasn't been easy. We've faced our fair share of obstacles, from family drama to career ups and downs intermixed with personal growth. And I'd like to think that through it all, our love has only grown stronger, but this last year of trying and failing to get pregnant has been the hardest test we've endured so far.

Mark tilts my chin up as if sensing my spiraling thoughts until I meet his darkened eyes. "No matter what, I love you, baby." His lips find mine, equal parts fierceness and reverence. "You're already my whole world, okay?"

His silent, I've got you, doesn't need to be said.

I cling tighter as Mark's finger runs across the lip firmly tucked beneath my teeth.

"Careful not to hurt that lip. I enjoy it too much."

I can't help but smile, even as anxiety spikes inside.

When the two-minute timer finally warns, I nudge Mark gently toward the test awaiting nearby, still too nervous to check myself. I don't know how I'll manage another no. He presses a kiss to my temple, lingering on my skin an extra second before retreating into the attached bathroom.

A moment later, his body is framed in the doorway, hands clutching the wood on either side, expressionless.

"Well?" I ask, my heart pounding.

Slowly, a grin spreads across his face, his eyes shining. "It's positive. We're pregnant. Well, you're pregnant."

I let out a sound that's half-laugh, half-sob as Mark pulls me into his arms. "Really? This is really happening?"

Mark cups my cheeks, his touch gentle and reassuring as he brushes away tears. "It's happening, babe. We're going to be parents."

I search his face, drinking in every detail of this moment. The joy in his eyes, the tender curve of his smile, the way he looks at me like I'm his entire world. "I love you so much," I whisper.

"I love you too," Mark says, his thumbs gently wiping away my tears. "More than I ever thought possible." His hand drifts to my stomach. "I always knew there'd be a little Bell-Cooper in our future."

I smile, recalling his comment from our talk at the cafe about our "rules."

Covering his hand with mine, a wave of emotion washes over me. "What do you think they'll be like?"

Mark pretends to ponder, but his eyes never leave mine. "Well, with your brains and my charm, they'll be unstoppable."

I laugh through my tears. "Poor kid won't stand a chance."

"Hey," Mark says softly, his expression turning serious. "We've got this. You're going to be an amazing mother, Arden."

I smile, overwhelmed by the love and certainty I see in his eyes. "And you're going to be an incredible father."

Our lips meet in a kiss that's tender and passionate all at once, filled with all the emotions words can't express. As Mark lifts me up, I wrap my legs around his waist, feeling the solid strength of him.

"I think," I murmur against his lips, "this calls for a celebration."

Mark grins, that cocky, irresistible grin that still makes my heart skip a beat. "I couldn't agree more, Mrs. Bell."

As he lays me on the bed, his touch reverent and loving, I'm struck by how far we've come. From that first night at the bar to this moment, creating a life together. It hasn't always been easy, but looking into Mark's eyes, feeling the love that surrounds us, I know without a doubt:

Every struggle, every moment of doubt, every leap of faith was worth it. Because it led us here, to this perfect moment, and to the beautiful future stretching out before us.

As Mark's lips trail down my neck, my whole body buzzing with love and desire, my phone suddenly blares to life. We both groan in frustration.

"Ignore it," Mark murmurs against my skin.

I'm tempted, so tempted, but a glance at the screen makes my heart skip. "It's Cora. I should... she hasn't called in months."

Mark sighs, but his eyes are understanding. "Of course. Go ahead."

I answer, my voice bright. "Cora! Hey—" But my smile falters as I hear muffled sobs on the other end. "Cora? What's wrong?"

Mark sits up, concern etching his features. His hand finds mine, a silent show of support.

"Slow down, honey," I say, trying to keep my voice calm. "Take a deep breath and tell me what happened."

As Cora's story unfolds between hiccups and broken sentences, my stomach drops. I meet Mark's questioning gaze and mouth, "Logan cheated." They'd been together three years and just got engaged last month. We didn't even have the chance to celebrate it together yet.

Mark's jaw clenches, but he doesn't say a word. Instead, he squeezes my hand, his eyes asking what I need.

"Listen, Cora," I say, my voice steady despite the anger and sadness churning inside me. "We're coming. Right now. Just...stay where you are, okay? We'll be there as soon as we can."

I end the call, and Mark's already on his feet, grabbing our jackets. "I'll drive," he says simply.

As we head out, I can practically hear the gears turning in Mark's head. "I know what you're thinking," I say softly. "But please, no 'I told you so' tonight."

Mark's eyes soften as he helps me into the car. "Hey, I'm here for you and Cora. No judgments, just support."

I lean into his touch, overwhelmed with gratitude. "Thank you."

As we drive, the silence is heavy with unspoken thoughts. Finally, Mark breaks it. "How are you holding up, Arden? It's been quite a rollercoaster the last hour."

I exhale heavily. "I'm... I don't know. I'm over the moon about us, about the baby." I glance at him, catching his eye briefly. "But Cora... God, I can't believe this happened. I really thought they were doing better after the engagement."

Mark nods, squeezing my hand. "Maybe it's for the best she found out now, before they got married."

"Best?" I frown. "Mark, she's heartbroken."

He sighs, choosing his words carefully. "He's a manipulator. We both knew it years ago. He's the reason she pushed you away. And it's hard…the way she's treated you, knowing how it makes you feel."

"What would you have done if it were Jake calling?" I regret the words the minute they slip from my mouth.

Mark's grip on the steering wheel tightens, his voice strained. "Jake's situation is different, Arden. He's been through hell and back, but he's trying to make amends. Cora keeps running back to the same toxic patterns. You can't compare the two."

I lean over, wrapping my arm around his shoulder. "You're right, Jake's had it rough. It isn't the same. Still, it's hard to watch how he's shut you out, too."

Mark takes a deep breath, clearly reframing his thoughts. "I know. I get it. They're family. And however this goes down with Cora, we face it together. Always."

His strong hand finds mine, thumb tracing my knuckles—a silent promise of unwavering partnership. Tears slip down my cheeks in gratitude. However chaotic our life becomes in welcoming this child, at least Cora will have Mark selflessly shielding her, too.

"Always, Mark." I lean closer, pressing kisses of wordless thanks to his cheek. "Who knows, maybe Jake will come around soon, too."

Mark nods, but I can see the flicker of doubt in his eyes. I think back to the day Jake's life forever changed, the day he pushed everyone away.

"We don't give up on family," I whisper.

Mark brings our joined hands to his lips, tenderly kissing my knuckles. "What did I do to deserve you, Arden Bell?"

"I ask myself the same thing every day," I murmur, glancing up to see his intense stare as we pull up to Cora's apartment. "I love you and our little family."

"Our growing, little family," he echoes, pressing his forehead to mine. "Now let's go take care of your sister."

My heart swells for the man at my side, the one who's already ready to catch me when I stumble. And no matter what challenges lie ahead, I know that together, we can face anything…even Cora's break-up and Jake's spiraling life choices.

Our family may be small and imperfect, but it's ours. And we'll fight for it, today and every day, forever and always.

Read more about Cora and Jake's story in
Rewriting December

Bonus Content

The day Mark Bell and Arden Cooper reunited at the hospital, was also the same day fate pulled together Jake Rhoades and Cora Cooper… What happened five years later after Mark and Arden picked her up? And why wasn't Jake speaking with Mark anymore?

Find out in

Rewriting December

Rewriting December
1

Cora

I stare at the final page on my screen, cringing as the protagonists ride off into the sunset for their happily ever after. If only editing romance novels aligned with reality—an epic love story that explodes like an overstuffed pillow.

No. The stories I'm assigned don't conclude with their sister, husband in tow, picking them up outside their apartment with only two suitcases and a box of tear-soaked tissues after discovering their fiancé had been cheating on them for months.

Bing!

I tap the notification without thinking. Logan's name mocks me from the tiny screen, my personal reminder why love isn't enough. And despite my best efforts, the tears fall as that familiar cocktail of humiliation, grief, and exhaustion hits once again.

Three damn weeks of this. Three weeks since I stormed out, leaving Logan silhouetted in the doorway, his tattered excuses echoing down the hall. How long until that image becomes a distant memory instead of the picture burned into my brain?

My sister appears in the doorway, interrupting my spiral. "Another bad day?"

"If, by bad, you mean I'm fresh out of wine and dignity? Then absolutely," I respond, bitterness seeping into my voice as I toss the phone out of view.

Arden winces, but her voice remains calm like always. *She's going to make an excellent mother.* "It's only been twenty days, hon. Go easy on yourself. You'll be back on your feet in no time."

I snort. Back on my feet? I'm holed up in my sister's guest room, and I've barely left it since I got here. I even skipped Thanksgiving last week just to cozy up under the covers solo. I'd be thrilled to 'see the light of day' at this rate.

As if reading my mind, Arden tugs at my arm. "Come on. We're going downstairs to the coffee shop. You need to get out of this apartment."

"Arden, no—" I start to protest, but she's already pulling me towards the door.

"Grab your computer. There's some nice space to work down there," she insists. "Consider this sisterly intervention."

Ten minutes later, I'm reluctantly perched on a stool at The Daily Grind, nursing a cappuccino I didn't really want. The cheerful jingle of bells every time the door opens feels like a personal attack on my fragile emotional state.

"See? Isn't this better than wallowing in that empty room?" Arden asks, her early pregnancy glow making me feel even more like a human dumpster fire by comparison.

"Jury's still out," I mutter. But I have to admit, the rich aroma of coffee and the gentle hum of conversation is not terrible.

"Get used to it," Arden says firmly. "I'm now requiring at least thirty minutes of playtime a day. Consider this your personal playground."

"Should I go back to calling you 'mom' like when we were teenagers, too?" I tease, trying to suppress a smirk as I eye her over my mug.

"Guess all that practice will come in handy soon enough," she says with a shrug, placing her hand over her not-at-all-showing stomach. Then again, she is only nine weeks along.

I look around the small café, taking in the faux fireplace and shelves of books. There are worse places I could be. Like with Logan.

"So, this will be my mandatory outing, huh?" I quip. Might need to brush up on my conversation skills because the only people I've spoken to in the last three weeks are the fictional characters in the books I'm reading.

My gaze wanders to the counter, where a barista is chatting with a customer. Was he here when we walked in? He's scruffy, with an unkempt beard and messy hair that looks like it hasn't seen a comb in days. But there's something about him—maybe the way his eyes crinkle when he smiles, or the easy grace of his movements—that catches my attention.

Arden follows my line of sight and lets out a bark of laughter. "See something you like?"

"Are you kidding?" I bite back. "I'm pretty sure the last thing I need right now is some hot, scruffy barista who will break my heart another six ways to Sunday."

"Hot and scruffy, huh? Sounds like progress," Arden teases. "Don't let Jake's appearance fool you. He can be a gentleman when he wants to be."

There's something in her tone—a hint of familiarity that goes beyond just knowing her local barista—but before I can question it, Jake looks our way. His eyes meet mine briefly, and I quickly refocus on the cappuccino, feeling my cheeks burn.

"The only progress I'm interested in is progressing back to your guest room and my date with a pint of ice cream," I reassure her. But as I peek over the rim of my mug, I catch Jake glancing our way again. This time, he offers a small, crooked smile that makes my heart do an unexpected flip.

Not your type, girl, I remind myself. Though I'm already involuntarily analyzing him for manuscript inspiration. With a hint of a tattoo showing on his bicep and killer waves, he's giving major wounded bad-boy character vibes. And God knows readers eat up that plotline—some inked hottie healing a broken heroine's ravaged heart, finding true love and blah blah blah.

My phone chimes mid-assessment, and I glance down, seeing Alyssa's name flash.

Alyssa: *Still on for our standard Monday happy hour? Or are you ditching me again for more Hallmark movies?*

I groan, not sure whether I should appreciate the one friend I'd managed to keep during my Logan-hazed relationship or keep pushing her away now that he's gone.

Arden glances at my phone with a raised brow. "Don't you dare cancel again," she warns. "You need this, Co. Besides, Alyssa's probably the only person who can match your cynicism about romance right now."

I sigh. "I'm not exactly in the mood for anything called 'happy hour.'"

Arden starts to argue, but she's cut off by the ringtone from her phone. She glances at the screen and grimaces. "It's work. I have to take this." She stands, gathering her things. "You'll be okay here for a bit?"

I wave her off. "Go. I'll just sit here in my 'personal playground' judging people's coffee order until I hit my required thirty minutes."

As Arden leaves, I pull out my laptop, figuring I might as well get some work done. You know, being Monday and all. I'm deep in the throes of editing a particularly cringe-worthy love scene when a voice startles me.

"Refill?"

I look up to find Jake standing there, coffee pot in hand, his blue eyes twinkling with amusement. Up close, his scruffiness is even more apparent, but somehow it works for him. I realize I've been staring without answering and quickly nod, pushing my mug towards him.

"Thanks," I manage, trying not to notice how his hands dwarf the coffee pot. "I'm going to need all the caffeine I can get to make it through this... literary masterpiece."

Jake's eyebrow quirks up. "Literary masterpiece, huh? Reading it for fun or..."

"Work," I finish. "I'm an associate editor. And let's just say if this is what passes for romance these days, I'm glad I'm swearing off men."

Jake's eyes widen slightly, and I feel my face heat up. *Great. Not only am I the creepy girl staring at the hot barista, but now I'm the bitter, man-hating creepy girl.*

But then Jake's lips twitch into a grin. "Well, on behalf of my gender, I apologize for whatever crime against literature you're suffering through."

A laugh escapes for the first time since... well, since before I called Arden that night. "Trust me, this goes way beyond a simple apology. We're talking reparations on a global scale."

Jake leans against the table, his eyes dancing. "That serious, huh? Maybe I should be taking notes. You know, in case I ever decide to pursue a career in terrible romance writing."

"Oh God, please don't," I groan, but I'm smiling despite myself. "The world can only handle so many 'throbbing members' and 'heaving bosoms.'"

Jake lets out a surprised bark of laughter, drawing curious glances from nearby tables. "Duly noted. I'll stick to coffee for now."

"I'm Cora, by the way," I say, meeting those piercing blues that look like they've already lived a lifetime.

"Jake," he says with a smile. "And you're Arden's..."

"Sister," I finish when he trails off. "I'm staying with her for a few weeks." *Or months*, I add silently. *However long it takes for me to reestablish how to function on my own again.*

"Well, nice to meet you, Cora."

There's a moment where we're just grinning at each other, and I feel something warm unfurl in my chest. *Am I... attracted to a man again?* The spell is broken by another customer calling for Jake's attention. He straightens up, looking almost reluctant. "Duty calls. But, uh, let me know if you need anything else. You know, to get through your literary ordeal."

I watch him go, my heart doing a little flip when he glances back and catches me looking. I shake my head, trying to clear it.

What am I doing? I'm not ready for... whatever this is. I have a pity party for one scheduled with Alyssa later, and the last thing I need is to complicate things with some espresso-slinging bad-boy type, no matter how cute or funny he might be.

Still, I'm smiling as I turn back to my laptop. Maybe getting out of the apartment wasn't such a bad idea after all.

Several hours and countless stolen glances later, I reluctantly pack up my laptop. As much as I'd like to camp out in this coffee shop forever (for purely professional reasons, of course), it's time to face the music. Or in this case, face Alyssa and her inevitable inquisition.

I give Jake a small wave as I leave, earning another one of those crooked smiles that does funny things to my insides. *Stop, Cora. He's just the first guy to show you attention after Logan. It means nothing*, I chastise myself as I drop my computer and head out into the chilly, late November air.

The bar Alyssa chose is already crowded when I arrive, the after-work crowd in full swing. I spot her at a high top, already nursing what I'm sure isn't her first cocktail of the night.

"Well," Alyssa drawls as I slide onto the stool across from her. "If it isn't the elusive Cora Cooper, finally emerging from her cave of misery and Ben & Jerry's."

I roll my eyes, despite the grin on my face. "Hello to you too, Lys."

She signals the waiter. "Two dirty martinis, extra olives. We're drowning sorrows tonight."

"I don't have any sorrows to drown," I protest weakly.

Alyssa fixes me with a look. "Honey, you've been wearing the same leggings for a week, and I'm pretty sure that hoodie has seen better days. Trust me, you've got sorrows."

I glance down at my outfit and wince. She's not wrong.

324 | Nicole Crystal

"So," Alyssa leans in, her eyes gleaming with a mix of concern and mischief, "tell me. How bad is it really?"

I take a long sip of the martini, letting the alcohol burn a path down my throat. "On a scale of one to 'contemplating joining a convent?' I'd say I'm hovering around 'seriously considering adopting seventeen cats.'"

Alyssa snorts. "Please. You're allergic to cats. Try again."

I sigh, fiddling with my olive skewer. "It's... it's bad, Lys. I keep thinking I'm over it, that I'm moving on, and then bam! I'll see something that reminds me of him, or I'll have a moment of weakness and check his Instagram, and it's like I'm right back where I started."

"Tell me you haven't been drunk texting him," Alyssa says, narrowing her eyes.

"No!" I exclaim, then pause. "Well, maybe a few times. Arden confiscates my phone most nights now." *Especially after Logan begged for me to come back and I started to pack my bags.* But I don't tell Alyssa that.

"Smart woman, your sister," Alyssa says approvingly. "Unlike that idiot ex of yours. God, I still can't believe he had the balls to cheat on you with a co-worker. Talk about a walking cliché."

I wince at the blunt reminder. "Yeah, well, apparently I have a type–'emotionally unavailable man-children with a desire to destroy my self-esteem.'"

"Screw that," Alyssa declares, signaling for another round. "Your type from now on is 'hot, emotionally stable men who worship the ground you walk on.' Or, you know, just 'hot.' We can work on the rest later."

I laugh into my glass. "Is that your type these days?"

Alyssa grins wickedly. "Honey, my type is 'breathing and between the ages of 25 and 45.' I'm an equal opportunity enjoyer of the male form."

"You're incorrigible," I say, shaking my head.

"And you love me for it," she retorts. "Now, enough sulking. We're going to find you a rebound tonight if it kills me."

I nearly choke on my olive. "What? No, absolutely not. I am not ready for... that."

Alyssa waves dismissively. "Nonsense. The best way to get over someone is to get under someone else. Trust me, I'm practically a doctor in this field."

"I think I'll stick to my ice cream therapy, thanks," I mutter.

"Suit yourself," Alyssa shrugs. "But don't come crying to me when you've forgotten how to flirt. Speaking of which..." Her eyes focus on something over my shoulder, a predatory grin spreading across her face. "Don't look now, but there's an extremely fuckable specimen at 3 o'clock who's been checking you out for the last five minutes."

Despite my protests, I find myself turning slightly, curiosity getting the better of me. Looky there, she's right again. The guy is hot, all sandy hair and tanned skin. But it only makes me picture another guy with dirty blonde hair who asked me to marry him two months ago, only to cheat on me weeks later.

"To Logan-ish," I murmur, taking another long sip of the drink to rid myself of the memory.

"Oh! I've got it!" Her eyes light up with an idea that I'm sure I'm going to hate. "How comfortable would you be with a blind date?"

"Lys, no. I can barely handle talking to men I know right now, let alone strangers."

"Hear me out," she insists. "I know this guy, Baker. He's cute, he's funny, and most importantly, he's nothing like Logan. It could be just what you need to remind yourself that not all men are lying, cheating scumbags."

I eye her skeptically. "I don't know..."

"Come on, Co," Alyssa pleads. "One date. If it's terrible, I'll personally buy you a year's supply of ice cream and swear off matchmaking forever."

"That's a pretty big promise."

"That's how confident I am," she says with a grin. "Besides, what's the worst that could happen?"

I raise an eyebrow. "Do you want that list alphabetically or chronologically?"

Alyssa rolls her eyes. "Okay, drama queen. But what else are you gonna do this weekend? Mope around your sister's apartment? Come on. You know you want to have a little fun! And trust me, this guy will knock your socks off."

I chew on my lip, considering. Maybe Alyssa has a point. If nothing else, it's something I can rub in Logan's face when he inevitably calls crying again.

"Fine," I sigh, already regretting my decision. "One date. But if he turns out to be a serial killer, you're testifying at the trial."

Alyssa squeals, clapping her hands together. "You won't regret this. Now, let's talk outfits. You can't meet your potential future husband in leggings and a ratty hoodie."

As Alyssa launches into a detailed analysis of my wardrobe (or lack thereof), I wonder what I've gotten myself into. But beneath the anxiety, there's a tiny spark of something else. Hope, maybe? Or at least the possibility of it.

Because my life needs more than a light edit—it needs a complete rewrite.

Rewriting December

2

Jake

I stare at my reflection in the coffee shop window, barely recognizing the guy looking back at me. Unkempt beard, hair that hasn't seen a comb in days, dark circles under eyes that have seen too much. I look like hell. But then again, I feel like it too. Just another day in the life of Jake Rhoades, professional screwup.

With a sigh, I slink into the coffee shop a solid fifteen minutes before my shift starts. Judging by the way my manager's eyes nearly pop out of her skull, she's probably wondering if I'm still riding the drunk train from last night's bender. But for once, I went to bed stone-cold sober.

I do a sweep of the room, finding her immediately. Cora. My guardian angel. My used-to-be best friend's sister-in-law. It's been two days since she first stumbled into the shop with Arden, and I still can't believe it's really her.

Slipping on my apron, I shake my head at the irony of it all. Six years ago, I was in a car wreck. Now? I'm a human coffee dispenser for the girl who saved my sorry ass–twice–and can't even pick me out of a lineup. Meanwhile, Mark's living the American Dream with Arden. Me? I'm living the American Meme. It's like a cosmic joke without a punchline. Or maybe it's the greatest hit I'll never write.

The café's mind-numbing rhythm takes over. Grind, tamp, brew. Repeat. It's about as exciting as watching paint dry, but hey, at least paint doesn't have to think.

I glance up, catching another glimpse of her. Her honey-colored hair is lit up like a halo, and suddenly I'm back in that smoking wreck. The acrid smell of burning rubber, my shoulder screaming bloody murder, and there she is–MY personal action hero with eyes that could melt steel.

I shake it off, trying to focus on the here and now. But those amber eyes are suddenly right in front of me, clearing their throat like they're about to deliver a sermon. They're the same eyes that kept me tethered to this mortal coil that night, the ones that haunted my morphine-addled dreams in the hospital, and–who am I kidding–the same ones I pictured this morning while brushing my teeth.

"Welcome back, Cora," I manage, plastering on a grin that feels about as genuine as a three-dollar bill. And damn if those eyes aren't even more stunning up close.

"Morning Jake," Cora responds, "Large coffee, please. Black."

"Rough night?" I ask casually, sneaking glances at her as I pour. *Rough night? Smooth, bud! I'm acting like I've never talked to a woman. Then again, I've never really talked to this one before.*

A wry smile twists on Cora's lips. Not that I'm looking at them. "More like a rough month. Or year. Take your pick," she says with a hint of bitterness.

I chuckle, the sound rusty from disuse. "I hear you. Life has a way of kicking you when you're down, doesn't it?" *I should know, I'm practically on a first-name basis with rock bottom at this point.*

"You have no idea," Cora sighs, then seems to catch herself. "Sorry, I'm sure you don't need to hear my sob story when you first get in."

I shrug, sliding her coffee across the counter. "Hey, misery loves company, right? Besides, I'm told I'm a pretty good listener." *Which is rich, coming from the guy who's spent the last five years avoiding any meaningful conversation.*

Those amber eyes tick up to mine, and an unfamiliar jolt of electricity runs through me. Is there a flicker of recognition? I want to say something, to thank her, to ask her where she's been all these years. But that would mean answering where I've been. And, well, I already know how that would end.

I hold my breath, waiting for... I don't know what. A miracle, maybe?

Cora blinks, and just like that, the moment's gone. "Thanks," she says, taking the mug.

"Yeah, no problem," I respond, pretending her showing back up doesn't have my world tilting on its axis.

As she returns to her table, my phone buzzes in my pocket. I pull it out to see a text from Lindsey, asking if I'm free tonight. Disappointment curdles at her misguided belief that we share some "friends with benefits" arrangement. Why'd I think getting involved with a twenty-one-year-old was a good idea? Then again, when do I ever think about anything I do?

But then my eyes land on Cora again, all furrowed brow and intense concentration, and suddenly I'm feeling things. Scary things. The kind of things I promised myself I'd never want again.

With a shake of my head, I pocket my phone without responding. I've got work to do, and a long shift at Sadie's tonight. I can't afford to get distracted, especially not by ghosts from my past. Even if those ghosts have eyes I could drown in and a smile that makes me forget how to breathe.

Throughout the day, my gaze keeps drifting back to Cora's table like it's magnetized. Each glance lightens the weight on my chest a bit. It's almost nice, until I remember that guys like me don't get second chances. We get to serve coffee, tend bar, and pretend we're not one sad country song away from a complete breakdown.

When she finally approaches the counter again, I nearly jump out of my skin.

"Hey," she says, sliding her mug across. "Me again. Could I get another refill? And maybe a muffin? Apparently, caffeine isn't a suitable replacement for actual food. Who knew?"

I chuckle, grabbing the pot. "Arden giving you a hard time about your eating habits?"

Cora's eyebrows shoot up. "You and her are on a first-name basis, huh?"

Shit. Backpedal, backpedal! "Oh, you know. She's a regular. You pick things up." *Smooth as sandpaper, Rhoades.*

She eyes me curiously, but mercifully lets it slide. "Right. Well, thanks for the coffee. And the muffin."

As she turns to go, my mouth decides to stage a coup against my brain. "I'm here most weekdays."

She pauses, a hint of a smile on her lips. "So I've been told. By Arden."

And then she's gone, leaving me to wonder what else Arden might have said. Probably my entire embarrassing life story, knowing my luck.

The rest of my shift crawls by slower than a snail on sedatives. By the time I drag myself into Sadie's that evening, I'm ready to perform a trust fall into the beer taps.

"Whoa there, sunshine," Natalie says as I slump against the bar. "Who pissed in your cornflakes this morning?"

I manage a grunt. "Just living the dream, Nat. One soul-crushing shift at a time."

Like always, Natalie sees through my bullshit. After more than five years, she might know me better than I know me.

"Seriously, Jake. What's up? You look like you've seen a ghost."

If only she knew how close to the truth that was.

"You ever have someone from your past show up out of nowhere and turn your whole world upside down?" I ask with a sigh.

Nat's eyebrows shoot up. "Honey, that's the plot of every rom-com ever made. But coming from you? This I gotta hear."

I give her the cliff notes version as we set up for the night. No way I'm sharing everything. The less she knows, the better.

"Let me get this straight," she says, hands on her hips. "The girl who saved your life six years ago, who happens to be your ex-best friend's sister-in-law, just waltzed back into your life, and you're what? Scared?"

Put like that, it sounds ridiculous. But then again, my whole life is pretty ridiculous at this point. "It's not that simple, Nat."

"Seems pretty simple to me. Girl saves boy. Boy's now pining for girl. Girl comes back. Cue happily ever after."

I snort. "Yeah, because my life is just one big fairy tale, right? In case you haven't noticed, I'm not exactly Prince Charming material."

Nat's expression softens like she's about to deliver a Hallmark card moment. "Jake, you've got to forgive yourself for what happened. You couldn't have known…"

Yeah, and I couldn't have known I'd be living the glamorous life of a bartender with a side of crippling guilt, but here we are.

Before I can dive headfirst into my pity party, the first customers start trickling in. And because the universe loves a good joke, Lindsey's among them, all tight clothes and shark-like smile. Fuck. I should've texted her back. Maybe then I could've avoided this train wreck in stilettos.

"Hey there, handsome," Lindsey purrs, leaning over the bar. "You never text me back."

I manage a weak smile. "Yeah, sorry about that. Got caught up with… stuff."

She pouts, but I can see the calculation behind her eyes. "Well, maybe we can make up for lost time later?"

For a hot second, I'm tempted. It'd be so easy to fall back into old habits, to lose myself in the familiar haze of booze and bad decisions. But then Cora's face flashes in my mind, and suddenly, I'm not so keen on my usual brand of self-destruction.

"Not tonight, Linds. I've got rehearsal tomorrow."

It's not a lie. Owen nearly bit my head off last week when I showed up an hour late for rehearsal, reeking of strawberries and regret. Ah, the joys of sorority bathrooms.

Still, Thursdays? They're my lifeline. For a few hours, I get to shed this skin of surly, damaged bartender and become someone else. Someone who isn't drowning in a sea of grief and Jack Daniels. Because when I'm on that stage with Owen and Chris, I'm the Jake I used to be— before Tessa and Thomas, before my life became a country song minus the pickup truck.

Lindsey huffs, clearly not used to rejection. Join the club, sweetheart. I've been rejected by life itself.

The rest of the night passes in a blur of drink orders and forced smiles. Six years of this, and I've got the act down pat. Oscar-worthy performance, really.

By last call, I'm running on fumes and considering the sweet embrace of my old friend, Mr. Whiskey. But instead of reaching for the bottle, I find myself thinking of amber eyes and second chances. What the hell?

Natalie's jaw drops like she's watching a pig sprout wings. "Wow, Jake, this girl really has your head spinning, huh?"

"Yeah, or maybe I've finally pickled my brain with all this booze," I reply with a small laugh. *Or maybe it's my savior showing up five days before the worst month of the year.*

When I finally stumble back to my apartment, I grab my guitar, hoping music might keep the nightmares at bay. But as I settle onto the couch, something weird happens. My fingers start moving, coaxing out a melody that doesn't sound like it was born in the bottom of a whiskey bottle.

Before I know it, I'm scribbling lyrics like a man possessed. And here's the kicker—they're not my usual doom and gloom greatest hits. They're... hopeful? Christ, I must be losing it.

But as I stare at the words, I can't help but think maybe, just maybe, my guardian angel's back for round three. And this time, hopefully, I'll give her something better to remember me by.

.

About the Author:

Nicole Crystal is a multi-passionate author who recently rediscovered her love for storytelling amidst a successful career in corporate America. With fifteen years of experience in sales management and a keen eye for marketing, Nicole brings a unique perspective to her writing.

When she's not writing or working, Nicole can be found exploring the suburbs of Chicago with her husband and children, seeking new adventures and inspiration for her next novel. With a passion for personal growth and a commitment to her craft, Nicole is excited to embark on this new chapter in her life as a published author.

BOOKS BY NICOLE CRYSTAL:

I Choose Us
Rewriting December
Rewriting the Rules

Follow her on Instagram @MsNicoleCrystal and Facebook @NicoleCrystal

Made in the USA
Columbia, SC
26 September 2024

43082667R00200